Patricia Cornwell's first novel, *Postmortem*, is the only novel to have won the Edgar, John Creasey, Anthony and MacAvity awards, and the Prix du Roman d'Aventure for the best first novel, and she subsequently won the Gold Dagger Award for *Cruel and Unusual*. The twelfth Dr Kay Scarpetta novel, *Blow Fly*, is due to be published in autumn 2003.

A former crime reporter and computer analyst in the Chief Medical Examiner's office in Virginia, she is acclaimed as the creator of the forensic detective novel. She is the biographer of Ruth Bell Graham, the wife of the evangelist, and author of the renowned work, *Portrait of a Killer*, in which she identifies Jack the Ripper as the artist Walter Sickert. She has helped to establish the Virginia Institute of Forensic Science and Medicine and serves as its Chairman of the Board.

PATRICIA CORNWELL

POSTMORTEM

timewarner
paperbacks

A *Time Warner* Paperback

First published in Great Britain in 1990
by Macdonald & Co (Publishers) Ltd
First Futura edition published in 1991
Reprinted 1991 (five times)
This edition published by Warner Books in 1992
Reprinted 1992 (four times), 1993 (five times), 1994 (four times),
1995 (four times), 1996 (three times), 1997 (three times), 1998 (three times),
1999, 2000 (twice), 2001 (twice)
Reprinted by Time Warner Paperbacks in 2002, 2003 (twice)

A CIP catalogue record for this book
is available from the British Library.

ISBN 0 7515 3043 3

Typeset by M Rules
Printed in Great Britain by
Clays Ltd, St Ives plc

Time Warner Paperbacks
An imprint of
Time Warner Books UK
Brettenham House
Lancaster Place
London WC2E 7EN

www.TimeWarnerBooks.co.uk

To Joe and Dianne

1

It was raining in Richmond on Friday, June 6.

The relentless downpour, which began at dawn, beat the lilies to naked stalks, and blacktop and sidewalks were littered with leaves. There were small rivers in the streets, and newborn ponds on playing fields and lawns. I went to sleep to the sound of water drumming the slate roof, and was dreaming a terrible dream as night dissolved into the foggy first hours of Saturday morning.

I saw a white face beyond the rain-streaked glass, a face formless and inhuman like the faces of misshapen dolls made of nylon hose. My bedroom window was dark when suddenly the face was there, an evil intelligence looking in. I woke up and stared blindly into the dark. I did not know what had awakened me until the telephone rang again. I found the receiver without fumbling.

"Dr. Scarpetta?"

"Yes." I reached for the lamp and switched it on. It was 2:33 A.M. My heart was drilling through my ribs.

"Pete Marino here. We got us one at 5602 Berkley Avenue. Think you better come."

The victim's name, he went on to explain, was Lori Petersen, a white female, thirty years old. Her husband had found her body about half an hour earlier.

Details were unnecessary. The moment I picked up the receiver and recognized Sergeant Marino's voice, I knew. Maybe I knew the instant the telephone rang. People who

1

believe in werewolves are afraid of a full moon. I'd begun to dread the hours between midnight and 3:00 A.M. when Friday becomes Saturday and the city is unconscious.

Ordinarily, the medical examiner on call is summoned to a death scene. But this wasn't ordinary. I had made it clear after the second case that no matter the hour, if there was another murder, I was to be called. Marino wasn't keen on the idea. Ever since I was appointed chief medical examiner for the Commonwealth of Virginia less than two years ago he'd been difficult. I wasn't sure if he didn't like women, or if he just didn't like me.

"Berkley's in Berkley Downs, Southside," he said condescendingly. "You know the way?"

Confessing I didn't, I scribbled the directions on the notepad I always kept by the phone. I hung up and my feet were already on the floor as adrenaline hit my nerves like espresso. The house was quiet. I grabbed my black medical bag, scuffed and worn from years of use.

The night air was like a cool sauna, and there were no lights in the windows of my neighbors' houses. As I backed the navy station wagon out of the drive, I looked at the light burning over the porch, at the first-story window leading into the guest bedroom where my ten-year-old niece, Lucy, was asleep. This would be one more day in the child's life I would miss. I had picked her up at the airport Wednesday night. Our meals together, so far, had been few.

There was no traffic until I hit the Parkway. Minutes later I was speeding across the James River. Taillights far ahead were rubies, the downtown skyline ghostly in the rearview mirror. Fanning out on either side were plains of darkness with tiny necklaces of smudged light at the edges. Out there, somewhere, is a man, I thought. He could be anybody, walks upright, sleeps with a roof over his head, and has the usual number of fingers and toes. He is probably white and much younger than my forty years. He is ordinary by most standards, and probably doesn't drive a BMW or grace the bars in the Slip or the finer clothing stores along Main Street.

2

But, then again, he could. He could be anybody and he was nobody. Mr. Nobody. The kind of guy you don't remember after riding up twenty floors alone with him inside an elevator.

He had become the self-appointed dark ruler of the city, an obsession for thousands of people he had never seen, and an obsession of mine. Mr. Nobody.

Because the homicides began two months ago, he may have been recently released from prison or a mental hospital. This was the speculation last week, but the theories were constantly changing.

Mine had remained the same from the start. I strongly suspected he hadn't been in the city long, he'd done this before somewhere else, and he'd never spent a day behind the locked doors of a prison or a forensic unit. He wasn't disorganized, wasn't an amateur, and he most assuredly wasn't "crazy."

Wilshire was two lights down on the left, Berkley the first right after that.

I could see the blue and red lights flashing two blocks away. The street in front of 5602 Berkley was lit up like a disaster site. An ambulance, its engine rumbling loudly, was alongside two unmarked police units with grille lights flashing and three white cruisers with light bars going full tilt. The Channel 12 news crew had just pulled up. Lights had blinked on up and down the street, and several people in pajamas and housecoats had wandered out to their porches.

I parked behind the news van as a cameraman trotted across the street. Head bent, the collar of my khaki raincoat turned up around my ears, I briskly followed the brick walk to the front door. I have always had a special distaste for seeing myself on the evening news. Since the stranglings in Richmond began, my office had been inundated, the same reporters calling over and over again with the same insensitive questions.

"If it's a serial killer, Dr. Scarpetta, doesn't that indicate it's quite likely to happen again?"

3

As if they wanted it to happen again.

"Is it true you found bite marks on the last victim, Doc?"

It wasn't true, but no matter how I answered such a question I couldn't win. "No comment," and they assume it's true. "No," and the next edition reads, "Dr. Kay Scarpetta denies that bite marks have been found on the victims' bodies . . ." The killer, who's reading the papers like everybody else, gets a new idea.

Recent news accounts were florid and frighteningly detailed. They went far beyond serving the useful purpose of warning the city's citizens. Women, particularly those who lived alone, were terrified. The sale of handguns and dead-bolt locks went up fifty percent the week after the third murder, and the SPCA ran out of dogs – a phenomenon which, of course, made the front page, too. Yesterday, the infamous and prize-winning police reporter Abby Turnbull had demonstrated her usual brass by coming to my office and clubbing my staff with the Freedom of Information Act in an unsuccessful attempt at getting copies of the autopsy records.

Crime reporting was aggressive in Richmond, an old Virginia city of 220,000, which last year was listed by the FBI as having the second-highest homicide rate per capita in the United States. It wasn't uncommon for forensic pathologists from the British Commonwealth to spend a month at my office to learn more about gunshot wounds. It wasn't uncommon for career cops like Pete Marino to leave the madness of New York or Chicago only to find Richmond was worse.

What was uncommon were these sex slayings. The average citizen can't relate to drug and domestic shootouts or one wino stabbing another over a bottle of Mad Dog. But these murdered women were the colleagues you sit next to at work, the friends you invite to go shopping or to stop by for drinks, the acquaintances you chat with at parties, the people you stand in line with at the checkout counter. They were someone's neighbor, someone's sister, someone's daughter, someone's lover. They were in their own homes, sleeping in

4

their own beds, when Mr. Nobody climbed through one of their windows.

Two uniformed men flanked the front door, which was open wide and barred by a yellow ribbon of tape, warning: CRIME SCENE – DO NOT CROSS.

"Doc." He could have been my son, this boy in blue who stepped aside at the top of the steps and lifted the tape to let me duck under.

The living room was immaculate, and attractively decorated in warm rose tones. A handsome cherry cabinet in a corner contained a small television and a compact disc player. Nearby a stand held sheet music and a violin. Beneath a curtained window overlooking the front lawn was a sectional sofa, and on the glass coffee table in front of it were half a dozen magazines neatly stacked. Among them were *Scientific American* and the *New England Journal of Medicine*. Across a Chinese dragon rug with a rose medallion against a field of cream stood a walnut bookcase. Tomes straight from a medical school's syllabi lined two shelves.

An open doorway led into a corridor running the length of the house. To my right appeared a series of rooms, to the left was the kitchen, where Marino and a young officer were talking to a man I assumed was the husband.

I was vaguely aware of clean countertops, linoleum and appliances in the off-white that manufacturers call "almond," and the pale yellow of the wallpaper and curtains. But my attention was riveted to the table. On top of it lay a red nylon knapsack, the contents of which had been gone through by the police: a stethoscope, a penlight, a Tupperware container once packed with a meal or a snack, and recent editions of the *Annals of Surgery*, *Lancet* and the *Journal of Trauma*. By now I was thoroughly unsettled.

Marino eyed me coolly as I paused by the table, then introduced me to Matt Petersen, the husband. Petersen was slumped in a chair, his face destroyed by shock. He was exquisitely handsome, almost beautiful, his features flawlessly chiseled, his hair jet-black, his skin smooth and hinting

5

of a tan. He was wide-shouldered with a lean but elegantly sculpted body casually clad in a white Izod shirt and faded blue jeans. His eyes were cast down, his hands stiffly in his lap.

"These are hers?" I had to know. The medical items might belong to the husband.

Marino's "Yeah" was a confirmation.

Petersen's eyes slowly lifted. Deep blue, bloodshot, they seemed relieved as they fixed on me. The doctor had arrived, a ray of hope where there was none.

He muttered in the truncated sentences of a mind fragmented, stunned, "I talked to her on the phone. Last night. She told me she'd be home around twelve-thirty, home from VMC, the ER. I got here, found the lights out, thought she'd already gone to bed. Then I went in there." His voice rose, quivering, and he took a deep breath. "I went in there, in the bedroom." His eyes were desperate and welling, and he was pleading with me. "Please. I don't want people looking at her, seeing her like that. *Please*."

I gently told him, "She has to be examined, Mr. Petersen."

A fist suddenly banged the top of the table in a startling outburst of rage. "I know!" His eyes were wild. "But all of them, the police and everybody!" His voice was shaking. "I know how it is! Reporters and everybody crawling all over the place. I don't want every son of a bitch and his brother staring at her!"

Marino didn't bat an eye. "Hey. I got a wife, too, Matt. I know where you're coming from, all right? You got my word she gets respect. The same respect I'd want if it was me sitting in your chair, okay?"

The sweet balm of lies.

The dead are defenseless, and the violation of this woman, like the others, had only begun. I knew it would not end until Lori Petersen was turned inside out, every inch of her photographed, and all of it on display for experts, the police, attorneys, judges and members of a jury to see. There would be thoughts, remarks about her physical attributes or lack of them. There would be sophomoric jokes and cynical asides as the victim, not the killer, went on trial, every aspect of her person and the way she lived, scrutinized, judged and, in some instances, degraded.

A violent death is a public event, and it was this facet of my profession that so rudely grated against my sensibilities. I did what I could to preserve the dignity of the victims. But there was little I could do after the person became a case number, a piece of evidence passed from hand to hand. Privacy is destroyed as completely as life.

Marino led me out of the kitchen, leaving the officer to continue questioning Petersen.

"Have you taken your pictures yet?" I asked.

"ID's in there now, dusting everything," he said, referring to the Identification section officers processing the scene. "I told 'em to give the body a wide berth."

We paused in the hallway.

On the walls were several nice watercolors and a collection of photographs depicting the husband's and the wife's respective graduating classes, and one artistic color shot of the young couple leaning against weathered piling before a backdrop of the beach, the legs of their trousers rolled up to their calves, the wind ruffling their hair, their faces ruddy from the sun. She was pretty in life, blond, with delicate features and an engaging smile. She went to Brown, then to Harvard for medical school. Her husband's undergraduate years were spent at Harvard. This was where they must have met, and apparently he was younger than she.

She. Lori Petersen. Brown. Harvard. Brilliant. Thirty years old. About to have it all realized, her dream. After eight grueling years, at least, of medical training. A physician. All of it destroyed in a few minutes of a stranger's aberrant pleasure.

Marino touched my elbow.

I turned away from the photographs as he directed my attention to the open doorway just ahead on the left.

"Here's how he got in," he said.

It was a small room with a white tile floor and walls

papered in Williamsburg blue. There was a toilet and a lava-tory, and a straw clothes hamper. The window above the toilet was open wide, a square of blackness through which cool, moist air seeped and stirred the starchy white curtains. Beyond, in the dark, dense trees, cicadas were tensely sawing.

"The screen's cut." Marino's face was expressionless as he glanced at me. "It's leaning against the back of the house. Right under the window's a picnic table bench. Appears he pulled it up so he could climb in."

I was scanning the floor, the sink, the top of the toilet. I didn't see dirt or smudges or footprints, but it was hard to tell from where I was standing, and I had no intention of running the risk of contaminating anything.

"Was this window locked?" I asked.

"Don't look like it. All the other windows are locked. Already checked. Seems like she would've gone to a lot of trouble to make sure this one was. Of all the windows, it's the most vulnerable, close to the ground, in back where no one can see what's going on. Better than coming in through the bedroom window because if the guy's quiet, she's not going to hear him cutting the screen and climbing in this far down the hall."

"And the doors? Were they locked when the husband got home?"

"He says so."

"Then the killer went out the same way he came in," I decided.

"Looks that way. Tidy squirrel, don't you think?" He was holding on to the door frame, leaning forward without step-ping inside. "Don't see nothing in here, like maybe he wiped up after himself to make sure he didn't leave footprints on the john or floor. It's been raining all day." His eyes were flat as they fixed on me. "His feet should've been wet, maybe muddy."

I wondered where Marino was going with this. He was hard to read, and I'd never decided if he was a good poker

8

player or simply slow. He was exactly the sort of detective I avoided when given a choice – a cock of the walk and absolutely unreachable. He was pushing fifty, with a face life had chewed on, and long wisps of graying hair parted low on one side and combed over his balding pate. At least six feet tall, he was bay-windowed from decades of bourbon or beer. His unfashionably wide red-and-blue-striped tie was oily around the neck from summers of sweat. Marino was the stuff of tough-guy flicks – a crude, crass gumshoe who probably had a foul-mouthed parrot for a pet and a coffee table littered with *Hustler* magazines.

I went the length of the hallway and stopped outside the master bedroom. I felt myself go hollow inside.

An ID officer was busy coating every surface with black dusting powder; a second officer was capturing everything on videotape.

Lori Petersen was on top of the bed, the blue-and-white spread hanging off the foot of the bed. The top sheet was kicked down and bunched beneath her feet, the cover sheet pulled free of the top corners, exposing the mattress, the pillows shoved to the right side of her head. The bed was the vortex of a violent storm, surrounded by the undisturbed civility of middle-class bedroom furnishings of polished oak.

She was nude. On the colorful rag rug to the right of the bed was her pale yellow cotton gown. It was slit from collar to hem, and this was consistent with the three previous cases. On the night stand nearest the door was a telephone, the cord ripped out of the wall. The two lamps on either side of the bed were out, the electrical cords severed from them. One cord bound her wrists, which were pinioned at the small of her back. The other cord was tied in a diabolically creative pattern also consistent with the first three cases. Looped once around her neck, it was threaded behind her through the cord around her wrists and tightly lashed around her ankles. As long as her knees were bent, the loop around her neck remained loose. When she straightened her legs, either in a reflex to pain or because of the assailant's

9

weight on top of her, the ligature around her neck tightened like a noose.

Death by asphyxiation takes only several minutes. That's a very long time when every cell in your body is screaming for air.

"You can come on in, Doc," the officer with the video camera was saying. "I've got all this on film."

Watching where I walked, I approached the bed, set my bag on the floor and got out a pair of surgical gloves. Next I got out my camera and took several photographs of the body *in situ*. Her face was grotesque, swollen beyond recognition and a dark bluish purple from the suffusion of blood caused by the tight ligature around her neck. Bloody fluid had leaked from her nose and mouth, staining the sheet. Her straw-blond hair was in disarray. She was moderately tall, no less than five foot seven, and considerably fleshier than the younger version captured in the photographs down the hall.

Her physical appearance was important because the absence of a pattern was becoming a pattern. The four strangling victims seemed to have had no physical characteristics in common, not even race. The third victim was black and very slender. The first victim was a redhead and plump, the second a brunette and petite. They had different professions: a schoolteacher, a freelance writer, a receptionist, and now a physician. They lived in different areas of the city.

Fetching a long chemical thermometer from my bag, I took the temperature of the room, then of her body. The air was 71 degrees, her body 93.5. Time of death is more elusive than most people think. It can't be pinned down exactly unless the death was witnessed or the victim's Timex stopped ticking. But Lori Petersen had been dead no more than three hours. Her body had been cooling between one and two degrees per hour, and rigor had started in the small muscles.

I looked for any obvious trace evidence that might not survive the trip to the morgue. There were no loose hairs on the skin, but I found a multitude of fibers, most of which, no doubt, were from the bedcovers. With forceps I collected a sampling of them, minuscule whitish ones and several seeming to have come from a dark blue or black material. These I placed in small metal evidence buttons. The most obvious evidence was the musky smell, the patches of a residue, transparent and dried like glue, on the upper front and back of her legs.

Seminal fluid was present in all of the cases, yet it was of little serological value. The assailant was one of the twenty percent of the population who enjoyed the distinction of being a nonsecreter. This meant his blood-type antigens could not be found in his other body fluids, such as saliva or semen or sweat. Absent a blood sample, in other words, he couldn't be typed. He could have been A, B, AB or anything.

As recently as two years earlier, the killer's nonsecreter status would have been a crushing blow to the forensic investigation. But now there was DNA profiling, newly introduced and potentially significant enough to identify an assailant to the exclusion of all other human beings, provided the police caught him first and obtained biological samples and he didn't have an identical twin.

Marino was inside the bedroom right behind me.

"The bathroom window," he said, looking at the body. "Well, according to the husband in there," jerking a thumb in the direction of the kitchen, "the reason it was unlocked's because he unlocked it last weekend."

I just listened.

"He says that bathroom's hardly ever used, unless they got company. Seems he was replacing the screen last weekend, says it's possible he forgot to relock the window when he finished. The bathroom's not used all week. She" – he glanced again at the body – "has no reason to give it a thought, just assumes it's locked." A pause. "Kind of interesting the only window the killer tried, it appears, was that window. The one unlocked. The screens to the rest of 'em aren't cut."

"How many windows are in the back of the house?" I asked.

11

"Three. In the kitchen, the half bath and the bathroom in here."

"And all of them have slide-up sashes with a latch lock at the top?"

"You got it."

"Meaning, if you shone a flashlight on the latch lock from the outside, you probably could see whether it's fastened or not?"

"Maybe." Those flat, unfriendly eyes again. "But only if you climbed up something to look. You couldn't see the lock from the ground."

"You mentioned a picnic bench," I reminded him.

"Problem with that's the backyard's soggy as hell. The legs of the bench should've left depressions in the lawn if the guy put it up against the other windows and stood on top of it to look. I got a couple men poking around out there now. No depressions under the other two windows. Don't look like the killer went near 'em. What it does look like is he went straight to the bathroom window down the hall."

"Is it possible it might have been open a crack, and that's why the killer went straight to it?"

Marino conceded, "Hey. Anything's possible. But if it was open a crack, maybe she would've noticed it, too, at some point during the week."

Maybe. Maybe not. It is easy to be observant retrospectively. But most people don't pay that much attention to every detail of their residences, especially to rooms scarcely used.

Beneath a curtained window overlooking the street was a desk containing other numbing reminders that Lori Petersen and I were of the same profession. Scattered over the blotter were several medical journals, the *Principles of Surgery* and Dorland's. Near the base of the brass gooseneck lamp were two computer diskettes. The labels were tersely dated "6/1" in felt-tip pen and numbered "I" and "II." They were generic double-density diskettes, IBM-compatible. Possibly they contained something Lori Petersen was working on at VMC, the

12

medical college, where there were numerous computers at the disposal of the students and physicians. There didn't appear to be a personal computer inside the house.

On a wicker chair in the corner between the chests of drawers and the window clothes were neatly laid: a pair of white cotton slacks, a red-and-white-striped short-sleeved shirt and a brassiere. The garments were slightly wrinkled, as if worn and left on the chair at the end of the day, the way I sometimes do when I'm too tired to hang up my clothes.

I briefly perused the walk-in closet and full bath. In all, the master bedroom was neat and undisturbed, except for the bed. By all indications, it was not part of the killer's *modus operandi* to ransack or commit burglary.

Marino was watching an ID officer open the dresser drawers.

"What else do you know about the husband?" I asked him.

"He's a grad student at Charlottesville, lives there during the week, comes home on Friday nights. Stays the weekend, then goes back to Charlottesville on Sunday night."

"What is his discipline?"

"Literature's what he said," Marino replied, glancing around at everything but me. "He's getting his Ph.D."

"In what?"

"Literature," he said again, slowly enunciating each syllable.

"What sort of literature?"

His brown eyes finally fixed unemphaticaly on me. "American's what he told me. But I get the impression his main interest is plays. Seems he's in one right now. Shakespeare. *Hamlet*, I think he said. Says he's done a lot of acting, including some bit parts in movies shot around here, a couple of TV commercials, too."

The ID officers stopped what they were doing. One of them turned around, his brush poised in midair.

Marino pointed toward the computer diskettes on the desk and exclaimed loudly enough to grab everybody's

13

attention, "Looks like we'd better take a peek at what's on these suckers. Maybe a play he's writing, huh?"

"We can take a look at them in my office. We've got a couple of IBM-compatible PCs," I offered.

"PCs," he drawled. "Yo. Beats the hell out of my RC: one Royal Crapola, standard issue, black, boxy, sticky keys, the whole nine yards."

An ID officer was pulling out something from beneath a stack of sweaters in a bottom drawer, a long-bladed survival knife with a compass built into the top of the black handle and a small whetstone in a pocket on the sheath. Touching as little of it as possible, he placed it inside a plastic evidence bag.

Out of the same dresser drawer came a box of Trojans, which, I pointed out to Marino, was a little unusual, since Lori Petersen, based on what I'd seen in the master bathroom, was on oral contraceptives.

Marino and the other officers began the expected cynical speculations.

I pulled off my gloves and stuffed them in the top of my bag. "The squad can move her," I said.

The men turned in unison, as if suddenly reminded of the brutalized, dead woman in the center of the rumpled turned-down bed. Her lips were pulled back, as if in pain, from her teeth; her eyes swollen to slits and staring blindly up.

A radio message was relayed to the ambulance, and several minutes later two paramedics in blue jumpsuits came in with a stretcher, which they covered with a clean white sheet and placed flush against the bed.

Lori Petersen was lifted as I directed, the bedclothes folded over her, the gloved hands not touching her skin. She was gently placed on the stretcher, the sheet pinned at the top to ensure no trace evidence was lost or added. Velcro straps made a loud ripping sound as they were peeled apart and fastened across the white cocoon.

Marino followed me out of the bedroom and I was surprised when he announced, "I'll walk you to your car."

14

Matt Petersen was on his feet as we came down the hall. His face wan, his eyes glassy, he stared at me, desperately, needing something only I could give. Assurance. A word of comfort. The promise his wife died quickly and did not suffer. That she was tied up and raped after the fact. There was nothing I could say to him. Marino led me back through the living room and out the door.

The front yard was lit up with television lights floating against the background of hypnotically flashing red and blue. The staccato voices of disembodied dispatchers competed with the throbbing engines as a gentle rain began to fall through a light fog.

Reporters with notepads and tape recorders were everywhere, waiting impatiently for the moment when the body was carried down the front steps and slid into the back of the ambulance. A television crew was on the street, a woman in a snappy belted trenchcoat talking into a microphone, her face serious as a grinding camera recorded her "at the scene" for Saturday's evening news.

Bill Boltz, the Commonwealth's attorney, had just pulled up and was getting out of his car. He looked dazed and half asleep and determined to elude the press. He didn't have anything to say because he didn't know anything yet. I wondered who notified him. Maybe Marino. Cops milled around, a few of them aimlessly probing the grass with their powerful Kel lights, some of them clustered by their white cruisers and talking. Boltz zipped up his windbreaker and nodded as he briefly met my eyes, then hurried up the walk.

The chief of police and a major sat inside an unmarked beige car, the interior light on, their faces pale as they periodically nodded and made remarks to reporter Abby Turnbull. She was saying something to them through an open window. Waiting until we were on the street, she trotted after us.

Marino warded her off with a flap of a hand, a "Hey, no comment" in a "screw yourself" tone of voice.

He stepped up the pace. He was almost a comfort.

"Ain't this the pits?" Marino said with disgust as he patted himself down for his cigarettes. "A regular three-ring circus. Jesus Christ."

The rain was soft and cool on my face as Marino held the station wagon door open for me. As I turned the ignition he leaned down and said with a smirk, "Drive real careful, Doc."

2

The white clock face floated like a full moon in the dark sky, rising high above the old domed train station, the railroad tracks and the I-95 overpass. The great clock's filigree hands stopped when the last passenger train did many years before. It was twelve-seventeen. It would always be twelve-seventeen in the city's lower end where Health and Human Services decided to erect its hospital for the dead.

Time has stopped here. Buildings are boarded up and torn down. Traffic and freight trains perpetually rumble and roar like a distant discontented sea. The earth is a poisoned shore of weed-patched raw dirt littered with debris where nothing grows and there are no lights after dark. Nothing moves here except the truckers and the travelers and the trains speeding along their tracks of concrete and steel.

The white clock face watched me as I drove through the darkness, watched me like the white face in my dream.

I nosed the station wagon through an opening in the chain-link fence and parked behind the stucco building where I'd spent virtually every day of the past two years. The only state vehicle in the lot aside from mine was the gray Plymouth belonging to Neils Vander, the fingerprints examiner. I had called him right after Marino called me. Set into effect after the second strangling was a new policy. If there was another, Vander was to meet me in the morgue immediately. By now he was inside the X-ray room and setting up the laser.

Light was spilling on the tarmac from the open bay, and

17

two paramedics were pulling a stretcher bearing a black body pouch out of the back of an ambulance. Deliveries went on throughout the night. Anybody who died violently, unexpectedly, or suspiciously in central Virginia was sent here, no matter the hour or the day.

The young men in their blue jumpsuits looked surprised to see me as I walked through the bay and held open the door leading inside the building.

"You're out early, Doc."

"Suicide from Mecklenburg," the other attendant volunteered. "Threw himself in front of a train. Scattered him over fifty feet of tracks."

"Yo. Pieces an' parts . . ."

The stretcher bumped through the open doorway and into the white-tiled corridor. The body pouch apparently was defective or torn. Blood leaked through the bottom of the stretcher and left a trail of speckled red.

The morgue had a distinctive odor, the stale stench of death no amount of air deodorizer could mask. Had I been led here blindfolded, I would have known exactly where I was. At this hour of the morning, the smell was more noticeable, more unpleasant than usual. The stretcher clattered loudly through the hollow stillness as the attendants wheeled the suicide into the stainless steel refrigerator.

I turned right into the morgue office where Fred, the security guard, was sipping coffee from a Styrofoam cup and waiting for the ambulance attendants to sign in the body and be on their way. He was sitting on the edge of the desk, ducking out of view, just as he always did when a body was delivered. A gun to his head wouldn't have been sufficient incentive to make him escort anybody inside the refrigerator. Toe tags dangling from cold feet protruding from sheets had a peculiar effect on him.

He shot a sidelong glance at the wall clock. His ten-hour shift was almost at an end.

"We've got another strangling coming in," I bluntly told him.

18

"Lord, Lord! Sure am sorry." Shaking his head. "I tell you. It's hard to imagine anybody doing something like that. All them poor young ladies." Head still shaking.

"It will be here any minute and I want you to make sure the bay door is shut and remains shut after the body's brought in, Fred. The reporters will be out in droves. I don't want anybody within fifty feet of this building. Is that clear?" I sounded hard and sharp, and I knew it. My nerves were singing like a power line.

"Yes, ma'am." A vigorous nod. "I'll keep an eye out, I sure will."

Lighting a cigarette, I reached for the telephone and stabbed out my home number.

Bertha picked up on the second ring and sounded drugged with sleep when she hoarsely asked, "Hello?"

"Just checking in."

"I'm here. Lucy hasn't budged, Dr. Kay. Sleeping like a log, didn't even hear me come in."

"Thank you, Bertha. I can't thank you enough. I don't know when I'll be home."

"I'll be here till I see you, then, Dr. Kay."

Bertha was on notice these days. If I got called out in the middle of the night, so did she. I'd given her a key to the front door and instructions about the operation of the burglar alarm. She probably arrived at my house just minutes after I left for the scene. It dully drifted through my mind that when Lucy got out of bed in several hours, she'd find Bertha inside the kitchen instead of her Auntie Kay.

I had promised to take Lucy to Monticello today.

On a nearby surgical cart was the blue power unit, smaller than a microwave oven, with a row of bright green lights across the front. It was suspended in the pitch darkness of the X-ray room like a satellite in empty space, a spiral cord running from it to a pencil-sized wand filled with seawater.

The laser we acquired last winter was a relatively simple device.

19

In ordinary light sources, atoms and molecules emit light independently and in many different wavelengths. But if an atom is excited by heat, and if light of a certain wavelength is impinged upon it, an atom can be stimulated to emit light in phase.

"Give me just another minute." Neils Vander was working various knobs and switches, his back to me. "She's slow to warm up this morning . . ." Adding in a despondent mumble, "So am I, for that matter."

I was standing on the other side of the X-ray table, watching his shadow through a pair of amber-tinted goggles. Directly below me was the dark shape of Lori Petersen's remains, the covers from her bed open but still underneath her. I stood in the darkness waiting for what seemed a very long time, my thoughts undistracted, my hands perfectly still, my senses undisturbed. Her body was warm, her life so recently ended it seemed to linger about her like an odor.

Vander announced "Ready" and flipped a switch.

Instantly spitting from the wand was a rapidly flashing synchronized light as brilliant as liquid chrysoberyl. It did not dispel darkness but seemed to absorb it. It did not glow but rather flowed over a small surface area. He was a flickering lab coat across the table as he began by directing the wand at her head.

We explored inches of the suffused flesh at a time. Tiny fibers lit up like hot wires and I began collecting them with forceps, my movements staccato in the strobe, creating the illusion of slow motion as I went from her body on the X-ray table to the evidence buttons and envelopes on a cart. Back and forth. Everything was disconnected. The laser's bombardment illuminated a corner of a lip, a rash of pinpoint hemorrhages on the cheekbone, or a wing of the nose, isolating each feature. My gloved fingers working the forceps seemed to belong to somebody else.

The rapidly alternating darkness and light were dizzying, and the only way I could maintain my equilibrium was to channel my concentration into one thought at a time, as if I, like the laser beam, was in phase, too – all of me in sync with what I was doing, the sum of my mental energy coalesced into a single wavelength.

"One of the guys who brought her in," Vander remarked, "told me she was a surgical resident at VMC."

I barely responded.

"Did you know her?"

The question took me by surprise. Something inside me tightened like a fist. I was on the faculty of VMC, where there were hundreds of medical students and residents. There was no reason I should have known her.

I didn't answer except to give directions such as "A little to the right," or "Hold it there for a minute." Vander was slow and deliberate and tense, as was I. A feeling of helplessness and frustration was getting to us. So far the laser had proven to be no better than a Hoover vacuum cleaner that collected miscellaneous debris.

We'd tried it on maybe twenty cases by now, only a few of which actually merited its use. In addition to its usefulness in finding fibers and other trace evidence, it reveals various components of perspiration that fluoresce like a neon sign when stimulated by a laser. Theoretically, a fingerprint left on human skin can emit light and may be identified in cases where traditional powder and chemical methods will fail. I knew of only one case where prints on skin were found, in south Florida, where a woman was murdered inside a health spa and the assailant had tanning oil on his hands. Neither Vander nor I was expecting our luck to be any better than it had been in the past.

What we saw didn't register at first.

The wand was probing several inches of Lori Petersen's right shoulder when directly over her right clavicle three irregular smudges suddenly leapt out as if they were painted with phosphorus. We both stood still and stared. Then he whistled through his teeth as a faint chill ran up my spine.

Retrieving a jar of powder and a Magna brush, Vander

delicately dusted what appeared to be three latent finger-prints left on Lori Petersen's skin.

I dared to hope. "Any good?"

"They're partials," he said abstractedly as he began taking photographs with an MP-4 Polaroid camera. "The ridge detail's damn good. Good enough to classify, I think. I'll run these babes through the computer right away."

"Looks like the same residue," I thought out loud. "The same stuff on his hands." The monster had signed his work again. It was too good to be true. The fingerprints were too good to be true.

"Looks the same, all right. But he must have had a lot more of it on his hands this time."

The killer had never left his prints in the past, but the glittery residue, which apparently caused them to fluoresce, was something we'd grown to expect. There was more of it. As Vander began probing her neck, a constellation of tiny white stars popped out like shards of glass hit by headlights on a dark street. He held the wand in place as I reached for a sterilized gauze pad.

We'd found the same glitter scattered over the bodies of the first three strangling victims, more of it in the third case than in the second, and the least amount found in the first. Samples had been sent to the labs. So far, the strange residue had not been identified beyond determining it was inorganic.

We weren't closer to knowing what it was, though by now we had quite a long list of substances it couldn't be. Over the past few weeks, Vander and I had run several series of tests, smearing everything from margarine to body lotions on our own forearms to see what reacted to the laser and what didn't. Fewer samples lit up than either of us had supposed, and nothing blazed as brightly as the unknown glittery residue.

I gently wedged a finger under the electrical cord ligature around Lori Petersen's neck, exposing an angry red furrow in the flesh. The margin wasn't clearly defined – the strangulation was slower than I'd originally thought. I could see the faint abrasions from the cord's having slipped in place several times. It was loose enough to keep her barely alive for a while. Then suddenly, it was jerked tight. There were two or three sparkles clinging to the cord, and that was all.

"Try the ligature around her ankles," I said quietly.

We moved down. The same white sparkles were there, too, but again, very few of them. There was none of this residue, whatever it was, anywhere on her face, none in her hair or on her legs. We found several of the sparkles on her forearms, and a spangling of them over her upper arms and breasts. A constellation of the tiny white stars clung to the cords savagely binding her wrists in back, and there was a scattering of the glitter over her cut gown as well.

I moved away from the table, lit a cigarette and began reconstructing.

The assailant had some material on his hands that was deposited wherever he touched his victim. After Lori Petersen's gown was off, perhaps he gripped her right shoulder and his fingertips left the smudges over her clavicle. One thing I felt sure of: For the concentration of this material to be so dense over her clavicle, he must have touched her there first.

This was puzzling, a piece that seemed to fit but didn't, really.

From the beginning, I'd assumed he was restraining his victims immediately, subduing them, perhaps at knifepoint, and then binding them before he cut off their clothing or did anything else. The more he touched, the less of the residue was left on his hands. Why this high concentration over her clavicle? Was this area of her skin exposed when he began his assault? I wouldn't have supposed so. The gown was an interlocking cotton material, soft and stretchy and fashioned to look almost exactly like a long-sleeved T-shirt. There were no buttons or zippers, and the only way for her to have put it on was to pull it over her head. She would have been covered to her neck. How could the killer touch the bare skin over her clavicle if she still had her gown on? Why was there such a

23

high concentration of the residue at all? We'd never found such a high concentration before.

I went out into the hallway where several uniformed men were leaning against the wall, chatting. I asked one of them to raise Marino on the radio and have him call me right away. I heard Marino's voice crackle back, "Ten fo'." I paced the hard tile floor inside the autopsy suite with its gleaming stainless steel tables and sinks and carts lined with surgical instruments. A faucet was dripping somewhere. Disinfectant smelled sweetly revolting, only smelled pleasant when there were worse smells lurking beneath it. The black telephone on the desk mocked me with its silence. Marino knew I was waiting by the phone. He was having a good time knowing that.

It was idle speculation to go back to the beginning and try to figure out what had gone wrong. Occasionally I thought about it anyway. What it was about me. I had been polite to Marino the first time we met, had offered him a firm and respectful handshake while his eyes went as flat as two tarnished pennies.

Twenty minutes passed before the telephone rang.

Marino was still at the Petersen house, he said, interviewing the husband, who was, in the detective's words, "as goofy as a shithouse rat."

I told him about the sparkles. I repeated what I'd explained to him in the past. It was possible they might be from some household substance consistent in all of the homicide scenes, some oddball something the killer looked for and incorporated into his ritual. Baby powder, lotions, cosmetics, cleansers.

So far, we had ruled out many things which, in a way, was the point. If the substance wasn't indigenous to the scenes, and in my heart I didn't think it was, then the killer was carrying it in with him, perhaps unaware, and this could be important and eventually lead us to where he worked or lived.

"Yeah," Marino's voice came over the line, "well, I'll poke

around in the cabinets and so forth. But I got my own thought."

"Which is?"

"The husband here's in a play, right? Has practice every Friday night, which is why he gets in so late, right? Correct me if I'm wrong, but actors wear greasepaint."

"Only during dress rehearsals or performances."

"Yeah," he drawled. "Well, according to him, a dress rehearsal's exactly what he had just before he came home and supposedly found his dead wife. My little bell's ringing. My little voice is talking to me –"

I cut him off. "Have you printed him?"

"Oh, yeah."

"Place his card inside a plastic bag and when you come in bring it straight to me."

He didn't get it.

I didn't elaborate. I was in no mood to explain.

The last thing Marino told me before hanging up was "Don't know when that will be, Doc. Got a feeling I'm going to be tied up out here most of the day. No pun intended."

It was unlikely I would see him or the fingerprint card until Monday. Marino had a suspect. He was galloping down the same trail every cop gallops down. A husband could be St. Anthony and in England when his wife is murdered in Seattle, and still the cops are suspicious of him first.

Domestic shootings, poisonings, beatings and stabbings are one thing, but a lust murder is another. Not many husbands would have the stomach for binding, raping and strangling their wives.

I blamed my disconcertedness on fatigue.

I had been up since 2:33 A.M. and it was now almost 6:00 P.M. The police officers who came to the morgue were long gone. Vander went home around lunchtime. Wingo, one of my autopsy technicians, left not long after that, and there was no one inside the building but me.

The quiet I usually craved was unnerving and I could not

seem to get warm. My hands were stiff, the fingernails almost blue. Every time the telephone rang in the front office, I started.

The minimal security in my office never seemed to worry anyone but me. Budget requests for an adequate security system were repeatedly refused. The commissioner thought in terms of property loss, and no thief was going to come into the morgue even if we put out welcome mats and left the doors open wide at all hours. Dead bodies are a better deterrent than guard dogs.

The dead have never bothered me. It is the living I fear.

After a crazed gunman walked into a local doctor's office several months back and sprayed bullets into a waiting room full of patients, I went to a hardware store and bought a chain and padlock myself, which after hours and on weekends were used to reinforce the front glass double doors.

Suddenly, while I was working at my desk, someone shook those front doors so violently the chain was still swaying when I forced myself to go down the hallway to check. No one was there. Sometimes street people tried to get in to use our restrooms, but when I looked out I didn't see anyone.

I returned to my office and was so jumpy that when I heard the elevator doors opening across the hall I had a large pair of scissors in hand and was prepared to use them. It was the day-shift security guard.

"Did you try to get in through the front glass doors a little while ago?" I asked.

He glanced curiously at the scissors I was clutching and said he didn't. I'm sure it seemed an inane question. He knew the front doors were chained, and he had a set of keys to the other doors throughout the building. He had no reason to try to get in through the front.

An uneasy silence returned as I sat at my desk trying to dictate Lori Petersen's autopsy report. For some reason, I couldn't say anything, couldn't bear to hear the words out loud. It began to dawn on me that no one should hear these words, not even Rose, my secretary. No one should hear about the glittery residue, the seminal fluid, the fingerprints, the deep tissue injuries to her neck – and worst of all, the evidence of torture. The killer was degenerating, becoming more hideously cruel.

Rape and murder were no longer enough for him. It wasn't until I'd removed the ligatures from Lori Petersen's body, and was making small incisions in suspicious reddish-tinted areas of skin and palpating for broken bones that I realized what went on before she died.

The contusions were so recent they were barely visible on the surface, but the incisions revealed the broken blood vessels under the skin, and the patterns were consistent with her having been struck with a blunt object, such as a knee or a foot. Three ribs in a row on the left side were fractured, as were four of her fingers. There were fibers inside her mouth, mostly on her tongue, suggesting that at some point she was gagged to prevent her from screaming.

In my mind I saw the violin on the music stand inside the living room, and the surgical journals and books on the desk in the bedroom. Her hands. They were her most prized instruments, something with which she healed and made music. He must have deliberately broken her fingers one by one after she was bound.

The microcassette recorder spun on, recording silence. I switched it off and swiveled my judge's chair around to the computer terminal. The monitor blinked from black to the sky blue of the word-processing package, and black letters marched across the screen as I began typing the autopsy report myself.

I didn't look at the weights and notes I'd scribbled on an empty glove packet when I was performing the autopsy. I knew everything about her. I had total recall. The phrase "within normal limits" was playing nonstop inside my head. There was nothing wrong with her. Her heart, her lungs, her liver. "Within normal limits." She died in perfect health. I typed on and on and on, full pages blinking out as I was automatically given new screens until I suddenly looked up. Fred, the security guard, was standing in my doorway.

I had no idea how long I'd been working. He was due back on duty at 8:00 P.M. Everything that had transpired since I saw him last seemed like a dream, a very bad dream.

"You still here?" Then hesitantly, "Uh, there's this funeral home downstairs for a pickup but can't find the body. Come all the way from Mecklenburg. Don't know where Wingo is . . ."

"Wingo went home hours ago," I said. "What body?"

"Someone named Roberts, got hit by a train."

I thought for a moment. Including Lori Petersen, there were six cases today. I vaguely recalled the train fatality. "He's in the refrigerator."

"They say they can't find 'im in there."

I slipped off my glasses and rubbed my eyes. "Did you look?"

His face broke into a sheepish grin. Fred backed away shaking his head. "You know, Dr. Sca'petta, I don't never go inside that box! Uh-uh."

3

I pulled into my driveway, relieved to find Bertha's boat of a Pontiac still there. The front door opened before I had a chance to select the right key.

"How's the weather?" I asked right off.

Bertha and I faced each other inside the spacious foyer. She knew exactly what I meant. We had this conversation at the end of every day when Lucy was in town.

"Been *bad*, Dr. Kay. That child been in your office all day banging on that computer of yours. I tell you! I as much as step foot in there to bring her a sandwich and ask how she be and she start hollerin' and carryin' on. But I know." Her dark eyes softened. "She just upset because you had to work."

Guilt seeped through my numbness.

"I seen the evenin' paper, Dr. Kay. Lord have mercy." She was working one arm at a time into the sleeves of her raincoat. "I know why you had to be doin' what you was doin' all day. Lord, Lord. I sure do hope the police catch that man. Meanness. Just plain meanness."

Bertha knew what I did for a living and she never questioned me. Even if one of my cases was someone from her neighborhood, she never asked.

"The evenin' paper's in there." She gestured toward the living room and collected her pocketbook from the table near the door. "I stuck it under the sofa cushion so she couldn't get hold of it. Didn't know if you'd want her to be readin' it or not, Dr. Kay." She patted my shoulder on her way out.

29

I watched her make her way to her car and slowly back out of the drive. God bless her. I no longer apologized for my family. Bertha had been insulted and bullied either face-to-face or over the phone by my niece, my sister, my mother. Bertha knew. She never sympathized or criticized, and I sometimes suspected she felt sorry for me, and that only made me feel worse. Shutting the front door, I went into the kitchen.

It was my favorite room, high-ceilinged, the appliances modern but few, for I prefer to do most things, such as making pasta or kneading dough, by hand. There was a maple butcher block in the center of the cooking area, just the right height for someone not a stitch over five foot three in her stocking feet. The breakfast area faced a large picture window overlooking the wooded backyard and the bird feeder. Splashing the monochrome blonds of wooden cabinets and countertops were loose arrangements of yellow and red roses from my passionately well attended garden.

Lucy was not here. Her supper dishes were upright in the drainboard and I assumed she was in my office again.

I went to the refrigerator and poured myself a glass of Chablis. Leaning against the counter, I shut my eyes for a moment and sipped. I didn't know what I was going to do about Lucy.

Last summer was her first visit here since I had left the Dade County Medical Examiner's Office and moved away from the city where I was born and where I had returned after my divorce. Lucy is my only niece. At ten she was already doing high-school-level science and math. She was a genius, an impossible little holy terror of enigmatic Latin descent whose father died when she was small. She had no one but my only sister, Dorothy, who was too caught up in writing children's books to worry much about her flesh-and-blood daughter. Lucy adored me beyond any rational explanation, and her attachment to me demanded energy I did not have at the moment. While driving home, I debated

30

changing her flight reservations and sending her back to Miami early. I couldn't bring myself to do it.

She would be devastated. She would not understand. It would be the final rejection in a lifelong series of rejections, another reminder she was inconvenient and unwanted. She had been looking forward to this visit all year. I'd been looking forward to it, too.

Taking another sip of wine, I waited for the absolute quiet to begin untangling my snarled nerves and smoothing away my worries.

My house was in a new subdivision in the West End of the city, where the large homes stood on wooded one-acre lots and the traffic on the streets was mostly station wagons and family cars. The neighbors were so quiet, break-ins and vandalism so rare, I couldn't recall the last time I had seen a police car cruise through. The stillness, the security, was worth any price, a necessity, a must, for me. It was soothing to my soul on early mornings to eat breakfast alone and know the only violence beyond my window would be a squirrel and a blue jay fighting over the feeder.

I took a deep breath and another sip of wine. I began to dread going to bed, dreading those moments in the dark before sleep, fearing what it would be like when I permitted my mind to be still, and therefore unguarded. I could not stop seeing images of Lori Petersen. A dam had broken and my imagination was rushing in, quickening the images into more terrible ones.

I saw him with her, inside that bedroom. I could almost see his face, but it had no features, just a glimpse of a facelike flash going by as he was with her. She would try to reason with him at first, after the paralyzing fear of waking up at the feel of cold flat steel to her throat, or at the chilling sound of his voice. She would say things, try to talk him out of it for God knows how long as he cut the cords from the lamps and began to bind her. She was a Harvard graduate, a surgeon. She would attempt to use her mind against a force that is mindless.

31

Then the images went wild, like a film at high speed, flapping off the reel as her attempts disintegrated into unmitigated terror. The unspeakable. I would not look. I could not bear to see any more. I had to control my thoughts.

My home office overlooked the woods in back and the blinds were typically drawn because it has always been hard for me to concentrate if I'm offered a view. I paused in the doorway, quietly letting my attention drift as Lucy vigorously tapped away on the keyboard on top of my sturdy oak desk, her back to me. I had not straightened up in here in weeks, and the sight of it was shameful. Books leaned this way and that in the bookcases, several *Law Reporters* were stacked on the floor and others were out of order. Propped against a wall were my diplomas and certificates: Cornell, Johns Hopkins, Georgetown, et al. I'd been meaning to hang them in my office downtown but had yet to get around to it. Sloppily piled on a corner of the deep blue T'ai-Ming rug were journal articles still waiting to be read and filed. Professional success meant I no longer had the time to be impeccably neat, and yet clutter bothered me as much as ever.

"How come you're spying on me?" Lucy muttered without turning around.

"I'm not spying on you." I smiled a little and kissed the top of her burnished red head.

"Yes, you are." She continued to type. "I saw you. I saw your reflection in the monitor. You've been standing in the doorway watching me."

I put my arms around her, rested my chin on the top of her head and looked at the black screen filled with chartreuse commands. It never occurred to me before this moment that the screen had a mirror effect, and I now understood why Margaret, my programming analyst, could hail by name people walking past her office though she had her back to the door. Lucy's face was a blur in the monitor. Mostly I saw a reflection of her grown-up, tortoise-rimmed glasses. She usually greeted me with a tree frog hug, but she was in a mood.

32

"I'm sorry we couldn't go to Monticello today, Lucy," I ventured.

A shrug.

"I'm as disappointed as you are," I said.

Another shrug. "I'd rather use the computer anyway."

She didn't mean it, but the remark stung.

"I had a shit-load of stuff to do," she went on, sharply striking the Return key. "Your data base needed cleaning up. Bet you haven't initialized it in a year." She swiveled around in my leather chair and I moved to one side, crossing my arms at my waist.

"So I fixed it up."

"You *what*?"

No, Lucy wouldn't do such a thing. Initializing was the same thing as formatting, obliterating, erasing all of the data on the hard disk. On the hard disk were – or had been – half a dozen statistical tables I was using for journal articles under deadline. The only backups were several months old.

Lucy's green eyes fixed on mine and looked owlish behind the thick lenses of her glasses. Her round, elfish face was hard as she said, "I looked in the books to see how. All you do is type IOR I at the C prompt, and after it's initialized, you do the Addall and Catalog.Ora. It's easy. Any dick head could figure it out."

I didn't say anything. I didn't reprimand her for her dirty mouth.

I was feeling weak in the knees.

I was remembering Dorothy calling me, absolutely hysterical, several years ago. While she was out shopping, Lucy had gone into her office and formatted every last one of her diskettes, erasing everything on them. On two of them was a book Dorothy was writing, chapters she hadn't gotten around to printing out or backing up yet. A homicidal event.

"Lucy. You didn't."

"Ohhhh, don't worry," she said sullenly. "I exported all

33

your data first. The book says to. And then I imported it back in and reconnected your grants. Everything's there. But it's cleaned up, space-wise, I mean."

I pulled up an ottoman and sat beside her. It was then I noticed what was beneath a layer of diskettes: the evening paper, folded the way papers are folded when they have been read. I slid it out and opened it to the front page. The banner headline was the last thing I wanted to see.

YOUNG SURGEON SLAIN: BELIEVED TO BE STRANGLER'S FOURTH VICTIM

A 30-year-old surgical resident was found brutally murdered inside her home in Berkley Downs shortly after midnight. Police say there is strong evidence that her death is related to the deaths of three other Richmond women who were strangled in their homes within the last two months.

The most recent victim has been identified as Lori Anne Petersen, a graduate of Harvard Medical School. She was last seen alive yesterday, shortly after midnight, when she left the VMC hospital emergency room, where she was currently completing a rotation in trauma surgery. It is believed she drove directly home from the hospital and was murdered sometime between twelve-thirty and two this morning. The killer apparently got inside her house by cutting a screen to a bathroom window that was unlocked . . .

It went on. There was a photograph, a grainy black-and-white tableau of paramedics carrying her body down the front steps, and a smaller photograph of a figure in a khaki raincoat I recognized as me. The caption read: "Dr. Kay Scarpetta, Chief Medical Examiner, Arriving at Murder Scene."

Lucy was staring wide-eyed at me. Bertha had been wise to hide the paper, but Lucy was resourceful. I didn't know what to say. What does a ten-year-old think when she reads something like this, especially if it is accompanied by a grim photograph of her "Auntie Kay"?

I'd never fully explained to Lucy the details of my profession. I'd restrained myself from preaching to her about the savage world in which we live. I didn't want her to be like me, robbed of innocence and idealism, baptized in the bloody waters of randomness and cruelty, the fabric of trust forever torn.

"It's like the *Herald*," she quite surprised me by saying. "All the time there's stuff in the *Herald* about people being killed. Last week they found a man in the canal and his head was cut off. He must have been a bad man for someone to cut his head off."

"He may have been, Lucy. But it doesn't justify someone's doing something like that to him. And not everyone who is hurt or murdered is bad."

"Mom says they are. She says good people don't get murdered. Only hookers and drug dealers and burglars do." A thoughtful pause. "Sometimes police officers, too, because they try to catch the bad people."

Dorothy would say such a thing and, what was worse, she would believe it. I felt a flare of the old anger.

"But the lady who got strangled," Lucy wavered, her eyes so wide they seemed to swallow me. "She was a doctor, Auntie Kay. How could she be bad? You're a doctor, too. She was just like you, then."

I was suddenly aware of the time. It was getting late. I switched off the computer, took Lucy's hand, and we walked out of the office and into the kitchen. When I turned to her to suggest a snack before bed, I was dismayed to see she was biting her bottom lip, her eyes welling.

"Lucy! Why are you crying?"

She wrapped around me, sobbing. Clinging to me with fierce desperation, she cried, "I don't want you to die! I don't want you to die!"

"*Lucy* . . ." I was stunned, bewildered. Her tantrums, her arrogant and angry outbursts were one thing. But this! I could feel her tears soaking through my blouse. I could feel the hot intensity of her miserable little body as she held on to me.

"It's all right, Lucy," was all I could think to say, and I pressed her close.

"I don't want you to die, Auntie Kay!"

"I'm not going to die, Lucy."

"Daddy did."

"Nothing is going to happen to me, Lucy."

She was not to be consoled. The story in the paper affected her in a deep and pernicious way. She read it with an adult intellect yet to be weaned from a child's fearful imagination. This in addition to her insecurities and losses.

Oh, Lord. I groped for the appropriate response and couldn't come up with a thing. My mother's accusations began throbbing in some deep part of my psyche. My inadequacies. I had no children. I would have made an awful mother. "You should have been a man," my mother had said during one of our less productive encounters in recent history. "All work and ambition. It's not natural for a woman. You'll dry out like a chinch bug, Kay."

And during my emptiest moments when I felt the worst about myself, damn if I wouldn't see one of those chinch bug shells that used to litter the lawn of my childhood home. Translucent, brittle, dried out. Dead.

It wasn't something I would ordinarily do, pour a ten-year-old a glass of wine.

I took her to her room and we drank in bed. She asked me questions impossible to answer. "Why do people hurt other people?" and "Is it a game for him? I mean, does he do it for fun, sort of like MTV? They do things like that on MTV, but it's make-believe. Nobody gets hurt. Maybe he doesn't mean to hurt them, Auntie Kay."

"There are some people who are evil," I quietly replied. "Like dogs, Lucy. Some dogs bite people for no reason. There's something wrong with them. They're bad and will always be bad."

36

"Because people were mean to them first. That's what makes them bad."

"In some instances, yes," I told her. "But not always. Sometimes there isn't a reason. In a way, it doesn't matter. People make choices. Some people would rather be bad, would rather be cruel. It's just an ugly, unfortunate part of life."

"Like Hitler," she muttered, taking a swallow of wine.

I began stroking her hair.

She rambled on, her voice thick with sleep, "Like Jimmy Groome, too. He lives on our street and shoots birds with his BB gun, and he likes to steal bird eggs out of nests and smash them on the road and watch the baby birds struggle. I hate him. I hate Jimmy Groome. I threw a rock at him once and hit him when he was riding by on his bike. But he doesn't know it was me because I was hiding behind the bushes."

I sipped wine and continued stroking her hair.

"God won't let anything happen to you, will He?" she asked.

"Nothing is going to happen to me, Lucy. I promise."

"If you pray to God to take care of you, He does, doesn't He?"

"He takes care of us." Though I wasn't sure I believed it.

She frowned. I'm not sure she believed it either. "Don't you ever get scared?"

I smiled. "Everybody gets scared now and then. I'm perfectly safe. Nothing's going to happen to me."

The last thing she mumbled before drifting off was "I wish I could always be here, Auntie Kay. I want to be just like you."

Two hours later, I was upstairs and still wide-awake and staring at a page in a book without really seeing the words when the telephone rang.

My response was Pavlovian, a startled reflex. I snatched up the receiver, my heart thudding. I was expecting, fearing, Marino's voice, as if last night were starting all over again.

"Hello."

Nothing.

"Hello?"

In the background I could hear the faint, spooky music I associated with early-morning foreign movies or horror films or the scratchy strains of a Victrola before the dial tone cut it off.

"Coffee?"

"Please," I said.

This sufficed for a "Good morning."

Whenever I stopped by Neils Vander's lab, his first word of greeting was "Coffee?" I always accepted. Caffeine and nicotine are two vices I've readily adopted.

I wouldn't think of buying a car that isn't as solid as a tank, and I won't start the engine without fastening my seat-belt. There are smoke alarms throughout my house, and an expensive burglar alarm system. I no longer enjoy flying and opt for Amtrak whenever possible.

But caffeine, cigarettes and cholesterol, the grim reapers of the common man – God forbid I should give them up. I go to a national meeting and sit at a banquet with three hundred other forensic pathologists, the world's foremost experts in disease and death. Seventy-five percent of us don't jog or do aerobics, don't walk when we can ride, don't stand when we can sit, and assiduously avoid stairs or hills unless they're on the decline. A third of us smoke, most of us drink, and all of us eat as if there is no tomorrow.

Stress, depression, perhaps a greater need for laughter and pleasure because of the misery we see – who can be sure of the reason? One of my more cynical friends, an assistant chief in Chicago, likes to say, "What the hell. You die. Everybody dies. So you die healthy. So what?"

Vander went to the drip coffee machine on the counter behind his desk and poured two cups. He had fixed my coffee countless times and could never remember I drink it black.

My ex-husband never remembered either. Six years I

38

lived with Tony and he couldn't remember that I drink my coffee black or like my steaks medium-rare, not as red as Christmas, just a little pink. My dress size, forget it. I wear an eight, have a figure that will accommodate most anything, but I can't abide fluff, froth and frills. He always got me something in a six, usually lacy and gauzy and meant for bed. His mother's favorite color was spring green. She wore a size fourteen. She loved ruffles, hated pullovers, preferred zippers, was allergic to wool, didn't want to bother with anything that had to be dry-cleaned or ironed, had a visceral antagonism toward anything purple, deemed white or beige impractical, wouldn't wear horizontal stripes or paisley, wouldn't have been caught dead in Ultrasuede, believed her body wasn't compatible with pleats and was quite fond of pockets – the more the better. When it came to his mother, Tony would somehow get it right.

Vander dumped the same heaping teaspoons of whitener and sugar into my cup as he dumped into his own.

Typically, he was disheveled, his wispy gray hair wild, his voluminous lab coat smeared with black fingerprint powder, a spray of ballpoint pens and felt-tip markers protruding from his ink-stained breast pocket. He was a tall man with long, bony extremities and a disproportionately round belly. His head was shaped remarkably like a light bulb, his eyes a washed-out blue and perpetually clouded by thought.

My first winter here he stopped by my office late one afternoon to announce it was snowing. A long red scarf was wrapped around his neck, and pulled over his ears was a leather flight helmet, possibly ordered from a Banana Republic catalogue and absolutely the most ridiculous winter hat I'd ever seen. I think he would have looked perfectly at home inside a Fokker fighter plane. "The Flying Dutchman," we appropriately called him around the office. He was always in a hurry, flying up and down the halls, his lab coat flapping around his legs.

"You saw the papers?" he asked, blowing on his coffee.

"The whole blessed world saw the papers," I dismally replied.

Sunday's front page was worse than Saturday evening's. The banner headline ran across the entire width of the top of the page, the letters about an inch high. The story included a sidebar about Lori Petersen and a photograph that looked as if it came from a yearbook. Abby Turnbull was aggressive enough, if not indecent, to attempt an interview with Lori Petersen's family, who lived in Philadelphia and "were too distraught to comment."

"It sure as hell isn't helping us any," Vander stated the obvious. "I'd like to know where the information's coming from so I could string a few people up by their thumbs."

"The cops haven't learned to keep their mouths shut," I told him. "When they learn to zip their lips, they won't have leaks to bitch about anymore."

"Well, maybe it's the cops. Whatever the case, the stuff's making my wife crazy. I think if we lived in the city, she'd make us move today."

He went to his desk, which was a jumble of computer printouts, photographs and telephone messages. There was a quart beer bottle and a floor tile with a dried bloody shoe print, both inside plastic bags and tagged as evidence. Randomly scattered about were ten small jars of formalin, each containing a charred human fingertip anatomically severed at the second joint. In cases of unidentified bodies that are badly burned or decomposed, it isn't always possible to get prints by the usual method. Incongruously stationed in the midst of this macabre mess was a bottle of Vaseline Intensive Care lotion.

Rubbing a dollop of the lotion on his hands, Vander pulled on a pair of white cotton gloves. The acetone, xylene and constant hand-washing that go with his trade were brutal on his skin, and I could always tell when he'd forgotten to put on gloves while using ninhydrin, a chemical helpful for visualizing latent prints, because he'd walk around with purple fingers for a week. His morning ritual complete, he motioned me to follow him out into the fourth-floor hallway.

Several doors down was the computer room, clean, almost sterile, and filled with light-silver modular hardware of various boxy shapes and sizes, bringing to mind a space-age Laundromat. The sleek, upright unit most closely resembling a set of washers and dryers was the fingerprint matching processor, its function to match unknown prints against the multimillion fingerprint data base stored on magnetic disks. The FMP, as it was known, with its advanced pipeline and parallel processing was capable of eight hundred matches per second. Vander didn't like to sit around and wait for the results. It was his habit to let the thing cook overnight so he had something to look forward to when he came to work the next morning.

The most time-consuming part of the process was what Vander did Saturday, feeding the prints into the computer. This required his taking photographs of the latent prints in question, enlarging them five times, placing a sheet of tracing paper over each photograph and with a felt-tip pen tracing the most significant characteristics. Next he reduced the drawing to a one-to-one-sized photograph, precisely correlating to the actual size of the print. He glued the photograph to a latent-print layout sheet, which he fed into the computer. Now it simply was a matter of printing out the results of the search.

Vander seated himself with the deliberation of a concert pianist about to perform. I almost expected him to flip up his lab coat in back and stretch his fingers. His Steinway was the remote input station, consisting of a keyboard, a monitor, an image scanner and a fingerprint image processor, among other things. The image scanner was capable of reading both ten-print cards and latent prints. The fingerprint image processor (or FIP, as Vander referred to it) automatically detected fingerprint characteristics.

I watched him type in several commands. Then he

punched the print button, and lists of potential suspects were rapidly hammered across the green-striped paper.

I pulled up a chair as Vander tore off the printout and ripped the paper into ten sections, separating his cases.

We were interested in 88-01651, the identification number for the latents found on Lori Petersen's body. Computerized print comparison is analogous to a political election. Possible matches are called candidates, and ranked according to score. The higher the score, the more points of comparison a candidate has in common with the unknown latents entered into the computer. In the case of 88-01651 there was one candidate leading by a wide margin of more than one thousand points. This could mean only one thing.

A hit.

Or as Vander glibly put it, "A hot one."

The winning candidate was impersonally listed as NIC112.

I really hadn't expected this.

"So whoever left the prints on her has prints on file with the data base?" I asked.

"That's right."

"Meaning it's possible he has a criminal record?"

"Possible, but not necessarily." Vander got up and moved to the verification terminal. He lightly rested his fingers on the keyboard and stared into the CRT display.

He added, "Could be he was printed for some other reason. If he's in law enforcement, or maybe applied for a taxi license once."

He began calling up fingerprint cards from the depths of image retrieval. Instantly, the search-print image, an enlarged aggregation of loops and whorls in turquoise blue, was juxtaposed to the candidate-print image. To the right was a column listing the sex, race, date of birth and other information revealing the candidate's identification. Producing a hard copy of the prints, he handed it over.

I studied it, read and reread the identity of NIC112.

Marino would be thrilled.

According to the computer, and there could be no mistake about it, the latents the laser picked up on Lori Petersen's shoulder were left by Matt Petersen, her husband.

4

I was not unduly surprised that Matt Petersen touched her body. Often it is a reflex to touch someone who appears dead, to feel for a pulse or to grip a shoulder lightly the way one does to wake up the person. What dismayed me were two things. First, the latents were picked up because the individual who left them had a residue of the perplexing sparkles on his fingers – evidence also found in the previous strangling cases. Second, Matt Petersen's ten-print card had not been turned in to the lab yet. The only reason the computer got a hit was he *already* had prints on file with the data base.

I was telling Vander we needed to find out why and when Petersen was printed in the past, if he had a criminal record, when Marino walked in.

"Your secretary said you was up here," he announced by way of a greeting.

He was eating a doughnut I recognized as having come from the box by the coffee machine downstairs. Rose always brought in doughnuts on Monday mornings. Glancing around at the hardware, he casually shoved a manila envelope my way. "Sorry, Neils," he mumbled. "But the Doc here says she's got first dibs."

Vander looked curiously at me as I opened the envelope. Inside was a plastic evidence bag containing Petersen's ten-print card. Marino had put me on the spot, and I didn't appreciate it. The card, under ordinary circumstances, should have been receipted directly to the fingerprints lab – not to

44

me. It is this very sort of maneuver that creates animosity on the part of one's colleagues. They assume you're violating their turf, assume you're preempting them when, in truth, you may be doing nothing of the sort.

I explained to Vander, "I didn't want this left on your desk, out in the open where it might be handled. Matt Petersen supposedly was using greasepaint before he came home. If there was a residue on his hands, it may also be on his card."

Vander's eyes widened. The thought appealed to him. "Sure. We'll run it under the laser."

Marino was staring sullenly at me.

I asked him, "What about the survival knife?"

He produced another envelope from the stack wedged between his elbow and waist. "Was on my way to take it to Frank."

Vander suggested, "We'll take a look at it with the laser first."

Then he printed out another hard copy of NIC112, the latents that Matt Petersen had left on his wife's body, and presented it to Marino.

He studied it briefly, muttering, "Ho-ly shit," and he looked up straight at me.

His eyes smiled in triumph. I was familiar with the look, which I had expected. It said, "So there, *Ms. Chief*. So maybe you got book-learning, but me, I know the street."

I could feel the investigative screws tightening on the husband of a woman who I still believed was slain by a man not known to any of us.

Fifteen minutes later, Vander, Marino and I were inside what was the equivalent of a darkroom adjoining the fingerprint lab. On a countertop near a large sink were the ten-print card and the survival knife. The room was pitch-black. Marino's big belly was unpleasantly brushing my left elbow as the dazzling pulses ignited a scattering of sparkles on the inky smudges of the card. In addition, there were sparkles on the handle of the knife, which was hard rubber and too coarse for prints.

On the knife's wide shiny blade was a smattering of virtually microscopic debris and several distinct partial prints that Vander dusted and lifted. He leaned closer to the tenprint card. A quick visual comparison with his eagle, expert eye was enough for him to tentatively say, "Based on an initial ridge comparison, they're his, the prints on the blade are Petersen's."

The laser went off, throwing us into complete blackness, and presently we were squinting in the rude glare of overhead lights that had suddenly returned us to the world of dreary cinder block and white Formica.

Pushing back my goggles, I began the litany of objective reminders as Vander fooled around with the laser and Marino lit a cigarette.

"The prints on the knife may not mean anything. If the knife belonged to Petersen, you'd expect to find his prints. As for the sparkling residue – yes, it's obvious he had something on his hands when he touched his wife's body and when he was fingerprinted. But we can't be sure the substance is the same as the glitter found elsewhere, particularly in the first three strangling cases. We'll give scanning electron microscopy a shot at it, hopefully determine if the elemental compositions or infrared spectrums are the same as those in the residues found on other areas of her body and in the previous cases."

"What?" Marino asked, incredulously. "You thinking Matt had one thing on his hands and the killer had something else, and they ain't the same but both look the same under the laser?"

"Almost everything that reacts strongly to the laser looks the same," I told him in slow, measured words. "It glows like white neon light."

"Yeah, but most people don't have white neon crap on their hands, to my knowledge."

I had to agree. "Most people don't."

"Sort of a weird little coincidence Matt just happens to have the stuff on his hands, whatever it is."

"You mentioned he'd just come home from a dress rehearsal," I reminded him.

"That's his story."

"It might not be a bad idea to collect the makeup he was using Friday night and bring it in for testing."

Marino stared disdainfully at me.

In my office was one of the few personal computers on the second floor. It was connected to the main computer down the hall, but it wasn't a dumb terminal. Even if the main computer was down, I could use my PC for word processing if nothing else.

Marino handed over the two diskettes found on the desk inside the Petersen bedroom. I slipped them into the drives and executed a directory command for each one.

An index of files, or chapters, of what clearly was Matt Petersen's dissertation appeared on the screen. The subject was Tennessee Williams, "whose most successful plays reveal a frustrating world in which sex and violence lie beneath the surface of romantic gentility," read the opening paragraph of the Introduction.

Marino was peering over my shoulder shaking his head.

"Jeez," he muttered, "this is only getting better. No wonder the squirrel freaked when I told him we was taking these disks in. Look at this stuff."

I rolled down the screen.

Flashing past were Williams's controversial treatments of homosexuality and cannibalism. There were references to the brutish Stanley Kowalski and to the castrated gigolo in *Sweet Bird of Youth*. I didn't need clairvoyant powers to read Marino's mind, which was as banal as the front page of a tabloid. To him, this was the stuff of garden-variety porn, the fuel of the psychopathic minds that feed on fantasies of sexual aberrancies and violence. Marino wouldn't know the difference between the street and the stage if he were pistol-whipped with a Drama 101 course.

The people like Williams, and even Matt Petersen, who

47

create such scenarios rarely are the individuals who go around living them.

I looked levelly at Marino. "What would you think if Petersen were an Old Testament scholar?"

He shrugged, his eyes shifting away from me, glancing back at the screen. "Hey. This ain't exactly Sunday school material."

"Neither are rapes, stonings, beheadings and whores. And in real life, Truman Capote wasn't a mass murderer, Sergeant."

He backed away from the computer and went to a chair. I swiveled around, facing him across the wide expanse of my desk. Ordinarily, when he stopped by my office he preferred to stand, to remain on his feet towering over me. But he was sitting, and we were eye to eye. I decided he was planning to stay awhile.

"How about seeing if you can print out this thing? You mind? Looks like good bedtime reading." He smiled snidely. "Who knows? Like, maybe this American lit freak quotes the Marquis-Sade-what's-his-face in there, too."

"The Marquis de Sade was French."

"Whatever."

I restrained my irritation. I was wondering what would happen if one of my medical examiner's wives were murdered. Would Marino look in the library and think he'd struck pay dirt when he found volume after volume on forensics and perverse crimes in history?

His eyes narrowed as he lit another cigarette and took a big drag. He waited until he'd blown out a thin stream of smoke before saying, "You've apparently got a high opinion of Petersen. What's it based on? The fact he's an artist or just that he's a hotshot college kid?"

"I have no opinion of him," I replied. "I know nothing about him except he doesn't profile right to be the person strangling these women."

He got thoughtful. "Well, I do know about him, Doc. You see, I talked to him for several hours. " He reached inside a

48

pocket of his plaid sports jacket and tossed two microcassette tapes on the blotter, within easy reach of me. I got out my cigarettes and lit one, too.

"Let me tell you how it went down. Me and Becker are in the kitchen with him, okay? The squad's just left with the body when bingo! Petersen's personality completely changes. He sits up straighter in the chair, his mind clears, and his hands start gesturing like he's on stage or something. It was friggin' unbelievable. His eyes tear up now and then, his voice cracks, he flushes and gets pale. I'm thinking to myself, this ain't an interview. It's a damn performance."

Settling back in the chair, he loosened his tie. "I'm thinking where I've seen this before, you know. Mainly back in New York with the likes of Johnny Andretti with his silk suits and imported cigarettes, charm oozing out his ears. He's so smooth you start falling all over yourself to accommodate 'im and begin suppressing the minor detail that he's whacked more than twenty people during his career. Then there's Phil the Pimp. He beat his girls with coat hangers, two of them to death, and tears up inside his restaurant, which is just a front for his escort service. Phil's all broken up about his dead hookers and he's leaning across the table, saying to me, 'Please find who did this to them, Pete. He has to be an animal. Here, try a little of this Chianti, Pete. It's nice.'

"Point is, Doc, I've been around the block more than once. And Petersen's setting off the same alarm toads like Andretti and Phil did. He's giving me this performance, I'm sitting there and asking myself, 'What's this Harvard highbrow think? I'm a bimbo or what?'"

I inserted a tape inside my microcassette player without saying anything.

Marino nodded for me to press the Play button. "Act one," he drolly announced. "The setting, the Petersen kitchen. The main character, Matt. The role, tragic. He's pale and wounded about the eyes, okay? He's staring off at the wall. Me? I'm seeing a movie in my head. Never been to Boston

49

and wouldn't know Harvard from a hole in the ground, but I'm seeing old brick and ivy."

He fell silent as the tape abruptly began with Petersen mid-sentence. He was talking about Harvard, answering questions about when he and Lori had met. I'd heard my share of police interviews over the years, and this one was perplexing me. Why did it matter? What did Petersen's courting of Lori back in their college days have to do with her murder? At the same time I think a part of me knew.

Marino was probing, drawing Petersen out. Marino was looking for anything – *anything* – that might show Petersen to be obsessive and warped and possibly capable of overt psychopathy.

I got up to shut the door so we wouldn't be interrupted, as the recorded voice quietly went on.

". . . I'd seen her before. On campus, this blonde carrying an armload of books and oblivious, as if she was in a hurry and had a lot on her mind."

Marino: "What was it about her that made you notice her, Matt?"

"It's hard to say. But she intrigued me from a distance. I'm not sure why. But part of it may have been that she was usually alone, in a hurry, on her way somewhere. She was, uh, confident and seemed to have purpose. She made me curious."

Marino: "Does that happen very often? You know, where you see some attractive woman and she makes you curious, from a distance, I'm saying?"

"Uh, I don't think so. I mean, I notice people just like everybody else does. But with her, with Lori, it was different."

Marino: "Go on. So you met her, finally. Where?"

"It was at a party. In the spring, early May. The party was in an off-campus apartment belonging to a buddy of my roommate, a guy who turned out to be Lori's lab partner, which was why she'd come. She walked in around nine, just about the time I was getting ready to leave. Her lab partner,

50

Tim, I think was his name, popped open a beer for her and they started talking. I'd never heard her voice before. Contralto, soothing, very pleasant to listen to. The sort of voice that makes you turn around to find the source of it. She was telling anecdotes about some professor and the people around her were laughing. Lori had a way of getting everybody's attention without even trying."

Marino: "In other words, you didn't leave the party after all. You saw her and decided to stick around."

"Yes."

"What did she look like back then?"

"Her hair was longer, and she was wearing it up, the way ballet dancers do. She was slender, very attractive . . ."

"You like slender blondes, then. You find those qualities attractive in a woman."

"I just thought she was attractive, that's all. And there was more to it. It was her intelligence. That's what made her stand out."

Marino: "What else?"

"I don't understand. What do you mean?"

Marino: "I'm just wondering what attracted you to her." A pause. "I find it interesting."

"I can't really answer that. It's mysterious, that element. How you can meet a person and be so aware. It's as if something inside you wakes up. I don't know why . . . God . . . I don't know."

Another pause, this one longer.

Marino: "She was the kind of lady people notice."

"Absolutely. All the time. Whenever we went places together, or if my friends were around. She'd upstage me, really. I didn't mind. In fact, I liked it. I enjoyed sitting back and watching it happen. I'd analyze it, try to figure out what it was that drew people to her. Charisma is something you have or you don't have. You can't manufacture it. You can't. She didn't try. It just was."

Marino: "You said when you used to see her on campus, she seemed to keep to herself. What about at other times?

What I'm wondering is if it was her habit to be friendly with strangers. You know, like if she was in a store or at a gas station, did she talk to people she didn't know? Or if someone came by the house, a deliveryman, for example, was she the type to invite the person in, be friendly?"

"No. She rarely talked to strangers, and I know she didn't invite strangers into the house. Never. Especially when I wasn't here. She'd lived in Boston, was acclimated to the dangers of the city. And she worked in the ER, was familiar with violence, the bad things that happen to people. She wouldn't have invited a stranger in or been what I consider particularly vulnerable to that sort of thing. In fact, when the murders started happening around here, it frightened her. When I'd come home on the weekends she hated it when I'd leave . . . hated it more than ever. Because she didn't like being alone at night. It bothered her more than it used to."

Marino: "Seems like she would have been careful about keeping all the windows locked if she was nervous because of the murders around here."

"I told you. She probably thought it was locked."

"But you accidentally left it, the bathroom window, unlocked last weekend when you was replacing the screen."

"I'm not sure. But that's the only thing I can figure . . ."

Becker's voice: "Did she mention anybody coming by the house, or an encounter somewhere, with someone who made her nervous? Anything at all? Maybe a strange car she noticed in your neighborhood, or the suspicion at some point that maybe she was being followed or observed? Maybe she meets some guy and he puts the move on her."

"Nothing like that."

Becker: "Would she have been likely to tell you if something like that had happened?"

"Definitely. She told me everything. A week, maybe two weeks ago, she thought she heard something in the backyard. She called the police. A patrol car came by. It was just a cat messing with the garbage cans. The point is, she told me everything."

Marino: "What other activities was she involved in besides work?"

"She had a few friends, a couple of other women doctors at the hospital. Sometimes she went out to dinner with them or shopping, maybe a movie. That was about it. She was so busy. In the main, she worked her shift and came home. She'd study, sometimes practice the violin. During the week, she generally worked, came home and slept. The weekends she kept open for me. That was our time. We were together on the weekends."

Marino: "Last weekend was the last time you saw her?"

"Sunday afternoon, around three. Right before I drove back to Charlottesville. We didn't go out that day. It was raining, raw. We stayed in, drank coffee, talked . . ."

Marino: "How often did you talk to her during the week?"

"Several times. Whenever we could."

Marino: "The last time was last night, Thursday night?"

"I called to tell her I'd be in after play practice, that I might be a few minutes later than usual because of dress rehearsal. She was supposed to be off this weekend. If it was nice, we were thinking of driving to the beach."

Silence.

Petersen was struggling. I could hear him taking a deep breath, trying to steady himself.

Marino: "When you talked to her last night, did she have anything to report, any problems, any mention of anybody coming by the house? Anyone bothering her at work, maybe weird phone calls, anything?"

Silence.

"Nothing. Nothing at all like that. She was in good spirits, laughing . . . looking forward, uh, looking forward to the weekend."

Marino: "Tell us a little more about her, Matt. Every little thing you can think of might help. Her background, her personality, what was important to her."

Mechanically, "She's from Philadelphia, her dad's an insurance salesman, and she has two brothers, both younger.

53

Medicine was the most important thing to her. It was her calling."

Marino: "What kind of doctor was she studying to be?"

"A plastic surgeon."

Becker: "Interesting. Why did she decide on that?"

"When she was ten, eleven, her mother got breast cancer, underwent two radical mastectomies. She survived but her self-esteem was destroyed. I think she felt deformed, worthless, untouchable. Lori talked about it sometimes. I think she wanted to help people. Help people who have been through things like that."

Marino: "And she played the violin."

"Yes."

Marino: "Did she ever give concerts, play in the symphony, anything public like that?"

"She could have, I think. But she didn't have time."

Marino: "What else? For example, you're big on acting, in a play right now. Was she interested in that kind of thing?"

"Very much so. That's one of the things that fascinated me about her when we first met. We left the party, the party where we met, and walked the campus for hours. When I started telling her about some of the courses I was taking, I realized she knew a lot about the theater, and we started talking about plays and such. I was into Ibsen then. We got into that, got into reality and illusion, what's genuine and what's ugly in people and society. One of his strongest themes is the feeling of alienation from home. Uh, of separation. We talked about that.

"And she surprised me. I'll never forget it. She laughed and said, 'You artists think you're the only ones who can relate to these things. Many of us have the same feelings, the same emptiness, the same loneliness. But we don't have the tools to verbalize them. So we carry on, we struggle. Feelings are feelings. I think people's feelings are pretty much the same all over the world.'

"We got into an argument, a friendly debate. I disagreed.

Some people feel things more deeply than others, and some people feel things the rest of us don't. This is what causes isolation, the sense of being apart, different . . ."

Marino: "This is something you relate to?"

"It is something I understand. I may not feel everything other people feel, but I understand the feelings. Nothing surprises me. If you study literature, drama, you get in touch with a vast spectrum of human emotions, needs and impulses, good and bad. It's my nature to step into other characters, to feel what they feel to act as they do, but it doesn't mean these manifestations are genuinely my own. I think if anything makes me feel different from others, it's my need to experience these things, my need to analyze and understand the vast spectrum of human emotions I just mentioned."

Marino: "Can you understand the emotions of the person who did this to your wife?"

Silence.

Almost inaudibly, "Good God, no."

Marino: "You sure about that?"

"No. I mean, yes, I'm sure! I don't want to understand it!"

Marino: "I know it's a hard thing for you to think about, Matt. But you could help us a lot if you had any ideas. For example, if you was designing the role for a killer like this, what would he be like –"

"I don't know! The filthy son of a bitch!" His voice was breaking, exploding with rage. "I don't know why you're asking me! You're the fucking cops! You're supposed to be the ones figuring it out!"

He abruptly fell silent, as if a needle had been lifted off a record.

The tape played a long stretch in which nothing was heard except Marino clearing his throat and a chair scraping back.

Then Marino asked Becker, "You wouldn't by chance have an extra tape in your car?"

It was Petersen who mumbled, and I think he was crying, "I've got a couple of them back in the bedroom."

55

"Well, now," Marino's voice coolly drawled, "that's mighty nice of you, Matt."

Twenty minutes later, Matt Petersen got to the subject of finding his wife's body.

It was awful to hear and not see. There were no distractions. I drifted on the current on his images and recollections. His words were taking me into dark areas where I did not want to go.

The tape played on.

". . . Uh, I'm sure of it. I didn't call first. I never did, just left. Didn't hang around or anything. As I was saying, uh, I left Charlottesville as soon as rehearsal was over and the props and costumes were put away. I guess this was close to twelve-thirty. I was in a hurry to get home. I hadn't seen Lori all week.

"It was close to two when I parked in front of the house, and my first reaction was to notice the lights out and realize she'd already gone to bed. Her schedule was very demanding. On twelve hours and off twenty-four, the shift out of sync with human biological clocks and never the same. She worked Friday until midnight, was to be off Saturday, uh, today. And tomorrow she would be on from midnight to noon Monday. Off Tuesday, and on Wednesday from noon to midnight again. That's how it went.

"I unlocked the front door and flipped on the living room light. Everything looked normal. Retrospectively, I can say that even though I had no reason to be looking for anything out of the ordinary. I do remember the hall light was off. I noticed because usually she left it on for me. It was my routine to go straight to the bedroom. If she wasn't too exhausted, and she almost never was, we would sit up in bed and drink wine and talk. Uh, stay up, and then sleep very late.

"I was confused. Uh. Something was confusing me. The bedroom. I couldn't see anything much at first because the lights . . . the lights, of course, were out. But something felt

56

wrong immediately. It's almost as if I sensed it before I saw it. Like an animal senses things. And I thought I was smelling something but I wasn't sure and it only added to my confusion."

Marino: "What sort of smell?"

Silence.

"I'm trying to remember. I was only vaguely aware of it. But aware enough to be puzzled. It was an unpleasant smell. Sort of sweet but putrid. Weird."

Marino: "You mean a body-odor-type smell?"

"Similar, but not exactly. It was sweetish. Unpleasant. Rather pungent and sweaty."

Becker: "Something you've smelled before?"

A pause. "No, it wasn't quite like anything I've ever smelled before, I don't think. It was faint, but maybe I was more aware of it because I couldn't see anything, couldn't hear anything the instant I walked into the bedroom. It was so quiet inside. The first thing that struck my senses was this peculiar odor. And it flickered in my mind, oddly, it flickered in my mind – maybe Lori had been eating something in bed. I don't know. It was, uh, it was like waffles, maybe syrupy. Pancakes. I thought maybe she was sick, had been eating junk and gotten sick. Uh, sometimes she went on binges. Uh, ate fattening things when she was stressed or anxious. She gained a lot of weight after I started commuting to Charlottesville . . ."

His voice was trembling very badly now.

"Uh, the smell was sick, unhealthy, as if maybe she was sick and had been in bed all day. Explaining why all the lights were out, why she hadn't waited up for me."

Silence.

Marino: "Then what happened, Matt?"

"Then my eyes began to adjust and I didn't understand what I was seeing. The bed materialized in the dimness. I didn't understand the covers, the way they were hanging off. And her. Lying on top in this strange position and not having anything on. God. My heart was coming out of my chest before it even registered. And when I flipped on the light, and saw her . . . I was screaming, but I couldn't hear my own voice. Like I was screaming inside my head. Like my brain was floating out of my skull. I saw the stain on the sheet, the red, the blood coming out of her nose and mouth. Her face. I didn't think it was her. It wasn't her. It didn't even look like her. It was somebody else. A prank, a terrible trick. It wasn't her."

Marino: "What did you do next, Matt? Did you touch her or disturb anything inside the bedroom?"

A long pause and the sound of Petersen's shallow, rapid breathing: "No. I mean, yes. I touched her. I didn't think. I just touched her. Her shoulder, her arm. I don't remember. She was warm. But when I started to feel for a pulse, I couldn't find her wrists. Because she was on top of them, they were behind her back, tied. And I started to touch her neck and saw the cord embedded in her skin. I think I tried to feel her heart beating or hear it but I don't remember. I knew it. I knew she was dead. The way she looked. She had to be dead. I ran into the kitchen. I don't remember what I said or even remember dialing the phone. But I know I called the police and then I paced. Just paced. I paced in and out of the bedroom. I leaned against the wall and cried and talked to her. I talked to her. I talked to her until the police got here. I told her not to let it be real. I kept going over to her and backing off and begging her not to let it be real. I kept listening for someone to get here. It seemed to take forever . . ."

Marino: "The electrical cords, the way she was tied. Did you disturb anything, touch the cords or do anything else? Can you remember?"

"No. I mean, I don't remember if I did. Uh, but I don't think I did. Something stopped me. I wanted to cover her. But something stopped me. Something told me not to touch anything."

Marino: "Do you own a knife?"

Silence.

Marino: "A knife, Matt. We found a knife, a survival

knife with a whetstone in the sheath and a compass in the handle."

Confused: "Oh. Uh-huh. I got it several years ago. One of those mail-order knives you could get for five-ninety-five or something. Uh, I used to take it with me when I went hiking. It's got fishing line, matches inside the handle."

Marino: "Where did you see it last?"

"On the desk. It's been on the desk. I think Lori was using it as a letter opener. I don't know. It's just been sitting there for months. Maybe it made her feel better to have it out. Being alone at night and all. I told her we could get a dog. But she's allergic."

Marino: "If I hear what you're saying, Matt, you're telling me the knife was on the desk last time you saw it. That would have been when? Last Saturday, Sunday, when you was home, the weekend when you replaced the screen in the bathroom window?"

No response.

Marino: "You know any reason your wife might've had to move the knife, like maybe tuck it in a drawer or something? She ever done that in the past?"

"I don't think so. It's been on the desk, near the lamp for months."

Marino: "Can you explain why we found this knife in the bottom dresser drawer, underneath some sweaters and beside a box of condoms? Your dresser drawer, I'm guessing?"

Silence.

"No. I can't explain it. That's where you found it?"

Marino: "Yes."

"The condoms. They've been in there a long time." A hollow laugh that was almost a gasp. "From before Lori went on the pill."

Marino: "You sure about that? About the condoms?"

"Of course I'm sure. She went on the pill about three months after we got married. We got married just before we moved here. Less than two years ago."

Marino: "Now, Matt, I've got to ask you several questions of a personal nature, and I want you to understand I'm not picking on you or trying to embarrass you. But I have reasons. There's things we got to know, for your own good, too. Okay?"

Silence.

I could hear Marino lighting a cigarette. "All right then. The condoms. Did you have any relations outside your marriage, with anybody else, I'm saying?"

"Absolutely not."

Marino: "You was living out of town during the week. Now me, I would have been tempted –"

"Well, I'm not you. Lori was everything to me. I had nothing with anybody else."

Marino: "No one in the play with you, maybe?"

"No."

Marino: "See, the point is, we do these little things. I mean, they're human nature, okay? A good-looking guy like you – hey, the women probably throw themselves at you. Who could blame you? But if you was seeing someone, we need to know. There could possibly be a connection."

Almost inaudibly, "No. I've told you, no. There could be no connection unless you're accusing me of something."

Becker: "No one's accusing you of anything, Matt."

There was the sound of something sliding across the table. The ashtray, perhaps.

And Marino was asking, "When was the last time you had sex with your wife?"

Silence.

Petersen's voice was shaking. "Jesus Christ."

Marino: "I know it's your business, personal. But you need to tell us. We got our reasons."

"Sunday morning. Last Sunday."

Marino: "You know there will be tests run, Matt. Scientists will be examining everything so we can get blood types, make other comparisons. We need samples from you just like we needed your prints. So we can sort things out

60

and know what's yours, what's hers, and what maybe's from –"

The tape abruptly ended. I blinked and my eyes focused for what seemed the first time in hours.

Marino reached for the recorder, turned it off and retrieved his tapes.

He concluded, "After that we took him down to Richmond General and got the suspect kit. Betty's examining his blood even as we speak to see how it compares."

I nodded, glancing at the wall clock. It was noon. I felt sick.

"Something, huh?" Marino stifled a yawn. "You see it don't you? I'm telling you, the guy's off. I mean there's something off about any guy who can sit there after finding his wife like that and talk the way he does. Most of 'em, they don't talk much. He would have rattled on till Christmas if I'd let 'im. A lot of pretty words and poetry, you ask me. He's slick. You want my opinion, that's it. He's so slick it gives me the willies."

I slipped off my glasses and kneaded my temples. My brain was heated up, the muscles in my neck on fire. The silk blouse beneath my lab coat was damp. My circuits were so overloaded that what I wanted to do was place my head on my arms and sleep.

"His world is words, Marino," I heard myself say. "An artist would have painted the picture for you. Matt painted it with words. This is how he exists, how he expresses himself, through words and more words. To think a thought is to express it verbally for people like him." I put my glasses back on and looked at Marino. He was perplexed, his meaty, shop-worn face flushed.

"Well, take the bit about the knife, Doc. It's got his prints on it, even though he says his wife's the one who's been using it for months. It's got that sparkle crap on the handle, just like he had on his hands. And the knife was in his dresser drawer, like maybe someone was hiding it. Now that gives you a pause, don't you think?"

"I think it is possible the knife was on top of Lori's desk just as it had been, that she rarely used it and had no reason to touch the blade when she did if she simply opened letters with it, occasionally." I was seeing this in my head, so vividly I almost believed the images were memories of an event that had actually occurred. "I think it's possible the killer saw the knife too. Perhaps he took it out of the sheath to look at it. Perhaps he used it –"

"Why?"

"Why not?" I asked.

A shrug.

"To jerk everyone around, perhaps," I suggested. "Perversity, if nothing else. We have no idea what went on, for God's sake. He may have asked her about the knife, tormented her with her own – or her husband's own – weapon. And if she talked with him as I suspect she did, then he may have learned the knife belongs to her husband. He thinks, 'I'll use it. I'll put it in a drawer where the cops are sure to find it.' Or maybe he doesn't think much about it at all. Maybe his reason was utilitarian. In other words, maybe it was a bigger knife than the one he'd brought in with him, it caught his eye, appealed to him, he used it, didn't want to take it out with him, stuck it in a drawer hoping we wouldn't know he'd used it – and it was that simple."

"Or maybe Matt did it all," Marino flatly said.

"Matt? Think about it. Could a husband rape and bind his wife? Could he fracture her ribs and break her fingers? Could he slowly strangle her to death? This is someone he loves or once loved. Someone he sleeps with, eats with, talks to, lives with. A person, Sergeant. Not a stranger or deper-sonalized object of lust and violence. How are you going to connect a husband murdering his wife with the first three stranglings?"

Clearly, he'd already thought about this. "They occurred after midnight, on early Saturday mornings. Right about the time Matt was getting home from Charlottesville. Maybe his wife got suspicious about him for some reason and he decides he's got to whack her. Maybe he does her like the others to make us think the serial killer did her. Or maybe the wife's who he was after all along, and he does the other three first to make it look like his wife was done by this anonymous and same killer."

"A wonderful plot for Agatha Christie." I was pushing back my chair and getting up. "But as you know in real life murder is usually depressingly simple. I think these murders are simple. They are exactly what they appear to be, impersonal random murders committed by someone who stalks his victims long enough to figure out when to strike."

Marino got up, too. "Yeah, well in real life, Doc-tor Scarpetta, bodies don't have freaky little sparkles all over 'em that match the same freaky sparkles found on the hands of the husband who discovers the body and leaves his prints all over the damn place. And the victims don't have pretty-boy actors for husbands, squirrels writing dissertations on sex and violence and cannibals and faggots."

I calmly asked him, "The odor Petersen mentioned. Did you smell anything like that when you arrived on the scene?"

"Naw. Didn't smell a damn thing. So maybe he was smelling seminal fluid, if he's telling the truth."

"I should think he would know what that smells like."

"But he wouldn't be expecting to smell it. No reason it should come to mind at first. Now me, when I went in the bedroom, I didn't smell nothing like he was describing."

"Do you recall smelling anything peculiar at the other strangling scenes?"

"No, ma'am. Which just further corroborates my suspicion that either Matt imagined it or is making it up, to throw us off track."

Then it came to me. "In the three previous cases, the women weren't found until the next day, after they'd been dead at least twelve hours."

Marino paused in the doorway, his face incredulous. "You

suggesting Matt got home just after the killer left, that the killer's got some weird case of B.O.?"

"I'm suggesting it's possible."

His face tightened with anger, and as he stalked down the hall I heard him mutter, "Goddam women . . ."

5

The Sixth Street Marketplace is a Bayside without the water, one of these open, sunny malls built of steel and glass, on the north edge of the banking district in the heart of downtown. It wasn't often I went out for lunch, and I certainly didn't have time for the luxury this afternoon. I had an appointment in less than an hour, and there were two sudden deaths and one suicide in transport, but I needed to unwind.

Marino bothered me. His attitude toward me reminded me of medical school.

I was one of four women in my class at Hopkins. I was too naïve in the beginning to realize what was happening. The sudden creaking of chairs and loud shuffling of paper when a professor would call on me were not coincidence. It was not chance when old tests made the rounds but were never available to me. The excuses – "You wouldn't be able to read my writing" or "Someone else is borrowing them right now" – were too universal when I went from student to student on the few occasions I missed a lecture and needed to copy someone else's notes. I was a small insect faced with a formidable male network web in which I might be ensnared but never a part.

Isolation is the cruelest of punishments, and it had never occurred to me that I was something less than human because I wasn't a man. One of my female classmates eventually quit, another suffered a complete nervous breakdown. Survival was my only hope, success my only revenge.

I'd thought those days were behind me, but Marino brought all of it back. I was more vulnerable now because these murders were affecting me in a way others had not. I did not want to be alone in this, but Marino seemed to have his mind made up, not only about Matt Petersen, but also about me.

The midday stroll was soothing, the sun bright and winking on windshields of the passing traffic. The double glass doors leading inside the Marketplace were open to let the spring breeze in, and the food court was as crowded as I knew it would be. Waiting my turn at the carry-out salad counter, I watched people go by, young couples laughing and talking and lounging at small tables. I was aware of women who seemed alone, preoccupied professional women wearing expensive suits and sipping diet colas or nibbling on pita bread sandwiches.

It could have been in a place like this he first spotted his victims, some large public place where the only thing the four women had in common was that he took their orders at one of the counters.

But the overwhelming and seemingly enigmatic problem was that the murdered women did not work or live in the same areas of the city. It was unlikely they shopped or dined out or did their banking or anything else in the same places. Richmond has a large land area with thriving malls and business areas in the four major quadrants. People who live Northside are catered to by the Northside merchants, the people south of the river patronize the Southside businesses, and the same is true in the eastern part of the city. I mainly restricted myself to the malls and restaurants in the West End, for example, except when I was at work.

The woman at the counter who took my order for a Greek salad paused for a moment, her eyes lingering on my face as if I looked familiar to her. I uncomfortably wondered if she'd seen my picture in the Saturday evening paper. Or she could have seen me in the television footage and court sketches the local television stations were constantly pulling out of their files whenever murder was big news in central Virginia.

It has always been my wish to be unnoticed, to blend. But I was at a disadvantage for several reasons. There were few women chief medical examiners in the country, and this prompted reporters to be unduly tenacious when it came to pointing cameras in my direction or excavating for quotes. I was easily recognized because I am "distinctive" in appearance, "blond" and "handsome" and Lord knows what else I've been called in print. My ancestors are from northern Italy where there is a segment of blue-eyed, fair natives who share blood with the people of Savoy, Switzerland and Austria.

The Scarpettas are a traditionally ethnocentric group, Italians who have married other Italians in this country to keep the bloodline pure. My mother's greatest failure, so she has told me numerous times, is that she bore no son and her two daughters have turned out to be genetic dead ends. Dorothy sullied the lineage with Lucy, who is half Latin, and at my age and marital status it wasn't likely I would be sullying anything.

My mother is prone to weeping as she bemoans the fact that her immediate family is at the end of its line. "All that good blood," she would sob, especially during the holidays, when she should have been surrounded by a bevy of adorable and adoring grandchildren. "Such a shame. All that good blood! Our ancestors! Architects, painters! Kay, Kay, to let that go to waste, like fine grapes on the vine."

We are traced back to Verona, the province of Romeo of Montague and Juliet Capulet, of Dante, Pisano, Titian, Bellini and Paolo Cagliari, according to my mother. She persists in believing we are somehow related to these luminaries, despite my reminders that Bellini, Pisano and Titian, at any rate, influenced the Veronese School but were really native to Venice, and the poet Dante was Florentine, exiled after the Black Guelf triumph and relegated to wandering from city to city, his stay in Verona but a pit stop along the way to Ravenna. Our direct ancestors, in truth, were with the railways or were farmers, a humble people who immigrated to this country two generations ago.

A white bag in hand, I eagerly embraced the warm afternoon again. Sidewalks were crowded with people wandering to and from lunch, and as I waited on a corner for the light to change, I instinctively turned toward the two figures emerging from the Chinese restaurant across the street. The familiar blond hair had caught my eye. Bill Boltz, the Commonwealth's attorney for Richmond City, was slipping on a pair of sunglasses and seemed in the midst of an intense discussion with Norman Tanner, the director of public safety. For a moment, Boltz was staring straight at me, but he didn't return my wave. Maybe he really didn't see me. I didn't wave again. Then the two men were gone, swept up in the congested flow of anonymous faces and scuffling feet.

When the light turned green after an interminably long time, I crossed the street, and Lucy came to mind as I approached a computer software store. Ducking in, I found something she was sure to like, not a video game but a history tutorial complete with art, music and quizzes. Yesterday we had rented a paddleboat in the park and drifted around the small lake. She ran us into the fountain to give me a tepid shower, and I found myself childishly paying her back. We fed bread to the geese and sucked on grape snow cones until our tongues turned blue. Thursday morning she would fly home to Miami, and I would not see her again until Christmas, if I saw her again at all this year.

It was quarter of one when I walked into the lobby of the Office of the Chief Medical Examiner, or OCME, as it was called. Benton Wesley was fifteen minutes early and sitting on the couch reading the *Wall Street Journal*.

"Hope you got something to drink in that bag," he said drolly, folding the newspaper and reaching for his briefcase.

"Wine vinegar. You'll love it."

"Hell. Ripple – I don't care. Some days I'm so desperate I fantasize the water cooler outside my door's full of gin."

"Sounds like a waste of imagination to me."

"Nawwww. Just the only fantasy I'm going to talk about in front of a lady."

Wesley was a suspect profiler for the FBI and located in Richmond's field office, where he actually spent very little time. When he wasn't on the road, he was usually at the National Academy in Quantico teaching death-investigation classes and doing what he could to coax VICAP through its rocky adolescence. VICAP is an acronym for Violent Criminal Apprehension Program. One of VICAP's most inno-vative concepts was regional teams, which yoke a Bureau profiler with an experienced homicide detective. Richmond P.D. called in VICAP after the second strangling. Marino, in addition to being a detective sergeant for the city, was Wesley's regional team partner.

"I'm early," Wesley apologized, following me into the hallway. "Came straight here from a dental appointment. Won't bother me if you eat while we talk."

"Well, it *will* bother me," I said.

His blank look was followed by a sheepish grin as it sud-denly occurred to him. "I forgot. You're not Doc Cagney. You know, he used to keep cheese crackers on the desk in the morgue. In the middle of a post he'd take a break for a snack. It was unbelievable."

We turned off into a room so small it was really an alcove, where there was a refrigerator, a Coke machine and a coffeemaker. "He's lucky he didn't get hepatitis or AIDS," I said.

"AIDS." Wesley laughed. "That would have been poetic justice."

Like a lot of good ole boys I've known, Dr. Cagney was reputed to be acutely homophobic. "Just some goddam queer," he was known to say when persons of a certain per-suasion were sent in for examination.

"AIDS . . ." Wesley was still enjoying the thought as I

tucked my salad inside the refrigerator. "Wouldn't I love to hear him explain his way out of that one."

I'd gradually warmed up to Wesley. The first time I met him I had my reservations. At a glance, he made one a believer in stereotypes. He was FBI right down to his Florsheim shoes, a sharp-featured man with prematurely silver hair suggesting a mellow disposition that wasn't there. He was lean and hard and looked like a trial lawyer in his precisely tailored khaki suit and blue silk paisley-printed tie. I couldn't recall ever seeing him in a shirt that wasn't white and lightly starched.

He had a master's degree in psychology and had been a high school principal in Dallas before enlisting in the Bureau, where he worked first as a field agent, then undercover in fingering members of the Mafia, before ending up where he'd started, in a sense. Profilers are academicians, thinkers, analysts. Sometimes I think they are magicians.

Carrying our coffees out, we turned left and stepped inside the conference room. Marino was sitting at the long table and going through a fat case file. I was mildly surprised. For some reason, I just assumed he would be late.

Before I had a chance to so much as pull out a chair, he launched in with the laconic announcement, "I stopped by serology a minute ago. Thought you might be interested in knowing Matt Petersen's A positive and a nonsecreter."

Wesley looked keenly at him. "This the husband you were telling me about?"

"Yo. *A nonsecreter*. Same as the guy snuffing these women."

"Twenty percent of the population is nonsecreter," I matter-of-factly stated.

"Yeah," Marino said. "Two out of ten."

"Or approximately forty-four thousand people in a city the size of Richmond. Twenty-two thousand if half of that number is male," I added.

Lighting a cigarette, Marino squinted up at me over the Bic flame. "You know what, Doc?" The cigarette wagged with each syllable. "You're beginning to sound like a damn defense attorney."

A half hour later I was at the head of the table, the two men on either side. Spread out before us were photographs of the four murdered women.

This was the most difficult and time-consuming part of the investigation – profiling the killer, profiling the victims, and then profiling the killer again.

Wesley was describing him. This was what he did best, and quite often was uncannily accurate when he read the emotion of a crime scene, which in these cases was cold, calculating rage.

"I'm betting he's white," he was saying. "But I won't stake my reputation on it. Cecile Tyler was black, and an interracial mix in victim selection is unusual unless the killer is rapidly decompensating." He picked up a photograph of Cecile Tyler, dark-skinned, lovely in life, and a receptionist at a Northside investment firm. Like Lori Petersen, she was bound, strangled, her nude body on top of the bed.

"But we're getting more of them these days. That's the trend, an increase of sexual slayings in which the assailant is black, the woman white, but rarely the opposite – white men raping and murdering black women, in other words. Hookers are an exception." He glanced blandly at the array of photographs. "These women certainly weren't hookers. I suppose if they had been," he muttered, "our job would be a little easier."

"Yeah, but theirs wouldn'ta been," Marino butted in.

Wesley didn't smile. "At least there would be a connection that maybe makes sense, Pete. The selection." He shook his head. "It's peculiar."

"So what does Fortosis have to say these days?" Marino asked, referring to the forensic psychiatrist who had been reviewing the cases.

"Not a whole hell of a lot," Wesley replied. "Talked to

71

him briefly this morning. He's being noncommittal. I think the murder of this doctor's causing him to rethink a few things. But he's still damn sure the killer's white."

The face from my dream violated my mind, the white face without features.

"He's probably between twenty-five and thirty-five." Wesley continued staring into his crystal ball. "Because the murders aren't related to any particular locality, he's got some way of getting around, a car versus a motorcycle or a truck or a van. My guess is he's stashing his wheels in some inconspicuous spot, going the rest of the way on foot. His car's an older model, probably American, dark or plain in color, such as beige or gray. It wouldn't be the least bit uncommon for him to drive, in other words, the very sort of car plainclothes law-enforcement officers drive."

He wasn't being funny. This type of killer is frequently fascinated by police work and may even emulate cops. The classic postoffense behavior for a psychopath is to become involved in the investigation. He wants to help the police, to offer insights and suggestions, and assist rescue teams in their search for a body he dumped in the woods somewhere. He's the kind of guy who wouldn't think twice about hanging out at the Fraternal Order of Police lounge clacking beer mugs with the off-duty cops.

It has been conjectured that at least one percent of the population is psychopathic. Genetically, these individuals are fearless; they are people users and supreme manipulators. On the right side, they are terrific spies, war heroes, five-star generals, corporate billionaires and James Bonds. On the wrong side, they are strikingly evil: the Neros, the Hitlers, the Richard Specks, the Ted Bundys, antisocial but clinically sane people who commit atrocities for which they feel no remorse and assume no blame.

"He's a loner," Wesley went on, "and has a difficult time with close relationships, though he may be considered pleasant or even charming to acquaintances. He wouldn't be close to any one person. He's the type to pick up a woman in a bar, have sex with her and find it frustrating and highly unsatis-factory."

"Don't I know the feeling," Marino said, yawning.

Wesley elaborated, "He would gain far more satisfaction from violent pornography, detective magazines, S&M, and probably entertained violent sexual fantasies long before he began to make the fantasies reality. The reality may have begun with his peeping into the windows of houses or apart-ments where women live alone. It gets more real. Next he rapes. The rapes get more violent, culminating in murder. This escalation will continue as he continues to become more violent and abusive with each victim. Rape is no longer the motive. Murder is. Murder is no longer enough. It has to be more sadistic."

His arm extended, exposing a perfect margin of stiff white cuff, he reached for Lori Petersen's photographs. Slowly he looked through them, one at a time, his face impassive. Lightly pushing the stack away from him, he turned to me. "It seems clear to me that in her case, in Dr. Petersen's case, the killer introduced elements of torture. An accurate assess-ment?"

"Accurate," I replied.

"What? Busting her fingers?" Marino posed the question as if looking for an argument. "The Mob does shit like that. Sex murderers usually don't. She played the violin, right? Busting her fingers seems kinda personal. Like the guy who did it knew her."

As calmly as possible I said, "The surgical reference books on her desk, the violin – the killer didn't have to be a genius to pick up a few clues about her."

Wesley considered, "Another possibility is her broken fin-gers and fractured ribs are defense injuries."

"They aren't." I was sure of this. "I didn't find anything to send me the message she struggled with him."

Marino turned his flat, unfriendly eyes my way. "Really? I'm curious. What do you mean by defense injuries? According to your report, she had plenty of bruises."

73

"Good examples of defense injuries" – I met his gaze and held it – "are broken fingernails, scratches or injuries found in areas of the hands and arms that would have been exposed had the victim attempted to ward off blows. Her injuries are inconsistent with this."

Wesley summarized, "Then we're all in agreement. He was more violent this time."

"Brutal's the word," Marino quickly said as if this were his favorite point to make. "That's what I'm talking about. Lori Petersen's different from the other three."

I suppressed my fury. The first three victims were tied up, raped and strangled. Wasn't that *brutal*? Did they need to have their bones broken, too?

Wesley grimly predicted, "If there's another one, there will be more pronounced signs of violence, of torture. He kills because it's a compulsion, an attempt to fill some need. The more he does it the stronger this need becomes and the more frustrated he gets, therefore the stronger the urge will become. He's becoming increasingly desensitized and it's taking more with each killing to satiate him. The satiation is temporary. Over the subsequent days or weeks, the tension builds until he finds his next target, stalks her and does it again. The intervals between each killing may get shorter. He may escalate, finally, into a spree murderer, as Bundy did."

I was thinking of the time frame. The first woman had been murdered on April 19, the second on May 10, the third on May 31. Lori Petersen was murdered a week later, on the seventh of June.

The rest of what Wesley said was fairly predictable. The killer was from a "dysfunctional home" and might have been abused either physically or emotionally, by his mother. When he was with a victim, he was acting out his rage, which was inextricably connected to his lust.

He was above average in intelligence, an obsessive-compulsive, and very organized and meticulous. He might be prone to obsessive behavior patterns, phobias or rituals, such as neatness, cleanliness, his diet – anything that maintained his sense of controlling his environment.

He had a job, which is probably menial – a mechanic, a repairman, a construction worker or some other labor-related occupation . . .

I noticed Marino's face getting redder by the moment. He was looking restlessly around the conference room.

"For him," Wesley was saying, "the best part of what he does is the antecedent phase, the fantasy plan, the environmental cue that activates the fantasy. Where was the victim when he became aware of her?"

We did not know. She may not have known were she alive to tell. The interface may have been as tenuous and obscure as a shadow crossing her path. He caught a glimpse of her somewhere. It may have been at a shopping mall or perhaps while she was inside her car and stopped at a red light.

"What triggered him?" Wesley went on. "Why this particular woman?"

Again, we did not know. We knew only one thing. Each of the women was vulnerable because she lived alone. Or was thought to live alone as in Lori Petersen's case.

"Sounds like your all-American Joe." Marino's acid remark stopped us cold.

Flicking an ash, he leaned aggressively forward. "Hey. This is all very good and nice. But me, I don't intend to be no Dorothy going down no Yellow Brick Road. They don't all lead to Emerald City, okay? We say he's a plumber or something, right? Well, Ted Bundy was a law student, and a couple years back there's this serial rapist in D.C. who turns out to be a dentist. Hell, the Green Valley strangler out there in the land of fruits and nuts could be a Boy Scout for all anybody knows."

Marino was getting around to what was on his mind. I'd been waiting for him to start in.

"I mean, who's to say he ain't a student? Maybe even an actor, a creative type whose imagination's gone apeshit. One lust murder don't look much different from another no

75

matter who's committed it unless the squirrel's into drinking blood or barbecuing people on spits – and this squirrel we're dealing with ain't a Lucas. The reason these brands of sex murders all profile pretty much the same, you want my opinion, is because, with few exceptions, people are people. Doctor, lawyer or Indian chief. People think and do pretty much the same damn things, going back to the days when cavemen dragged women off by their hair."

Wesley was staring off. He slowly looked over at Marino and quietly asked, "What's your point, Pete?"

"I'll tell you what the hell my point is!" His chin was jutted out, the veins in his neck standing out like cords. "This goddam crap about who profiles right and who don't. It frosts me. What I got here is a guy writing his friggin' dissertation on sex and violence, cannibals, queers. He's got glitter crap on his hands that looks like the same stuff found on all the bodies. His prints are on his dead wife's skin and on the knife stashed in one of his drawers – a knife that also has this glitter crap on the handle. He gets home every weekend right about the time the women get whacked. But no. Hell, no. He can't be the guy, right? And why? 'Cause he ain't blue collar. He ain't trashy enough."

Wesley was staring off again. My eyes fell to the photographs spread out before us, full-blown color shots of women who never in their worst nightmares would have believed anything like this could happen to them.

"Well, let me just lay this one on you." The tirade wasn't about to end. "Pretty-boy Matt, here – it just so happens he ain't exactly pure as the driven snow. While I was upstairs checking with serology, I buzzed by Vander's office again to see if he'd turned up anything else. Petersen's prints are on file, right? You know why?" He stared hard at me. "I'll tell you why. Vander looked into it, did his thing with his gizmos. Pretty-boy Matt got arrested six years ago in New Orleans. This was the summer before he went off to college, long before he met his surgeon lady. She probably never even knew about it."

"Knew about what?" Wesley asked.

"Knew her lover-boy actor was charged with rape, that's what."

No one said anything for a very long time.

Wesley was slowly turning his Mont Blanc pen end over end on the table top, his jaw firmly set. Marino wasn't playing by the rules. He wasn't sharing information. He was ambushing us with it as if this were court and Wesley and I were opposing counsel.

I finally proposed, "If Petersen was, in fact, charged with rape, then he was acquitted. Or else the charges were dropped."

Those eyes of his fixed on me like two gun barrels. "You know that, do you? I ain't run a record check on him yet."

"A university like Harvard, Sergeant Marino, doesn't make it a practice to accept convicted felons."

"If they know."

"True," I agreed. "If they know. It's hard to believe they wouldn't know, if the charge stuck."

"We'd better run it down" was all Wesley had to say about the matter.

With that, Marino abruptly excused himself.

I assumed he was going to the men's room.

Wesley acted as if there was nothing out of the ordinary about Marino's outburst or anything else. He casually asked, "What's the word from New York, Kay? Anything back from the lab yet?"

"DNA testing takes a while," I abstractedly replied. "We didn't send them anything until the second case. I should be getting those results soon. As for the second two, Cecile Tyler and Lori Petersen, we're talking next month at the earliest."

He persisted in his "nothing's wrong" mode. "In all four cases the guy's a nonsecreter. That much we know."

"Yes. We know that much."

"There's really no doubt in my mind it's the same killer."

"Nor in mine," I concurred.

Nothing more was said for a while.

We sat tensely, waiting for Marino's return, his angry words still ringing in our ears. I was perspiring and could feel my heart beating.

I think Wesley must have been able to read the look on my face that I wanted nothing more to do with Marino, that I had relegated him to the oblivion I reserve for people who are impossible and unpleasant and professionally dangerous.

He said, "You have to understand him, Kay."

"Well, I don't."

"He's a good detective, a very fine one."

I didn't comment.

We sat silently.

My anger began to rise. I knew better, but there was no stopping the words from boiling out. "Damn it, Benton! These women deserve our best effort. We screw it up and someone else may die. I don't want him screwing it up because he's got some problem!"

"He won't."

"He already is." I lowered my voice. "He's got a noose around Matt Petersen's neck. It means he's not looking at anybody else."

Marino, thank God, was taking his sweet time coming back. Wesley's jaw muscles were flexing and he wouldn't meet my eyes. "I haven't dismissed Petersen yet either. I can't. I know killing his wife doesn't fit with the other three. But he's an unusual case. Take Gacy. We've got no idea how many people he murdered. Thirty-three kids. Possibly it was hundreds. Strangers, all of them strangers to him. Then he does his mother and stuffs pieces of her down the garbage disposal . . ."

I couldn't believe it. He was giving me one of his "young agents" lectures, rattling on like a sweaty-palmed sixteen-year-old on his first date.

"Chapman's toting around *Catcher in the Rye* when he wastes John Lennon. Reagan, Brady get shot by some jerk who's obsessed with an actress. Patterns. We try to predict. But we can't always. It isn't always predictable."

Next he began reciting statistics. Twelve years ago the clearance rate for homicides averaged at ninety-five, ninety-six percent. Now it was more like seventy-four percent, and dropping. There were more stranger killings as opposed to crimes of passion, and so on. I was barely hearing a word of it.

". . . Matt Petersen worries me, to tell you the truth, Kay." He paused.

He had my attention.

"He's an artist. Psychopaths are the Rembrandts of murderers. He's an actor. We don't know what roles he's played out in his fantasies. We don't know that he isn't making them reality now. We don't know that he isn't diabolically clever. His wife's murder might have been utilitarian."

"*Utilitarian*?" I stared at him with wide, disbelieving eyes, stared at the photographs taken of Lori Petersen at the scene. Her face a suffused mask of agony, her legs bent, the electrical cord as taut as a bowstring in back and wrenching her arms up and cutting into her neck. I was seeing everything the monster did to her. Utilitarian? I wasn't hearing this.

Wesley explained, "Utilitarian in the sense he may have had a need to get rid of her, Kay. If, for example, something happened to make her suspect he'd killed the first three women, he may have panicked, decided he had to kill her. How can he do that and get away with it? He can make her death look like the other ones."

"I've heard shades of this before," I said evenly. "From your partner."

His words were slow and steady like the beat of a metronome, "All possible scenarios, Kay. We have to consider them."

"Of course we do. And that's fine as long as Marino considers *all* possible scenarios and doesn't wear blinders because he's getting obsessed or has a problem."

Wesley glanced toward the open door. Almost inaudibly, he said, "Pete's got his prejudices. I won't deny that."

"I think you'd better tell me exactly what they are."

"Let it suffice to say that when the Bureau decided he was a good candidate for a VICAP team, we did some checking into his background. I know where he grew up, how he grew up. Some things you never get over. They set you off. It happens."

He wasn't telling me anything I hadn't already figured out. Marino grew up poor on the wrong side of the tracks. He was uncomfortable around the sort of people who had always made him uncomfortable. The cheerleaders and homecoming queens never gave him a second glance because he was a social misfit, because his father had dirt under his nails, because he was "common."

I'd heard these cop sob stories a thousand times before. The guy's only advantage in life is he's big and white, so he makes himself bigger and whiter by carrying a gun and a badge.

"We don't get to excuse ourselves, Benton," I said shortly. "We don't excuse criminals because they had screwed-up childhoods. We don't get to use the powers entrusted to us to punish people who remind us of our own screwed-up childhoods."

I wasn't lacking in compassion. I understood exactly where Marino was coming from. I was no stranger to his anger. I'd felt it many times when facing a defendant in court. No matter how convincing the evidence, if the guy's nice-looking, clean-cut and dressed in a two-hundred-dollar suit, twelve working men and women don't, in their hearts, believe he's guilty.

I could believe just about anything of anybody these days. But only if the evidence was there. Was Marino looking at the evidence? Was he even looking at all?

Wesley pushed back his chair and stood up to stretch. "Pete has his spells. You get used to it. I've known him for years." He stepped into the open doorway and looked up and down the hall. "Where the hell is he, anyway? He fall in the john?"

Wesley concluded his depressing business with my office and disappeared into the sunny afternoon of the living where other felonious activities demanded his attention and his time.

We'd given up on Marino. I had no idea where he'd gone, but his trip to the men's room apparently took him out of the building. Nor did I have a chance to wonder about it for very long, because Rose came through the doorway linking my office with hers just as I was locking the case files back inside my desk.

I knew instantly by her weighty pause and the grim set of her mouth that she had something on her mind I didn't want to hear.

"Dr. Scarpetta, Margaret's been looking for you and asked me to tell you the minute you came out of your meeting."

My impatience showed before I could check it. There were autopsies to look in on downstairs and innumerable phone calls to return. I had enough to do to keep half a dozen people busy and I wanted nothing else added to the list.

Handing me a stack of letters to be signed, she looked like a formidable headmistress as she peered at me over her reading glasses and added, "She's in her office, and I don't think the matter can wait."

Rose wasn't going to tell me, and though I really couldn't fault her, I was annoyed. I think she knew everything that went on throughout the entire statewide system, but it was her style to direct me to the source instead of filling me in directly. In a word, she assiduously avoided being the bearer of bad news. I suppose she'd learned the hard way after working for my predecessor Cagney most of her life.

Margaret's office was midway down the hall, a small Spartan room of cinder-block walls painted the same insipid crème-de-menthe color as the rest of the building. The dark green tile floor always looked dusty no matter how often it was swept, and spilling over her desktop and every other surface were reams of computer printouts. The bookcase was crammed with instruction manuals and printer cables, extra ribbons and boxes of diskettes. There were no personal touches, no photographs, posters or knick-knacks. I don't know how Margaret lived with the sterile mess, but I'd never seen a computer analyst's office that wasn't.

She had her back to the door and was staring at the monitor, a programmer manual opened in her lap. Swiveling around, she rolled the chair to one side when I came in. Her face was tense, her short black hair ruffled as if she'd been raking her fingers through it, her dark eyes distracted.

"I was at a meeting most of the morning," she launched in. "When I got here after lunch I found this on the screen."

She handed me a printout. On it were several SQL commands that allowed one to query the data base. At first my mind was blank as I stared at the printout. A Describe had been executed on the case table, and the upper half of the page was filled with column names. Below this were several simple Select statements. The first one asked for the case number where the last name was "Petersen," the first name "Lori." Under it was the response, "No Records Found." A second command asked for the case numbers and first names of every decedent whose record was in our data base and whose last name was "Petersen."

Lori Petersen's name was not included in the list because her case file was inside my desk. I had not handed it over to the clerks up front for entry yet.

"What are you saying, Margaret? You didn't type in these commands?"

"I most certainly didn't," she replied with feeling. "Nobody did it up front either. It wouldn't have been possible."

She had my complete attention.

"When I left Friday afternoon," she went on to explain, "I did the same thing I always do at the end of the day. I left the computer in answer mode so you could dial in from home if you wanted to. There's no way anyone used my computer, because you can't use it when it's in answer mode unless you're at another PC and dialing in by modem."

That much made sense. The office terminals were networked to the one Margaret worked on, which we referred to as the "server." We were not linked to the Health and Human Services Department's mainframe across the street, despite the commissioner's ongoing pressure for us to do so. I had refused and would continue to do so because our data was highly sensitive, many of the cases under active criminal investigation. To have everything dumped in a central computer shared by dozens of other HHSD agencies was an invitation to a colossal security problem.

"I didn't dial in from home," I told her.

"I never assumed you did," she said. "I couldn't imagine why you would type in these commands. You of all people would know Lori Petersen's case isn't in yet. Someone else is responsible, someone other than the clerks up front or the other doctors. Except for your PC and the one in the morgue, everything else is a dumb terminal."

A dumb terminal, she went on to remind me, is rather much what it sounds like – a brainless unit consisting of a monitor and a keyboard. The dumb terminals in our office were linked to the server in Margaret's office. When the server was down or frozen, as was true when it was in answer mode, the dumb terminals were down or frozen, too. In other words, they'd been out of commission since late Friday – *before* Lori Petersen's murder.

The data base violation had to have occurred over the weekend or at some point earlier today.

Someone, an outsider, got in.

This someone had to be familiar with the relational data base we used. A popular one, I reminded myself, and not impossible to learn. The dial-up number was Margaret's extension, which was listed in the HHSD's in-house directory. If you had a computer loaded with a communications software package, if you had a compatible modem, and if you knew Margaret was the computer analyst and tried her number, you could dial in. But that's as far as you would get. You couldn't access any office applications or data. You

83

couldn't even get into the electronic mailboxes without knowing the user names and passwords.

Margaret was staring at the screen through her tinted glasses. Her brow was slightly furrowed and she was nipping at a thumbnail.

I pulled up a chair and sat down. "How? The user name and password. How did anyone have access to these?"

"That's what I'm puzzling over. Only a few of us know them, Dr. Scarpetta. You, me, the other doctors, and the people who enter the data. And our user names and passwords are different from the ones I assigned to the districts."

Though each of my other districts was computerized with a network exactly like ours, they kept their own data and did not have on-line access to the Central Office data. It wasn't likely – in fact, I did not think it was possible – that one of my deputy chiefs from one of the other offices was responsible.

I made a lame suggestion.

"Maybe someone guessed and got lucky."

She shook her head. "Next to impossible. I know. I've tried before when I've changed someone's electronic mail password and can't remember what it is. After about three tries, the computer isn't very forgiving, the phone line's disconnected. In addition, this version of the data base doesn't like illegal log-ons. If you type in enough of them when you're trying to get into SQL or into a table, you get a context error, whack the pointers out of alignment and crash the data base."

"There's no other place the passwords might be?" I asked. "No other place in the computer, for example, where someone might be able to find out what they are? What if the person were another programmer . . .?"

"Wouldn't work." She was sure. "I've been careful about it. There *is* a system table where the user names and passwords are listed, but you could get into that only if you know what you're doing. And it doesn't matter anyway because I dropped that table a long time ago to prevent this very sort of problem."

I didn't say anything.

She was tentatively searching my face, looking for a sign of displeasure, for a glint in my eyes telling her I was angry or blaming her.

"It's awful," she blurted out. "Really. I don't have a clue, don't know what all the person did. The DBA isn't working, for example."

"Isn't working?" The DBA, or data base administrator, was a grant giving select persons, such as Margaret or me, authority to access all tables and do anything we wished with them. For the DBA not to be working was the equivalent of being told the key to my front door no longer fit. "What do you mean *it isn't working*?" It was getting very difficult to sound calm.

"Exactly that. I couldn't get into any of the tables with it. The password was invalid for some reason. I had to reconnect the grant."

"How could *that* have happened?"

"I don't know." She was getting more upset. "Maybe I should change all of the grants, for security reasons, and assign new passwords?"

"Not now," I automatically replied. "We'll simply keep Lori Petersen's case out of the computer. Whoever the person is, at least he didn't find what he was looking for." I got out of the chair.

"This time he didn't."

I froze, staring down at her.

Two spots of color were forming on her cheeks. "I don't know. If it's happened before, I have no way of knowing, because the echo was off. These commands here" – she pointed to the printout – "are the echo of the commands typed on the computer that dialed up this one. I always leave the echo off so if you're dialing in from home, whatever you're doing isn't echoed on this screen. Friday I was in a hurry. Maybe I inadvertently left the echo on or set it on. I don't remember, but it was on." Ruefully she added, "I guess it's a good thing –"

85

We both turned around at the same time.

Rose was standing in the doorway.

That look on her face – *Oh, no, not again.*

She waited for me to come out into the hallway, then said, "The ME in Colonial Heights is on line one. A detective from Ashland's on line two. And the commissioner's secretary just called –"

"What?" I interrupted. Her last remark was the only one I really heard. "Amburgey's secretary?"

She handed me several pink telephone slips as she replied, "The commissioner wants to see you."

"About what, for God's sake?" If she told me one more time I'd have to hear the details for myself, I was going to lose my temper.

"I don't know," Rose replied. "His secretary didn't say."

6

I couldn't bear to sit at my desk. I had to move about and distract myself before I lost my composure.

Someone had broken into my office computer, and Amburgey wanted to see me in an hour and forty-five minutes. It wasn't likely that he was merely inviting me to tea.

So I was making evidence rounds. Usually this entailed my receipting evidence to the various labs upstairs. Other times I simply stopped by to see what was going on with my cases – the good doctor checking in on her patients. At the moment, my routine was a veiled and desperate peregrination.

The Forensic Science Bureau was a beehive, a honeycomb of cubicles filled with laboratory equipment and people wearing white lab coats and plastic safety glasses.

A few of the scientists nodded and smiled as I passed their open doorways. Most of them didn't look up, too preoccupied with whatever they were doing to pay a passerby any mind. I was thinking about Abby Turnbull, about other reporters I didn't like.

Did some ambitious journalist pay a computer hack to break into our data?

How long had the violations been going on?

I didn't even realize I'd turned in to the serology lab until my eyes were suddenly focusing on black countertops cluttered with beakers, test tubes, and Bunsen burners. Jammed on glass-enclosed shelves were bags of evidence and jars of chemicals, and in the center of the room was a long table covered with the spread and sheets removed from Lori Petersen's bed.

"You're just in time," Betty greeted me. "If you want acid indigestion, that is."

"No, thanks."

"Well, I'm getting it already," she added. "Why should you be immune?"

Close to retirement, Betty had steel-gray hair, strong features and hazel eyes that could be unreadable or shyly sensitive depending on whether you took the trouble to get to know her. I liked her the first time I met her. The chief serologist was meticulous, her acumen as sharp as a scalpel. In private she was an ardent bird-watcher and an accomplished pianist who had never been married or sorry about the fact. I think she reminded me of Sister Martha, my favorite nun at St. Gertrude's parochial school.

The sleeves of her long lab coat were rolled up to her elbows, her hands gloved. Arranged over her work area were test tubes containing cotton-tipped swabs, and a physical evidence recovery kit – or PERK – comprising the cardboard folder of slides and the envelopes of hair samples from Lori Petersen's case. The file of slides, the envelopes and the test tubes were identified by computer-generated labels initialed by me, the fruits of yet one more of Margaret's programs.

I vaguely recalled the gossip at a recent academy meeting. In the weeks following the mayor of Chicago's sudden death, there were some ninety attempts at breaking into the medical examiner's computer. The culprits were thought to be reporters after the autopsy and toxicology results.

Who? Who broke into my computer?

And why?

"He's coming along well," Betty was saying.

"I'm sorry . . ." I smiled apologetically.

She repeated, "I talked with Dr. Glassman this morning. He's coming along well with the samples from the first two cases and should have results for us in a couple of days."

"You sent up the samples from the last two yet?"

"They just went out." She was unscrewing the top of a small brown bottle. "Bo Friend will be hand-delivering them –"

"*Bo Friend*?" I interrupted.

"Or Officer Friendly, as he's known by the troops. That's his name. Bo Friend. Scout's honor. Let's see, New York's about a six-hour drive. He should get them to the lab sometime this evening. I think they drew straws."

I looked blankly at her. "Straws?"

What could Amburgey want? Maybe he was interested in how the DNA testing was going. It was on everyone's mind these days.

"The cops," Betty was saying. "Going to New York and all. Some of them have never been."

"Once will be enough for most of them," I commented abstractedly. "Wait until they try changing lanes or finding a parking place."

But he could have just sent a memo through the electronic mail if he'd had a question about DNA tests or anything else. That's what Amburgey usually did. In fact, that's what he'd always done in the past.

"Huh. That's the least of it. Our man Bo was born and bred in Tennessee and never goes anywhere without his piece."

"He went to New York without his piece, I hope." My mouth was talking to her. The rest of me was elsewhere.

"Huh," she said again. "His captain told him to, told him about the gun laws up there in Yankeeville. Bo was smiling when he came up to get the samples, smiling and patting what I presume was a shoulder holster under his jacket. He's got one of these John Wayne revolvers with a six-inch barrel. These guys and their guns. It's so Freudian it's boring . . ."

The back of my brain was recalling news accounts of virtual children who had broken into the computers of major corporations and banks.

Beneath the telephone on my desk at home was a modem

enabling me to dial up the computer here. It was off-limits, strictly verboten. Lucy understood the seriousness of her ever attempting to access the OCME data. Everything else she was welcome to do, despite my inward resistance, the strong sense of territory that comes from living alone.

I recalled the evening paper Lucy found hidden under the sofa cushion. I recalled the expression on her face as she questioned me about the murder of Lori Petersen, and then the list of my staff's office and home telephone numbers – including Margaret's extension – tacked to the cork bulletin board above my home desk.

I realized Betty hadn't said anything for quite a long time. She was staring strangely at me.

"Are you all right, Kay?"

"I'm sorry," I said again, this time with a sigh.

Silent for a moment, she spoke sympathetically. "No suspects yet. It's eating at me, too."

"I suppose it's hard to think of anything else." Even though I'd hardly given the subject a thought in the last hour or so, and I should be giving it my full attention, I silently chastised myself.

"Well, I hate to tell you, but DNA's not worth a tinker's damn unless they catch *somebody*."

"Not until we reach the enlightened age where genetic prints are stored in a central data base like fingerprint records," I muttered.

"Will never happen as long as the ACLU has a thing to say about it."

Didn't anybody have anything positive to offer today? A headache was beginning to work its way up from the base of my skull.

"It's weird." She was dripping naphthyl acid phosphate on small circles of white filter paper. "You would think somebody *somewhere* has seen this guy. He's not invisible. He doesn't just beam into the women's houses, and he's got to have seen them at some point in the past to have picked them and followed them home. If he's hanging out in parks or malls or the likes, someone should have noticed him, seems to me."

"If anybody's seen anything, we don't know about it. It isn't that people aren't calling," I added. "Apparently the Crime Watch hot lines are ringing off the hook morning, noon and night. But so far, based on what I've been told, nothing is panning out."

"A lot of wild goose chases."

"That's right. A lot of them."

Betty continued to work. This stage of testing was relatively simple. She took the swabs from the test tubes I'd sent up to her, moistened them with water and smeared filter paper with them. Working in clusters, she first dripped naphthyl acid phosphate, and then added drops of fast-blue B salt, which caused the smear to pop up purple in a matter of seconds if seminal fluid was present.

I looked at the array of paper circles. Almost all of them were coming up purple.

"The bastard," I said.

"A lousy shot at that." She began describing what I was seeing.

"These are the swabs from the back of her thighs," she said, pointing. "They came up immediately. The reaction wasn't quite as quick with the anal and vaginal swabs. But I'm not surprised. Her own body fluids would interfere with the tests. In addition, the oral swabs are positive."

"The bastard," I repeated quietly.

"But the ones you took of the esophagus are negative. Obviously, the most substantial residues of seminal fluid were left outside the body. Misfires, again. The pattern's almost identical to what I found with Brenda, Patty and Cecile."

Brenda was the first strangling, Patty the second, Cecile the third. I was startled by the note of familiarity in Betty's voice as she referred to the slain women. They had, in an odd way, become part of our family. We'd never met them in life and yet now we knew them well.

As Betty screwed the medicine dropper back inside its small brown bottle, I went to the microscope on a nearby counter, stared through the eyepiece and began moving the wetmount around on the stage. In the field of polarized light were several multicolored fibers, flat and ribbon-shaped with twists at irregular intervals. The fibers were neither animal hair nor man-made.

"These what I collected from the knife?" I almost didn't want to ask.

"Yes. They're cotton. Don't be thrown off by the pinks and greens and white you're seeing. Dyed fabrics are often made up of a combination of colors you can't detect with the naked eye."

The gown cut from Lori Petersen was cotton, a pale yellow cotton.

I adjusted the focus. "I don't suppose there's any chance they could be from a cotton rag paper, something like that. Lori apparently was using the knife as a letter opener."

"Not a chance, Kay. I've already looked at a sample of fibers from her gown. They're consistent with the fibers you collected from the knife blade."

That was expert-witness talk. Consistent-this and reasonable-that. Lori's gown was cut from her body with her husband's knife. Wait until Marino gets this lab report, I thought. Damn.

Betty was going on, "I can also tell you right off the fibers you're looking at aren't the same as some of the ones found on her body and on the frame of the window the police think the killer came through. Those are dark – black and navy blue with some red, a polyester-and-cotton blend."

The night I'd seen Matt Petersen he was wearing a white Izod shirt that I suspected was cotton and most certainly would not have contained black, red or navy blue fibers. He was also wearing jeans, and most denim jeans are cotton.

It was highly unlikely he left the fibers Betty just mentioned, unless he changed his clothes before the police arrived.

"Yeah, well, Petersen ain't stupid," I could hear Marino say. "Ever since Wayne Williams half the world knows fibers can be used to nail your ass."

I went out and followed the hallway to the end, turning left into the tool marks and firearms lab, with its countertops and tables cluttered with handguns, rifles, machetes, shotguns and Uzis, all tagged as evidence and waiting their day in court. Handgun and shotgun cartridges were scattered over desktops, and in a back corner was a galvanized steel tank filled with water and used for test fires. Floating placidly on the water's surface was a rubber duck.

Frank, a wiry white-haired man retired from the army's CID, was hunched over the comparison microscope. He relit his pipe when I came in and didn't tell me anything I wanted to hear.

There was nothing to be learned from the cut screen removed from Lori Petersen's window. The mesh was a synthetic, and therefore useless as far as tool marks or even the direction of the cut was concerned. We couldn't know if it had been cut from the inside or the outside of the house because plastic, unlike metal, doesn't bend.

The distinction would have been an important one, something I very much would have liked to know. If the screen was cut from the *inside* of the house, then all bets were off. It would mean the killer didn't break in but out of the Petersen house. It would mean, quite likely, Marino's suspicions of the husband were correct.

"All I can tell you," Frank said, puffing out swirls of aromatic smoke, "is it's a clean cut, made with something sharp like a razor or a knife."

"Possibly the same instrument used to cut her gown?"

He absently slipped off his glasses and began cleaning them with a handkerchief. "Something sharp was used to cut her gown but I can't tell you if it was the same thing used to cut the screen. I can't even give you a classification, Kay. Could be a stiletto. Could be a saber or a pair of scissors."

The severed electrical cords and survival knife told another story.

Based on a microscopic comparison, Frank had good reason to believe the cords had been cut with Matt Petersen's knife. The tool marks on the blade were consistent with those left on the severed ends of the cords. Marino, I dismally thought again. This bit of circumstantial evidence wouldn't amount to much had the survival knife been found out in the open and near the bed instead of hidden inside Matt Petersen's dresser drawer.

I was still envisioning my own scenario. The killer saw the knife on top of Lori's desk and decided to use it. But why did he hide it afterward? Also, if the knife was used to cut Lori's gown and if it was also used to cut the electrical cords, then this changed the sequence of events as I had imagined them.

I'd assumed when the killer entered Lori's bedroom he had his own cutting instrument in hand, the knife or sharp instrument he used to cut the window screen. If so, then why didn't he cut her gown and the electrical cords with it? How is it he ended up with the survival knife? Did he instantly spot it on the desk when he entered her bedroom?

He couldn't have. The desk was nowhere near the bed, and when he first came in, the bedroom was dark. He couldn't have seen the knife.

He couldn't have seen it until the lights were on, and by then Lori should have been subdued, the killer's knife at her throat. Why should the survival knife on the desk have mattered to him? It didn't make any sense.

Unless something interrupted him.

Unless something happened to disrupt and alter his ritual, unless an unexpected event occurred that caused him to change course.

Frank and I batted this around.

"This is assuming the killer's not her husband," Frank said.

"Yes. This is assuming the killer is a stranger to Lori. He

has his pattern, his MO. But when he's with Lori, something catches him off guard."

"Something she does . . ."

"Or says," I replied, then proposed, "She may have said something that momentarily stalled him."

"Maybe." He looked skeptical. "She may have stalled him long enough for him to see the knife on the desk, long enough for him to get the idea. But it's more likely, in my opinion, he found the knife on the desk earlier in the evening because he was already inside her house when she got home."

"No. I really don't think so."

"Why not?"

"Because she was home for a while before she was assaulted."

I'd gone through it many times.

Lori drove home from the hospital, unlocked her front door and relocked it from the inside. She went into the kitchen and placed her knapsack on the table. Then she had a snack. Her gastric contents indicated she'd eaten several cheese crackers very close to the time she was assaulted. The food had scarcely begun to digest. Her terror when she was attacked would have caused her digestion to completely shut down. It's one of the body's defense mechanisms. Digestion shuts down to keep blood flowing to the extremities instead of to the stomach, preparing the animal for fight or flight.

Only it hadn't been possible for her to fight. It hadn't been possible for her to flee anywhere.

After her snack, she went from the kitchen to the bedroom. The police had found out it was her habit to take her oral contraceptive at night, right before bed. Friday's tablet was missing from the foil pack inside the master bathroom. She took her tablet, perhaps brushed her teeth and washed her face, then changed into her gown and placed her clothing neatly on the chair. I believed she was in bed when he attacked her not long afterward. He may have been watching her house from the darkness of the trees or the shrubbery. He may have waited until the lights were out, until he assumed she was asleep. Or he may have observed her in the past and known exactly what time she came home from work and went to bed.

I remembered the bedcovers. They were turned down as if she'd been under them, and there was no evidence of a struggle anywhere else in the house.

There was something else coming to me.

The smell Matt Petersen mentioned, the sweaty, sweet smell.

If the killer had a peculiar and pronounced body odor, it was going to be wherever he was. It would have lingered inside her bedroom had he been hiding there when Lori got home.

She was a physician.

Odors are often indications of diseases and poisons. Physicians are trained to be very sensitive to smells, so sensitive I can often tell by the odor of blood at a scene that the victim was drinking shortly before he was shot or stabbed. Blood or gastric contents reminiscent of musky macaroons, of almonds, may indicate the presence of cyanide. A patient's breath smelling of wet leaves may indicate tuberculosis –

Lori Petersen was a physician, like me.

Had she noticed a peculiar odor the moment she walked into her bedroom, she would not have undressed or done anything else until she determined the source of it.

Cagney did not have my worries, and there were times when I felt haunted by the spirit of the predecessor I had never met, a reminder of a power and invulnerability I would never have. In an unchivalrous world he was an unchivalrous knight who wore his position like a panache, and I think a part of me envied him.

His death was sudden. He literally dropped dead as he was crossing the living room rug to switch on the Super Bowl. In the predawn silence of an overcast Monday morning he became the subject of his own instruction, a towel draped over his face, the autopsy suite sealed off from everyone but the pathologist whose lot it was to examine him. For three months, no one touched his office. It was exactly as he'd left it, except, I suppose, that Rose had emptied the cigar butts out of the ashtray.

The first thing I did when I moved to Richmond was to strip his inner sanctum to a shell and banish the last remnant of its former occupant – including the hard-boiled portrait of him dressed in his academic gown, which was beneath a museum light behind his formidable desk. That was relegated to the Pathology Department at VMC, as was an entire bookcase filled with macabre mementos forensic pathologists are expected to collect, even if most of us don't.

His office – my office, now – was well-lighted and carpeted in royal blue, the walls arranged with prints of English landscapes and other civilized scenes. I had few mementos, and the only hint of morbidity was the clay facial reconstruction of a murdered boy whose identity remained a mystery. I'd arranged a sweater around the base of his neck and perched him on top of a filing cabinet where he watched the open doorway with plastic eyes and waited in sad silence to be called by name.

Where I worked was low-profile, comfortable but businesslike, my impedimenta deliberately unrevealing and bland. Though I somewhat smugly assured myself it was better to be viewed as a professional than as a legend, I secretly had my doubts.

I still felt Cagney's presence in this place.

People were constantly reminding me of him through stories that became more apocryphal the longer they lived on. He rarely wore gloves while doing a post. He was known to arrive at scenes eating his lunch. He went hunting with the cops, he went to barbecues with the judges, and the previous commissioner was obsequiously accommodating because he was absolutely intimidated by Cagney.

I paled by comparison and I knew comparisons were

constantly being made. The only hunts and barbecues I was invited to were courtrooms and conferences in which targets were drawn on me and fires lit beneath my feet. If Dr. Alvin Amburgey's first year in the commissioner's office was any indication, his next three promised to be the pits. My turf was his to invade. He monitored what I did. Not a week went by that I didn't get an arrogant electronic memo from him requesting statistical information or demanding an answer as to why the homicide rate continued to rise while other crimes were slightly on the decline – as if somehow it was my fault people killed each other in Virginia.

What he had never done to me before was to schedule an impromptu meeting.

In the past, when he had something to discuss, if he didn't send a memo he sent one of his aides. There was no doubt in my mind his agenda was not to pat me on the back and tell me what a fine job I was doing.

I was abstractedly looking over the piles on my desk and trying to find something to arm myself with – files, a notepad, a clipboard. For some reason, the thought of going in there empty-handed made me feel undressed. Emptying my lab-coat pockets of the miscellaneous debris I had a habit of collecting during the day, I settled for tucking in a pack of cigarettes, or "cancer sticks," as Amburgey was known to call them, and I went out into the late afternoon.

He reigned across the street on the twenty-fourth floor of the Monroe Building. No one was above him except an occasional pigeon roosting on the roof. Most of his minions were located below on floor after floor of HHSD agencies. I'd never seen his office. I'd never been invited.

The elevator slid open onto a large lobby where his receptionist was ensconced within a U-shaped desk rising from a great field of wheat-colored carpet. She was a bosomy redhead barely out of her teens, and when she looked up from her computer and greeted me with a practiced, perky smile, I almost expected her to ask if I had reservations and needed a bellhop to manage my bags.

I told her who I was, which didn't seem to fan the smallest spark of recognition.

"I have a four o'clock appointment with the commissioner," I added.

She checked his electronic calendar and cheerily said, "Please make yourself comfortable, Mrs. Scarpetta. Dr. Amburgey will be with you shortly."

As I settled myself on a beige leather couch, I searched the sparkling glass coffee and end tables bearing magazines and arrangements of silk flowers. There wasn't an ashtray, not a single one, and at two different locations were "Thank You for Not Smoking" signs.

The minutes crept by.

The redheaded receptionist was sipping Perrier through a straw and preoccupied with her typing. At one point she thought to offer me something to drink. I smiled a "no, thank you," and her fingers flew again, keys rapidly clicked, and the computer complained with a loud beep. She sighed as if she'd just gotten grave news from her accountant.

My cigarettes were a hard lump in my pocket and I was tempted to find a ladies' room and light up.

At four-thirty her telephone buzzed. Hanging up – that cheery, vacant smile again – she announced, "You may go in, Mrs. Scarpetta."

Defrocked and decidedly out of sorts, "Mrs." Scarpetta took her at her word.

The commissioner's door opened with a soft click of its rotating brass knob and instantly on their feet were three men – only one of whom I was expecting to see. With Amburgey were Norman Tanner and Bill Boltz, and when it came Boltz's turn to offer his hand, I looked him straight in the eye until he glanced away uncomfortably.

I was hurt and a little angry. Why hadn't he told me he was going to be here? Why hadn't I heard a word from him since our paths had crossed briefly at Lori Petersen's home?

Amburgey granted me a nod that seemed more a

dismissal, and added "Appreciate your coming" with the enthusiasm of a bored traffic court judge.

He was a shifty-eyed little man whose last post had been in Sacramento, where he picked up enough West Coast ways to disguise his North Carolina origins; he was the son of a farmer, and not proud of the fact. He had a penchant for string ties with silver slides, which he wore almost religiously with a pin-striped suit, and on his right ring finger was a hunk of silver set with turquoise. His eyes were hazy gray, like ice, the bones of his skull sharply pronounced through his thin skin. He was almost bald.

An ivory wing chair had been pulled out from the wall and seemed to be there for me. Leather creaked, and Amburgey stationed himself behind his desk, which I had heard of but never seen. It was a huge, ornately carved masterpiece of rosewood, very old and very Chinese.

Behind his head was an expansive window affording him a vista of the city, the James River a glinting ribbon in the distance and Southside a patchwork. With a loud snap he opened a black ostrich-skin briefcase before him and produced a yellow legal pad filled with his tight, snarled scrawl. He had outlined what he was going to say. He never did anything without his cue cards.

"I'm sure you're aware of the public distress over these recent stranglings," he said to me.

"I'm very aware of it."

"Bill, Norm and I had an emergency summit meeting, so to speak, yesterday afternoon. This was apropos of several things, not the least of which was what was in the Saturday evening and Sunday morning papers, Dr. Scarpetta. As you may know, because of this fourth tragic death, the murder of the young surgeon, the news has gone out over the wire."

I didn't know. But I wasn't surprised.

"No doubt you've been getting inquiries," Amburgey blandly went on. "We've got to nip this in the bud or we're going to have sheer pandemonium on our hands. That's one of the things the three of us have been discussing."

"If you can nip the murders in the bud," I said just as blandly, "you'll deserve a Nobel Prize."

"Naturally, that's our top priority," said Boltz, who had unbuttoned his dark suit jacket and was leaning back in his chair. "We've got the cops working overtime on them, Kay. But we're all in agreement there's one thing we must control for the time being – these leaks to the press. The news stories are scaring the hell out of the public and letting the killer know everything we're up to."

"I couldn't agree more." My defenses were going up like a drawbridge, and I instantly regretted what I said next: "You can rest assured I have issued no statements from my office other than the obligatory information of cause and manner."

I'd answered a charge not yet made, and my legal instincts were bridling at my foolishness. If I were here to be accused of indiscretion, I should have forced them – forced Amburgey, anyway – to introduce such an outrageous subject. Instead, I'd sent up the flare I was on the run and it gave them justification to pursue.

"Well, now," Amburgey commented, his pale, unfriendly eyes resting briefly on me, "you've just laid something on the table I think we need to examine closely."

"I haven't laid anything on the table," I unemphatically replied. "I'm just stating a fact, for the record."

With a light knock, the redheaded receptionist came in with coffee, and the room abruptly froze into a mute tableau. The heavy silence seemed completely lost on her as she went to considerable lengths to make sure we had everything we needed, her attention hovering about Boltz like a mist. He may not have been the best Commonwealth's attorney the city had ever known, but he was by far the best looking – one of those rare blond men to whom the passing years were generous. He was losing neither his hair nor his physique, and the fine lines at the corners of his eyes were the only indication he was creeping close to forty.

When she was gone, Boltz said to no one in particular, "We all know the cops occasionally have a problem with kiss

101

and tell. Norm and I have had a few words with the brass. No one seems to know exactly where the leaks are coming from."

I restrained myself. What did they expect? One of the majors is in tight with Abby Turnbull or whoever and this guy's going to confess, "Yeah, sorry about that. I squawked"?

Amburgey flipped a page in his legal pad. "So far a leak cited as 'a medical source' has been quoted seventeen times in the papers since the first murder, Dr. Scarpetta. This makes me a little uneasy. Clearly, the most sensational details, such as the ligatures, the evidence of sexual assault, how the killer got in, where the bodies were found, and the fact DNA testing is in the works have been attributed to this medical source." He glanced up at me. "Am I to assume the details are accurate?"

"Not entirely. There were a few minor discrepancies."

"Such as?"

I didn't want to tell him. I didn't want to talk about these cases at all with him. But he had the right to the furniture inside my office if he wanted it. I reported to him. He reported to no one but the governor.

"For example," I replied, "in the first case, the news reported there was a tan cloth belt tied around Brenda Steppe's neck. The ligature was actually a pair of pantyhose."

Amburgey was writing this down. "What else?"

"In Cecile Tyler's case, it was reported her face was bleeding, that the bedspread was covered with blood. An exaggeration, at best. She had no lacerations, no injuries of this nature. There was a little bloody fluid coming out of her nose and mouth. A postmortem artifact."

"These details," Amburgey asked as he continued to write, "were they mentioned in the CME-1 reports?"

I had to take a moment to compose myself. It was becoming clear what was going through his mind. The CME-1's were the medical examiner's initial report of investigation. The responding ME simply wrote down what he saw at the scene and learned from the police. The details were not always completely accurate because the ME on call was surrounded by confusion, and the autopsy hadn't been performed yet.

In addition, ME's were not forensic pathologists. They were physicians in private practice, virtual volunteers who got paid fifty dollars a case to be jerked out of bed in the middle of the night or have their weekends wrecked by car crashes, suicides and homicides. These men and women provided a public service; they were the troops. Their primary job was to determine whether the case merited an autopsy, to write everything down and take a lot of photographs. Even if one of my ME's had confused a pair of pantyhose with a tan belt, it wasn't relevant. My ME's didn't talk to the press.

Amburgey persisted, "The bit about the tan cloth belt, the bloody bedspread. I'm wondering if these were mentioned in the CME-1's."

"In the manner the press made reference to the details," I firmly replied, "no."

Tanner drolly remarked, "We all know what the press does. Takes a mustard seed and turns it into a mountain."

"Listen," I said, looking around at the three men, "if your point is that one of my medical examiners is leaking details about these cases, I can tell you with certainty you're way off base. It isn't happening. I know both of the ME's who responded to the first two scenes. They've been ME's in Richmond for years and have always been unimpeachable. I myself responded to the third and fourth scenes. The information is not coming from my office. The details, all of them, could have been divulged by anyone who was there. Members of the rescue squads who responded, for example."

Leather quietly creaked as Amburgey shifted in his chair. "I've looked into that. Three different squads responded. No one paramedic was present at all four scenes."

I said levelly, "Anonymous sources are often a blend of numerous sources. A medical source could have been a combination of what a squad member said, what a police officer said, and what the reporter overheard or saw while waiting around outside the residence where the body was found."

"True." Amburgey nodded. "And I don't believe any of us really think the leaks are coming from the Medical Examiner's Office – at least not intentionally –"

"*Intentionally*?" I broke out. "Are you implying the leaks may be coming from my office *unintentionally*?" Just as I was about to retort self-righteously what a lot of nonsense this was, I was suddenly struck silent.

A flush began creeping up my neck as it came back to me with swift simplicity. My office data base. It had been violated by an outsider. Was this what Amburgey was alluding to? How could he possibly know about it?

Amburgey went on as if he hadn't heard me, "People talk, employees talk. They tell their family, their friends, and they don't intend any harm in most instances. But you never know where the buck stops – maybe on a reporter's desk. These things happen. We're objectively looking into the matter, turning over every stone. We have to. As you must realize, some of what's been leaked has the potential of doing serious damage to the investigation."

Tanner laconically added, "The city manager, the mayor, they aren't pleased with this type of exposure. The homicide rate's already given Richmond a black eye. Sensational national news accounts of a serial murderer are the last thing the city needs. All these new hotels going up are dependent on big conferences, visitors. People don't want to come to a city where they fear for their lives."

"No, they don't," I coldly agreed. "Nor would people want to think the city's major concern over these murders is they're an inconvenience, an embarrassment, a potential obstruction to the tourist trade."

"Kay," Boltz quietly reasoned, "nobody's implying anything outrageous like that."

"Of course not," Amburgey was quick to add. "But we have to face certain hard realities, and the fact is there's a lot simmering beneath the surface. If we don't handle the matter with extreme care, I'm afraid we're in for a major eruption."

"Eruption? Over what?" I warily asked, and automatically looked at Boltz.

His face was tight, his eyes hard with restrained emotion. Reluctantly he said, "This last murder's a powder keg. There are certain things about Lori Petersen's case no one's talking about. Things that, thank God, the reporters don't know yet. But it's just a matter of time. Someone's going to find out, and if we haven't handled the problem first, sensibly and behind the scenes, the situation's going to blow sky-high."

Tanner took over, his long, lantern-shaped face very grim, "The city is at risk for, well, litigation." He glanced at Amburgey, who signaled him with a nod to proceed.

"A very unfortunate thing happened, you see. Apparently Lori Petersen called the police shortly after she got home from the hospital early Saturday morning. We learned this from one of the dispatchers on duty at the time. At eleven minutes before one A.M., a 911 operator got a call. The Petersen residence came up on the computer screen but the line was immediately disconnected."

Boltz said to me, "As you may recall from the scene, there was a telephone on the bedside table, the cord ripped out of the wall. Our conjecture is Dr. Petersen woke up when the killer was inside her house. She reached for the phone and got as far as dialing 911 before he stopped her. Her address came up on the computer screen. That was it. No one said anything. Nine-one-one calls of this nature are dispatched to the patrolmen. Nine times out of ten they're cranks, kids playing with the phone. But we can't ever be sure of that. Can't be sure the person isn't suffering a heart attack, a seizure. In mortal danger. Therefore the operator's supposed to give the call a high priority. Then the dispatcher broadcasts it to the units on the street without delay, prompting an officer to drive past the residence and at least check to make sure everything's all right. This wasn't done. A certain 911 operator, who even as we speak is suspended from duty, gave the call a priority four."

Tanner interjected, "There was a lot of action on the street that night. A lot of radio traffic. The more calls there are, the easier it is to rank something lower in importance than you maybe otherwise would. Problem is, once something's been given a number, there's no going back. The dispatcher's looking at the numbers on his screen. He's not privy to the nature of the calls until he gets to them. He's not going to get to a four anytime soon when he's got a backlog of ones and twos and threes to send out to the men on the street."

"No question the operator dropped the ball," Amburgey mildly said. "But I think one can see how such a thing could have happened."

I was sitting so rigidly I was barely breathing.

Boltz resumed in the same dull tone, "It was some forty-five minutes later when a patrol car finally cruised past the Petersen residence. The officer says he shone his spotlight over the front of the house. The lights were out, everything looked, quote, 'secure.' He gets a call of a domestic fight in progress, speeds off. It wasn't long after this Mr. Petersen apparently came home and found his wife's body."

The men continued to talk, to explain. References were made to Howard Beach, to a stabbing in Brooklyn, in which the police were negligent in responding and people died.

"Courts in D.C., New York, have ruled a government can't be held liable for failing to protect people from crime."

"Makes no difference what the police do or don't do."

"Doesn't matter. We win the suit, if there is one, we still lose because of the publicity."

I was scarcely hearing a word of it. Horrible images were playing crazily inside my mind. The 911 call, the fact it was aborted, made me see it.

I knew what happened.

Lori Petersen was exhausted after her ER shift, and her husband had told her he would be in later than usual that night. So she went to bed, perhaps planning to sleep just awhile, until he got home – as I used to do when I was a resident and waiting for Tony to come home from the law library at Georgetown. She woke up at the sound of someone inside the house, perhaps the quiet sound of this person's footsteps coming down the hallway toward the bedroom. Confused, she called out the name of her husband.

No one answered.

In that instant of dark silence that must have seemed an eternity, she realized there was someone inside the house and it wasn't Matt.

Panicking, she flicked on the bedside lamp so she could see to dial the phone.

By the time she'd stabbed out 911, the killer had gotten to her. He jerked the phone line from the wall before she had a chance to cry out for help.

Maybe he grabbed the receiver out of her hand. Maybe he yelled at her or she began to plead with him. He'd been interrupted, momentarily knocked off guard.

He was enraged. He may have struck her. This may be when he fractured her ribs, and as she cowered in stunned pain he wildly looked around. The lamp was on. He could see everything inside the bedroom. He could see the survival knife on her desk.

Her murder was preventable. It could have been stopped!

Had the call been given a priority one, had it immediately been dispatched over the air, an officer would have responded within minutes. He would have noticed the bedroom light was on – the killer couldn't see to cut cords and tie up his victim in the dark. The officer might have gotten out of his car and heard something. If nothing else, had he taken the time to shine his light over the back of her house, the removed window screen, the picnic bench, the open window would have been noticed. The killer's ritual took time. The police might have been able to get inside before he killed her!

My mouth was so dry I had to take several sips of coffee before I could ask, "How many people know this?"

Boltz replied, "No one's talking about it, Kay. Not even Sergeant Marino knows. Or at least it's doubtful he does. He wasn't on duty when the call was broadcast. He was contacted at home after a uniform man had already arrived at the scene. The word's out in the department. Those cops aware of what happened are not to discuss the matter with anyone."

I knew what that meant. Loose lips would send the guy back to traffic or stick him behind a desk in the uniform room.

"The only reason we're apprising you of this unfortunate situation" – Amburgey carefully chose his words – "is because you need the background in order to understand the steps we feel compelled to take."

I sat tensely, looking hard at him. The point of all this was about to be made.

"I had a conversation with Dr. Spiro Fortosis last night, the forensic psychiatrist who has been good enough to share his insights with us. I've discussed the cases with the FBI. It's the opinion of the people who are experts in profiling this type of killer that publicity exacerbates the problem. This type of killer gets off on it. He gets excited, hyper, when he reads about what he's done. It pushes him into overdrive."

"We can't curtail the freedom of the press," I bluntly reminded him. "We have no control over what reporters print."

"We do." Amburgey was gazing out the window. "They can't print much if we don't give them much. Unfortunately, we've given them a lot." A pause. "Or at least someone has."

I wasn't sure where Amburgey was going but the road signs definitely pointed in my direction.

He continued, "The sensational details – the leaks – we've already discussed have resulted in graphic, grisly stories, banner headlines. It's the expert opinion of Dr. Fortosis this may be what prompted the killer to strike again so soon. The publicity excites him, puts him under incredible stress. The urge peaks again and he has to find release in selecting another victim. As you know, there was only a week between the slayings of Cecile Tyler and Lori Petersen –"

"Have you talked to Benton Wesley about this?" I interrupted.

"Didn't have to. Talked to Susling, one of his colleagues at the Behavioral Science Unit in Quantico. He's well known in the field, has published quite a lot on the subject."

Thank God. I couldn't endure knowing Wesley had just been sitting in my conference room several hours before and had made no mention of what I was now being told. He would be just as incensed as I was, I thought. The commissioner was wedging his foot in the investigation. He was going around me, around Wesley, around Marino, and taking matters into his own hands.

"The probability that sensational publicity, which has been ignited by loose talk, by leaks," Amburgey went on, "the fact the city may be liable because of the 911 mishap, means we have to take serious measures, Dr. Scarpetta. All information dispensed to the public, from this point forward, will be channeled through Norm or Bill, as far as the police end of it goes. And nothing will be coming from your office unless it is released by me. Are we clear?"

There had never been a problem with my office before, and he knew it. We had never solicited publicity, and I'd always been circumspect when releasing information to the press.

What would the reporters – what would anybody – think when they were told they were being referred to the commissioner for information that historically had come from my agency? In the forty-two-year history of the Virginia medical examiner system, this had never happened. By gagging me it would appear I'd been relieved of my authority because I couldn't be trusted.

I looked around. No one would meet my eyes. Boltz's jaw was firmly set as he absently studied his coffee cup. He refused to grant me so much as a reassuring smile.

Amburgey began perusing his notes again. "The worst offender is Abby Turnbull, which isn't anything new. She doesn't win prizes for being passive." This to me: "Are you two acquainted?"

"She rarely gets past my secretary."

"I see." He casually flipped another page.

"She's dangerous," Tanner volunteered. "The *Times* is part of one of the biggest chains in the country. They have their own wire service."

"Well, there's no question that Miss Turnbull is the one doing the damage. All the other reporters are simply reprinting her scoops and kicking the stuff around on the air," Boltz slowly commented. "What we've got to find out is where the hell she's getting the goods." This to me: "We'd be wise to consider all channels. Who else, for example, has access to your records, Kay?"

"Copies are sent to the CA and to the police," I replied evenly – he and Tanner *were* the CA and the police.

"What about the families of the victims?"

"So far I've gotten no requests from the women's families, and in cases such as these I most likely would refer the relative to your office."

"What about insurance companies?"

"If requested. But after the second homicide I instructed my clerks to refrain from sending out any reports, except to your office and to the police. The reports are provisional. I've been stalling for as long as possible to keep them out of circulation."

Tanner asked, "Anybody else? What about Vital Statistics? Didn't they used to keep your data on their mainframe, requiring you to send them copies of all your CME-1's and autopsy reports?"

Startled, I didn't respond right away. Tanner certainly had done his homework. There was no reason he should have been privy to such a mundane housekeeping concern.

"We stopped sending VS any paper reports after we became computerized," I told him. "They'll get data from us eventually. When they begin working on their annual report –"

Tanner interrupted with a suggestion that had the impact of a pointed gun.

"Well, that leaves your computer." He began idly swirling the coffee in his Styrofoam cup. "I assume you have very restricted access to the data base."

"That was my next question," Amburgey muttered.

The timing was terrible.

I almost wished Margaret hadn't told me about the computer violation.

I was desperately trying to think what to say as I was seized by panic. Was it possible the killer might have been caught earlier and this gifted young surgeon might still be alive had these leaks not occurred? Was it possible the anonymous "medical source" wasn't a person after all, but my office computer?

I think it was one of the worst moments in my life when I had no choice but to admit, "Despite all precautions, it appears someone has gotten into our data. Today we discovered evidence that someone tried to pull up Lori Petersen's case. It was a fruitless attempt because she hasn't been entered into the computer yet."

No one spoke for a few moments.

I lit a cigarette. Amburgey stared angrily at it, then said, "But the first three cases are in there."

"Yes. "

"You're sure it wasn't a member of your staff, or perhaps one of your deputy chiefs from one of the districts?"

"I'm reasonably sure."

Silence again. Then he asked, "Could it be, whoever this infiltrator is, he may have gotten in before?"

"I can't be sure it hasn't happened before. We routinely leave the computer in answer mode so either Margaret or I can dial in after hours. We have no idea how an outsider gained access to the password."

"How did you discover the violation?" Tanner looked confused. "You discovered it today. Seems like you would have discovered it in the past if it's happened before."

"My computer analyst discovered it because the echo was inadvertently left on. The commands were on the screen. Otherwise we would never have known."

Something flickered in Amburgey's eyes and his face was turning an angry red. Idly picking up a cloisonné letter opener, he ran his thumb along the blunt edge for what seemed a long moment. "Well," he decided, "I suppose we'd better take a look at your screens. See what sort of data this individual might have looked at. It may not have anything to do with what's been in the papers. I'm sure this's what we'll discover. I also want to review the four strangling cases, Dr. Scarpetta. I'm getting asked a lot of questions. I need to know exactly what we're dealing with."

I sat helplessly. There was nothing I could do. Amburgey was usurping me, opening the private, sensitive business carried on in my office to bureaucratic scrutiny. The thought of him going through these cases, of him staring at the photographs of these brutalized, murdered women made me tremble with rage.

"You may review the cases across the street. They are not to be photocopied, nor are they to leave my office." I added coldly, "For security reasons, of course."

"We'll take a look at them now." Glancing around. "Bill, Norm?"

The three men got up. As we filed out, Amburgey told his receptionist he would not be back today. Her gaze longingly followed Boltz out the door.

7

We waited in the bright sun for a break in rush-hour traffic and hurried across the street. No one talked, and I walked several paces ahead of them, leading them around to the back of the building. The front doors would be chained by now.

Leaving them inside the conference room, I went to collect the files from a locked drawer in my desk. I could hear Rose shuffling paper next door. It was after five and she was still here. This comforted me a little. She was lingering because she sensed something bad was going on for me to have been summoned to Amburgey's office.

When I returned to the conference room, the three men had pulled their chairs close together. I sat across from them, quietly smoking and silently daring Amburgey to ask me to leave. He didn't. So I sat.

Another hour went by.

There was the sound of pages turning, of reports being riffled through, of comments and observations made in low voices. Photographs were fanned out on the table like playing cards. Amburgey was busily taking notes in his niggling, fussy scrawl. At one point several case files slid off Boltz's lap and splashed on the carpet.

"I'll pick it up." Tanner unenthusiastically scooted his chair to one side.

"I've got it." Boltz seemed disgusted as he began to collect the paperwork scattered under and around the table. He and Tanner were considerate enough to sort everything by the proper case numbers while I numbly looked on. Amburgey, meanwhile, continued to write as if nothing had happened.

The minutes took hours to go by, and I sat.

Sometimes I was asked a question. Mostly, the men just looked and talked among themselves as if I were not there.

At half past six we moved into Margaret's office. Seating myself before the computer, I deactivated answer mode, and momentarily the case screen was before us, a pleasing orange and blue construction of Margaret's design. Amburgey glanced at his notes and read me the case number of Brenda Steppe, the first victim.

Entering it, I hit the query key. Almost instantly, her case was up.

The case screen actually comprised more than half a dozen tables which were joined. The men began scanning the data filling the orange fields, glancing at me each time they were ready for me to page-down.

Two pages later, we all saw it at the same time.

In the field called "Clothing, Personal Effects, etc." was a description of what came in with Brenda Steppe's body, including the ligatures. Written in black letters as big as life was "tan fabric belt around neck."

Amburgey leaned over me and silently ran his finger across the screen.

I opened Brenda Steppe's case file and pointed out that this was not what I had dictated in the autopsy protocol, that typed in my paper record was "a pair of nude pantyhose around her neck."

"Yes," Amburgey jogged my memory, "but take a look at the rescue squad's report. A tan cloth belt is listed, is it not?"

I quickly found the squad sheet and scanned it. He was right. The paramedic, in describing what he had seen, mentioned the victim was bound with electrical cords around the wrists and ankles, and a "tannish cloth beltlike article" was around her neck.

Boltz suggested, as if trying to be helpful, "Perhaps one of your clerks was going through this record as she typed

114

it, and she saw the squad sheet and mistakenly typed in the bit about the belt – in other words, she didn't notice this was inconsistent with what you dictated in the autopsy report."

"It's not likely," I objected. "My clerks know to get the data only from the autopsy and lab reports and the death certificate."

"But it's possible," Amburgey said, "because this belt is mentioned. It's in the record."

"Of course it's possible."

"Then it's also possible," Tanner decided, "the source of this tan belt, which was cited in the paper, came from your computer. That maybe a reporter has been getting into your data base, or has been getting someone else to get into it for him. He printed inaccurate information because he read an inaccuracy in your office's data."

"Or he got the information from the paramedic who listed the belt in his squad report," I countered.

Amburgey backed away from the computer. He said coldly, "I'll trust you to do something to ensure the confidentiality of your office records. Get the girl who looks after your computer to change the password. Whatever it takes, Dr. Scarpetta. And I'll expect a written statement from you pertaining to the matter."

He moved to the doorway, hesitating long enough to toss back at me, "Copies will be given to the appropriate parties, and then it remains to be seen if any further measures will have to be taken."

With that he was gone, Tanner at his heels.

When all else fails, I cook.

Some people go out after a god-awful day and slam a tennis ball around or jog their joints to pieces on a fitness course. I had a friend in Coral Gables who would escape to the beach with her folding chair and burn off her stress with sun and a slightly pornographic romance she wouldn't have been caught dead reading in her professional world – she was a district court judge. Many of the cops I know wash away their miseries with beer at the FOP lounge.

I've never been particularly athletic, and there wasn't a decent beach within reasonable driving distance. Getting drunk never solved anything. Cooking was an indulgence I didn't have time for most days, and though Italian cuisine isn't my only love, it has always been what I do best.

"Use the finest side of the grater," I was saying to Lucy over the noise of water running in the sink.

"But it's so hard," she complained, blowing in frustration.

"Aged parmigiano-reggiano is hard. And watch your knuckles, okay?"

I finished rinsing green peppers, mushrooms and onions, patted them dry and placed them on the cutting board. Simmering on the stove was sauce made last summer from fresh Hanover tomatoes, basil, oregano and several cloves of crushed garlic. I always kept a good supply in the freezer for times like these. Luganega sausage was draining on paper towels near other towels of browned lean beef. High-gluten dough was on the counter rising beneath a damp dish towel, and crumbled in a bowl was whole-milk mozzarella imported from New York and still packed in its brine when I'd bought it at my favorite deli on West Avenue. At room temperature the cheese is soft like butter, when melted is wonderfully stringy.

"Mom always gets the boxed kind and adds a bunch of junk to it," Lucy said breathlessly. "Or she buys the kind already made in the grocery store."

"That's deplorable," I retorted, and I meant it. "How can she eat such a thing?" I began to chop. "Your grandmother would have let us starve first."

My sister has never liked cooking. I've never understood why. Some of the happiest times when we were growing up were spent around the dinner table. When our father was well, he would sit at the head of the table and ceremoniously serve our plates with great mounds of steaming spaghetti or fettuccine or – on Fridays – frittata. No matter how poor we

116

were, there was always plenty of food and wine, and it was always a joy when I came home from school and was greeted by delicious smells and promising sounds coming from the kitchen.

It was sad and a violation of tradition that Lucy knew nothing of these things. I assumed when she came home from school most days she walked into a quiet, indifferent house where dinner was a drudgery to be put off until the last minute. My sister should never have been a mother. My sister should never have been Italian.

Greasing my hands with olive oil, I began to knead the dough, working it hard until the small muscles in my arms hurt.

"Can you twirl it like they do on TV?" Lucy stopped what she was doing, staring wide-eyed at me.

I gave her a demonstration.

"Wow!"

"It's not so hard." I smiled as the dough slowly spread out over my fists. "The trick is to keep your fingers tucked in so you don't poke holes in it."

"Let me do it."

"You haven't finished grating the cheese," I said with mock severity.

"Please . . ."

She got down from her footstool and came over to me. Taking her hands in mine, I bathed them with olive oil and folded them into fists. It surprised me that her hands were almost the size of mine. When she was a baby her fists were no bigger than walnuts. I remembered the way she would reach out to me when I was visiting back then, the way she would grab my index finger and smile while a strange and wonderful warmth spread through my breast. Draping the dough over Lucy's fists, I helped her flop it around awkwardly.

"It gets bigger and bigger," she exclaimed. "This is neat!"

"The dough spreads out because of the centrifugal force – similar to the way people used to make glass. You know, you've seen the old glass windows with ripples in them?"

Nodding.

"The glass was spun into a large, flat disk –"

We both looked up as gravel crunched beneath tires in the drive. A white Audi was pulling in and Lucy's mood immediately began to sink.

"Oh," she said unhappily. "*He's* here."

Bill Boltz was getting out of the car and collecting two bottles of wine from the passenger's seat.

"You'll like him very much." I was deftly laying the dough in the deep pan. "He very much wants to meet you, Lucy."

"He's your boyfriend."

I washed my hands. "We just do things together, and we work together . . ."

"He's not married?" She was watching him follow the walkway to the front door.

"His wife died last year."

"Oh." A pause. "How?"

I kissed the top of her head and went out of the kitchen to answer the door. Now was not the time for me to answer such a question. I wasn't sure how Lucy would take it.

"You recovering?" Bill smiled and lightly kissed me.

I shut the door. "Barely."

"Wait till you've had a few glasses of this magic stuff," he said holding up the bottles as if they were prize catches from a hunt. "From my private stock – you'll love it."

I touched his arm and he followed me to the kitchen.

Lucy was grating cheese again, up on her footstool, her back to us. She didn't even glance around when we walked in.

"Lucy?"

Still grating.

"Lucy?" I led Bill over to her. "This is Mr. Boltz, and Bill, this is my niece."

Reluctantly, she stopped what she was doing and looked

118

straight at me. "I scraped my knuckle, Auntie Kay. See?" She held up her left hand. A knuckle was bleeding a little.

"Oh, dear. Here, I'll get a Band-Aid . . ."

"Some of it got in the cheese," she went on, as if suddenly on the verge of tears.

"Sounds to me like we need an ambulance," Bill announced and he quite surprised Lucy by plucking her off the stool and locking his arms under her thighs. She was in a ridiculously funny sitting position. "Rerrrrrr – RERRRRRRRRRRR . . ." He was wailing like a siren and carrying her over to the sink. "Three-one-six, bringing in an emergency – cute little girl with a bleeding knuckle." He was talking to a dispatcher now. "Please have Dr. Scarpetta ready with a Band-Aid . . ."

Lucy was shrieking with laughter. Momentarily her knuckle was forgotten and she was staring with open adoration at Bill as he uncorked a bottle of wine.

"You have to let it breathe," he was gently explaining to her. "See, it's sharper now than it will be in an hour or so. Like everything else in life, it gets mellower with time."

"Can I have some?"

"Well, now," he replied with exaggerated gravity, "all right by me if your Auntie Kay says so. But we wouldn't want you getting silly on us."

I was quietly putting the pizza together, spreading the dough with sauce and overlaying this with the meats, vegetables and parmesan cheese. Topping it with the crumbled mozzarella, I slid it into the oven. Soon the rich garlicky aroma was filling the kitchen and I was busying myself with the salad and setting the table while Lucy and Bill chatted and laughed.

We didn't eat until late, and Lucy's glass of wine turned out to be a good thing. By the time I was clearing the table, her eyes were half shut and she was definitely ready for bed, despite her unwillingness to say good-night to Bill, who had completely won her heart.

"That was rather amazing," I said to him after I'd tucked

her in and we were sitting at the kitchen table. "I don't know how you managed it. I was worried about her reaction . . ."

"You thought she'd view me as competition." He smiled a little.

"Let's just put it this way. Her mother's in and out of relationships with just about anything on two legs."

"Meaning she doesn't have much time for her daughter." He refilled our glasses.

"To put it mildly."

"That's too damn bad. She's something, smart as hell. Must have inherited your brains." He slowly sipped his wine, adding, "What does she do all day long while you're working?"

"Bertha's here. Mostly Lucy stays in my office hours on end banging on the computer."

"Playing games on it?"

"Hardly. I think she knows more about the damn thing than I do. Last time I checked, she was programming in Basic and reorganizing my data base."

He began studying his wineglass. Then he asked, "Can you use your computer to dial up the one downtown?"

"Don't even suggest it!"

"Well." He looked at me. "You'd be better off. Maybe I was hoping."

"Lucy wouldn't do such a thing," I said with feeling. "And I'm not sure how I would be better off were it true."

"Better your ten-year-old niece than a reporter. It would get Amburgey off your back. "

"Nothing would get him off my back," I snapped.

"That's right," he said dryly. "His reason for getting up in the morning is to jerk you around."

"I'm frankly beginning to wonder that."

Amburgey was appointed in the midst of the city's black community publicly protesting that the police were indifferent to homicides unless the victims were white. Then a black city councilman was shot in his car, and Amburgey and the mayor considered it good public relations, I supposed, to appear unannounced at the morgue the next morning.

Maybe it wouldn't have turned out so badly had Amburgey thought to ask questions while he watched me perform the autopsy, had he kept his mouth shut afterward. But the physician combined with the politician, compelling him to confidently inform the press waiting outside my building that the "spread of pellet wounds" over the dead councilman's upper chest "indicates a shotgun blast at close range." As diplomatically as possible, I explained when the reporters questioned me later that the "spread" of holes over the chest was actually marks of therapy made when ER attendants inserted large-gauge needles into the subclavian arteries to transfuse blood. The councilman's lethal injury was a small-caliber gunshot wound to the back of the head.

The reporters had a field day with Amburgey's blunder.

"The problem is he's a physician by training," I was saying to Bill. "He knows just enough to think he's an expert in forensic medicine, to think he can run my office better than I can, and a lot of his opinions are flat-out full of shit."

"Which you make the mistake of pointing out to him."

"What am I supposed to do? Agree and look as incompetent as he is?"

"So it's a simple case of professional jealousy," he said with a shrug. "It happens."

"I don't know *what* it is. How the hell do you explain these things? Half of what people do and feel doesn't make a damn bit of sense. For all I know, I could remind him of his mother."

My anger was mounting with fresh intensity, and I realized by the expression on his face that I was glaring at him.

"Hey," he objected, raising his hand, "don't be pissed at me. I didn't do anything."

"You were there this afternoon, weren't you?"

"What do you expect? I'm supposed to tell Amburgey and Tanner I can't be in on the meeting because you and I have been seeing each other?"

121

"Of course you couldn't tell them that," I said in a miserable way. "But maybe I wanted you to. Maybe I wanted you to punch Amburgey's lights out or something."

"Not a bad idea. But I don't think it would help me much come reelection time. Besides, you'd probably let my ass rot in jail. Wouldn't even post my bond."

"Depends on how much it was."

"Shit."

"Why didn't you tell me?"

"Tell you what?"

"About the meeting. You must have known about it since yesterday." Maybe you'd known about it longer, I started to say, and that's why you didn't so much as call me over the weekend! Restraining myself, I stared tensely at him.

He was studying his wineglass again. After a pause, he replied, "I didn't see any point in telling you. All it would have done was worry you, and it was my impression the meeting was *pro forma* –"

"*Pro forma*?" I looked incredulously at him. "Amburgey's gagged me and spent half the afternoon tearing apart my office and that's *pro forma*?"

"I feel sure some of what he did was sparked by your disclosure of the computer violation, Kay. And I didn't know about that yesterday. Hell, you didn't even know about that yesterday."

"I see," I said coldly. "No one knew about it until I told them."

Silence.

"What are you implying?"

"It just seemed an incredible coincidence we discovered the violation just hours before he called me to his office. I had the peculiar thought that maybe he knew . . ."

"Maybe he did."

"That certainly reassures me."

"It's moot anyway," he easily went on. "So what if Amburgey knew about the violation by the time you came to his office this afternoon? Maybe somebody talked – your computer analyst, for example. And the rumor drifted up to the twenty-fourth floor." He shrugged. "It just gave him one more worry, right? You didn't trip yourself up, if that's the case, because you were smart enough to tell the truth."

"I always tell the truth."

"Not always," he remarked slyly. "You routinely lie about us – by omission –"

"So maybe he knew," I cut him off. "I just want to hear you didn't."

"I didn't." He looked intensely at me. "I swear. If I'd heard anything about it, I would have forewarned you, Kay. I would have run to the nearest phone booth –"

"And charged out as Superman."

"Hell," he muttered, "now you're making fun of me."

He was in his boyish wounded manifestation. Bill had a lot of roles and he played all of them extraordinarily well. Sometimes it was hard for me to believe he was so smitten with me. Was that a role as well?

I think he had a starring role in the fantasies of half the city's women, and his campaign manager was shrewd enough to take advantage of it. Photographs of Bill had been plastered over restaurant and storefronts, and nailed to telephone poles on virtually every city block. Who could resist that face? He was stunningly handsome, his hair streaked straw-blond, his complexion perpetually sunburned from the many hours he spent each week at his tennis club. It was hard not to stare openly at him.

"I'm not making fun of you," I said wearily. "Really, Bill. And let's not fight."

"Fine by me."

"I'm just sick. I don't have any idea what to do."

Apparently he'd already thought about this, and he said, "It would be helpful if you could figure out who's been getting into your data." A pause. "Or better, if you could prove it."

"Prove it?" I looked warily at him. "Are you suggesting you have a suspect?"

"Not based on any fact."

"Who?" I lit a cigarette.

His attention drifted across the kitchen. "Abby Turnbull is top on my list."

"I thought you were going to tell me something I couldn't have figured out on my own."

"I'm dead serious, Kay."

"So she's an ambitious reporter," I said irritably. "Frankly, I'm getting a little tired of hearing about her. She's not as powerful as everyone makes her out to be."

Bill set his wineglass on the table with a sharp click. "The hell she isn't," he retorted, staring at me. "The woman's a goddam snake. I know she's an ambitious reporter and all that shit. But she's worse than anybody imagines. She's vicious and manipulative and extremely dangerous. The bitch would stoop to anything."

His vehemence startled me into silence. It was uncharacteristic of him to use such vitriolic terms in describing anyone. Especially someone I assumed he scarcely knew.

"Remember that story she did on me a month or so back?"

Not long ago the *Times* finally got around to the obligatory profile of the city's new Commonwealth's attorney. The story was a rather lengthy spread that ran in the Sunday paper, and I didn't remember in detail what Abby Turnbull had written except that the piece struck me as unusually colorless considering its author.

I said as much to him, "As best I recall, the story was toothless. It did no harm; neither did it do any good."

"There's a reason for that," he fired back at me. "I suspect it wasn't something she wanted to write, particularly."

He wasn't hinting that the assignment had been a boring one. Something else was coming and my nerves were coiling tightly again.

"My session with her was pretty damn terrible. She spent an entire day with me, riding around in my car, going from meeting to meeting, hell, even to my dry cleaner's. You know how these reporters are. They'll follow you into the men's room if you let them. Well, let's just say that as the evening progressed, things took a rather unfortunate and definitely unexpected turn."

He hesitated to see if I got his implication.

I got it all too well.

Glancing at me, his face hard, he said, "It completely broadsided me. We got out of the last meeting around eight. She insisted we go to dinner. You know, it was on the paper and she had a few questions to finish up. We'd no sooner pulled out of the restaurant's parking lot when she said she wasn't feeling well. Too much wine or something. She wanted me to drop her off at her house instead of taking her back to the paper, where her car was parked. So I did. Took her home. And when I pulled in front of her house, she was all over me. It was awful."

"And?" I asked as if I didn't care.

"And I didn't handle it worth a damn. I think I humiliated her without intending to. She's been out to jerk the hell out of me ever since."

"What? She's calling you, sending you threatening letters?" I wasn't exactly serious. Nor was I prepared for what he said next.

"This shit she's been writing. The fact maybe it's coming from your computer. As crazy as it may sound, I think her motivation is mostly personal –"

"The *leaks*? Are you suggesting she's breaking into my computer and writing lurid details about these cases to jerk you around?"

"If these cases are compromised in court, who the hell gets hurt?"

I didn't respond. I was staring in disbelief at him.

"*I* do. I'll be the one prosecuting the cases. Cases as sensational and heinous as these get screwed up because of all this shit in the papers, and no one's going to be sending me flowers or thank-you notes. She sure as hell knows that, Kay. She's sticking it to me, that's what she's doing."

"Bill," I said, lowering my voice, "it's her job to be an

aggressive reporter, to print everything she can get her hands on. More important, the cases would get screwed up in court only if the sole evidence was a confession. Then the defense gets to make him change his mind. He takes it all back. The party line is the guy's psychotic and knows the details of the murders because he read about them in the paper. He imagined he committed the crimes. That sort of rubbish. The monster who's killing these women isn't about to turn himself in or confess to anything."

He drained his glass and refilled it. "Maybe the cops develop him as a suspect and get him to talk. Maybe that's the way it happens. And it might be the only thing linking him to the crimes. There isn't a shred of physical evidence that's amounted to anything –"

"No shred of physical evidence?" I interrupted. Surely I hadn't heard him right. Was the wine dulling his senses? "He's leaving a load of seminal fluid. He gets caught and DNA will nail him to –"

"Oh, yeah. *Sure* it will. DNA printing's only gone to trial a couple of times in Virginia. There are very few precedents, very few convictions nationwide – every damn one of them still being appealed. Try explaining to a Richmond jury the guy's guilty because of DNA. I'll be lucky if I can find a juror who can *spell* DNA. Anybody's got an IQ over forty and the defense will find a reason to exclude him, that's what I put up with week after week . . ."

"Bill . . ."

"Hell." He began to pace the kitchen floor. "It's hard enough to get a conviction if fifty people swear they saw the guy pull the trigger. The defense will drag in a herd of expert witnesses to muddy the waters and hopelessly confuse everything. You of all people know how complicated this DNA testing is."

"Bill, I've explained just as difficult things to juries in the past."

He started to say something but caught himself. Staring across the kitchen again, he took another swallow of wine.

The silence was drawn out and heavy. If the outcome of the trials depended solely on the DNA results, this placed me in the position of being a key witness for the prosecution. I'd been in such a position many times in the past and I couldn't recall it ever unduly worrying Bill.

Something was different this time.

"What is it?" I forced myself to ask. "Are you unsettled because of our relationship? You're thinking someone's going to figure it out and accuse us of being professionally in bed together – accuse me of rigging the results to suit the prosecution?"

He glanced at me, his face flushed. "I'm not thinking that at all. It's a fact we've been together, but big deal? So we've gone out to dinner and taken in a few plays . . ."

He didn't have to complete the sentence. Nobody knew about us. Usually he came to my house or we went to some distant place, such as Williamsburg or D.C., where it wasn't likely we would run into anybody who would recognize us. I'd always been more worried about the public seeing us together than he seemed to be.

Or was he alluding to something else, something far more biting?

We were not lovers, not completely, and this remained a subtle but uncomfortable tension between us.

I think we'd both been aware of the strong attraction, but we'd completely avoided doing anything about it until several weeks ago. After a trial that didn't end until early evening, he casually offered to buy me a drink. We walked to a restaurant near the courthouse and two Scotches later we were heading to my house. It was that sudden. It was adolescent in its intensity, our lust as tangible as heat. The forbiddenness of it made it all the more frantic, and then quite suddenly while we were in the dark on my living room couch, I panicked.

His hunger was too much. It exploded from him, invaded instead of caressed as he pushed me down hard into the couch. It was at that moment I had a vivid image of his wife

127

slumped against pale blue satin pillows in bed like some lovely life-size doll, the front of her white negligee stained dark red, the nine-millimeter automatic just inches from her limp right hand.

I'd gone to the suicide scene knowing only that the wife of the man running for Commonwealth's attorney apparently had committed suicide. I did not know Bill then. I examined his wife. I literally held her heart in my hands. Those images, all of them, flashed graphically behind my eyes in my dark living room so many months later.

Physically, I withdrew from him. I'd never told him the real reason why, although in the days that followed he continued to pursue me even more vigorously. Our mutual attraction remained but a wall had gone up. I could not seem to tear it down or climb over it much as I wanted to.

I was scarcely hearing a word he was saying.

". . . and I don't see how you could rig DNA results unless you're involved in a conspiracy that includes the private lab conducting the tests and half the forensic bureau, too –"

"What?" I asked, startled. "Rig DNA results?"

"You haven't been listening," he blurted out impatiently.

"Well, I missed something, that's certain."

"I'm saying no one could accuse you of rigging anything – that's my point. So our relationship has nothing to do with what I'm thinking."

"Okay."

"It's just . . ." He faltered.

"Just *what*?" I asked. Then, as he drained his glass again, I added, "Bill, you have to drive . . ."

He waved it off.

"Then what is it?" I demanded again. "What?"

He pressed his lips together and wouldn't look at me. Slowly, he drew it out. "It's just I'm not sure where you'll be in the eyes of the jurors by then."

I couldn't have been more stunned had he struck me with his open palm.

"My God . . . You do know something. What? What! What

128

is that son of a bitch plotting? He's going to fire me because of this goddam computer violation, is this what he's said to you?"

"Amburgey? He's not plotting anything. Hell, he doesn't have to. If your office gets blamed for the leaks, and if the public eventually believes the inflammatory news stories are why the killer's striking with increased frequency, then your head will be on the block. People need someone to blame. I can't afford my star witness to have a credibility or popularity problem."

"Is this what you and Tanner were discussing so intensely after lunch?" I was just a blink away from tears. "I saw you on the sidewalk, coming out of The Peking . . ."

A long silence. He had seen me, too, then but had pretended otherwise. Why? Because he and Tanner probably were talking about me!

"We were discussing the cases," he replied evasively. "Discussing a lot of things."

I was so enraged, so stung, I didn't trust myself to say a word.

"Listen," he said wearily as he loosened his tie and unfastened the top button of his shirt. "This didn't go right. I didn't mean for it to come out like this. I swear to God. Now you're all upset, and I'm all upset. I'm sorry."

My silence was stony.

He took a deep breath. "It's just we have real things to worry about and we should be working on them together. I'm painting worst-case scenarios so we can be prepared, okay?"

"What exactly do you expect me to do?" I measured each word to keep my voice steady.

"Think five times about everything. Like tennis. When you're down or psyched you've got to play it careful. Concentrate on every shot, don't take your eye off the ball for a second."

His tennis analogies got on my nerves sometimes. Right now was a good example. "I always think about what I'm doing," I said testily. "You don't need to tell me how to do my job. I'm not known for missing shots."

"It's especially important now. Abby Turnbull's poison. I think she's setting us up. Both of us. Behind the scenes. Using you or your office computer to get to me. Not giving a damn if she maims justice in the process. The cases get blown out of the water and you and I are both blown out of office. It's that simple."

Maybe he was right, but I was having a hard time accepting that Abby Turnbull could be so evil. Surely if she had even a drop of human blood in her veins she would want the killer punished. She wouldn't use four brutally murdered young women as pawns in her vindictive machinations if she were guilty of vindictive machinations, and I wasn't convinced she was.

I was about to tell him he was exaggerating, his bad encounter with her had momentarily distorted his reason. But something stopped me.

I didn't want to talk about this anymore.

I was afraid to.

It was nagging at me. He'd waited until now to say anything. Why? His encounter with her was weeks ago. If she were setting us up, if she were so dangerous to both of us, then why hadn't he told me this before now?

"I think what you need is a good night's sleep," I said quietly. "I think we'd be wise to strike this conversation, at least certain portions of it, go on as if it never happened."

He pushed back from the table. "You're right. I've had it. So have you. Christ, I didn't mean for it to go like this," he said again. "I came over here to cheer you up. I feel terrible . . ."

His apologies continued as we went down the hall. Before I could open the door, he was kissing me and I could taste the wine on his breath and feel his heat. My physical response was always immediate, a frisson of spine-tingling desire and fear running through me like a current. I involuntarily pulled away from him and muttered, "Good night."

He was a shadow in the darkness heading to his car, his profile briefly illuminated by the interior light as he opened the door and climbed in. I was still standing numbly on the porch long after red taillights had burned along the vacant street and disappeared behind trees.

8

The inside of Marino's silver Plymouth Reliant was as cluttered and slovenly as I would have expected it to be – had I ever given the matter a moment's thought.

On the floor in back were a chicken-dinner box, crumpled napkins and Burger King bags, and several coffee-stained Styrofoam cups. The ashtray was overflowing, and dangling from the rearview mirror was an evergreen-scented air freshener shaped like a pine tree and about as effective as a shot of Glade aimed inside a Dumpster. Dust and lint and crumbs were everywhere, and the windshield was practically opaque with smoker's soot.

"You ever give this thing a bath?" I was fastening my seatbelt.

"Not anymore I don't. Sure, it's assigned to me, but it ain't mine. They don't let me take it home at night or over the weekend or nothing. So I wax it to a spit shine and use up half a bottle of Armor All on the inside and what happens? Some drone's going to be in it while I'm off duty. I get it back looking just like this. Never fails. After a while, I started saving everybody the trouble. Started trashing it myself."

Police traffic quietly crackled as the scanner light blinked from channel to channel. He pulled out of the parking lot behind my building. I hadn't heard a word from him since he abruptly left the conference room on Monday. It was late Wednesday afternoon now, and he had mystified me moments ago by suddenly appearing in my doorway with the announcement that he wanted to take me on a "little tour."

The "tour," it turned out, entailed a retrospective visit to the crime scenes. The purpose, as best I could ascertain, was for me to fix a map of them in my head. I couldn't argue. The idea was a good one. But it was the last thing I was expecting from him. Since when did he include me in anything unless he absolutely had no choice?

"Got a few things you need to know," he said, as he adjusted the side mirror.

"I see. I suppose the implication is had I not agreed to your 'little tour' then you might never have gotten around to telling me these few things I need to know?"

"Whatever."

I waited patiently as he returned the lighter to its socket. He took his time settling more comfortably behind the wheel.

"Might interest you to know," he began, "we gave Petersen a polygraph yesterday and the sucker passed it. Pretty telling, but it don't completely let him off the hook. It's possible to pass it if you're one of these psychopaths who can lie as easy as other people breathe. He's an actor. He probably could say he's Christ crucified and his hands wouldn't sweat, his pulse would be steadier than yours and mine when we're in church."

"That would be highly unusual," I said. "It's pretty hard, close to impossible, to beat a polygraph. I don't care who you are."

"It's happened before. That's one reason it's not admissible in court."

"No, I won't go so far as to say it's infallible."

"Point is," he went on, "we don't have probable cause to pop him or even tell him not to skip town. So I've got him under surveillance. What we're really looking for is his activities after hours. Like, what he does at night. Like, maybe does he get in his car and drive through various neighborhoods, cruising, getting the lay of the land."

"He hasn't gone back to Charlottesville?"

Marino flicked an ash out the window. "He's hanging around for a while, says he's too upset to go back. He's moved, staying in an apartment on Freemont Avenue, says he can't set foot in the house after what happened. I think he's gonna sell the joint. Not that he'll need the money." He glanced over at me and I was briefly faced with a distorted image of myself in his mirrored shades. "Turns out the wife had a hefty life insurance policy. Petersen's going to be about two hundred grand richer. Guess he'll be able to write his plays and not have to worry about making a living."

I didn't say anything.

"And I guess we just let it slide he was brought up on rape charges the summer after he graduated from high school."

"You've looked into that?" I knew he had or he wouldn't have mentioned it.

"Turns out he was doing summer theater in New Orleans and made the mistake of taking some groupie too seriously. I've talked with the cop who investigated the case. According to him, Petersen's the lead actor in some play, and this babe in the audience gets the hots for him, comes to see him night after night, leaves him notes, the whole nine yards. Then she turns up backstage and they end up bar-hopping in the French Quarter. Next thing you know, she's calling the cops at four in the morning, all hysterical, claiming she's been raped. He's in hot water because her PERK's positive and the fluids pop up nonsecreter, which is what he is."

"Did the case go to court?"

"Damn grand jury threw it out. Petersen admitted having sex with her inside her apartment. Said it was consensual, she came on to him. The girl was pretty bruised up, even had a few marks on her neck. But no one could prove how fresh the bruises were and if Petersen caused 'em by working her over. See, the grand jury takes one look at a guy like him. They take into account he's in a play and this girl initiated the encounter. He still had her notes inside the dressing room, which clearly showed the girl had a thing for him. And he

134

was real convincing when he testified she had bruises when he was with her, that she supposedly told him she'd been in a fight several days earlier with some guy she was in the process of breaking up with. Nobody's going to throw the book at Petersen. The girl had the morals of a guppy and was either a Froot Loop or else she made a stupid mistake, laid herself wide open, so to speak, for getting a number done on her."

"Those kinds of cases," I quietly commented, "are almost impossible to prove."

"Well, you just never know. It's also sort of coincidental," he added as a by-the-way for which I was completely unprepared, "that Benton called me up the other night to tell me the big mother computer in Quantico got a hit on the MO of whoever's whacking these women here in Richmond."

"Where?"

"Waltham, Massachusetts, as a matter of fact," he replied, glancing over at me. "Two years ago, right at the time Petersen was a senior at Harvard, which is about twenty miles east of Waltham. During the months of April and May, two women was raped and strangled inside their apartments. Both lived alone in first-floor apartments, was tied up with belts, electrical cords. The killer apparently got in through unsecured windows. Both times it occurred on the weekend. The crimes are a carbon copy of what's been happening here."

"Did the murders stop after Petersen graduated and moved here?"

"Not exactly," he replied. "There was one more later that summer which Petersen couldn't have committed because he was living here, his wife just starting at VMC. But there were a few differences in the third case. The victim was a teenager and lived about fifteen miles from where the other two homicides occurred. She didn't live alone, was shacked up with a guy who was out of town at the time. The cops speculated her murder was a copycat – some squirrel read about the first two in the papers and got the idea. She wasn't

135

found for about a week, was so decomposed there wasn't a hope in hell of finding seminal fluid. Typing the killer wasn't possible."

"What about typing the first two cases?"

"Nonsecreter," he slowly said, staring straight ahead.

Silence. I reminded myself there are millions of men in the country who are nonsecreters and sex slayings happen every year in almost every major city. But the parallels were jolting.

We had turned onto a narrow, tree-lined street in a recently developed subdivision where all of the ranch-style houses looked alike and hinted of cramped space and low-budget building materials. There were realtor signs scattered about, and some of the homes were still under construction. Most of the lawns were newly seeded and landscaped with small dogwoods and fruit trees.

Two blocks down on the left was the small gray house where Brenda Steppe had been slain not quite two months ago. The house had not been rented or sold. Most people in the market for a new home aren't keen on the idea of moving into a place where someone has been brutally murdered. Planted in the yards of the houses on either side were "For Sale" signs.

We parked in front and sat quietly, the windows rolled down. There were few streetlights, I noted. At night it would be very dark, and if the killer was careful and wearing dark clothing, he wasn't going to be seen.

Marino said, "He got in the kitchen window around back. It appears she got home at nine, nine-thirty that night. We found a shopping bag in the living room. The last item she bought had the computer-printed time on it of eight-fifty P.M. She goes home and cooks a late dinner. That weekend it was warm, and I'm assuming she left the window open to air out the kitchen. Especially since it appears she'd been frying ground beef and onions."

I nodded, recalling Brenda Steppe's gastric contents.

"Cooking hamburger and onions usually smokes or

smells up the kitchen. Least it does in my damn house. And there was a ground-beef wrapper, an empty spaghetti sauce jar, onion skins, in the trash under the sink, plus a greasy frying pan soaking." He paused, adding thoughtfully, "Kind of weird to think her choice of what to cook for dinner maybe resulted in her ending up murdered. You know, maybe if she'd had a tuna casserole, a sandwich or something, she wouldn't have left the window open."

This was a favorite rumination of death investigators: What if? What if the person had not decided to buy a pack of cigarettes at a convenience store where two armed robbers were holding the clerk hostage in the back? What if someone hadn't decided to step outside and empty the cat-litter box at the very moment a prison escapee was nearing the house? What if someone hadn't had a fight with his lover, resulting in his driving off in a huff at the exact moment a drunk driver was rounding a curve on the wrong side of the road?

Marino asked, "You notice the turnpike's less than a mile from here?"

"Yes. There's a Safeway on the corner, just before you turn off in this neighborhood," I recalled. "A possible place for him to have left his car, assuming he came the rest of the way on foot."

He cryptically observed, "Yeah, the Safeway. It closes at midnight."

I lit another cigarette and played on the adage that in order for a detective to be good, he has to be able to think like the people he's out to get.

"What would you have done," I asked, "if it were you?"

"If what were me?"

"If you were this killer."

"Depending on whether I'm some squirrely artist like Matt Petersen or just your run-of-the-mill maniac who gets off on stalking women and strangling them?"

"The latter," I evenly said. "Let's assume the latter."

He was baiting me, and he laughed rather rudely. "See, you missed it, Doc. You should've asked how it would be different. Because it wouldn't be. What I'm telling you is if I was either type, I'd pretty much do it the same way – don't matter who or what I am during my regular hours when I'm working and acting like everybody else. When I get into it, I'm just every other drone who's ever done it or ever will. Doctor, lawyer or Indian chief."

"Go on."

He did.

"It starts with me seeing her, having some sort of contact with her somewhere. Maybe I'm coming to her house, selling something or delivering flowers, and when she comes to the door, that little voice in my head says, 'This is the one.' Maybe I'm doing construction in the neighborhood and see her coming and going alone. I fix on her. I might follow her for as long as a week, learning as much about her, about her habits, as possible. Like what lights left on means she's up, what lights off means she's asleep, what her car looks like."

"Why her?" I asked. "Of all the women in the world, why this one?"

He briefly considered this. "She sets something off in me."

"Because of the way she looks?"

He was still thinking. "Maybe. But maybe it's her attitude. She's a working woman. Got a pretty nice crib, meaning she's smart enough to earn a decent living. Sometimes career women are snooty. Maybe I didn't like the way she treated me. Maybe she assaulted my masculinity, like I'm not good enough for her or something."

"All of the victims are career women," I said, adding, "but then, most women who live alone work."

"That's right. And I'm going to know she lives alone, going to make sure of it, going to think I'm sure of it, anyway. I'm going to fix her, show her who's got the power. The weekend comes and I'm feeling like doing it. So I get in the car late, after midnight. I've already cased the area, have the whole scenario planned. Yeah. I might leave my car in the Safeway parking lot, but the problem is it's after hours. The lot's going to be empty, meaning my ride's going to stick out

138

like a sore thumb. Now, it just so happens there's an Exxon station on the same corner as the grocery store. Me, I'd probably leave my car there. Why? Because the service station closes at ten and you expect to see cars waiting for repairs left in service station lots after hours. No one's going to think twice about it, not even the cops, and that's who I'm most worried about. Some cop on patrol seeing my car in an empty parking lot and maybe checking it out or calling in a ten-twenty-eight to find out who owns it."

He described in chilling detail every move. Dressed in dark clothing, he stayed in the shadows as he walked through the neighborhood. When he got to this address his adrenaline began to pump as he realized the woman, whose name he probably did not know, was home. Her car was in the drive. All the lights, except the porch light, were out. She was asleep.

Taking his time, he stayed out of sight as he assessed the situation. He looked around, making sure no one spotted him, then went around to the back of the house where he began to feel a surge of confidence. He was invisible from the street, and the houses one row over are an acre away, the lights out, not a sign of anybody stirring. It was pitch dark in back.

Quietly, he approached the windows and immediately noted the one open. It was simply a matter of running a knife through the screen and releasing the latches inside. Within seconds, the screen was off and on the grass. He slid the window open, pulled himself up and found himself staring at the shadowy shapes of kitchen appliances.

"Once inside," Marino was saying, "I stand still for a minute, listening. Once satisfied I don't hear nothing, I find the hallway and start looking for the room where she's at. A crib small as this," a shrug, "and there aren't too many possibilities. I find the bedroom right off and can hear her sleeping inside. By now I got something over my head, a ski mask, for example . . ."

"Why bother?" I asked. "She isn't going to live to identify you."

"Hairs. Hey, I ain't stupid. I probably pick forensic science books for bedtime reading, probably have memorized all the cop's ten codes. No chance anybody's going to be finding my hairs on her or anywhere else."

"If you're so smart" – now I was the one baiting him – "why aren't you worried about DNA? Don't you read the newspapers?"

"Well, I'm not going to wear no damn rubber. And you aren't ever going to develop me as a suspect because I'm too damn slick. No suspect, no comparison, and your DNA hocus-pocus isn't worth a dime. Hairs are a little more personal. You know, maybe I don't want you to know if I'm black or white, a blond or a redhead."

"What about fingerprints?"

He smiled. "Gloves, babe. The same as you wear when you're examining my victims."

"Matt Petersen wasn't wearing gloves. If he had been, he wouldn't have left his prints on his wife's body."

Marino said easily, "If Matt's the killer, he wouldn't worry about leaving prints in his own house. His prints are gonna be all over the place anyway." A pause. "*If.* Fact is, we're looking for a squirrel. Fact is, Matt's a squirrel. Fact is, he ain't the only squirrel in the world – there's one behind every bush. Fact is, I really don't know who the hell whacked his wife."

I saw the face from my dreams, the white face with no features. The sun breaking through the windshield was hot but I couldn't seem to get warm.

He continued, "The rest's pretty much what you'd imagine. I'm not going to startle her. Going to ease my way to the edge of the bed and wake her up by putting one hand over her mouth, the knife to her throat. I'm probably not going to carry a gun because if she struggles and it goes off maybe I get shot, maybe she does before I've had a chance to do my thing. That's real important to me. It's got to go down the way I planned or I'm real upset. Also, I can't take the chance of anyone hearing gunfire and calling the cops."

"Do you say anything to her?" I asked, clearing my throat.

"I'm going to talk low, tell her if she screams I'll kill her. I'll tell her that over and over again."

"What else? What else will you say to her?"

"Probably nothing."

He shoved the car in gear and turned around. I took one last look at the house where what he just described happened, or at least I almost believed it happened exactly as he said. I was seeing it as he was saying it. It did not seem speculation but an eyewitness revelation. An unemotional, unremorseful confession.

I was formulating a different opinion of Marino. He wasn't slow. He wasn't stupid. I think I liked him less than ever.

We headed east. The sun was caught in the leaves of the trees and rush hour was at its peak. For a while we were trapped in a sluggish flow of congestion, cars occupied by anonymous men and women on their way home from work. As I looked at the passing faces I felt out of sync, detached, as if I did not belong in the same world other people lived in. They were thinking about supper, perhaps the steaks they would cook on the grill, their children, the lover they would soon be seeing, or some event that had taken place during the day.

Marino was going down the list.

"Two weeks before her murder UPS delivered a package. Already checked out the delivery guy. Zip," he said. "Not long before that some guy came by to work on the plumbing. He squares okay, too, best we can tell. So far, we've come up with nothing to suggest any service person, delivery guy, what have you, is the same in the four cases. Not a single common denominator. No overlapping or similarities where the victims' jobs are concerned either."

Brenda Steppe was a fifth-grade teacher who taught at Quinton Elementary, not far from where she lived. She moved to Richmond five years ago, and had recently broken off her engagement to a soccer coach. She was a full-figured

141

redhead, bright and good-humored. According to her friends and her former fiancé, she jogged several miles every day and neither smoked nor drank.

I probably knew more about her life than her family in Georgia did. She was a dutiful Baptist who attended church every Sunday and the suppers every Wednesday night. A musician, she played the guitar and led the singing at the youth group retreats. Her college major was English, which was also what she taught. Her favorite form of relaxation, in addition to jogging, was reading, and she was reading Doris Betts, it appeared, before switching off her bedside light that Friday night.

"The thing that sort of blew my mind," Marino told me, "is something I recently found out, one possible connection between her and Lori Petersen. Brenda Steppe was treated in the VMC ER about six weeks ago."

"For what?" I asked, surprised.

"A minor traffic accident. She got hit when she was backing out of her driveway one night. No big deal. She called the cops herself, said she'd bumped her head, was a little dizzy. An ambulance was dispatched. She was held a few hours in the ER for observation, X rays. It was nothing."

"Was she treated during a shift when Lori Petersen was working?"

"That's the best part, maybe the only hit we've gotten so far. I checked with the supervisor. Lori Petersen was on that night. I'm running down everybody else who might've been around, orderlies, other doctors, you name it. Nothing so far except the freaky thought the two women may have met, having no idea that this very minute their murders would be in the process of being discussed by you and yours truly."

The thought went through me like a low-voltage shock. "What about Matt Petersen? Any chance he might have been at the hospital that night, perhaps to see his wife?"

Marino replied, "Says he was in Charlottesville. This was a Wednesday, around nine-thirty, ten P.M."

The hospital certainly could be a connection, I thought.

Anyone who works there and has access to the records could have been familiar with Lori Petersen and might also have seen Brenda Steppe, whose address would be listed on her ER chart.

I suggested to Marino that everyone who may have been working at VMC the night she was treated should be turned inside out.

"We're only talking five thousand people," he replied. "And for all we know, the squirrel who took her out might've been treated in the ER that night, too. So I'm juggling that ball, too, and it don't look real promising at the moment. Half the people treated that shift was women. The other half was either old geezers suffering heart attacks or a couple of young Turks who was tanked when they got in their cars. They didn't make it, or else are hanging around in comas even as we speak. A lot of people was in and out, and just between you and me, the record-keeping in that joint stinks. I may never know who was there. I'm never going to know who might've wandered in off the street. Could be the guy's some vulture who drifts in and out of hospitals, looking for victims – nurses, doctors, young women with minor problems." He shrugged. "Could be he delivers flowers and is in and out of hospitals."

"You've mentioned this twice," I commented. "The bit about flower deliveries."

Another shrug. "Hey. Before I became a cop, I delivered flowers for a while, okay? Most flowers is sent to women. If I was going around wanting to meet women to whack, me, I'd deliver flowers."

I was sorry I'd asked.

"That's how I met my wife, as a matter of fact. Delivered a Sweetheart Special to her, nice arrangement of red and white carnations and a couple of sweetheart roses. From some drone she was dating. She ends up more impressed with me than with the flowers, and her boyfriend's gesture puts him out of business. This was in Jersey, a couple years before I moved to New York and signed on with the P.D."

I was seriously considering never accepting delivered flowers again.

"It's just something that jumps into my mind. Whoever he is, he's got some gig going. It puts him in touch with women. That's it, plain and simple."

We crept past Eastland Mall and took a right.

Soon we were out of traffic and gliding through Brookfield Heights, or the Heights, as it's usually called. The neighborhood is situated on a rise that almost passes for a hill. It's one of the older parts of town the young professionals have begun to take over during the last ten years. The streets are lined with row houses, some of them dilapidated and boarded up, most of them beautifully restored, with intricate wrought-iron balconies and stained-glass windows. Just a few blocks north the Heights deteriorates into a skid row; a few blocks beyond are federal housing projects.

"Some of these cribs are going for a hundred g's and up," Marino said as he slowed the car to a crawl. "I wouldn't take one if you gave it to me. I've been inside a few of 'em. Incredible. But no way you'd catch me living in this neighborhood. A fair number of single women here, too. Crazy. Just crazy."

I'd been eyeing the odometer. Patty Lewis's row house was exactly 6.7 miles from where Brenda Steppe lived. The neighborhoods were so different, so far from each other, I couldn't imagine anything about the locations that might link the crimes. There was construction going on here just as there was in Brenda's neighborhood, but it wasn't likely the companies or the crews were the same.

Patty Lewis's house was squeezed between two others, a lovely brownstone with a stained-glass window over the red front door. The roof was slate, the front porch girdled in freshly painted wrought iron. In back was a walled-in yard dense with big magnolias.

I'd seen the police photographs. It was hard to look at the graceful elegance of this turn-of-the-century home and believe anything so horrible happened inside it. She came from old money in the Shenandoah Valley, which was why, I assumed, she was able to afford living here. A free-lance writer, she struggled over a typewriter for many years and was just reaching the tier where rejection letters were war stories from the past. Last spring a story was published by *Harper's*. A novel was due out this fall. It would be a posthumous work.

Marino reminded me the killer, once again, got in through a window, this one leading into her bedroom, which faced the backyard.

"It's the one there on the end, on the second story," he was saying.

"Your theory is he climbed that magnolia closest to the house, got up on the porch roof and then through the window?"

"It's more than a theory," he retorted. "I'm sure of it. No other way he could've done it unless he had a ladder. It's more than possible to climb the tree, get on the porch roof and reach over to slide up the window. I know. I tried it myself to see if it could be done. Did it without a hitch. All the guy needs is sufficient upper-body strength to grab the edge of the roof from that thick lower tree branch," he pointed, "and pull himself up."

The brownstone had ceiling fans but no air-conditioning. According to an out-of-town friend who used to come to visit several times a year, Patty often slept with the bedroom window open. Simply put, it was a choice between being comfortable or being secure. She chose the former.

Marino made a lazy U-turn in the street and we headed northeast.

Cecile Tyler lived in Ginter Park, the oldest residential neighborhood in Richmond. There are monstrous three-story Victorian houses with wraparound porches wide enough to roller-skate on, and turrets, and dentil work along the eaves. Yards are thick with magnolias, oaks and rhododendrons. Grape vines climb over porch posts and arbors in back. I was envisioning dim living rooms beyond the blank windows, faded Oriental rugs, ornate furniture and cornices, and knick-knacks jammed in every nook and cranny. I wouldn't have wanted to live here. It was giving me the same claustrophobic case of the creeps that ficus trees and Spanish moss do.

Hers was a two-story brick house, modest by her neighbors' standards. It was exactly 5.8 miles from where Patty Lewis lived. In the waning sun the slate roof glinted like lead. Shutters and doors were naked, stripped to the wood and still waiting for the fresh paint Cecile would have applied had she lived long enough.

The killer got in through a basement window behind a boxwood hedge on the north wing of the house. The lock was broken and, like everything else, waiting to be repaired.

She was a lovely black woman, recently divorced from a dentist now living in Tidewater. A receptionist at an employment agency, she was attending college classes at night to complete a degree in business. The last time she'd been seen alive was at approximately 10:00 P.M., a week ago Friday, about three hours before her death, I had estimated. She had dinner that night with a woman friend at a neighborhood Mexican restaurant, then went straight home.

Her body was found the next afternoon, Saturday. She was supposed to go shopping with her friend. Cecile's car was in the drive, and when she didn't answer the phone or the door, her friend got worried and peered through the slightly parted curtains of the bedroom window. The sight of Cecile's nude, bound body on top of the disarrayed bed wasn't something the friend was likely ever to forget.

"Bobbi," Marino said. "She's white, you know."

"Cecile's friend?" I'd forgotten her name.

"Yo. Bobbi. The rich bitch who found Cecile's body. The two of 'em was always together. Bobbi's got this red Porsche, a dynamite-looking blonde, works as a model. She's at Cecile's crib all the time, sometimes don't leave until early morning. Think the two of 'em were sweet on each other, you want my opinion. Blows my mind. I mean, it's hard to figure. Both of 'em goodlooking enough to pop your eyes out. You'd think men would be hitting on 'em all the time . . ."

"Maybe that's your answer," I said in annoyance. "If your suspicions about the women are founded."

Marino smiled slyly. He was baiting me again.

"Well, my point is," he went on, "maybe the killer's cruising the neighborhood and sees Bobbi climbing into her red Porsche late one night. Maybe he thinks she lives here. Or maybe he follows her one night when she's on her way to Cecile's house."

"And he murders Cecile by mistake? Because he thought Bobbi lived here?"

"I'm just running it up the pole. Like I said, Bobbi's white. The other victims are white."

We sat in silence for a moment, staring at the house.

The racial mix continued to bother me, too. Three white women and one black woman. Why?

"One more thing I'll run up the pole," Marino said. "I've been wondering if the killer's got several candidates for each of these murders, like he chooses from the menu, ends up getting what he can afford. Sort of strange each time he sets out to kill one of 'em, she just happens to have a window unlocked or open or broke. It's either, in my opinion, a random situation, where he cruises and looks for anyone who seems to be alone and whose house is insecure, or else he's got access to a number of women and their addresses, and maybe makes the rounds, maybe cases a lotta residences in one night before finding the one that'll work for him."

I didn't like it.

"I think he stalked each of these women," I said, "that they were specific targets. I think he may have cased their homes before and either not found them in or found the windows locked. It may be the killer habitually visits the place where his next victim lives and then strikes when the opportunity presents itself."

He shrugged, playing with the idea. "Patty Lewis was

murdered several weeks after Brenda Steppe. And Patty also was out of town visiting a friend the week prior to her murder. So it's possible he tried the weekend before and didn't find her home. Sure. Maybe it happened like that. Who's to say? Then he hits Cecile Tyler three weeks later. But he got to Lori Petersen exactly one week after that – who knows? Maybe he scored right off. A window was unlocked because the husband forgot to lock it. The killer could have had some sort of contact with Lori Petersen as recently as several days before he murdered her, and if her window hadn't been unlocked last weekend he'd be back this week-end, trying again."

"The weekend," I said. "That seems to be important to him, important to strike on a late Friday night or in the first hour or so of Saturday morning."

Marino nodded. "Oh, yeah. It's calculated. Me, I think it's because he works Monday through Friday, has the weekend off to chill out after he's done it. Probably he likes the pattern for another reason, too. It's a way of jerking us around. Friday comes and he knows the city, people like you and me, are nervous as a cat in the middle of a freeway."

I hesitated, then broached the subject. "Do you think his pattern is escalating? That the murders are more closely spaced because he's getting more stressed, perhaps by all the publicity?"

He didn't comment right away. Then he spoke very seri-ously, "He's a friggin' addict, Doc. Once he starts, he can't stop."

"You're saying the publicity has nothing to do with his pattern?"

"No," he replied, "I'm not saying that. His pattern's to lay low and keep his mouth shut, and maybe he wouldn't be so cool if the reporters wasn't making it so damn easy for him. The sensational stories are a gift. He don't have to do any work. The reporters are rewarding him, giving it to him free. Now if nobody was writing up nothing, he'd get frustrated, more reckless maybe. After a while, maybe he'd start sending

148

notes, making phone calls, doing something to get the reporters going. He might screw up."

We were quiet awhile.

Then Marino caught me off guard.

"Sounds like you been talking to Fortosis."

"Why?"

"The stuff about it escalating and the news stories stressing him, making his urge peak quicker."

"Is this what he's told you?"

He casually slipped off his sunglasses and set them on the dash. When he looked at me his eyes were faintly glinting with anger. "Nope. But he's told a couple people near and dear to my heart. Boltz, for one. Tanner, for another."

"How do you know that?"

"Because I got as many snitches inside the department as I got on the street. I know exactly what's going down and where it's going to end – maybe."

We sat in silence. The sun had dipped below rooftops and long shadows were creeping over the lawns and street. In a way, Marino had just cracked the door that would take us into each other's confidence. He knew. He was telling me he knew. I wondered if I dared push the door open wider.

"Boltz, Tanner, the powers-that-be are very upset by the leaks to the press," I said cautiously.

"May as well have a nervous breakdown over the rain. It happens. 'Specially when you got 'Dear Abby' living in the same city."

I smiled ruefully. How appropriate. Spill your secrets to "Dear Abby" Turnbull and she prints every one of them in the paper.

"She's a big problem," he went on. "Has the inside track, a line hooked straight into the heart of the department. I don't think the chief takes a whiz without her knowing it."

"Who's telling her?"

"Let's just say I got my suspicions but I haven't got the goods yet to go nowhere with them, okay?"

"You know someone's been getting into my office computer," I said as if it were common knowledge.

He glanced sharply at me. "Since when?"

"I don't know. Several days ago someone got in and tried to pull up Lori Petersen's case. It was luck we discovered it – a onetime oversight made by my computer analyst resulted in the perpetrator's commands appearing on the screen."

"You're saying someone could've been getting in for months and you wouldn't know?"

"That's what I'm saying."

He got quiet, his face hard.

I pressed him. "Changes your suspicions?"

"Huh," he said shortly.

"That's it?" I asked in exasperation. "You don't have anything to say?"

"Nope. Except your ass must be getting close to the fire these days. Amburgey know?"

"He knows."

"Tanner, too, I guess."

"Yes."

"Huh," he said again. "Guess that explains a couple things."

"Like what?" My paranoia was smoldering and I knew Marino could see I was squirming. "What things?"

He didn't reply.

"What things?" I demanded.

He slowly looked over at me. "You really want to know?"

"I think I'd better." My steady voice belied my fear, which was quickly mounting into panic.

"Well, I'll put it to you like this. If Tanner knew you and me was riding around together this afternoon, he'd probably jerk my badge."

I stared at him in open bewilderment. "What are you saying?"

"See, I ran into him at HQ this morning. He called me aside for a little chat, said he and some of the brass are clamping down on the leaks. Tanner told me to be real tight-lipped

150

about the investigation. As if I needed to be told that. Hell. But he said something else that didn't make a whole lot of sense at the time. Point is, I'm not supposed to be telling anyone at your office – meaning you – shit about what's going on anymore."

"What –"

He went on, "How the investigation's going and what we're thinking, I'm saying. You're not supposed to be told squat. Tanner's orders are for us to get the medical info from you but not give you so much as the time of day. He said too much has been floating around and the only way to put a stop to it is not say a word to anyone except those of us who got to know in order to work the cases . . ."

"That's right," I snapped. "And that includes me. These cases are within my jurisdiction – or has everyone suddenly forgotten that?"

"Hey," he said quietly, staring at me. "We're sitting here, right?"

"Yes," I replied more calmly. "We are."

"Me, I don't give a shit what Tanner says. So maybe he's just antsy because of your computer mess. Doesn't want the cops blamed for giving out sensitive information to Dial-a-Leak at the ME's office."

"Please . . ."

"Maybe there's another reason," he muttered to himself.

Whatever it was, he had no intention of telling me.

He roughly shoved the car in gear and we were off toward the river, south to Berkley Downs.

For the next ten, fifteen, twenty minutes – I wasn't really aware of the time – we didn't say a word to each other. I was left sitting in a miserable silence, watching the roadside flash by my window. It was like being the butt of a cruel joke or a plot to which everyone was privy but me. My sense of isolation was becoming unbearable, my fears so acute I no longer was sure of my judgment, my acumen, my reason. I don't think I was sure of anything.

All I could do was picture the debris of what just days ago

was a desirable professional future. My office was being blamed for the leaks. My attempts at modernization had undermined my own rigid standards of confidentiality.

Even Bill was no longer sure of my credibility. Now the cops were no longer supposed to talk to me. It wouldn't end until I had been turned into the scapegoat for all the atrocities caused by these murders. Amburgey probably would have no choice but to ease me out of office if he didn't outright fire me.

Marino was glancing over at me.

I'd scarcely been aware of his pulling off the road and parking.

"How far is it?" I asked.

"From what?"

"From where we just were, from where Cecile lived?"

"Exactly seven-point-four miles," he replied laconically, without a glance at the odometer.

In the light of day, I almost didn't recognize Lori Petersen's house.

It looked empty and unlived in, wearing the patina of neglect. The white clapboard siding was dingy in the shadows, the Wedgwood shutters seeming a dusky blue. The lilies beneath the front windows had been trampled, probably by investigators combing every inch of the property for evidence. A tatter of yellow crime-scene tape remained tacked to the door frame, and in the overgrown grass was a beer can that some thoughtless passerby had tossed out of his car.

Her house was the modest tidy house of middle-class America, the sort of place found in every small town and every small neighborhood. It was the place where people got started in life and migrated back to during their later years: young professionals, young couples and, finally, older people retired and with children grown and gone.

It was almost exactly like the Johnsons' white clapboard house where I rented a room during my medical school years in Baltimore. Like Lori Petersen, I had existed in a grueling oblivion, out the door at dawn and often not returning until the following evening. Survival was limited to books, labs, examinations, rotations, and sustaining the physical and emotional energy to get through it all. It would never have occurred to me, just as it never occurred to Lori, that someone I did not know might decide to take my life.

"Hey . . ."

I suddenly realized Marino was talking to me.

His eyes were curious. "You all right, Doc?"

"I'm sorry. I didn't catch what you were saying."

"I asked what you thought. You know, you got a map in your head. What do you think?"

I abstractedly replied, "I think their deaths have nothing to do with where they lived."

He didn't agree or disagree. Snatching up his hand mike, he told the dispatcher he was EOT. He was marking off for the day. The tour was over.

"Ten-four, seven-ten," the cocky voice crackled back. "Eighteen-forty-five hours, watch the sun in your eyes, same time tomorrow they'll be playing our song . . ."

Which was sirens and gunfire and people crashing into each other, I assumed.

Marino snorted. "When I was coming along, you so much as gave a 'Yo' instead of a ten-four the inspector'd write up your ass."

I briefly shut my eyes and kneaded my temples.

"Sure ain't what it used to be," he said. "Hell, nothing is."

9

The moon was a milk-glass globe through gaps in the trees as I drove through the quiet neighborhood where I lived.

Lush branches were moving black shapes along the roadside and the mica-flecked pavement glittered in the sweep of my headlights. The air was clear and pleasantly warm, perfect for convertibles or windows rolled down. I was driving with my doors locked, my windows shut, and the fan on low.

The very sort of evening I would have found enchanting in the past was now unsettling.

The images from the day were before me, as the moon was before me. They haunted me and wouldn't let me go. I saw each of those unassuming houses in unrelated parts of the city. How had he chosen them? And why? It wasn't chance. I strongly believed that. There had to be some element consistent with each case, and I was continually drawn back to the sparkling residue we'd been finding on the bodies. With absolutely no evidence to go on, I was profoundly sure this glitter was the missing link connecting him to each of his victims.

That was as far as my intuition would take me. When I attempted to envision more, my mind went blank. Was the glitter a clue that could lead us to where he lived? Was it related to some profession or recreation that gave him his initial contact with the women he would murder? Or stranger yet, did the residue originate with the women themselves?

Maybe it *was* something each victim had in her house – or even on her person or in her workplace. Maybe it was something each woman purchased from him. God only knew. We couldn't test every item found in a person's house or office or some other place frequently visited, especially if we had no idea what we were looking for.

I turned into my drive.

Before I'd parked my car, Bertha was opening the front door. She stood in the glare of the porch light, her hands on her hips, her purse looped over a wrist. I knew what this meant – she was in one big hurry to leave. I hated to think what Lucy had been like today.

"Well?" I asked when I got to the door.

Bertha started shaking her head. "Terrible, Dr. Kay. That child. Uh-uh! Don't know what in the world's got in her. She been bad, bad, bad."

I'd reached the ragged edge of this worn-out day. Lucy was in a decline. In the main, it was my fault. I hadn't handled her well. Or perhaps I'd *handled* her, period, and that was a better way to state the problem.

Not accustomed to confronting children with the same forthrightness and bluntness that I used with relative impunity on adults, I hadn't questioned her about the computer violation, nor had I so much as alluded to it. Instead, after Bill left my house Monday night, I had disconnected the telephone modem in my office and carried it upstairs to my closet.

My rationale was Lucy would assume I took it downtown, in for repairs, or something along these lines, if she noticed its absence at all. Last night she made no mention of the missing modem, but was subdued, her eyes fleeting and hinting of hurt when I caught her watching me instead of the movie I'd inserted in the VCR.

What I did was purely logical. If there were even the slightest chance it was Lucy who broke into the computer downtown, then the removal of the modem obviated her doing it again without my accusing her or instigating a

155

painful scene that would tarnish our memories of her visit. If the violation did recur, it would prove Lucy couldn't be the perpetrator, should there ever be a question.

All this when I know human relationships are not founded on reason any more than my roses are fertilized with debate. I know seeking asylum behind the wall of intellect and rationality is a selfish retreating into self-protectiveness at the expense of another's well-being.

What I did was so intelligent it was as stupid as hell.

I remembered my own childhood, how much I hated the games my mother used to play when she would sit on the edge of my bed and answer questions about my father. He had a "bug" at first, something that "gets in the blood" and causes relapses every so often. Or he was fighting off "something some colored person" or "Cuban" carried into his grocery store. Or "he works too hard and gets himself run down, Kay." Lies.

My father had chronic lymphatic leukemia. It was diagnosed before I entered the first grade. It wasn't until I was twelve and he deteriorated from stage-zero lymphocytosis to stage-three anemia that I was told he was dying.

We lie to children even though we didn't believe the lies we were told when we were their age. I don't know why we do that. I didn't know why I'd been doing it with Lucy, who was as quick as any adult.

By eight-thirty she and I were sitting at the kitchen table. She was fiddling with a milk shake and I was drinking a much-needed tumbler of Scotch. Her change in demeanor was unsettling and I was fast losing my nerve.

All the fight in her had vanished; all of the petulance and resentment over my absences had retreated. I couldn't seem to warm her or cheer her up, not even when I said Bill would be dropping by just in time to say good-night to her. There was scarcely a glimmer of interest. She didn't move or respond, and she wouldn't meet my eyes.

"You look sick," she finally muttered.

"How would you know? You haven't looked at me once since I've been home."

"So. You still look sick."

"Well, I'm not sick," I told her. "I'm just very tired."

"When Mom gets tired she doesn't look sick," she said, halfway accusing me. "She only looks sick when she fights with Ralph. I hate Ralph. He's a dick head. When he comes over, I make him do 'Jumble' in the paper just because I know he can't. He's a stupid-ass dick head."

I didn't admonish her for her dirty mouth. I didn't say a word. "So," she persisted, "you have a fight with a Ralph?"

"I don't know any Ralphs."

"Oh." A frown. "Mr. Boltz is mad at you, I bet."

"I don't think so."

"I bet he is too. He's mad because I'm here –"

"Lucy! That's ridiculous. Bill likes you very much."

"Ha! He's mad 'cause he can't *do it* when I'm here!"

"Lucy . . ." I warned.

"That's it. Ha! He's mad 'cause he's gotta keep his pants on."

"Lucy," I spoke severely. "Stop it this minute!"

She finally gave me her eyes and I was startled by their anger. "See. I knew it!" She laughed in a mean way. "And you wish I wasn't here so I couldn't get in the way. Then he wouldn't have to go home at night. Well, I don't care. So there. Mom sleeps with her boyfriends all the time and I don't care!"

"*I'm not your Mom!*"

Her lower lip quivered as if I'd slapped her. "I never said you were! I wouldn't want you to be anyway! I hate you!"

Both of us sat very still.

I was momentarily stunned. I couldn't remember anyone's ever saying he hated me, even if it was true.

"Lucy," I faltered. My stomach was knotted like a fist. I felt sick. "I didn't mean it like that. What I meant was I'm not like your mother. Okay? We're very different. Always have been very different. But this doesn't mean I don't care very much for you."

She didn't respond.

157

"I know you don't really hate me."

She remained stonily silent.

I dully got up to refresh my drink. Of course she didn't really hate me. Children say that all the time and don't mean it. I tried to remember. I never told my mother I hated her. I think I secretly did, at least when I was a child, because of the lies, and because when I lost my father I lost her, too. She was as consumed by his dying as he was consumed by his disease. There was nothing warm-blooded left for Dorothy and me.

I had lied to Lucy. I was consumed, too, not by the dying but by the dead. Every day I did battle for justice. But what justice was there for a living little girl who didn't feel loved? Dear Lord. Lucy didn't hate me but maybe I couldn't blame her if she did. Returning to the table, I approached the forbidden subject as delicately as possible.

"I guess I look worried because I am, Lucy. You see, someone got into the computer downtown."

She was quiet, waiting.

I sipped my drink. "I'm not sure this person saw anything that matters, but if I could explain how it happened or who did it, it would be a big load off my mind."

Still, she said nothing.

I forced it.

"If I don't get to the bottom of it, Lucy, I might be in trouble." This seemed to alarm her.

"Why would you be in trouble?"

"Because," I calmly explained, "my office data is very sensitive, and important people in city and state government are concerned over the information that is somehow ending up in the newspapers. Some people are worried the information might be coming from my office computer."

"Oh."

"If a reporter somehow got in, for example . . ."

"Information about what?" she asked.

"These recent cases."

"The lady doctor who got killed."

I nodded.

Silence.

Then she said sullenly, "That's why the modem's gone, isn't it, Auntie Kay? You took it because you think I did something bad."

"I don't think you did anything bad, Lucy. If you dialed into my office computer, I know you didn't do it to be bad. I wouldn't blame you for being curious."

She looked up at me, her eyes welling. "You took away the modem 'cause you don't trust me anymore."

I didn't know how to respond to this. I couldn't lie to her, and the truth would be an admission that I didn't really trust her.

Lucy had lost all interest in her milk shake and was sitting very still, chewing her bottom lip as she stared down at the table.

"I did remove the modem because I wondered if it was you," I confessed. "That wasn't the right thing for me to do. I should have just asked you. But maybe I was hurt. It hurt me to think you might have broken our trust."

She looked at me for a long time. She seemed strangely pleased, almost happy when she asked, "You mean my doing something bad hurt your feelings?" – as if this gave her some sort of power or validation she desperately wanted.

"Yes. Because I love you very much, Lucy," I said, and I think it was the first time I'd ever told her that so clearly. "I didn't intend to hurt your feelings any more than you intended to hurt mine. I'm sorry."

"It's okay."

The spoon clacked the side of the glass as she stirred her milk shake and cheerfully exclaimed, "Besides, I knew you hid it. You can't hide things from me, Auntie Kay. I saw it in your closet. I looked while Bertha was making lunch. I found it on the shelf right next to your .38."

"How did you know it's a .38?" I blurted without thinking.

"'Cause Andy has a .38. He was before Ralph. Andy has a

159

.38 on his belt, right here," pointing to the small of her back. "He owns a pawnshop and that's why he always wears a .38. He used to show it to me and how it works. He'd take all the bullets out and let me shoot it at the TV. Bang! Bang! It's really neat! Bang! Bang!" Shooting her finger at the refrigerator. "I like him better than Ralph but Mom got tired of him, I guess."

This was what I was sending her home to tomorrow? I started lecturing her on handguns, reciting all the lines about how they aren't toys and can hurt people, when the telephone rang.

"Oh, yeah," Lucy remembered as I got out of the chair. "Grans called before you got home. Twice."

She was the last person I wanted to talk to right now. No matter how well I disguised my moods she always managed to sense them and wouldn't let them alone.

"You sound depressed," my mother said two sentences into the conversation.

"I'm just tired." That shopworn line again.

I could see her as if she were before me. No doubt she was sitting up in bed, several pillows behind her back, the television softly playing. I have my father's coloring. My mother is dark, her black hair white now and softly framing her round, full face, her brown eyes large behind her thick glasses.

"Of course you're tired," she started in. "All you do is work. And those horrible cases in Richmond. There was a story about them in the *Herald* yesterday, Kay. I've never been so surprised in my life. I didn't even see it until this afternoon when Mrs. Martinez dropped by with it. I stopped getting the Sunday paper. All those inserts and coupons and ads. It's so fat I can't be bothered. Mrs. Martinez came by with it because your picture's in it."

I groaned.

"Can't say I would have recognized you. It's not very good, taken at night, but your name's under it, sure enough. And wearing no hat, Kay. Looked like it was raining or wet and nasty out and here you are not wearing a hat. All those hats I've crocheted for you and you can't even bother to wear one of your mother's hats so you don't catch pneumonia . . ."

"Mother . . ."

She went on.

"Mother!"

I couldn't stand it, not tonight. I could be Maggie Thatcher and my mother would persist in treating me like a five-year-old who doesn't have sense enough to come out of the rain.

Next came the run of questions about my diet and whether I was getting enough sleep.

I abruptly derailed her. "How's Dorothy?"

She hesitated. "Well, that's why I'm calling."

I scooted over a chair and sat down as my mother's voice went up an octave and she proceeded to tell me Dorothy had flown to Nevada – to get married.

"Why Nevada?" I stupidly asked.

"You tell me! You tell me why your only sister meets with some book person she's only talked to over the phone in the past, and suddenly calls her mother from the airport to say she's on her way to Nevada to get married. You tell me how my daughter could do something like that. You think she has macaroni for brains . . ."

"What sort of book person?" I glanced at Lucy. She was watching me, her face stricken.

"I don't know. Some illustrator she called him, I guess he draws the pictures for her books, was in Miami a few days ago for some convention and got with Dorothy to discuss her current project or something. Don't ask me. His name's Jacob Blank. Jewish, I just know it. Though Dorothy certainly couldn't tell me. Why should she tell her mother she's marrying a Jew I've never met who's twice her age and draws kiddy pictures, for crummy sake?"

I didn't even ask.

To send Lucy home in the midst of yet another family crisis was unthinkable. Her absences from her mother had been prolonged before, whenever Dorothy had to dash out of

161

town for an editorial meeting or a research trip or one of her numerous "book talks" that always seemed to detain her longer than anyone had supposed. Lucy would remain with her grandmother until the wandering writer eventually made it back home. Maybe we had learned to accept these lapses into blatant irresponsibility. Maybe even Lucy had. But eloping? Good God.

"She didn't say when she'd be back?" I turned away from Lucy and lowered my voice.

"What?" my mother said loudly. "Tell *me* such a thing? Why should she tell her mother that? Oh! How could she do this again, Kay! He's *twice* her age! Armando was twice her age and look what happened to him! He drops dead by the pool before Lucy's even old enough to ride a bicycle . . ."

It took me a while to ease her out of hysteria. After I hung up, I was left with the fallout.

I couldn't think of a way to cushion the news. "Your mother's gone out of town for a little while, Lucy. She's gotten married to Mr. Blank, who illustrates her books for her . . ."

She was as still as a statue. I reached out my arms to pull her into an embrace.

"They're in Nevada at the moment –"

The chair jerked back and fell against the wall as she wrenched away from me and fled to her room.

How could my sister do this to Lucy? I was sure I would never forgive her, not this time. It was bad enough when she married Armando. She was barely eighteen. We warned her. We did everything to talk her out of it. He hardly spoke English, was old enough to be her father, and we were uneasily suspicious of his wealth, of his Mercedes, his gold Rolex and his posh waterfront apartment. Like a lot of people who appear mysteriously in Miami, he enjoyed a high-rolling life-style that couldn't be explained logically.

Damn Dorothy. She knew about my work, knew how demanding and relentless it was. She knew I'd been hesitant about Lucy's coming at all right now because of these cases!

But it was planned, and Dorothy cajoled and convinced with her charms.

"If it gets too inconvenient, Kay, you can just send her back and we'll reschedule," she had said sweetly. "*Really*. She's so desperately looking forward to it. It's all she talks about these days. She simply *adores* you. A genuine case of hero worship if I ever saw it."

Lucy was sitting stiffly on the edge of her bed, staring at the floor.

"I hope they get killed in a plane crash" was the only thing she said to me as I helped her into her pajamas.

"You don't mean that, Lucy." I smoothed the daisy-spangled spread beneath her chin. "You can stay with me for a while. That will be nice, won't it?"

She squeezed her eyes shut and turned her face to the wall.

My tongue felt thick and slow. There were no words that would ease her pain, so I sat looking helplessly at her for a while. Hesitantly, I moved closer to her and began to rub her back. Gradually her misery seemed to fade, and eventually she began breathing the deep, regular breaths of sleep. I kissed the top of her head and softly shut her door.

Halfway back to the kitchen, I heard Bill pull in.

I got to the door before he had a chance to ring the bell.

"Lucy's asleep," I whispered.

"Oh," he playfully whispered back. "Too bad – so I wasn't worth waiting up for –"

He suddenly turned, following my startled eyes out to the street. Headlights cut around the bend and were instantly extinguished at the same time a car I could not make out came to an abrupt stop. Now it was accelerating in reverse, the engine loudly straining.

Pebbles and grit popped as it turned around beyond the trees and sped away.

"Expecting company?" Bill muttered, staring out into the darkness.

I slowly shook my head.

163

He stole a glance at his watch and lightly nudged me into the foyer.

Whenever Marino came to the OCME, he never failed to needle Wingo, who was probably the best autopsy technician I'd ever worked with and by far the most fragile.

". . . Yo. It's what's known as a close encounter of the *Ford* kind . . ." Marino was loudly going on.

A bay-windowed state trooper who arrived at the same time Marino did guffawed again.

Wingo's face was bright red as he stabbed the plug of the Stryker saw into the yellow cord reel dangling over the steel table.

Up to my wrists in blood, I mumbled under my breath, "Ignore it, Wingo."

Marino cut his eyes at the trooper, and I waited for the limp wrist act to follow.

Wingo was much too sensitive for his own good and I sometimes worried about him. He so keenly identified with the victims it wasn't uncommon for him to cry over unusually heinous cases.

The morning had presented one of life's cruel ironies. A young woman had gone to a bar in a rural area of a neighboring county last night, and as she started walking home around 2:00 A.M. she was struck by a car that kept on going. The state trooper, examining her personal effects, had just discovered inside her billfold a slip of paper from a fortune cookie which predicted, "You will soon have an encounter that will change the course of your life."

"Or maybe she was looking for Mr. HOODbar . . ."

I was just on the verge of blowing up at Marino when his voice was drowned out by the Stryker saw, which sounded like a loud dentist's drill as Wingo began cutting through the dead woman's skull. A bony dust unpleasantly drifted on the air and Marino and the trooper retreated to the other end of the suite where the autopsy of Richmond's latest shooting homicide was being performed on the last table.

When the saw was silenced and the skull cap removed I stopped what I was doing to make a quick inspection of the brain. No subdural or subarachnoid hemorrhages . . .

"It isn't funny," Wingo began his indignant litany, "not the least bit funny. How can anybody laugh at something like that . . ."

The woman's scalp was lacerated but that was it. What killed her were multiple pelvic fractures, the blow to her buttocks so violent the pattern of the vehicle's grille was clearly visible on her skin. She wasn't struck by something low to the ground, such as a sports car. Might have been a truck.

"She saved it because it meant something to her. Like it was something she wanted to believe. Maybe that's why she went to the bar last night. She was looking for someone she'd been waiting for all her life. Her *encounter*. And it turns out to be some drunk driver who knocks her fifty feet into a ditch."

"Wingo," I said wearily as I began taking photographs, "it's better if you don't imagine some things."

"I can't help it . . ."

"You have to learn to help it."

He cast wounded eyes in the direction of Marino, who was never satisfied unless he got a rise out of him. Poor Wingo. Most members of the rough-and-tumble world of law enforcement were more than a little put off by him. He didn't laugh at their jokes or particularly relish their war stories, and more to the point, he was, well, different.

Tall and lithely built, he had black hair cropped close on the sides with a cockatoo spray on top and a rat tail curling at the nape of his neck. Delicately handsome, he looked like a model in the loose-fitting designer clothes and soft leather European shoes he wore. Even his indigo-blue scrubs, which he bought and laundered himself, were stylish. He didn't flirt. He didn't resent having a woman tell him what to do. He never seemed remotely interested in what I looked like beneath my lab coat or all-business Britches of Georgetown suits. I'd grown so comfortable around him that on the few occasions when he accidentally walked into the locker room while I was changing into my scrubs, I was scarcely aware of him.

I suppose if I'd wondered about his proclivities when he interviewed for the job several months ago I might have been less enthusiastic about hiring him. It was something I didn't like to admit.

But it was all too easy to stereotype because I saw the worst example of every sort in this place. There were the transvestites with their falsies and padded hips, and the gays who flew into jealous rages and murdered their lovers, and the chicken hawks who cruised parks and video arcades and got carved up by homophobic rednecks. There were the prisoners with their obscene tattoos and histories of sodomizing anything on two legs inside the cell blocks, and there were the profligate purveyors in bathhouses and bars who didn't care who else got AIDS.

Wingo didn't fit. Wingo was just Wingo.

"You can handle it from here?" He was angrily rinsing off his gloved and bloody hands.

"I'll finish up," I replied abstractedly as I resumed measuring a large tear of the mesentery.

Walking off to a cabinet, he began to collect spray bottles of disinfectants, rags and the other odds and ends he used for cleaning. Slipping a small set of headphones over his ears, he switched on the tape player attached to the waistband of his scrubs, momentarily shutting out the world.

Fifteen minutes later he was cleaning out the small refrigerator where evidence was stored inside the autopsy suite over the weekend. I vaguely noticed him pulling something out and looking at it for a long moment.

When he came over to my table, he was wearing his headphones around his neck like a collar, and he had a puzzled, uneasy expression on his face. In his hand was a small cardboard slide folder from a PERK.

"Uh, Dr. Scarpetta," he said, clearing his throat, "this was inside the fridge."

He didn't explain.

He didn't need to.

I set down the scalpel as my stomach tightened. Printed on the slide folder label was the case number, name and date of the autopsy of Lori Petersen – whose evidence, all of it, had been turned in four days earlier.

"You found this in the refrigerator?"

There had to be some mistake.

"In the back, on the bottom shelf." Hesitantly, he added, "Uh, it's not initialed. I mean, you didn't initial it."

There had to be an explanation.

"Of course I didn't initial it," I said sharply. "I collected only one PERK in her case, Wingo."

Even as I said the words, doubt wavered deep inside me like a windblown flame. I tried to remember.

I stored Lori Petersen's samples in the refrigerator over the weekend, along with the samples from all of Saturday's cases. I distinctly remembered receipting her samples in person to the labs Monday morning, including a cardboard folder of slides smeared with anal, oral and vaginal swabs. I was sure I used only one cardboard folder of slides. I never sent up a slide folder bare – it was always enclosed inside a plastic bag containing the swabs, envelopes of hair, test tubes and everything else.

"I have no idea where this came from," I told him too adamantly.

He uncomfortably shifted his weight to his other foot and averted his eyes. I knew what he was thinking. I'd screwed up and he hated to be the one who had to point it out to me.

The threat had always been there. Wingo and I had gone over it numerous times in the past, ever since Margaret loaded the PC in the autopsy suite with the label programs.

Before one of the pathologists started a case he went to that PC and typed in information about the decedent whose autopsy he was about to perform. A run of labels was generated for every sample one might possibly collect, such as blood, bile, urine, stomach contents and a PERK. It saved a lot of time and was perfectly acceptable provided the pathologist was careful to stick the right label on the right tube and remembered to initial it.

There was one feature of this bit of automated enlightenment that had always made me nervous. Inevitably there were leftover labels because one didn't, as a rule, collect every possible sample, especially when labs were overworked and understaffed. I wasn't going to send fingernail clippings to trace evidence, for example, if the decedent was an eighty-year-old man who died of a myocardial infarct while cutting his grass.

What to do with leftover labels? You certainly didn't want to leave them lying around where they might find their way onto the wrong test tubes. Most of the pathologists tore them up. It was my habit to file them with the person's case folder. It was a quick way to know what was tested for, what wasn't, and how many tubes of this or that I'd actually sent upstairs.

Wingo had trotted across the suite and was running a finger down the pages of the morgue log. I could feel Marino staring across the suite at me as he waited to collect the bullets from his homicide case. He wandered my way just as Wingo got back.

"We had six cases that day," Wingo reminded me as if Marino were not there. "Saturday. I remember. There were a lot of labels on the counter over there. Maybe one of them –"

"No," I said loudly. "I don't see how. I didn't leave any leftover labels from her case lying around. They were with my paperwork, clipped to my clipboard –"

"Shit," Marino said in surprise. He was looking over my shoulder. "That what I think it is?"

Frantically pulling off my gloves, I took the folder from Wingo and slit the tape with a thumbnail. Inside were four slides, three of which were definitely smeared with something, but they were not hand-marked with the standard "O," "A," or "V," designating which samples they were. They weren't marked at all, except by the computer label on the outside of the folder.

'So, maybe you labeled this thinking you were going to use it, changed your mind or something?" Wingo suggested.

I didn't reply right away. I couldn't remember!

"When was the last time you went inside the refrigerator?" I asked him.

A shrug. "Last week, maybe a week ago Monday when I got out the stuff so the doctors could take it up. I wasn't in this past Monday. This is the first time I've looked in the fridge this week."

I slowly recalled that Wingo had taken comp time on Monday. I myself had gotten Lori Petersen's evidence out of the refrigerator before making evidence rounds. Was it possible I overlooked this cardboard folder? Was it possible I was so fatigued, so distracted, I got her evidence mixed up with evidence from one of the five other cases we had that day? If so, which cardboard folder of slides was really from her case – the one I receipted upstairs, or this one? I couldn't believe this was happening. I was always so careful!

I rarely wore my scrubs out of the morgue. Almost never. Not even when there was a fire drill. Several minutes later, lab workers glanced curiously at me as I walked briskly down the third-floor hall in my blood-spattered greens. Betty was inside her cramped office taking a coffee break. She took one look at me and her eyes froze.

"We've got a problem," I said right off.

She stared at the cardboard folder, at the label on it.

"Wingo was cleaning out the evidence refrigerator. He found it a few minutes ago."

"Oh, God," was all she said.

As I followed her into the serology lab, I was explaining I had no recollection of labeling two folders from PERKs in Lori's case. I was clueless.

Working her hands into a pair of gloves, she reached for bottles inside a cabinet as she attempted to reassure me. "I think the ones you sent me, Kay, have to be right. The slides were consistent with the swabs, with everything else you receipted. Everything came up as nonsecreter, was consistent. This must be an extra you don't remember taking."

Another tremor of doubt. I had taken only one folder of slides, or had I? Could I swear to it? Last Saturday seemed a blur. I couldn't retrace my every step with certainty.

"No swabs with this, I take it?" she asked.

"None," I replied. "Just this folder of slides. That's all Wingo found."

"Hmm." She was thinking. "Let's see what we have here." She placed each slide under the phase microscope, and after a long silence, said. "We've got big squamous cells, meaning these could be oral or vaginal, but not anal. And" – she looked up – "I'm not seeing any sperm."

"Lord," I groaned.

"We'll try again," she answered.

Tearing open a packet of sterilized swabs, she moistened them with water and began gently rolling one at a time over a portion of each smear on each slide – three in all. Next she smeared the swabs over small circles of white filter paper.

Getting out the medicine droppers, she began deftly dripping naphthyl acid phosphate over the filter paper. Then came the fast-blue B salt. We stared, waiting for the first hint of purple.

The smears didn't react. They sat there in tiny wet stains tormenting me. I continued to stare beyond the brief period of time the smears needed to react as if I could somehow will them into testing positive for seminal fluid. I wanted to believe this was an extra file of slides. I wanted to believe I *had* taken two PERKs in Lori's case and just didn't remember. I wanted to believe anything except what was becoming patently clear.

The slides Wingo had found were not from Lori's case. They couldn't be.

Betty's impassive face told me she was worried, too, and doing her best not to let it show.

I shook my head.

She was forced to conclude, "Then it doesn't seem likely

these are from Lori's case." A pause. "I'll do what I can to group them, of course. See if there are any Barr bodies present, that sort of thing."

"Please." I took a deep breath.

She went on, trying to make me feel better, "The fluids I separated out from the killer's fluids are consistent with Lori's blood samples. I don't think you have a worry. There's no doubt in my mind about the first file sent in . . ."

"The question has been raised," I said, miserable.

Lawyers would love it. Good God, would they love it. They'd have a jury doubting any of the samples were Lori's, including the tubes of blood. They'd have a jury wondering if the samples sent to New York for DNA testing were the right ones. Who was to say that they weren't from some other dead body?

My voice was on the verge of trembling when I told her, "We had six cases that day, Betty. Three of them merited PERKs, were potential sexual assaults."

"All female?"

"Yes," I muttered. "All of them women."

What Bill said Wednesday night when he was stressed, his tongue lubricated by liquor, was branded in my mind. What would happen to these cases should my credibility be compromised? Not only would Lori's case come into question, all of them would. I was cornered, absolutely and with no way out. I couldn't pretend this file didn't exist. It did exist and what it meant was I couldn't honestly swear in court the chain of evidence was intact.

There was no second chance. I couldn't collect the samples again, start from scratch. Lori's samples had already been hand-delivered to the New York lab. Her embalmed body had been buried Tuesday. An exhumation, forget it. It wouldn't be profitable. It would be, however, a sensational event sparking enormous public curiosity. Everyone would want to know why.

Betty and I both glanced toward the door at the same time as Marino casually walked in.

"I just had a freaky little thought, Doc." He paused, his face hard as his eyes wandered to the slides and filter paper on the countertop.

I stared numbly at him.

"Me, I'd take this PERK here over to Vander. Maybe you left it in the fridge. Then again, maybe you didn't."

A sense of alarm fluttered through my blood before the jolt of comprehension.

"What?" I asked, as if he were crazy. "Someone else put it there?"

He shrugged. "I'm just suggesting you consider every possibility."

"Who?"

"Got no idea."

"How? How could that be possible? Someone would have to have gotten inside the autopsy suite, had access to the refrigerator. And the file is labeled . . ."

The labels: it was coming to me. The computer-generated labels left over from Lori's autopsy. They were inside her case file. No one had been inside her file except me – and Amburgey, Tanner and Bill.

When the three men left my office early Monday evening, the front doors were chained. All of them went out through the morgue. Amburgey and Tanner had left first, and Bill a little later.

The autopsy suite was locked, but the walk-in refrigerator was not. We had to leave the refrigerator unlocked so funeral homes and rescue squads could deliver bodies after hours. The walk-in refrigerator had two doors, one opening onto the hallway, another leading into the autopsy suite. Had one of the men gone through the refrigerator and into the suite? On a shelf near the first table were stacks of evidence kits, including dozens of PERKs. Wingo always kept the shelves fully stocked.

I reached for the phone and instructed Rose to unlock my desk drawer and open Lori Petersen's case file.

"There should be some evidence labels inside," I told her.

While she checked, I tried to remember. There were six, maybe seven labels left over, not because I didn't collect a lot of samples but because I collected so many of them – almost twice as many as usual, resulting in my generating not one, but two runs of computerized labels. Left over should be labels for heart, lung, kidneys and other organs, and an extra one for a PERK.

"Dr. Scarpetta?" Rose was back. "The labels are here."

"How many?"

"Let me see. Five."

"For what?"

She replied, "Heart, lung, spleen, bile and liver."

"And that's all."

"Yes. "

"You're sure there isn't one for a PERK?"

A pause. "I'm sure. Just these five."

Marino said, "You slapped the label on this PERK, and your prints should be on it, seems to me."

"Not if she was wearing gloves," said Betty, who was watching all this with dismay.

"I generally don't wear gloves when I'm labeling things," I muttered. "They're bloody. The gloves would be bloody."

Marino blandly went on, "Okay. So you wasn't wearing gloves and Dingo was –"

"Wingo," I irritably said. "His name's Wingo!"

"Whatever." Marino turned to leave. "Point is, you touched the PERK with bare hands, meaning your prints should be on it." He added from the hall, "But maybe nobody else's should be."

173

10

Nobody else's were. The only identifiable prints on the cardboard file were mine.

There were a few smudges – and something else so completely unexpected that I had, for the moment, completely forgotten the unhappy reason for coming to see Vander at all.

He was bombarding the file with the laser and the cardboard was lit up like a night sky of pinpoint stars.

"This is just crazy," he marveled for the third time.

"The damn stuff must have come from my hands," I said incredulously. "Wingo was wearing gloves. So was Betty . . ."

Vander flipped on the overhead light and shook his head from side to side. "If you were male, I'd suggest the cops take you in for questioning."

"And I wouldn't blame you."

His face was intense: "Rethink what you've been doing this morning, Kay. We've got to make sure this residue's from you. If it is, we might have to reconsider our assumptions about the strangling cases, about the glitter we've been finding –"

"No," I interrupted. "It isn't possible I've been leaving the residue on the bodies, Neils. I wore gloves the entire time I worked with them. I took my gloves *off* when Wingo found the PERK. I was touching the file with my bare hands."

He persisted, "What about hair sprays, cosmetics? Anything you routinely use?"

"Not possible," I repeated. "This residue hasn't shown up

when we've examined other bodies. It's shown up only in the strangling cases."

"Good point."

We thought for a minute.

"Betty and Wingo were wearing gloves when they handled this file?" He wanted to make sure.

"Yes, they were, which is why they left no prints."

"So it isn't likely the residue came from their hands?"

"Had to have come from mine. Unless someone else touched the file."

"Some other person who may have planted it in the refrigerator, you're still thinking." Vander looked skeptical. "Yours were the only prints, Kay."

"But the smudges, Neils. Those could be from anyone."

Of course they could be. But I knew he didn't believe it.

He asked, "What exactly were you doing just before you came upstairs?"

"I was posting a hit-and-run."

"Then what?"

"Then Wingo came over with the slide folder and I took it straight to Betty."

He glanced unemphatically at my bloodstained scrubs and observed, "You were wearing gloves while doing the post."

"Of course, and I took them off when Wingo brought me the file, as I've already explained –"

"The gloves were lined with talc."

"I don't think that could be it."

"Probably not, but it's a place to start."

I went back down to the autopsy suite to fetch an identical pair of latex gloves. Several minutes later, Vander was tearing open the packet, turning the gloves inside out, and shooting them with the laser.

Not even a glimmer. The talc didn't react, not that we really thought it would. In the past we'd tested various body powders from the murdered women's scenes in hopes of identifying the glittery substance. The powders, which had a talc base, hadn't reacted either.

The lights went on again. I smoked and thought. I was trying to envision my every move from the time Wingo showed me the slide file to when I ended up in Vander's office. I was engrossed in coronary arteries when Wingo walked up with the PERK. I set down the scalpel, peeled off my gloves and opened the file to look at the slides. I walked over to the sink, hastily washed my hands and patted them dry with a paper towel. Next I went upstairs to see Betty. Did I touch anything inside her lab? I didn't recall if I had.

It was the only thing I could think of. "The soap I used downstairs when I washed up. Could that be it?"

"Unlikely," Vander said without pause. "Especially if you rinsed off. If your everyday soap reacted even after rinsing we'd be finding the glittery stuff all the time on bodies and clothes. I'm pretty certain this residue is coming from something granular, a powdery substance of some sort. The soap you used downstairs is a disinfectant, a liquid, isn't it?"

It was, but that wasn't what I'd used. I was in too big of a rush to go back to the locker room and wash with the pink disinfectant kept in bottles by the sinks. Instead, I went to the sink nearest me, the one in the autopsy suite where there was a metal dispenser filled with the same grainy, gray soap powder used throughout the rest of the building. It was cheap. It was what the state purchased by the truckload. I had no idea what was in it. It was almost odorless and didn't dissolve or lather. It was like washing up with wet sand.

There was a ladies' room down the hall. I left for a moment and returned with a handful of the grayish powder. Lights out and Vander switched on the laser again.

The soap went crazy, blazing neon white.

"I'll be damned . . ."

Vander was thrilled. I wasn't exactly feeling the same way. I desperately wanted to know the origin of the residue we'd been finding on the bodies. But I'd never, not in my

176

wildest fantasies, hoped it would turn out to be something found in every bathroom inside my building.

I still wasn't convinced. Did the residue on this file come from my hands? What if it didn't?

We experimented.

Firearms examiners routinely conduct a series of test fires to determine distance and trajectory. Vander and I were conducting a series of test washings to determine how thoroughly one had to rinse his hands in order for none of the residue to show up in the laser.

He vigorously scrubbed with the powder, rinsed well, and carefully dried his hands with paper towels. The laser picked up one or two sparkles, and that was it. I tried to reenact my handwashing, doing it exactly as I did it when I was downstairs. The result was a multitude of sparkles that were easily transferred to the countertop, the sleeve of Vander's lab coat, anything I touched. The more I touched, obviously, the fewer sparkles there were left on my hands.

I returned to the ladies' room and presently was back with a coffee cup full of the soap. We washed and washed, over and over again. Lights went on and off, the laser spitting, until the entire area of the sink looked like Richmond from the air after dark.

One interesting phenomenon became apparent. The more we washed and dried, the more the sparkles accumulated. They got under our nails, clung to our wrists and the cuffs of our sleeves. They ended up on our clothing, found their way to our hair, our faces, our necks – everywhere we touched. After about forty-five minutes of dozens of experimental washings, Vander and I looked perfectly normal in normal light. In the laser, we looked as if we'd been decorated with Christmas glitter.

"Shit," he exclaimed in the dark. It was an expletive I'd never heard him use. "Would you look at this stuff? The bastard must be a clean freak. To leave as much of the stuff as he does, he must be washing his hands twenty times a day."

"*If* this soap powder's the answer," I reminded him.

"Of course, of course."

I prayed the scientists upstairs could make their magic work. But what couldn't be determined by them or anyone else, I thought, was the origin of the residue on the slide file – and how the file had gotten inside the refrigerator to begin with.

My anxious inner voice was nagging at me again.

You just can't accept you made a mistake, I admonished myself. You just can't handle the truth. You mislabeled this PERK, and the residue on it came from your own hands.

But what if? What if the scenario were a more pernicious one? I silently argued. What if someone maliciously planted the file inside the refrigerator, and what if the glittery residue was from this person's hands instead of mine? The thought was strange, the poison of an imagination gone berserk.

So far a similar residue had been found on the bodies of four murdered women.

I knew Wingo, Betty, Vander and I had touched the file. The only other people who might have touched it were Tanner, Amburgey or Bill.

His face drifted through my mind. Something unpleasant and chilling shifted inside me as Monday afternoon slowly replayed in my memory. Bill was so distant during the meeting with Amburgey and Tanner. He was unable to look at me then, or later when the three men were going through the cases inside my conference room.

I saw case files slipping off Bill's lap and falling to the floor in a commingled, god-awful mess. Tanner quickly offered to pick them up. His helpfulness was so automatic. But it was Bill who picked up the paperwork, paperwork that would have included leftover labels. Then he and Tanner sorted through everything. How easy it would have been to tear off a label and slip it into a pocket . . .

Later, Amburgey and Tanner left together, but Bill remained with me. We talked in Margaret's office for ten or fifteen minutes. He was affectionate and full of promises that a couple of drinks and an evening together would soothe my nerves.

He left long before I did, and when he went out of the building he was alone and unwatched . . .

I blanked the images out of my mind, refused to see them anymore. This was outrageous. I was losing control. Bill would never do such a thing. In the first place, there would be no point. I couldn't imagine how such an act of sabotage could possibly profit him. Mislabeled slides could only damage the very cases he eventually would be prosecuting in court. Not only would he be shooting himself in the foot, he'd be shooting himself in the head.

You want someone to blame because you can't face the fact that you probably screwed up!

These strangling cases were the most difficult of my career, and I was gripped by the fear I was becoming too caught up in them. Maybe I was losing my rational, methodical way of doing things. Maybe I was making mistakes.

Vander was saying, "We've got to figure out the composition of this stuff."

Like thoughtful shoppers, we needed to find a box of the soap and read the ingredients.

"I'll hit the ladies' rooms," I volunteered.

"I'll hit the men's."

What a scavenger hunt this turned out to be.

After wandering in and out of the ladies' rooms throughout the building I got smart and found Wingo. One of his jobs was to fill all the soap dispensers in the morgue. He directed me to the janitor's closet on the first floor, several doors down from my office. There, on a top shelf, right next to a pile of dusting rags, was an industrial-sized gray box of Borawash hand soap.

The main ingredient was borax.

A quick check in one of my chemical reference books hinted at why the soap powder lit up like the Fourth of July. Borax is a boron compound, a crystalline substance that conducts electricity like a metal at high temperatures. Industrial uses of it range from the making of ceramics, special glass, washing powders and disinfectants, to the manufacturing of abrasives and rocket fuels.

Ironically, a large percentage of the world's supply of borax is mined in Death Valley.

Friday night came and went, and Marino did not call.

By seven o'clock the following morning I had parked behind my building and uneasily began checking the log inside the morgue office.

I shouldn't have needed convincing. I knew better. I would have been one of the first to be alerted. There were no bodies signed in I wasn't expecting, but the quiet seemed ominous.

I couldn't shake the sensation another woman was waiting for me to tend to her, that it was happening again. I kept expecting Marino to call.

Vander rang me up from his home at seven-thirty.

"Anything?" he asked.

"I'll call you immediately if there is."

"I'll be near the phone."

The laser was upstairs in his lab, loaded on a cart and ready to be brought down to the X-ray room should we need it. I'd reserved the first autopsy table, and late yesterday afternoon Wingo had scrubbed it mirror-bright and set up two carts with every conceivable surgical tool and evidence-collection container and device. The table and carts remained unused.

My only cases were a cocaine overdose from Fredericksburg and an accidental drowning from James City County.

Just before noon Wingo and I were alone, methodically finishing up the morning's work.

His running shoes squeaked across the damp tile floor as he leaned a mop against the wall and remarked to me, "Word is they had a hundred cops working overtime last night."

I continued filling out a death certificate. "Let's hope it makes a difference."

"Would if I was the guy." He began hosing down a bloody table. "The guy'd be crazy to show his face. One cop told me they're stopping everybody out on the street. They see you walking around late they're going to check you out. Taking plate numbers, too, if they see your car parked somewhere late."

"What cop?" I looked up at him. We had no cases from Richmond this morning, no cops in from Richmond either. "What cop told you this?"

"One of the cops who came in with the drowning."

"From James City County? How did he know what was going on in Richmond last night?"

Wingo glanced curiously at me. "His brother's a cop here in the city."

I turned away so he couldn't see my irritation. Too many people were talking. A cop whose brother was a cop in Richmond just glibly told Wingo, a stranger, this? What else was being said? There was too much talk. Too much. I was reading the most innocent remark differently, becoming suspicious of everything and everybody.

Wingo was saying, "My opinion's the guy's gone under. He's cooling his heels for a while, until everything quiets down." He paused, water drumming down on the table. "Either that or he hit last night and no one's found the body yet."

I said nothing, my irritation becoming acute.

"Don't know, though." His voice was muffled by splashing water. "Kind of hard to believe he'd try it. Too risky, you ask me. But I know some of the theories. They say some guys like this get really bold after a while. Like they're jerking everybody around, when the truth is they want to be caught. Could be he can't help himself and is begging for someone to stop him . . ."

"Wingo . . ." I warned.

He didn't seem to hear me and went on, "Has to be

some kind of sickness. He knows he's sick. I'm pretty sure of it. Maybe he's begging someone to save him from himself . . ."

"Wingo!" I raised my voice and spun around in my chair. He'd turned off the water but it was too late. My words were out and startlingly loud in the still, empty suite –

"He doesn't want to be caught!"

His lips parted in surprise, his face stricken by my sharpness. "Gee. I didn't mean to upset you, Dr. Scarpetta. I . . ."

"I'm not upset," I snapped. "But people like this bastard don't want to be caught, okay? He isn't *sick*, okay? He's anti-social, he's evil and he does it because he *wants to*, okay?"

Shoes quietly squeaking, he slowly got a sponge out of a sink and began wiping down the sides of the table. He wouldn't look at me.

I stared after him in a defeated way.

He didn't look up from his cleaning.

I felt bad. "Wingo?" I pushed back from the desk. "Wingo?" He reluctantly came over to me, and I lightly touched his arm. "I apologize. I have no reason to be short with you."

"No problem," he said, and the uneasiness in his eyes unnerved me. "I know what you're going through. With what's been happening and all. Makes me crazy, you know. Like I'm sitting around all the time trying to figure out something to do. All this stuff you're getting hit with these days and I can't figure out anything. I just, well, I just wish I could do something . . ."

So that was it! I hadn't hurt his feelings as much as I had reinforced his worries. Wingo was worried about *me*. He knew I wasn't myself these days, that I was strung tight to the point of breaking. Maybe it was becoming apparent to everyone else, too. The leaks, the computer violation, the mislabeled slides. Maybe no one would be surprised if I were eventually accused of incompetence . . .

"We saw it coming," people would say. "She was getting unhinged."

For one thing, I wasn't sleeping well. Even when I tried to relax, my mind was a machine with no Off switch. It ran on and on until my brain was overheated and my nerves were humming like power lines.

Last night I had tried to cheer up Lucy by taking her out to dinner and a movie. The entire time we were inside the restaurant and the theater I was waiting for my pager to go off, and every so often I tested it to make sure the batteries were still charged. I didn't trust the silence.

By 3:00 P.M. I'd dictated two autopsy reports and demolished a stack of micro dictations. When I heard my phone ring as I was getting on the elevator, I dashed back to my office and snatched up the receiver.

It was Bill.

"We still on?"

I couldn't say no. "Looking forward to it," I replied with enthusiasm I didn't feel. "But I'm not sure my company is worth writing home about these days."

"I won't write home about it, then."

I left the office.

It was another sunny day, but hotter. The grass border around my building was beginning to look parched, and I heard on the radio as I was driving home that the Hanover tomato crop was going to be damaged if we didn't get more rain. It had been a peculiar and volatile spring. We had long stretches of sunny, windy weather, and then quite out of nowhere, a fierce black army of clouds would march across the sky. Lightning would knock out electricity all over the city, and the rain would billow down in sheets. It was like dashing a bucket of water in the face of a thirsty man – it happened too fast for him to drink a drop.

Sometimes I was struck by certain parallels in life. My relationship with Bill had been little different from the weather. He marched in with an almost ferocious beauty, and I discovered all I wanted was a gentle rain, something quiet to quench the longing of my heart. I was looking forward to seeing him tonight, and yet I wasn't.

He was punctual, as always, and drove up at five exactly.

"It's good and it's bad," he remarked when we were on my back patio lighting the grill.

"Bad?" I asked. "I don't think you mean it quite like that, Bill."

The sun was at a sharp angle and still very hot, but clouds were streaming across the face of it, throwing us into intervals of shade and white light. The wind had whipped up and the air was pregnant with change.

He wiped his forehead on his shirtsleeve and squinted at me. A gust of wind bent the trees and sent a paper towel fluttering across the patio. "Bad, Kay, because his getting quiet may mean he's left the area."

We backed away from the smoldering coals and sipped from bottles of beer. I couldn't endure the thought that the killer might have moved on. I wanted him here. At least we were familiar with what he was doing. My nagging fear was he might begin striking in other cities where the cases would be worked by detectives and medical examiners who did not know what we knew. Nothing could foul up an investigation like a multijurisdictional effort. Cops were jealous of their turf. Each investigator wanted to make the arrest, and he thought he could work the case better than anyone else. It got to the point one thought a case belonged to him.

I supposed I was not above feeling possessive either. The victims had become my wards, and their only hope for justice was for their killer to be caught and prosecuted here. A person can be charged with only so many capital murders, and a conviction somewhere else might preclude a trial here. It was an outrageous thought. It would be as if the deaths of the women in Richmond were practice, a warm-up, and utterly in vain. Maybe it would turn out that everything happening to me was in vain, too.

Bill was squirting more lighter fluid on the charcoal. He backed away from the grill and looked at me, his face flushed from the heat. "How about your computer?" he asked. "Anything new?"

I hesitated. There was no point in my being evasive. Bill knew very well that I'd ignored Amburgey's orders and hadn't changed the password or done anything else to, quote, "secure" my data. Bill was standing right over me last Monday night when I activated answer mode and set the echo on again as if I were inviting the perpetrator to try again. Which was exactly what I was doing.

"It doesn't appear anyone else has gotten in, if that's what you mean."

"Interesting," he mused, taking another swallow of beer. "It doesn't make much sense. You'd think the person would try to get into Lori Petersen's case."

"She isn't in the computer," I reminded him. "Nothing new is going into the computer until these cases are no longer under active investigation."

"So the case isn't in the computer. But how's the person getting in going to know that unless she looks?"

"*She*?"

"She, he – whoever."

"Well, she – he – whoever looked the first time and couldn't pull up Lori's case."

"Still doesn't make a lot of sense, Kay," he insisted. "Come to think of it, it doesn't make a lot of sense someone would have tried in the first place. Anybody who knows much about computer entry would have realized a case autopsied on a Saturday isn't likely to be in the office data base by Monday."

"Nothing ventured, nothing gained," I muttered.

I was edgy around Bill. I couldn't seem to relax or give myself up to what should have been a lovely evening.

Inch-thick ribeyes were marinating in the kitchen. A bottle of red wine was breathing on the counter. Lucy was making the salad, and she was in fine spirits considering we hadn't heard a word from her mother, who was off somewhere with her illustrator. Lucy seemed perfectly content. In her fantasies she was beginning to believe she would never leave, and it troubled me that she'd begun hinting at how nice it would be "when Mr. Boltz" and I "got married."

Sooner or later I would have to dash her dreams against the hard rock of reality. She would be going home just as soon as her mother returned to Miami, and Bill and I were not going to get married.

I'd begun scrutinizing him as though for the first time. He was staring pensively at the flaming charcoal, his beer absently cradled in both hands, the hair on his arms and legs gold like pollen in the sun. I saw him through a veil of rising heat and smoke, and it seemed a symbol of the distance growing between us.

Why did his wife kill herself with his gun? Was it simply utilitarian, that his gun was the most convenient means of instantly snuffing herself out? Or was it her way of punishing him for sins I knew nothing of?

His wife shot herself in the chest while she was sitting up in bed – in their bed. She pulled the trigger that Monday morning just hours, maybe even minutes, after they made love. Her PERK was positive for sperm. The faint scent of perfume still lingered on her body when I examined her at the scene. What was the last thing Bill said to her before he left for work?

"Earth to Kay . . ."

My eyes focused. Bill was staring at me. "Off some-where?" he asked, slipping an arm around my waist, his breath close to my cheek. "Can I come?"

"I was just thinking."

"About what? And don't tell me it's about the office . . ."

I came out with it. "Bill, there's some paperwork missing from one of the case files you, Amburgey and Tanner were looking through the other day . . ."

His hand kneading the small of my back went still. I could feel the anger in the pressure of his fingers. "What paperwork?"

"I'm not real sure," I nervously replied. I didn't dare get specific, didn't dare mention the PERK label missing from

186

Lori Petersen's file. "I was just wondering if you may have noticed anyone accidentally picking up anything –"

He abruptly removed his arm and blurted out, "Shit. Can't you push these goddam cases out of your mind for one goddam evening?"

"Bill . . ."

"Enough, all right?" He plunged his hands into the pockets of his shorts and wouldn't look at me. "Jesus, Kay. You're going to make me crazy. They're dead. The women are fucking dead. Dead. Dead! You and I are alive. Life goes on. Or at least it's supposed to. It's going to do you in – it's going to do *us* in – if you don't stop obsessing over these cases."

But for the rest of the evening, while Bill and Lucy were chatting about inconsequential matters at the dinner table, my ear was turned toward the phone. I kept expecting it to ring. I was waiting for Marino's call.

When it rang early in the morning the rain was lashing my house and I was sleeping restlessly, my dreams fragmented, worrisome.

I fumbled for the receiver.

No one was there.

"Hello?" I said again as I flicked on the lamp.

In the background a television was faintly playing. I could hear the murmur of distant voices reciting lines I could not make out, and as my heart thudded against my ribs I slammed down the receiver in disgust.

It was Monday now, early afternoon. I was going over the preliminary lab reports of the tests the forensic scientists were conducting upstairs.

They had given the strangling cases a top priority. Everything else – blood alcohol levels, street drugs and bar-biturates – was temporarily on hold. I had four very fine scientific minds focused on trace amounts of a glittery residue that might be a cheap soap powder found in public restrooms all over the city.

The preliminary reports weren't exactly thrilling. So far, we couldn't even say very much about the known sample, the Borawash soap we used in the building. It was approximately twenty-five percent "inert ingredient, an abrasive," and seventy-five percent sodium borate. We knew this because the manufacturer's chemists had told us so. Scanning electron microscopy wasn't so sure. Sodium borate, sodium carbonate and sodium nitrate, for example, all came up as flat-out sodium in SEM. The trace amounts of the glittery residue came up the same way – as sodium. It's about as specific as saying something contains trace elements of lead, which is everywhere, in the air, in the soil, in the rain. We never tested for lead in gunshot residues because a positive result wouldn't mean a thing.

In other words, all that glitters isn't borax.

The trace evidence we'd found on the slain women's bodies could be something else, such as a sodium nitrate with uses ranging from fertilizer to a component of dynamite. Or it could be a crystal carbonate used as a constituent in photography developers. Theoretically, the killer could spend his working hours in a darkroom or in a greenhouse or on a farm. How many substances out there contain sodium? God only knows.

Vander was testing a variety of other sodium compounds in the laser to see if they sparkled. It was a quick way to mark items off our list.

Meanwhile, I had my own ideas. I wanted to know who else in the greater Richmond metropolitan area ordered Borawash, who in addition to the Health and Human Services Department. So I called the distributor in New Jersey. I got some secretary who referred me to sales who referred me to accounting who referred me to data processing who referred me to public relations who referred me back to accounting.

Next, I got an argument.

"Our list of clients is confidential. I'm not allowed to release that. You're what kind of examiner?"

"Medical examiner," I measured out each word. "This is Dr. Scarpetta, chief medical examiner in Virginia."

"Oh. You grant licenses to physicians, then –"

"No. We investigate deaths."

A pause. "You mean a coroner?"

There was no point in explaining that, no, I was not a coroner. Coroners are elected officials. They usually aren't forensic pathologists. You can be a gas station attendant and get elected coroner in some states. I let him think he was in the right ballpark and this only made matters worse.

"I don't understand. Are you suggesting someone is saying Borawash is fatal? That just isn't possible. To my knowledge, it isn't toxic, absolutely not. We've never had any problems of that nature. Did someone eat it? I'm going to have to refer you to my supervisor . . ."

I explained a substance that may be Borawash had been found at several related crime scenes but the cleanser had nothing to do with the deaths, the potential toxicity of the soap wasn't my concern. I told him I could get a court order, which would only waste more of his time and mine. I heard keys clicking as he went into a computer.

"I think you're going to want me to send this to you, ma'am. There are seventy-three names here, clients in Richmond."

"Yes, I would very much appreciate it if you would send me a printout as quickly as possible. But if you would, read me the list over the phone, please."

Decidedly lacking in enthusiasm, he did, and a lot of good it did. I didn't recognize most of the businesses except for the Department of Motor Vehicles, Central Supply for the city, and of course, HHSD. Collectively speaking, they included probably ten thousand employees, everyone from judges to public defenders to prosecutors to the entire police force to mechanics at the state and city garages. Somewhere within this great pool of people was a Mr. Nobody with a fetish for cleanliness.

I was returning to my desk a little after 3:00 P.M. with

another cup of coffee when Rose buzzed me and transferred a call.

"She's been dead awhile," Marino was saying.

I grabbed my bag and was out the door.

11

According to Marino, the police had yet to find any neighbors who had seen the victim over the weekend. A friend she worked with tried to call Saturday and Sunday and didn't get an answer. When the woman didn't show up to teach her one o'clock class the friend called the police. An officer arrived at the scene and went around to the back of the house. A window on the third floor was wide open. The victim had a roommate who apparently was out of town.

The address was less than a mile from downtown and on the fringes of Virginia Commonwealth University, a sprawling physical plant with more than twenty thousand students. Many of the schools that made up the university were located in restored Victorian homes and brownstones along West Main. Summer classes were in session, and students were walking and riding bicycles along the street. They lingered at small tables on restaurant terraces, sipping coffee, their books stacked by their elbows as they talked with friends and luxuriated in the sunny warmth of a lovely June afternoon.

Henna Yarborough was thirty-one and taught journalism at the university's School of Broadcasting, Marino had told me. She had moved to the city from North Carolina last fall. We knew nothing more about her except that she was dead and had been dead for several days.

Cops, reporters were all over the place.

Traffic was slow rolling past the dark red brick, three-story house, with a blue-and-green handmade flag fluttering over the entrance. There were windowboxes bright with pink and white geraniums, and a blue-steel slate roof with an Art Nouveau flower design in pale yellow.

The street was so congested I was forced to park almost half a block away, and it didn't escape my notice that the reporters were more subdued than usual. They scarcely stirred as I passed. They didn't jam cameras and microphones in my face. There was something almost militaristic in their bearing – stiff, quiet, definitely not at ease – as if they sensed this was another one. Number five. Five women like themselves or their wives and lovers who had been brutalized and murdered.

A uniformed man lifted the yellow tape barring the front doorway at the top of the worn granite steps. I went into a dim foyer and up three flights of wooden stairs. On the top landing I found the chief of police, several high-ranking officers, detectives and uniformed men. Bill was there, too, closest to an open doorway and looking in. His eyes briefly met mine, his face ashen.

I was hardly aware of him as I paused in the doorway and looked inside the small bedroom filled with the pungent stench of decomposing human flesh that is unlike any other odor on earth. Marino's back was to me. He was squatting on his heels and opening dresser drawers, his hands deftly shuffling through layers of neatly folded clothing.

The top of the dresser was sparsely arranged with bottles of perfume and moisturizers, a hairbrush and a set of electric curlers. Against the wall to the left of it was a desk, and the electric typewriter on top of it was an island in the midst of a sea of paper and books. More books were on a shelf overhead and stacked on the hardwood floor. The closet door was open a crack, the light off inside. There were no rugs or knick-knacks, no photographs or paintings on the walls – as if the bedroom had not been lived in very long or else her stay was temporary.

Far to my right was a twin bed. From a distance I saw disarrayed bedcovers and a splay of dark, tangled hair. Watching where I stepped, I went to her.

Her face was turned toward me, and it was so suffused, so bloated by decomposition, I could not tell what she had looked like in life except she was white, with shoulder-length dark brown hair. She was nude and resting on her left side, her legs drawn up, her hands behind her and tightly bound. It appeared the killer used the cords from venetian blinds, and the knots, the pattern, were joltingly familiar. A dark blue bedspread was thrown over her hips in a manner still ringing of careless cold contempt. On the floor at the foot of the bed was a pair of shorty pajamas. The top was buttoned, and it was slit from the collar to the hem. The bottoms appeared to be slit along the sides.

Marino slowly crossed the bedroom and stood next to me. "He climbed up the ladder," he said.

"What ladder?" I asked.

There were two windows. The one he was staring at was open and nearer the bed. "Against the brick outside," he explained, "there's an old iron fire escape ladder. That's how he got in. The rungs are rusty. Some of it flaked off and is on the sill, probably from his shoes."

"And he went out that way, too," I assumed aloud.

"Can't say for sure, but it would appear so. The door downstairs was locked. We had to bust it open. But out-side," he added looking toward the window again, "there's tall grass under the ladder. No footprints. It rained cats and dogs Saturday night so that don't help our cause worth a damn either."

"This place air-conditioned?" My skin was crawling, the airless room hot and damp and bristling with decay.

"Nope. No fans either. Not a single one. " He wiped his flushed face with his hand. His hair was clinging like gray string to his wet forehead, his eyes bloodshot and darkly ringed. Marino looked as if he hadn't been to bed or changed his clothes in a week.

"Was the window locked?" I asked.

"Neither of them was –" He got a surprised look on his face as we turned in unison toward the doorway. "What the hell . . .?"

A woman had started screaming in the foyer two floors below. Feet were scuffing, male voices were arguing.

"Get out of my house! Oh, God . . . Get out of my house, you goddam son of a bitch!" screamed the woman.

Marino abruptly brushed past me, and his steps thudded loudly on the wooden stairs. I could hear him saying something to someone, and almost immediately the screaming stopped. The loud voices faded to a murmur.

I began the external examination of the body.

She was the same temperature as the room, and rigor had already come and gone. She got cool and stiff right after death, and then as the temperature outside rose so did the temperature of her body. Finally, her stiffness passed, as if the initial shock of death vanished with time.

I did not have to pull back the bedspread much to see what was beneath it. For an instant, I wasn't breathing and my heart seemed to stop. I gently laid the spread back in place and began peeling off my gloves. There was nothing more I could do with her here. Nothing.

When I heard Marino coming back up the stairs, I turned to tell him to be sure the body came to the morgue wrapped in the bedcovers. But the words stuck in my throat. I stared in speechless astonishment.

In the doorway next to him was Abby Turnbull. What in God's name did Marino think he was doing? Had he lost his mind? Abby Turnbull, the ace reporter, the shark that made Jaws seem like a goldfish.

Then I noticed she was wearing sandals, a pair of blue jeans and a white cotton blouse that wasn't tucked in. Her hair was tied back. She wasn't wearing makeup. She carried no tape recorder or notepad, just a canvas tote bag.

Her wide eyes were riveted to the bed, her face twisted by terror.

"*God, no!*" As she placed her hand over her open mouth.

"It's her, then," Marino said in a low voice.

She moved closer, staring. "My God. Henna. Oh, my God . . ."

"This was her room?"

"Yes. Yes. Oh, please, God . . ."

Marino jerked his head, motioning a uniformed man I couldn't see to come upstairs and escort Abby Turnbull out. I heard their feet on the stairs, heard her moaning.

I quietly asked Marino, "You know what you're doing?"

"Hey. I always know what I'm doing."

"That was her screaming," I numbly went on. "Screaming at the police?"

"Nope. Boltz had just come down. She was yelling at him."

"Boltz?" I couldn't think.

"Can't say I blame her," he replied unemphatically. "It's her house. Can't blame her for not wanting us crawling all over the damn place, telling her she can't come in . . ."

"Boltz?" I asked idiotically. "Boltz told her she couldn't come in?"

"And a couple of the guys." Shrugging. "She's going to be something to talk to. Totally off the wall." His attention drifted to the body on the bed, and something flickered in his eyes. "This lady here's her sister."

The living room was filled with sunlight and potted plants. It was on the second floor, and had been recently and expensively refurbished. The polished hardwood floor was almost completely covered with a dhurrie rug of pale blue and green geometrical designs against a field of white, and the furniture was white and angular with small pillows in pastels. On the whitewashed walls was an enviable collection of abstract monotype prints by Richmond artist Gregg Carbo. It was an impractical room, one Abby designed with no one in mind but herself, I suspected. An impressive frosty lair, it bespoke success and a lack of sentiment and seemed very much in character with what I'd always thought of its creator.

Curled up in a corner of the white leather couch, she was nervously smoking a long thin cigarette. I'd never seen Abby up close, and she was so peculiar looking she was striking. Her eyes were irregular, one slightly greener than the other, and her full lips did not seem to belong on the same face as the prominent, narrow nose. She had brown hair, which was graying and just brushing her shoulders, and her cheekbones were high, her complexion finely lined at the corners of her eyes and mouth. Long-legged and slender, she was my age, perhaps a few years younger.

She stared at us with the unblinking glassy eyes of a frightened deer. A uniformed man left and Marino quietly shut the door.

"I'm real sorry. I know how hard this is . . ." Marino started in with the usual windup. He calmly explained the importance that she answer all questions, remember everything about her sister – her habits, her friends, her routines – in as much detail as she could. Abby sat woodenly and said nothing. I sat opposite her.

"I understand you've been out of town," he was saying.

"Yes." Her voice trembled and she shivered as if she were cold. "I left Friday afternoon for a meeting in New York."

"What sort of meeting?"

"A book. I'm in the process of negotiating a book contract. Had a meeting with my agent. Stayed over with a friend."

The microcassette recorder on top of the glass coffee table silently turned. Abby stared blindly at it.

"So, you have any contact with your sister while you was in New York?"

"I tried to call her last night to tell her what time my train was coming in." She took a deep breath. "When I

196

didn't get an answer, I was puzzled, I guess. Then I just assumed she'd gone out somewhere. I didn't try after I pulled into the station. The train station. I knew she had classes this afternoon. I got a cab. I had no idea. It wasn't until I got here and saw all the cars, the police . . ."

"How long's your sister been living with you?"

"Last year she and her husband separated. She wanted a change, time to think. I told her to come here. Told her she could live with me until she got settled or went back to him. That was fall. Late August. She moved in with me last August and started her job at the university."

"When was the last time you saw her?"

"Friday afternoon." Her voice rose and caught. "She drove me to the train station." Her eyes were welling.

Marino pulled a rumpled handkerchief out of a back pocket and handed it to her. "You have any idea what her plans for the weekend were?"

"Work. She told me she was going to stay in, work on class preparations. As far as I know, she didn't have any plans. Henna wasn't very outgoing, had one or two good friends, other professors. She had a lot of class preparation, told me she would do the grocery shopping on Saturday. That's all."

"And where was that? What store?"

"I have no idea. It doesn't matter. I know she didn't go. The other policeman in here a minute ago had me check the kitchen. She didn't go to the grocery store. The refrigerator's as bare as it was when I left. It must have happened Friday night. Like the other ones. All weekend I've been in New York and she's been here. Been here like this."

No one said anything for a moment. Marino was looking around the living room, his face unreadable. Abby shakily lit a cigarette and turned to me.

I knew what she was going to ask before the words were out.

"Is it like the other ones? I know you looked at her." She hesitated, trying to compose herself. She was like a violent

197

storm about to break when she quietly asked, "What did he do to her?"

I found myself giving her the "I won't be able to tell you anything until I've examined her in a good light" response.

"For God's sake, she's my sister!" she cried. "I want to know what the animal did to her! Oh, God! Did she suffer? Please tell me she didn't suffer . . ."

We let her cry, deep, heaving moans of naked anguish. Her pain carried her far beyond the realm where any mortal could reach her. We sat. Marino watched her with unwavering, unreadable eyes.

I hated myself at times like this, cold, clinical, the consummate professional unmoved by another person's pain. What was I supposed to say? Of course she suffered! When she found him inside her room, when she began to realize what was going to happen, her terror, which would have been that much worse because of what she'd read in the papers about the other murdered women, chilling accounts written by her own sister. And her pain, her physical pain.

"Fine. Of course you're not going to tell me," Abby began in rapid jerky sentences. "I know how it is. You're not going to tell me. She's my sister. And you're not going to tell me. You keep all your cards close to your vest. I know how it goes. And for what? How many does the bastard have to murder? Six? Ten? Fifty? Then maybe the cops figure it out?"

Marino continued to stare blandly at her. He said, "Don't blame the police, Miss Turnbull. We're on your side, trying to help –"

"Right!" She cut him off. "You and your help! Like a lot of help you were last week! Where the shit were you then?"

"Last week? What are you referring to, exactly?"

"I'm referring to the redneck who tailed me all the way home from the newspaper," she exclaimed. "He was right on top of me, turning everywhere I did. I even stopped at a store to get rid of him. Then I come out twenty minutes later and there he is again. The same goddam car! Following me! I get

198

home and immediately call the cops. And what do they do? *Nothing.* Some officer stops by *two hours later* to make sure everything's all right. I give him a description, even the plate number. Did he ever follow up? Hell no, I never heard a word. For all I know, the pig in the car's the one who did it! My sister's dead. Murdered. Because some cop couldn't be bothered!"

Marino was studying her, his eyes interested. "When exactly was this?"

She faltered. "Tuesday, I think. A week ago Tuesday. Late, maybe ten, ten-thirty at night. I worked late in the newsroom, finishing up a story . . ."

He looked confused. "Uh, correct me if I'm wrong, but I thought you was on the graveyard beat, six to two A.M., or something."

"That Tuesday one of the other reporters was working my beat. I had to come in early, during the day, to finish up something the editors wanted for the next edition."

"Yeah," Marino said. "Okay, so this car. When did it start following you?"

"It's hard to know. I didn't really notice it until several minutes after I'd pulled out of the parking deck. He could have been waiting for me. Maybe he saw me at some point. I don't know. But he was right on my rear bumper, his high beams on. I slowed down, hoping he'd go around me. He slowed down, too. I speeded up. Same thing. I couldn't shake him. I decided to go to Farm Fresh. I didn't want him following me home. He did anyway. He must have gone by and come back, waited for me in the parking lot or on a nearby street. Waited until I came back out and drove off."

"You positive it was the same car?"

"A new Cougar, black. I'm absolutely sure. I got a contact at DMV to run the plate number since the cops couldn't be bothered. It's a rental car. I've got the address of the dealership, the car's plate number written down if you're interested."

"Yeah, I'm interested," Marino told her.

She dug inside her tote bag and found a folded piece of notepaper. Her hand trembled as she gave it to him.

He glanced at it and tucked it inside a pocket. "So what then? The car followed you. It followed you all the way home?"

"I had no choice. I couldn't drive around all night. Couldn't do a damn thing. He saw where I live. I came in and went straight to the phone. I guess he drove past, went on. When I looked out the window, I didn't see him anywhere."

"You ever seen the car before?"

"I don't know. I've seen black Cougars before. But I can't say that I've ever seen that exact car before."

"You get a look at the driver?"

"It was too dark and he was behind me. But there was definitely just one person inside the car. Him, the driver."

"Him? You're sure about that?"

"All I saw was a big shape, someone with short hair, okay? Of course it was a *him*. It was awful. He was sitting rigidly, staring straight at the back of my head. Just this shape, staring. Right on my bumper. I told Henna. I told her about it. I told her to be careful, to keep an eye out for a black Cougar and if she saw a car like that near the house to call 911. She knew what was going on in the city. The murders. We talked about it. Dear God! I can't believe it! She knew! I told her not to leave her windows unlocked! To be careful!"

"So it was normal for her to have a window or two unlocked, maybe open."

Abby nodded and wiped her eyes. "She's always slept with windows open. It's hot in here sometimes. I was going to get air-conditioning, have it installed by July. I just moved in right before she came. In August. There was so much else to do and fall, winter, wasn't that far off. Oh, God. I told her a thousand times. She was always off in her own world. Just oblivious. I couldn't get it to sink in. Just like I never could get her to fasten her seatbelt. She's my baby sister. She's never liked me telling her what to do. Things slid right over her, it's like she didn't even hear them. I'd tell her. I'd tell her the things that go on, the crimes. Not just the murders, but the rapes, the robberies, all of it. And she'd get impatient. She didn't want to hear it. She'd say, 'Oh, Abby, you see only the horrible things. Can't we talk about something else?' I have a handgun. I told her to keep it by her bed when I wasn't here. But she wouldn't touch it. No way. I offered to teach her how to shoot it, to get her one of her own. But no way. No way! And now this! She's gone! Oh, God! And all these things I'm supposed to tell you about her, about her habits and everything, it doesn't matter!"

"It does matter. Everything matters . . ."

"None of it matters because I know it wasn't her he was after! He didn't even know about her! He was after me!"

Silence.

"What makes you think that?" Marino calmly asked.

"If it was him in the black car, then I know he was after me. No matter who he is, I'm the one who's been writing about him. He's seen my byline. He knows who I am."

"Maybe."

"Me! He was after me!"

"You may have been his target," Marino matter-of-factly told her. "But we can't know that for sure, Miss Turnbull. Me, I've got to consider all possibilities, like maybe he seen your sister somewhere, maybe on the campus or in a restaurant, a shop. Maybe he didn't know she lived with somebody, especially if he followed her while you was at work – if he followed her at night and saw her come in when you weren't home, I'm saying. He may not have had any idea you're her sister. It could be a coincidence. Was there any place she frequented, a restaurant, a bar, any place?"

Wiping her eyes again, she tried to remember. "There's a deli on Ferguson within walking distance of the school.

The School of Broadcasting. She ate lunch there once or twice a week, I think. She didn't go to bars. Now and then we ate out at Angela's on Southside but we were always together on those occasions – she wasn't alone. She may have gone other places, shops, I mean. I don't know. I don't know every single thing she did every minute of the day."

"You say she moved in last August. She ever leave, maybe for the weekend, take any trips, that sort of thing?"

"Why?" She was bewildered. "You thinking someone followed her, someone from out of town?"

"I'm just trying to ascertain when she was here and when she wasn't."

She said shakily, "Last Thursday she went back to Chapel Hill to see her husband and spend some time with a friend. She was gone most of the week, got back on Wednesday. Today classes started, the first day of classes for the summer session."

"He ever come here, the husband?"

"No," she warily replied.

"He have any history of being rough with her, of violence –"

"No!" she blurted out. "Jeff didn't do this to her! They both wanted a trial separation! There wasn't any animosity between them! The pig who did this is the same pig who's been doing it!"

Marino stared at the tape recorder on the table. A tiny red light was flashing. He checked the pockets of his jacket and looked irritated. "I'm gonna have to go out to the car for a minute."

He left Abby and me alone in the bright white living room.

There was a long, uncomfortable silence before she looked at me.

Her eyes were bloodshot, her face puffy. Bitterly, miserably, she said to me, "All those times I've wanted to talk to you. And now, here it is. This. You're probably secretly glad. I know what your opinion of me is. You probably think I deserve it. I get a dose of what the people I write about must feel. Poetic justice."

The remark cut me to the bone. I said with feeling, "Abby, you don't deserve this. I would never wish this on you or anyone."

Staring down at her tightly clenched hands, she painfully went on, "Please take care of her. Please. My sister. Oh, God. Please take care of Henna . . ."

"I promise I'll take care of her . . ."

"You can't let him get away with this! You can't!"

I didn't know what to say.

She looked up at me and I was startled by the terror in her eyes. "I don't understand anything anymore. I don't understand what's going on. All these things I've been hearing. And this happens. I tried. I tried to find out, tried to find out from you. Now this. I don't know who's us or them anymore!"

Quietly, I said, "I don't think I understand, Abby. *What* did you try to find out from me?"

She talked very fast. "That night. Earlier in the week. I tried to talk to you about it. But he was there . . ."

It was coming to me. I dully asked, "What night?"

She looked confused, as if she couldn't remember. "Wednesday," she said. "Wednesday night."

"You drove to my house late that night and then quickly drove off? Why?"

She stammered, "You . . . you had company."

Bill. I remembered we stood in the glare of the front porch light. We were in plain view and his car was parked in my drive. It was her. Abby was the one who drove up that night, and she saw me with Bill, but this didn't explain her reaction. Why did she panic? It seemed a frightened visceral reflex when she extinguished her headlights and slammed the car into reverse.

She was saying, "These investigations. I've heard things. Rumors. Cops can't talk to you. Nobody's supposed to talk to you. Something's screwed up and that's why all calls are being referred to Amburgey. I had to ask you! And now they're saying you screwed up the serology in the surgeon . . . Lori Petersen's case. That the entire investigation's screwed up because of your office and if it wasn't for that the cops might have caught the killer by now . . ." She was angry and uncertain, staring wildly at me. "I have to know if it's true. I have to know! I have to know what's going to happen to my sister!"

How did she know about the mislabeled PERK? Surely Betty wouldn't tell her. But Betty had concluded her serology tests on the slides, and copies – all copies of all lab reports – were being sent straight to Amburgey. Did he tell Abby? Did someone in his office tell her? Did he tell Tanner? Did he tell Bill?

"Where did you hear this?"

"I hear a lot of things." Her voice trembled.

I looked at her miserable face, at her body drawn in by grief, by horror. "Abby," I said very calmly, "I'm quite sure you hear a lot of things. I'm also quite sure a lot of them aren't true. Or even if there is a grain of truth, the interpretation is misleading, and perhaps you might ask yourself why someone would tell you these things, what this person's real motive is."

She wavered. "I just want to know if it's true, what I've heard. If your office is at fault."

I couldn't think how to respond.

"I'm going to find out anyway, I'll tell you that right now. Don't underestimate me, Dr. Scarpetta. The cops have screwed up big time. Don't think I don't know. They screwed up with me when that damn redneck followed me home. And they screwed up with Lori Petersen when she dialed 911 and no one responded until almost an hour later. When she was already dead!"

My surprise was visible.

"When this breaks," she went on, her eyes bright with tears, with rage, "the city's going to rue the day I was ever born! People are going to pay! I'll make sure certain people pay, and you want to know why?"

I was staring dumbly at her.

"Because nobody who counts gives a damn when women are raped and murdered! The same bastards who work the cases go out on the town and watch movies about women being raped, strangled, slashed. To them it's sexy. They like to look at it in magazines. They fantasize. They probably get their rocks off by looking at the scene photographs. The cops. They make *jokes* about it. I hear it. I hear them laughing at scenes, hear them laughing inside the ER!"

"They don't really mean it like that." My mouth was dry. "It's one of the ways they cope."

Footsteps were coming up the stairs.

Glancing furtively toward the door, she went into her tote bag and clumsily got out a business card and scribbled a number on it. "Please. If there's anything you can tell me after it's – it's done . . ." She took a deep breath. "Will you call me?" She handed me the card. "It's got my pager number. I don't know where I'll be. Not in this house. Not for a while. Maybe never."

Marino was back.

Abby's eyes fixed angrily on him. "I know what you're going to ask," she said as he shut the door. "And the answer's no. There weren't any men in Henna's life, nobody here in Richmond. She wasn't seeing anyone, she wasn't sleeping with anyone."

Wordlessly, he clicked in a new tape and depressed the Record button.

He slowly looked up at her. "What about you, Miss Turnbull?"

Her breath caught in her throat. Stammering, "I have a close relationship, am close to someone in New York. Nobody here. Just a lot of business associations."

"I see. And just what exactly's your definition of a business association?"

"What do you mean?" Her eyes got wide with fear.

He looked thoughtful for a moment, then casually said,

"What I'm wondering is if you're aware that this 'redneck' who followed you home the other night, has, in fact, been keeping an eye on you for several weeks now. The guy in the black Cougar. Well, he's a cop. Plainclothes, works out of Vice."

She stared at him in disbelief.

"See," Marino laconically went on, "that's why nobody got real upset when you called in the complaint, Miss Turnbull. Well, strike that. It would've upset me, if I'd known about it at the time – because the guy's supposed to be better than that. If he's following you, you're not supposed to know it, is what I'm saying."

He was getting chillier by the second, his words beginning to bite.

"But this particular cop don't like you none too well. Fact is, when I went out to the car a minute ago, I raised him on the radio, got the straight skinny from him. He admits he was hassling you deliberately, lost his cool a little bit when he was tailing you that night."

"What is this?" she cried in a spasm of panic. "He was harassing me because I'm a *reporter*?"

"Well, it's a little more personal than that, Miss Turnbull." Marino casually lit a cigarette. "You remember a couple years back you did that big exposé on the Vice cop who was dipping into the contraband and got himself hooked on coke? Sure, you remember that. He ended up eating his service revolver, blew his damn brains out. You gotta remember that clear as a bell. That particular Vice cop was the partner of the guy following you. Thought his interest in you would motivate him to do a good job. Looks like he went a little overboard . . ."

"*You!*" she cried incredulously. "You asked him to follow me? Why?"

"I'll tell you. Since it appears my friend overplayed his hand, the gig's up. You would have found out eventually he's a cop. May as well put all of it out on the table, right here in front of the doc, since, in a way, it concerns her, too."

Abby glanced frantically at me. Marino took his time tapping an ash.

He took another drag and said, "Just so happens the ME's office is taking a lot of heat right now because of these alleged leaks to the press, which translates directly into leaks to you, Miss Turnbull. Someone's been breaking into the doc's computer. Amburgey's twisting the blade in the doc, here, causing a lot of problems and making a lot of accusations. Me, I'm of a different opinion. I think the leaks got nothing to do with the computer. I think someone's breaking into the computer to make it look like that's where the information's coming from in order to disguise the fact that the only data base being violated is the one between Bill Boltz's ears."

"That's insane!"

Marino smoked, his eyes fixed on her. He was enjoying watching her squirm.

"I absolutely had nothing to do with any computer violations!" she exploded. "Even if I knew how to do such a thing, I would never, never, do it! I can't believe this! My sister's dead . . . Jesus Christ . . ." Her eyes were wild and swimming in tears. "Oh, God! What does any of this have to do with Henna?"

Marino coldly said, "I'm to the point of not having any idea who or what's got to do with anything. I do know some of the stuff you've been printing ain't common knowledge. Someone in the know's singing, singing to you. Someone's screwing up the investigation behind the scenes. I'm curious why anybody would be doing that unless he's got something to hide or something to gain."

"I don't know what you're getting –"

"See," he interrupted, "I just think it's a little strange that about five weeks ago, right after the second strangling, you did a big spread on Boltz, a day-in-the-life-of story. A big profile of the city's favorite golden boy. The two of you spend a day together, right? It just so happens I was out that night, saw the two of you driving away from Franco's

207

around ten o'clock. Cops is nosy, especially if we've got nothing better to do, you know, if it's slow on the street. And it just so happens I tagged along after you . . ."

"Stop it," she whispered, shaking her head side to side. "Stop it!"

He ignored her. "Boltz don't drop you off at the newspaper. See, he takes you to your house and when I breeze by several hours later – bingo! The fancy white Audi's still there, all the lights in the house off. What do you know? Right after that, all these juicy details start showing up in your stories. I guess that's your definition of a *professional association*."

Abby was trembling all over, her face in her hands. I couldn't look at her. I couldn't look at Marino. I was knocked so off balance it was barely penetrating – the unwarranted cruelty of his hitting her with this now, after all that had happened.

"I didn't sleep with him." Her voice shook so badly she could barely talk. "I didn't. I didn't want to. He . . . he took advantage of me."

"Right." Marino snorted.

She looked up and briefly shut her eyes. "I was with him all day. The last meeting we went to wasn't over until seven that night. I offered dinner, said the newspaper would buy him dinner. We went to Franco's. I had one glass of wine, that was all. One glass. I start getting woozy, just incredibly woozy. I hardly remember leaving the restaurant. The last thing I remember is getting into his car. Him reaching for my hand, saying something about how he'd never made it with a police reporter before. What happened that night, I don't remember any of it. I woke up early the next morning. He was there . . ."

"Which reminds me." Marino stabbed out the cigarette. "Where was your sister during all this?"

"Here. She was in her room, I guess. I don't remember. It doesn't matter. We were downstairs. In the living room. On the couch, on the floor, I don't remember – I'm not sure she even knew!"

He looked disgusted.

She hysterically went on, "I couldn't believe it. I was terrified, sick like I'd been poisoned. All I can figure is when I got up to go to the ladies' room at one point during dinner he slipped something in my drink. He knew he had me. He knew I wouldn't go to the cops. Who would believe me if I called and said the Commonwealth's attorney . . . he did such a thing? No one! No one would believe me!"

"You got that straight," Marino butted in. "Hey, he's a good-looking guy. He don't need to slip a lady a mickey to get her to give up the goods."

Abby screamed, "He's scum! He's probably done it a thousand times and gotten away with it! He threatened me, told me if I mentioned a word he'd make me out to be a slut, he'd ruin me!"

"Then what?" Marino demanded. "Then he feels guilty and starts leaking information to you?"

"No! I've had nothing to do with the bastard! If I got within ten feet of him I'd be afraid I'd blow his goddam head off! None of my information has come from him!"

It couldn't be true.

What Abby was saying. It couldn't be true. I was trying to ward off the statements. They were terrible, but they were adding up despite my desperate inward denials.

She must have recognized Bill's white Audi on the spot. That was why she panicked when she saw it parked in my drive. Earlier she found Bill inside her house and shrieked at him to leave because she hated the very sight of him.

Bill warned me she would stoop to anything, that she was vengeful, opportunistic and dangerous. Why did he tell me that? Why really? Was he laying the groundwork for his own defense should Abby ever accuse him?

He had lied to me. He didn't spurn her so-called advances when he drove her to her house after the interview. His car was still parked there early the next morning . . .

Images were flashing through my mind of the few occasions early on when Bill and I were alone on my living

209

room couch. I became sickened by the memory of his sudden aggression, the raw brute force that I attributed to whisky. Was this the dark side of him? Was the truth that he found pleasure only in overpowering? In taking?

He was here, inside this house, at the scene, when I arrived. No wonder he was so quick to respond. His interest was more than professional. He wasn't merely doing his job. He would have recognized Abby's address. He probably knew whose house it was before anybody else did. He wanted to see, to make sure.

Maybe he was even hoping the victim was Abby. Then he would never have to worry this moment would happen, that she would tell.

Sitting very still, I willed my face to turn to stone. I couldn't let it show. The wrenching disbelief. The devastation. Oh, God, don't let it show.

A telephone started ringing in some other room. It rang and rang and nobody answered it.

Footsteps were coming up the stairs, metal making muffled clangs against wood and radios blaring unintelligible static. Paramedics were carrying a stretcher up to the third floor.

Abby was fumbling with a cigarette and she suddenly threw it and the burning match into the ashtray.

"If it's true you've been having me followed" – she lowered her voice, the room filled with her scorn – "and if your reason was to see if I was meeting him, sleeping with him to get information, then you ought to know what I'm saying is true. After what happened that night I haven't been anywhere near the son of a bitch. "

Marino didn't say a word.

His silence was his answer.

Abby had not been with Bill since.

Later, as paramedics were carrying the stretcher down, Abby leaned against the door frame, clutching it with white-knuckled emotion. She watched the white shape of her sister's body go past, stared after the retreating men, her face a pallid mask of abject grief.

I gripped her arm with unspoken feeling and went out in the wake of her incomprehensible loss. The odor lingered on the stairs, and when I stepped into the dazzling sunshine on the street, for a moment I was blind.

12

Henna Yarborough's flesh, wet from repeated rinsings, glistened like white marble in the overhead light. I was alone inside the morgue with her, suturing the last few inches of the Y incision, which ran in a wide seam from her pubis to her sternum and forked over her chest.

Wingo took care of her head before he left for the night. The skullcap was exactly in place, the incision around the back of her scalp neatly closed and completely covered by her hair, but the ligature mark around her neck was like a rope burn. Her face was bloated and purple, and neither my efforts nor those of the funeral home were ever going to change that.

The buzzer sounded rudely from the bay. I glanced up at the clock. It was shortly after 9:00 P.M.

Cutting the twine with a scalpel, I covered her with a sheet and peeled off my gloves. I could hear Fred, the security guard, saying something to someone down the hall as I pulled the body onto a gurney and began to wheel it into the refrigerator.

When I re-emerged and shut the great steel door, Marino was leaning against the morgue desk and smoking a cigarette.

He watched me in silence as I collected evidence and tubes of blood and began to initial them.

"Find anything I need to know?"

"Her cause of death is asphyxiation due to strangulation due to the ligature around her neck," I said mechanically.

"What about trace?" He tapped an ash on the floor.

"A few fibers –"

"Well," he interrupted, "I gotta couple of things."

"Well," I said in the same tone, "I want to get the hell out of here."

"Yo, Doc. Exactly what I had in mind. Me, I'm thinking of taking a ride."

I stopped what I was doing and stared at him. His hair was clinging damply to his pate, his tie was loose, his short-sleeved white shirt was badly wrinkled in back as if he'd been sitting for a long time in his car. Strapped under his left arm was his tan shoulder holster with its long-barreled revolver. In the harsh glare of the overhead light he looked almost menacing, his eyes deeply set in shadows, his jaw muscles flexing.

"Think you need to come along," he added unemphatically. "So, I'll just wait while you get out of your scrubs there and call home."

Call home? How did he know there was anyone at home I needed to call? I'd never mentioned my niece to him. I'd never mentioned Bertha. As far as I was concerned, it was none of Marino's goddam business I even had a home.

I was about to tell him I had no intention of riding anywhere with him when the hard look in his eyes stopped me cold.

"All right," I muttered. "All right."

He was still leaning against the desk smoking as I walked across the suite and went into the locker room. Washing my face in the sink, I got out of my gown and back into skirt and blouse. I was so distracted, I opened my locker and reached for my lab coat before I realized what I was doing. I didn't need my lab coat. My pocketbook, briefcase and suit jacket were upstairs in my office.

Somehow I collected all of these things and followed Marino to his car. I opened the passenger door and the interior light didn't go on. Slipping inside, I groped for the shoulder harness and brushed crumbs and a wadded paper napkin off the seat.

He backed out of the lot without saying a word to me. The scanner light blinked from channel to channel as dispatchers transmitted calls Marino didn't seem interested in and which often I didn't understand. Cops mumbled into the microphone. Some of them seemed to eat it.

"Three-forty-five, ten-five, one-sixty-nine on chan'l three."

"One-sixty-nine, switchin' ov'."

"You free?"

"Ten-ten. Ten-seventeen the breath room. With subj't."

"Raise me whenyurten-twen-fo'."

"Ten-fo'."

"Four-fifty-one."

"Four-fifty-one X."

"Ten-twenty-eight on Adam Ida Lincoln one-seven-zero . . ."

Calls went out and alert tones blared like a bass key on an electric organ. Marino drove in silence, passing through downtown where storefronts were barred with the iron curtains drawn at the end of the day. Red and green neon signs in windows garishly advertised pawnshops and shoe repairs and greasy-spoon specials. The Sheraton and Marriott were lit up like ships, but there were very few cars or pedestrians out, just shadowy clusters of peripatetics from the projects lingering on corners. The whites of their eyes followed us as we passed.

It wasn't until several minutes later that I realized where we were going. On Winchester Place we slowed to a crawl in front of 498, Abby Turnbull's address. The brownstone was a black hulk, the flag a shadow limply stirring over the entrance. There were no cars in front. Abby wasn't home. I wondered where she was staying now.

Marino slowly pulled off the street and turned into the narrow alleyway between the brownstone and the house next door. The car rocked over ruts, the headlights jumping and illuminating the dark brick sides of the buildings, sweeping over garbage cans chained to posts and broken bottles and other debris. About twenty feet inside this claustrophobic

214

passageway he stopped and cut the engine and the lights. Directly left of us was the backyard of Abby's house, a narrow shelf of grass girdled by a chain-link fence with a sign warning the world to "Beware" of a "Dog" I knew didn't exist.

Marino had the car searchlight out and the beam was licking over the rusting fire escape against the back of the house. All of the windows were closed, the glass glinting darkly. The seat creaked as he moved the light around the empty yard.

"Go on," he said. "I'm waiting to hear if you're thinking what I am."

I stated the obvious. "The sign. The sign on the fence. If the killer thought she had a dog, it should have given him pause. None of his victims had dogs. If they had, the women would probably still be alive."

"Bingo."

"And," I went on, "my suspicion is you're concluding the killer must have known the sign didn't mean anything, that Abby – or Henna – didn't have a dog. And how could he know that?"

"Yo. How could he know that," Marino echoed slowly, "unless he had a reason to know it?"

I said nothing.

He jammed in the cigarette lighter. "Like if maybe he'd been inside the house before."

"I don't think so . . ."

"Cut the playing-dumb act, Doc," he said quietly.

I got out my cigarettes, too, and my hands were trembling.

"I'm picturing it. I think you're picturing it. Some guy who's been inside Abby Turnbull's house. He don't know her sister's here, but he does know there ain't no damn dog. And Miss Turnbull here's someone he don't like none too well because she knows something he don't want anybody in the whole goddam world to know."

He paused. I could feel him glancing over at me, but I refused to look at him or say a word.

215

"See, he's already had his piece of her, right? And maybe he couldn't help himself when he did his number because he's got some kind of compulsion, some screw loose, so to speak. He's worried. He's worried she's going to tell. Shit. She's a goddam reporter. She *gets paid* to tell people's dirty secrets. It's going to come out, what he did."

Another glance my way, and I remained stonily silent.

"So what's he do? He decides to whack her and make her look like the other ones. Only little problem is he don't know about Henna. Don't know where Abby's bedroom is either, see, because when he's been inside the house in the past, he never got any farther than the living room. So he goes in the wrong bedroom – Henna's bedroom – when he breaks in last Friday night. Why? Because that's the one with the lights on, because Abby's out of town. Well, it's too late. He's committed himself. He's got to go through with it. He murders her . . ."

"He couldn't have done it." I was trying to keep my voice from shaking. "Boltz would never do such a thing. He's not a murderer, for God's sake."

Silence.

Then Marino slowly looked over at me and flicked an ash. "Interesting. I didn't mention no names. But since you did, maybe we ought to pursue the subject, go a little deeper."

I was quiet again. It was catching up to me and I could feel my throat swelling. I refused to cry. Dammit! I wasn't going to let Marino see me cry!

"Listen, Doc," he said, and his voice was considerably calmer, "I'm not trying to jerk you around, all right? I mean, what you do in private's none of my damn business, all right? You're both consenting adults, unattached. But I know about it. I've seen his car at your place . . ."

"My house?" I asked, bewildered. "What –"

"Hey. I'm all over this goddam city. You live in the city, right? I know your state car. I know your damn address, and I know his white Audi. I know when I seen it at your house on several occasions over the past few months he wasn't there taking a deposition . . ."

"That's right. Maybe he wasn't. And it's none of your business, either."

"Well, it is." He flicked the cigarette butt out the window and lit another one. "It is my business now because of what he done to Miss Turnbull. That makes me wonder what else he's been doing."

"Henna's case is virtually the same as the other ones," I coldly told him. "There's no doubt in my mind she was murdered by the same man."

"What about her swabs?"

"Betty will work on them first thing in the morning. I don't know . . ."

"Well, I'll save you the trouble, Doc. Boltz is a nonsecreter. I think you know that, too, have known it for months."

"There are thousands of men in the city who are nonsecreters. You could be one, for all I know."

"Yeah," he said shortly. "Maybe I could be, for all you know. But fact is, you don't know. Fact is, you do know about Boltz. When you posted his wife last year, you PERKed her and found sperm, her husband's sperm. It's right there on the damn lab report that the guy she had sex with right before she took herself out is a nonsecreter. Hell, even I remember that. I was at the scene, remember?"

I didn't respond.

"I wasn't going to rule out nothing when I first walked into that bedroom and found her sitting up in her pretty little nightie, a big hole in her chest. Me, I always think murder first. Suicide's last on my list because if you don't think murder first, it's a little late after the fact. The only friggin' mistake I made back then was not taking a suspect's kit from Boltz. Suicide seemed so obvious after you did the post I marked the case exceptionally cleared. Maybe I shouldn't have. Back then I had a good reason to get his blood, to make sure the sperm inside her was his. He said it was, said they had sex early that morning. I let it go. I didn't

217

get squat from him. Now I can't even ask. I don't got probable cause."

"You have to get more than blood," I said idiotically. "If he's A negative, B negative in the Lewis blood group system, you can't tell if he's a nonsecreter – you have to get saliva . . ."

"Yo. I know how to take a suspect kit, all right? It don't matter. We know what he is, right?"

I said nothing.

"We know the guy whacking these women is a nonsecreter. And we know Boltz would know the details of the crimes, know 'em so well he could take out Henna and make it look like the other ones."

"Well, get your kit and we'll get his DNA," I said angrily. "Just go ahead. That will tell you definitely."

"Hey. Maybe I will. Maybe I'll run him under the damn laser, too, and see if he sparkles."

The glittery residue on the mislabeled PERK flashed in my mind. Did the residue really come from my hands? Did Bill routinely wash his hands with Borawash soap?

"You found the sparkles on Henna's body?" Marino was asking.

"On her pajamas. The bedcovers, too."

Neither of us spoke for a while.

Then I said, "It's the same man. I know what my findings are. It's the same man."

"Yeah. Maybe it is. But that don't make me feel any better."

"You're sure what Abby said is true?"

"I buzzed by his office late this afternoon."

"You went to see him, to see Boltz?" I stammered.

"Oh, yeah."

"And did you get your confirmation?" My voice was rising.

"Yeah." He glanced over at me. "I got it more or less."

I didn't say anything. I was afraid to say anything.

"'Course, he denied everything and got right hot about it. Threatened to sue her for slander, the whole nine yards. He won't, though. No way he'll make a peep about it because he's lying and I know it and he knows I know it."

I saw his hand go toward his left outer thigh and I suddenly panicked. His microcassette recorder!

"If you're doing what I think you're doing . . ." I blurted out. "What?" he asked, surprised.

"If you've got a goddam tape recorder going . . ."

"Hey!" he protested. "I was scratching, all right? Hell, pat me down. Do a strip search if it'll make you feel better."

"You couldn't pay me enough."

He laughed. He was honestly amused.

He went on, "Want to know the truth? It makes me wonder what really happened to his wife."

I swallowed hard and said, "There was nothing suspicious about the physical findings. She had powder residues on her right hand –"

He cut me off. "Oh, sure. She pulled the trigger. I don't doubt that, but maybe we know why now, huh? Maybe he's been doing this for years. Maybe she found out."

Cranking the engine, he turned on his lights. Momentarily, we were rocking between houses and emerging on the street.

"Look." He wasn't going to give it a rest. "I don't mean to pry. Better put, it ain't my idea of a good time, okay? But you know him, Doc. You been seeing him, right?"

A transvestite was sashaying along a sidewalk, his yellow skirt swishing around his shapely legs, his false breasts firm and high, the false nipples erect beneath a tight white shell. Glassy eyes glanced our way.

"You been seeing him, right?" he asked again.

"Yes." My voice was almost inaudible.

"What about last Friday night?"

I couldn't remember at first. I couldn't think. The transvestite languidly turned around and went the other way.

"I took my niece to dinner and a movie."

"He with you?"

"No."

219

"You know where he was last Friday night?"

I shook my head.

"He didn't call or nothing?"

"No."

Silence.

"Shit," he muttered in frustration. "If only I'd known about it then, known what I know about him now. I would've driven past his crib. You know, checked to see where the hell he was. Shit."

Silence.

He tossed the cigarette butt out the window and lit up again. He was smoking one right after another. "So, how long you been seeing him?"

"Several months. Since April."

"He seeing any other ladies, or just you?"

"I don't think he's been seeing anybody else. I don't know. Obviously there's a lot about him I don't know."

He went on with the relentlessness of a threshing machine, "You ever pick up on anything? Anything *off* about him, I'm saying?"

"I don't know what you mean." My tongue was getting thick. I was almost slurring my words as if I were falling asleep.

"*Off*," he repeated. "Sex-wise."

I said nothing.

"He ever rough with you? Force anything?" A pause. "What's he like? He the animal Abby Turnbull described? Can you see him doing something like that, like what he done to her?"

I was hearing him and not hearing him. My thoughts were ebbing and flowing as if I were slipping in and out of consciousness.

". . . like aggression, I'm saying. Was he aggressive? You notice anything strange . . .?"

The images. Bill. His hands crushing me, tearing at my clothes, pushing me down hard into the couch.

". . . guys like that, they have a pattern. It ain't sex they're really after. They have to *take* it. You know, a conquest . . ."

He was so rough. He was hurting me. He thrust his tongue into my mouth. I couldn't breathe. It wasn't he. It was as if he'd become somebody else.

"Don't matter a damn he's good-looking, could have it when he wants it. You see that? People like that, they're *off*. OFF . . ."

Like Tony used to do when he was drunk and angry with me.

". . . I mean, he's a *friggin' rapist*, Doc. I know you don't want to hear it. But, goddam it, it's true. Seems like you might have picked up on something . . ."

He drank too much, Bill did. He was worse when he had too much to drink.

". . . happens all the time. You wouldn't believe the reports I get, these young ladies calling me to their cribs two months after the fact. They finally get around to telling someone. Maybe a friend convinces them to come forward with the info. Bankers, businessmen, politicians. They meet some babe in a bar, buy her a drink and slip in a little chloral hydrate. Boom. Next thing, she's waking up with this animal in her bed, feels like a friggin' truck's been run through her . . ."

He would never have tried such a thing with me. He cared about me. I wasn't an object, a stranger . . . Or maybe he'd simply been cautious. I know too much. He would never have gotten away with it.

". . . the toads get away with it for years. Some of 'em get away with it their whole lives. Go to their graves with as many notches on their belts as Jack the Giant Killer . . ."

We were stopped at a red light. I had no idea how long we'd been sitting here, not moving.

"That's the right allusion, ain't it? The drone who killed flies, put a notch on his belt for each one . . ."

The light was a bright red eye.

"He ever do it to you, Doc? Boltz ever rape you?"

"What?" I slowly turned toward him. He was staring straight ahead, his face pale in the red glow of the traffic light.

221

"What?" I asked again. My heart was pounding.

The light blinked from red to green, and we were moving again.

"Did he ever rape you?" Marino demanded, as if I were someone he didn't know, as if I were one of the "babes" whose "cribs" he was called to in the past.

I could feel the blood creeping up my neck.

"He ever hurt you, try to choke you, anything like . . ."

Rage exploded from me. I was seeing flecks of light. As if something were shorting out. Blinded as blood pounded inside my head. *"No! I've told you every goddam thing I know about him! Every goddam thing I'm going to tell you! PERIOD!"*

Marino was stunned into silence.

I didn't know where we were at first.

The great white clock face floated directly ahead as shadows and shapes materialized into the small trailer park of mobile unit laboratories beyond the back parking lot. There was no one else around as we crept to a halt beside my state car.

I unfastened my seatbelt. I was trembling all over.

Tuesday it rained. Water poured from gray skies and my wipers couldn't clear the windshield fast enough. I was part of the barely moving string of traffic creeping along the interstate.

The weather mirrored my mood. The encounter with Marino left me feeling physically sick, hung over. How long had he known? How often had he seen the white Audi parked in my drive? Was it more than idle curiosity when he cruised past my house? He wanted to see how the uppity lady chief lived. He probably knew what the Commonwealth paid me and what my mortgage was each month.

Spitting flares forced me to merge into the left lane, and as I crept past an ambulance, and police directing traffic around a badly mangled van, my dark thoughts were interrupted by the radio.

". . . Henna Yarborough was sexually assaulted and strangled, and it is believed she was murdered by the same man who has killed four other Richmond women in the past two months . . ."

I turned up the volume and listened to what I'd already heard several times since leaving my house. Murder seemed to be the only news in Richmond these days.

". . . the latest development. According to a source close to the investigation, Dr. Lori Petersen may have attempted to dial 911 just before she was murdered . . ."

This juicy revelation had been on the front page of the morning newspaper.

". . . Director of Public Safety Norman Tanner was reached at his home . . ."

Tanner read an obviously prepared statement. "The police bureau has been apprised of the situation. Due to the sensitivity of these cases, I can't make any comment . . ."

"Do you have any idea who the source of this information is, Mr. Tanner?" the reporter asked.

"Not at liberty to make any comments about that . . ."

He couldn't comment because he didn't know.

But I did.

The so-called source close to the investigation had to be Abby herself. Her byline was nowhere to be found. Obviously, her editors would have taken her off the stories. She was no longer reporting the news, now she was making it, and I remembered her threat: "Someone will pay . . ." She wanted Bill to pay, the police to pay, the city to pay, God Himself to pay. I was waiting for news of the computer violation and the mislabeled PERK. The person who would pay was going to be me.

I didn't get to the office until almost eight-thirty, and by then the phones were already ringing up and down the hall.

"Reporters," Rose complained as she came in and deposited a wad of pink telephone message slips on my blotter. "Wire services, magazines and a minute ago some guy from New Jersey who says he's writing a book."

I lit a cigarette.

"The bit about Lori Petersen calling the police," she added, her face lined with anxiety. "How awful, if it's true . . ."

"Just keep sending everybody across the street," I interrupted. "Anybody who calls about these cases gets directed to Amburgey."

He had already sent me several electronic memos demanding I have a copy of Henna Yarborough's autopsy report on his desk "immediately." In the most recent memo, "immediately" was underlined and included was the insulting remark "Expect explanation about *Times* release."

Was he implying I was somehow responsible for this latest "leak" to the press? Was he accusing me of telling a reporter about the aborted 911 call?

Amburgey would get no explanation from me. He wasn't going to get a damn thing from me today, not even if he sent twenty memos and appeared in person.

"Sergeant Marino's here," Rose quite unnerved me by adding. "Do you want to see him?"

I knew what he wanted. In fact, I'd already made a copy of my report for him. I supposed I was hoping he'd stop by later in the day, when I was gone.

I was initialing a stack of toxicology reports when I heard his heavy footsteps down the hall. When he came in, he was wearing a dripping-wet navy blue rain slicker. His sparse hair was plastered to his head, his face haggard.

"About last night . . ." he ventured as he approached my desk.

The look in my eyes shut him up.

Ill at ease, he glanced around as he unsnapped his slicker and dug inside a pocket for his cigarettes. "Raining cats and dogs out there," he muttered. "Whatever the hell that means. Don't make any sense, when you think of it." A pause. "'Sposed to burn off by noon."

Wordlessly, I handed him a photocopy of Henna Yarborough's autopsy report, which included Betty's preliminary serological findings. He didn't take the chair on the other side of my desk but stood where he was, dripping on my rug, as he began to read.

When he got to the gross description, I could see his eyes riveted about halfway down the page. His face was hard when he looked at me and asked, "Who all knows about this?"

"Hardly anybody."

"The commissioner seen it?"

"No."

"Tanner?"

"He called a while ago. I told him only her cause of death. I made no mention of her injuries."

He perused the report a little while longer. "Anybody else?" he asked without looking up.

"No one else has seen it."

Silence.

"Nothing in the papers," he said. "Not on the radio or the tube either. In other words, our leak out there don't know these details."

I stared stonily at him.

"Shit." He folded the report and tucked it inside a pocket. "The guy's a damn Jack the Ripper." Glancing at me, he added, "I take it you ain't heard a peep from Boltz. If you do, dodge him, make yourself scarce."

"And what's that supposed to mean?" The mere mention of Bill's name physically bit into me.

"Don't take his call, don't see him. Whatever's your style. I don't want him having a copy of anything right now. Don't want him seeing this report or knowing anything more than he already knows."

"You're still considering him a suspect?" I asked as calmly as possible.

"Hell, I'm not sure what I'm considering anymore," he retorted. "Fact is, he's the CA and has a right to whatever he wants, okay? Fact also is I don't give a rat's ass if he's the damn governor. I don't want him getting squat. So I'm just asking you to do what you can to avoid him, to give him the slip."

Bill wouldn't be by. I knew I wouldn't hear from him. He knew what Abby had said about him, and he knew I was present when she said it.

"And the other thing," he went on, snapping up his slicker and turning the collar up around his ears, "if you're gonna be pissed at me, then be pissed. But last night I was just doing my job and if you're thinking I enjoyed it, you're flat-out wrong."

He turned around at the sound of a throat clearing. Wingo hesitated in my doorway, his hands in the pockets of his stylish white linen trousers.

A look of disgust passed over Marino's face, and he rudely brushed past Wingo and left.

Nervously jingling change, Wingo came to the edge of my desk and said, "Uh, Dr. Scarpetta, there's another camera crew in the lobby . . ."

"Where's Rose?" I asked, slipping off my glasses. My eyelids felt as if they were lined with sandpaper.

"In the ladies' room or something. Uh, you want me to tell the guys to leave or what?"

"Send them across the street," I said, adding irritably, "just like we did to the last crew and the crew before that."

"Sure," he muttered, and he made no move to go anywhere. He was nervously jingling change again.

"Anything else?" I asked with forced patience.

"Well," he said, "there's something I'm curious about. It's about him, uh, about Amburgey. Uh, isn't he an antismoker and makes a lot of noise about it, or have I got him mixed up with somebody else?"

My eyes lingered on his grave face. I couldn't imagine why it mattered as I replied, "He's strongly opposed to smoking and frequently takes public stands on the issue."

"Thought so. Seems like I've read stuff about it on the editorial page, heard him on TV, too. As I understand it, he plans to ban smoking from all HHSD buildings by next year."

"That's right," I replied, my irritation flaring. "By this time

226

next year, your chief will be standing outside in the rain and cold to smoke – like some guilt-ridden teenager." Then I looked quizzically at him and asked, "Why?"

A shrug. "Just curious." Another shrug. "I take it he used to smoke and got converted or something."

"To my knowledge, he has never smoked," I told him.

My telephone rang again, and when I glanced up from my call sheet, Wingo was gone.

If nothing else, Marino was right about the weather. That afternoon I drove to Charlottesville beneath a dazzling blue sky, the only evidence of this morning's storm the mist rising from the rolling pastureland on the roadsides.

Amburgey's accusations continued to gnaw at me, so I intended to hear for myself what he had actually discussed with Dr. Spiro Fortosis. At least this was my rationale when I had made an appointment with the forensic psychiatrist. Actually, it wasn't my only reason. We'd known each other from the beginning of my career, and I'd never forgotten he had befriended me during those chilly days when I attended national forensic meetings and scarcely knew a soul. Talking to him was the closest I could comfortably get to unburdening myself without going to a shrink. He was in the hallway of the dimly lit fourth floor of the brick building where his department was located. His face broke into a smile, and he gave me a fatherly hug, planting a light peck on the top of my head.

Professor of medicine and psychiatry at UVA, he was older by fifteen years, his hair white wings over his ears, his eyes kindly behind rimless glasses. Typically, he was dressed in a dark suit, a white shirt and a narrow striped tie that had been out of fashion long enough to come into vogue again. I'd always thought he could be a Norman Rockwell painting of the "town doctor."

"My office is being repainted," he explained, opening a dark wooden door halfway down the hall. "So if it won't bother you being treated like a patient, we'll go in here."

"Right now I feel like one of your patients," I said as he shut the door behind us.

The spacious room had all the comforts of a living room, albeit a somewhat neutral, emotionally defused one.

I settled into a tan leather couch. Scattered about were pale abstract watercolors and several nonflowering potted plants. Absent were magazines, books and a telephone. The lamps on end tables were switched off, the white designer blinds drawn just enough to allow sunlight to seep peacefully into the room.

"How's your mother, Kay?" Fortosis said as he pulled up a beige wing chair.

"Surviving. I think she'll outlive all of us."

He smiled. "We always think that of our mothers, and unfortunately it's rarely true."

"Your wife and daughters?"

"Doing quite well." His eyes were steady on me. "You look very tired."

"I suppose I am."

He was quiet for a moment.

"You're on the faculty of VMC," he began, in his mild unthreatening way. "I've been wondering if you might have known Lori Petersen in life."

With no further prompting, I found myself telling him what I had not admitted to anyone else. My need to verbalize it was overwhelming.

"I met her once," I said. "Or at least I'm fairly sure of it."

I had probed my memory exhaustively, especially during those quiet, introspective times when I was driving to or from work, or when I was out in my yard, tending to my roses. I would see Lori Petersen's face and try to superimpose it on the vague image of one of the countless VMC students gathered around me at labs, or in the audiences at lectures. By now, I'd convinced myself that when I studied the photographs of her inside her house, something clicked. She looked familiar.

Last month I had given a Grand Rounds lecture, "Women

228

in Medicine." I remembered standing behind the podium and looking out over a sea of young faces lining the tiers rising up to the back of the medical college auditorium. The students had brought their lunches and were sitting comfortably in the red-cushioned seats as they ate and sipped their soft drinks. The occasion was like all others before it, nothing extraordinary or particularly memorable about it, except retrospectively.

I did not know for a fact but believed Lori was one of the women who came forward afterward to ask questions. I saw the hazy image of an attractive blonde in a lab coat. The only feature I remembered clearly was her eyes, dark green and tentative, as she asked me if I really thought it was possible for a woman to manage a family and a career as demanding as medicine. This stood out because I momentarily faltered. I managed one but certainly not the other.

Obsessively I'd replayed that scene, going over and over it in my mind, as if the face would come into focus if I conjured it up enough. Was it she or wasn't it? I would never be able to walk the halls of VMC again without looking for that blond physician. I did not think I would find her. I think she was Lori briefly appearing before me like a ghost from a future horror that would relegate her to nothing but a past.

"Interesting," Fortosis remarked in his thoughtful way. "Why do you suppose it's important that you met her then or at any other time?"

I stared at the smoke drifting up from my cigarette. "I'm not sure, except that it makes her death more real."

"If you could go back to that day, would you?"

"Yes."

"What would you do?"

"I would somehow warn her," I said. "I would somehow undo what he did."

"What her killer did?"

"Yes."

"Do you think about him?"

229

"I don't want to think about him. I just want to do everything I can to make sure he is caught."

"And punished?"

"There's no punishment equal to the crime. No punishment would be enough."

"If he's put to death, won't that be punishment enough, Kay?"

"He can die only once."

"You want him to suffer, then." His eyes wouldn't let me go.

"Yes," I said.

"How? Pain?"

"Fear," I said. "I want him to feel the fear they felt when they knew they were going to die."

*

I wasn't aware of how long I'd talked but the inside of the room was darker when I finally stopped.

"I suppose it's getting beneath my skin in a way other cases haven't," I admitted.

"It's like dreams." He leaned back in the chair and lightly tapped his fingertips together. "People often say they don't dream, when it's more accurate to say that they *don't remember* their dreams. It gets under our skin, Kay. All of it does. We just manage to cage in most of the emotions so they don't devour us."

"Obviously, I'm not managing that too well these days, Spiro."

"Why?"

I suspected he knew very well but he wanted me to say it. "Maybe because Lori Petersen was a physician. I relate to her. Maybe I'm projecting. I was her age once."

"In a sense, you *were* her once."

"In a sense."

"And what happened to her – it could have been you?"

"I don't know if I've pushed it that far."

"I think you have." He smiled a little. "I think you've been pushing a lot of things pretty far. What else?"

230

Amburgey. What did Fortosis actually say to him?

"There are a lot of peripheral pressures."

"Such as?"

"Politics." I brought it up.

"Oh, yes." He was still tapping his fingertips together. "There's always that."

"The leaks to the press. Amburgey's concerned they might be coming from my office." I hesitated, looking for any sign that he was already privy to this.

His impassive face told me nothing.

"According to him, it's your theory the news stories are making the killer's homicidal urge peak more quickly, and therefore the leaks could be indirectly responsible for Lori's death. And now Henna Yarborough's death, too. I'll be hearing that next, I'm sure."

"Is it possible the leaks are coming from your office?"

"Someone – an outsider – broke into our computer data base. That makes it possible. Better put, it places me in a somewhat indefensible position."

"Unless you find out who's responsible," he matter-of-factly stated.

"I don't see a way in the world to do that." I pressed him "You talked to Amburgey."

He met my eyes. "I did. But I think he's overemphasized what I said, Kay. I would never go so far as to claim information allegedly leaked from your office is responsible for the last two homicides. The two women would be alive, in other words, were it not for the news accounts. I can't say that. I didn't say that."

I was sure my relief was visible.

"However, if Amburgey or anyone else intends to make a big deal of the so-called leaks that may have come from your office computer, I'm afraid there isn't much I can do about it. In truth, I feel strongly there's a significant link between publicity and the killer's activity. If sensitive information is resulting in more inflammatory stories and bigger headlines, then yes, Amburgey – or anybody else for that matter – may

231

take what I objectively say and use it against your office." He looked at me for a long moment. "Do you understand what I'm saying?"

"You're saying you can't defuse the bomb," I replied, my spirits falling.

Leaning forward, he flatly told me, "I'm saying I can't defuse a bomb I can't even see. What bomb? Are you suggesting someone's setting you up?"

"I don't know," I replied carefully. "All I can tell you is the city stands to have a lot of egg on its face because of the 911 call Lori Petersen made to the police right before she was murdered. You read about that?"

He nodded, his eyes interested.

"Amburgey called me in to discuss the matter long before this morning's story. Tanner was there. So was Boltz. They said there might be a scandal, a lawsuit. At this point, Amburgey mandated that all further information to the press would have to be routed through him. No comments whatsoever are to come from me. He said you think the leaks to the press, the subsequent stories are escalating the killer's activities. I was questioned at length about the leaks, about the potentiality of their source being my office. I had no choice but to admit someone's gotten into our data base."

"I see."

"As all this progressed," I continued, "I began to get the unsettling impression that if any scandal erupts, it's going to be over what's supposedly been happening inside my office. The implication: I've hurt the investigation, perhaps indirectly caused more women to die . . ." I paused. My voice was starting to rise. "In other words, I have visions of everyone ignoring the city's screwup with the 911 call because everyone's so busy being enraged with the OCME, with me."

He made no comment.

I lamely added, "Maybe I'm getting bent over nothing."

"Maybe not."

It wasn't what I wanted to hear.

"Theoretically," he explained, "it could happen exactly as

you've just outlined it. If certain parties want it to happen that way, because they're trying to save their own skins. The medical examiner is an easy scapegoat. The public, in the main, doesn't understand what the ME does, has rather ghastly, objectionable impressions and assumptions. People tend to resist the idea of someone cutting up a loved one's body. They see it as mutilation, the final indignity –"

"Please," I broke out.

He mildly went on, "You get my point."

"All too well."

"It's a damn shame about the computer break-in."

"Lord. It makes me wish we were still using typewriters."

He stared thoughtfully at the window. "To get lawyerly with you, Kay." His eyes drifted toward me, his face grim. "I propose you be very careful. But I strongly advise you not to get so caught up in this that you let it distract you from the investigation. Dirty politics, or the fear of them, can be unsettling to the point you can make mistakes sparing your antagonists the trouble of manufacturing them."

The mislabeled slides flashed in my mind. My stomach knotted.

He added, "It's like people on a sinking ship. They can become savage. Every man for himself. You don't want to be in the way. You don't want to put yourself in a vulnerable position when people are panicking. And people in Richmond are panicking."

"Certain people are," I agreed.

"Understandably. Lori Petersen's death was preventable. The police made an unforgivable error when they didn't give her 911 call a high priority. The killer hasn't been caught. Women are continuing to die. The public is blaming the city officials, who in turn have to find someone else to blame. It's the nature of the beast. If the police, the politicians, can pass the buck on down the line, they will."

"On down the line and right to my doorstep," I said bitterly, and I automatically thought of Cagney.

Would this have happened to him?

I knew what the answer was, and I voiced it out loud. "I can't help but think I'm an easy mark because I'm a woman."

"You're a woman in a man's world," Fortosis replied. "You'll always be considered an easy mark until the ole boys discover you have teeth. And you do have teeth." He smiled. "Make sure they know it."

"How?"

He asked, "Is there anyone in your office you trust implicitly?"

"My staff is very loyal . . ."

He waved off the remark. "*Trust*, Kay. I mean trust with your life. Your computer analyst, for example?"

"Margaret's always been faithful," I replied hesitantly. "But trust with my life? I don't think so. I scarcely know her, not personally."

"My point is, your security – your best defense, if you want to think of it as such – would be to somehow determine who's been breaking into your computer. It may not be possible. But if there's a chance, then I suspect it would take someone who's sufficiently trained in computers to figure it out. A technological detective, someone you trust. I think it would be unwise to involve someone you scarcely know, someone who might talk."

"No one comes to mind," I told him. "And even if I found out, the news might be bad. If it *is* a reporter getting in, I don't see how finding that out will solve my problem."

"Maybe it wouldn't. But if it were I, I'd take the chance."

I wondered where he was pushing me. I was getting the feeling he had his own suspicions.

"I'll keep all this in mind," he promised, "if and when I get calls about these cases, Kay. If someone pressures me, for example, about the news accounts escalating the killer's peaks, that sort of thing." A pause. "I have no intention of being used. But I can't lie, either. The fact is, this killer's reaction to publicity, his MO, in other words, is a little unusual."

I just listened.

"Not all serial killers love to read about themselves, in truth. The public tends to believe the vast majority of people who commit sensational crimes want recognition, want to feel important. Like Hinckley. You shoot the President and you're an instant hero. An inadequate, poorly integrated person who can't keep a job and maintain a normal relationship with anyone is suddenly internationally known. These types are the exception, in my opinion. They are one extreme.

"The other extreme is your Lucases and Tooles. They do what they do and often don't even stick around in the city long enough to read about themselves. They don't want anybody to know. They hide the bodies and cover their tracks. They spend much of their time on the road, drifting from place to place, looking for their next targets along the way. It's my impression, based on a close examination of the Richmond killer's MO, that he's a blend of both extremes: He does it because it's a compulsion, and he absolutely doesn't want to be caught. But he also thrives on the attention, he wants everyone to know what he's done."

"This is what you told Amburgey?" I asked.

"I don't think it was quite this clear in my mind when I talked to him or anyone else last week. It took Henna Yarborough's murder to convince me."

"Because of Abby Turnbull."

"Yes."

"If she was the intended victim," I went on, "what better way to shock the city and make national news than to kill the prizewinning reporter who's been covering the stories."

"If Abby Turnbull was the intended victim, her selection strikes me as rather personal. The first four, it appears, were impersonal, stranger killings. The women were unknown to the assailant, he stalked them. They were targets of opportunity."

"The DNA test results will confirm whether it's the same man," I said, anticipating where I assumed his thoughts were going. "But I'm sure of it. I don't for a minute believe Henna was murdered by somebody else, a different person who might have been after her sister."

Fortosis said, "Abby Turnbull is a celebrity. On the one hand, I asked myself, if she was the intended victim, does it fit that the killer would make a mistake and murder her sister instead? On the other, if the intended victim was Henna Yarborough, isn't the coincidence she's Abby's sister somewhat overwhelming?"

"Stranger things have happened."

"Of course. Nothing is certain. We can conjecture all our lives and never pin it down. Why this or why that? Motive, for example. Was he abused by his mother, was he molested, et cetera, et cetera? Is he paying back society, showing his contempt for the world? The longer I'm in this profession the more I believe the very thing most psychiatrists don't want to hear, which is that many of these people kill because they enjoy it."

"I reached that conclusion a long time ago," I angrily told him.

"I think the killer in Richmond is enjoying himself," he calmly continued. "He's very cunning, very deliberate. He rarely makes mistakes. We're not dealing with some mental misfit who has damage to his right frontal lobe. Nor is he psychotic, absolutely not. He is a psychopathic sexual sadist who is above average in intelligence and able to function well enough in society to maintain an acceptable public persona. I think he's gainfully employed in Richmond. Wouldn't surprise me in the least if he's involved in an occupation, a hobby, that brings him in contact with distraught or injured people, or people he can easily control."

"What sort of occupation, exactly?" I asked uneasily.

"Could be just about anything. I'm willing to bet he's shrewd enough, competent enough, to do just about anything he likes."

"Doctor, lawyer, Indian chief," I heard Marino say.

I reminded Fortosis, "You've changed your mind. Originally you assumed he might have a criminal record or history of mental illness, maybe both. Someone who was just let out of a mental institution or prison –"

He interrupted, "In light of these last two homicides, particularly if Abby Turnbull figures in, I don't think that at all. Psychotic offenders rarely, if ever, have the wherewithal to repeatedly elude the police. I'm of the opinion that the killer in Richmond is experienced, has probably been murdering for years in other places, and has escaped apprehension as successfully in the past as he's escaping it now."

"You're thinking he moves to a new place and kills for several months, then moves on?"

"Not necessarily," he replied. "He may be disciplined enough to move to a new place and get himself settled in his job. It's possible he can go for quite a while until he starts. When he starts, he can't stop. And with each new territory it's taking more to satisfy him. He's becoming increasingly daring, more out of control. He's taunting the police and enjoying making himself the major preoccupation of the city, that is, through the press – and possibly through his victim selection."

"Abby," I muttered. "If he really was after her."

He nodded. "That was new, the most daring, reckless, thing he's done – if he set out to murder a highly visible police reporter. It would have been his greatest performance. There could be other components, ideas of reference, projection. Abby writes about him and he thinks he has something personal with her. He develops a relationship with her. His rage, his fantasies, focus on her."

"But he screwed up," I angrily retorted. "His so-called greatest performance and he completely screwed it up."

"Exactly. He may not have been familiar enough with Abby to know what she looks like, know that her sister moved in with her last fall." His eyes were steady as he added, "It's entirely possible he didn't know until he watched the news or read the papers that the woman he murdered wasn't Abby."

I was startled by the thought. It hadn't occurred to me.

"And this worries me considerably." He leaned back in the chair.

"What? He might come after her again?" I seriously doubted it.

"It worries me." He seemed to be thinking out loud now. "It didn't happen the way he planned. In his own mind, he made a fool of himself. This may only serve to make him more vicious."

"How violent does he have to be to qualify as 'more vicious'?" I blurted out loudly. "You know what he did to Lori. And now Henna . . ."

The look on his face stopped me.

"I rang up Marino shortly before you got here, Kay."

Fortosis knew.

He knew Henna Yarborough's vaginal swabs were negative.

The killer probably misfired. Most of the seminal fluid I collected was on the bedcovers and her legs. Or else the only instrument he successfully inserted was his knife. The sheets beneath her were stiff and dark with dried blood. Had he not strangled her, she probably would have bled to death.

We sat in oppressive silence with the terrible image of a person who could take pleasure in causing such horrendous pain to another human being.

When I looked at Fortosis his eyes were dull, his face drained. I think it was the first time I'd ever realized he was old beyond his years. He could hear, he could see what happened to Henna. He knew these things even more vividly than I. The room closed in on us.

We both got up at the same time.

I took the long way back to my car, veering across the campus instead of following the direct route of the narrow road leading to the parking deck. The Blue Ridge Mountains were a hazy frozen ocean in the distance, the dome of the rotunda bright white, and long fingers of shadow were spreading across the lawn. I could smell the scent of trees and grass still warm in the sun.

Knots of students drifted past, laughing and chatting and paying me no attention. As I walked beneath the spreading arms of a giant oak, my heart jumped into my throat at the sudden sound of running feet behind me. I abruptly spun around, and a young jogger met my startled gaze, his lips parting in surprise. He was a flash of red shorts and long brown legs as he cut across a sidewalk and was gone.

13

The next morning I was at the office by six. No one else was in, the phones up front still coded to roll over to the state switchboard.

While coffee was dripping, I stepped into Margaret's office. The computer in answer mode was still daring the perpetrator to try again. He hadn't.

It didn't make sense. Did he know we had discovered the break in after he tried to pull up Lori Petersen's case last week? Did he get spooked? Did he suspect nothing new was being entered?

Or was there some other reason? I stared at the dark screen. Who are you? I wondered. What do you want from me?

The ringing started again down the hall. Three rings and abrupt silence as the state operator intervened.

"He's very cunning, very deliberate . . ."

Fortosis didn't need to tell me that.

"We're not dealing with some mental misfit . . .

I wasn't expecting him to be anything like us. But he could be.

Maybe he was.

". . . able to function well enough in society to maintain an acceptable public persona . . ."

He might be competent enough to work in any profession. He might use a computer on his job or he might have one at home.

He would want to get inside my mind. He would want to get inside my mind as much as I wanted to get inside his. I was the only real link between him and his victims. I was the only living witness. When I examined the contusions, the fractured bones, and the deep tissue cuts, I alone realized the force, the savageness required to inflict the injuries. Ribs are flexible in young, healthy people. He broke Lori's ribs by smashing his knees down on top of her rib cage with all of his weight. She was on her back then. He did this after he jerked the telephone cord out of the wall.

The fractures to her fingers were twist fractures, the bones violently wrenched out of joint. He gagged and tied her, then broke her fingers one by one. He had no reason except to cause her excruciating pain and give her a taste of what was to come.

All the while, she was panicking for air. Panicking as the constricted blood flow ruptured vessels like small balloons and made her head feel as if it were going to explode. Then he forced himself inside her, into virtually every orifice.

The more she struggled, the more the electrical cord tightened around her neck until she blacked out for the last time and died.

I had reconstructed all of it. I had reconstructed what he did to all of them.

He was wondering what I knew. He was arrogant. He was paranoid.

Everything was in the computer, everything he did to Patty, to Brenda, to Cecile . . . The description of every injury, every shred of evidence we'd found, every laboratory test I'd instigated.

Was he reading the words I dictated? Was he reading my mind?

My low-heeled shoes clicked sharply along the empty hallway as I ran back to my office. In a burst of frantic energy, I emptied the contents of my billfold until I found the business card, offwhite with the *Times* masthead in raised black

241

Gothic print across the center. On the back was the ballpoint scribbling of an unsteady hand.

I dialed Abby Turnbull's pager number.

I scheduled the meeting for the afternoon because when I spoke to Abby her sister's body had not yet been released. I didn't want Abby inside the building until Henna was gone and in the care of the funeral home.

Abby was on time. Rose quietly showed her to my office and I just as quietly shut both doors.

She looked terrible. Her face was more deeply lined, her color almost gray. Her hair was loose and bushy over her shoulders, and she was dressed in a wrinkled white cotton blouse and khaki skirt. When she lit a cigarette, I noticed she was shaking. Somewhere deep within the emptiness of her eyes was a glint of grief, of rage.

I began by telling her what I told the loved ones of any of the victims whose cases I worked.

"The cause of your sister's death, Abby, was strangulation due to the ligature around her neck."

"How long?" She blew out a tremulous stream of smoke. "How long did she live after . . . after he got to her?"

"I can't tell you exactly. But the physical findings lead me to suspect her death was quick."

Not quick enough, I did not say. I found fibers inside Henna's mouth. She had been gagged. The monster wanted her alive for a while and he wanted her quiet. Based on the amount of blood loss, I'd classified her cutting injuries as perimortem, meaning I could say with certainty only that they were inflicted around the time of death. She bled very little into surrounding tissues after the assault with the knife. She may already have been dead. She may have been unconscious.

More likely it was worse than that. I suspected the cord from the venetian blinds was jerked tight around her neck when she straightened her legs in a violent reflex to pain.

"She had petechial hemorrhages in the conjunctivae, and

facial and neck skin," I said to Abby. "In other words, rupture of the small, superficial vessels of the eyes and face. This is caused by pressure, by cervical occlusion of the jugular veins due to the ligature around her neck."

"How long did she live?" she dully asked again.

"Minutes," I repeated.

That's as far as I intended to go. Abby seemed slightly relieved. She was seeking solace in the hope her sister's suffering was minimal. Someday, when the case was closed and Abby was stronger, she would know. God help her, she would know about the knife.

"That's all?" she asked shakily.

"That's all I can say now," I told her. "I'm sorry. I'm so terribly sorry about Henna."

She smoked for a while, taking nervous jerky drags as if she didn't know what to do with her hands. She was biting her lower lip, trying to keep it from trembling.

When she finally met my eyes, her own were uneasy, suspicious.

She knew I hadn't asked her here for this. She sensed there was something else.

"It's really not why you called, is it?"

"Not entirely," I replied frankly.

Silence.

I could see the resentment, the anger building.

"What?" she demanded. "What is it you want from me?"

"I want to know what you're going to do."

Her eyes flashed. "Oh, I get it. You're worried about your goddam self. Jesus Christ. You're just like the rest of them!"

"I'm not worried about myself, " I said very calmly. "I'm beyond that, Abby. You have enough to cause me trouble. If you want to run my office and me into the ground, then do it. That's your decision."

She looked uncertain, her eyes shifting away.

"I understand your rage."

"You couldn't possibly understand it."

"I understand it better than you might imagine." Bill

flashed in my mind. I could understand Abby's rage very well.

"You couldn't. Nobody could!" she exclaimed. "He stole my sister from me. He stole a part of my life. I'm so damn tired of people taking things from me! What kind of world is this," she choked, "where someone can do something like that? Oh, Jesus I *don't know* what I'm going to do . . ."

I said firmly, "I know you intend to investigate your sister's death on your own, Abby. Don't do it."

"Somebody's got to!" she cried out. "What? I'm supposed to leave it up to the Keystone Kops?"

"Some matters you must leave to the police. But you can help. You can if you really want to."

"Don't patronize me!"

"I'm not."

"I'll do it my own way . . ."

"No. You won't do it your own way, Abby. Do it for your sister."

She stared blankly at me with red-rimmed eyes.

"I asked you here because I'm taking a gamble. I need your help."

"Right! You need me to help by leaving town and keeping the hell out of it . . ."

I was slowly shaking my head.

She looked surprised.

"Do you know Benton Wesley?"

"The profiler," she replied hesitantly. "I know who he is."

I glanced up at the wall clock. "He'll be here in ten minutes."

She stared at me for a long time. "What? What is it, exactly, you want me to do?"

"Use your journalistic connections to help us find him."

"*Him*?" Her eyes widened.

I got up to see if there was any coffee left.

Wesley was reluctant when I had explained my plan over the telephone, but now that the three of us were in my office it seemed clear to me he'd accepted it.

"Your complete cooperation is non-negotiable," he said to Abby emphatically. "I've got to have your assurance you'll do exactly what we agree upon. Any improvisation or creative thinking on your part could blow the investigation right out of the water. Your discretion is imperative."

She nodded, then pointed out, "If it's the killer breaking into the computer, why's he done it only once?"

"Once we're aware of," I reminded her.

"Still, it hasn't happened again since you discovered it."

Wesley suggested, "He's been running like hell. He's murdered two women in two weeks and there's probably been sufficient information in the press to satisfy his curiosity. He could be sitting pretty, feeling smug, because by all news accounts we don't have anything on him."

"We've got to inflame him," I added. "We've got to do something to make him so paranoid he gets reckless. One way to do this is to make him think my office has found evidence that could be the break we've been waiting for."

"If he's the one getting into the computer," Wesley summarized, "this could be sufficient incentive for him to try again to discover what we supposedly know." He looked at me.

The fact was we had no break in the case. I'd indefinitely banished Margaret from her office and the computer was to be left in answer mode. Wesley had set up a tracer to track all calls made to her extension. We were going to use the computer to lure the murderer by having Abby's paper print a story claiming the forensic investigation had come up with a "significant link."

"He's going to be paranoid, upset enough to believe it," I predicted. "If he's ever been treated in a hospital around here, for example, he's going to worry now that we might track him through old charts. If he gets any special medications from a pharmacy, he's got that to worry about, too."

All of this hinged on the peculiar odor Matt Petersen mentioned to the police. There was no other "evidence" to which we could safely allude.

The one piece of evidence the killer would have trouble with was DNA.

I could bluff him from hell to breakfast with it, and it might not even be a bluff.

Several days ago, I had gotten copies of the reports from the first two cases. I studied the vertical array of bands of varying shades and widths, patterns that looked remarkably like the bar codes stamped on supermarket packaged foods. There were three radioactive probes in each case, and the position of the bands in each probe for Patty Lewis's case was indistinguishable from the position of the bands in the three probes in Brenda Steppe's.

"Of course this doesn't give us his identity," I explained to Abby and Wesley. "All we can say is if he's black, then only one out of 135 million men theoretically can fit the same pattern. If he's Caucasian, only one out of 500 million men."

DNA is the microcosm of the total person, his life code. Genetic engineers in a private laboratory in New York had isolated the DNA from the samples of seminal fluid I collected. They snipped the samples at specific sites, and the fragments migrated to discrete regions of an electrically charged surface covered with a thick gel. A positively charged pole was at one end of the surface, a negatively charged pole at the other.

"DNA carries a negative charge," I went on. "Opposites attract."

The shorter fragments traveled farther and faster in the positive direction than the longer ones did, and the fragments spread out across the gel, forming the band pattern. This was transferred to a nylon membrane and exposed to a probe.

"I don't get it," Abby interrupted. "What *probe*?"

I explained. "The killer's double-stranded DNA fragments were broken, or denatured, into single strands. In more simplistic terms, they were unzipped like a zipper. The probe is a solution of single-stranded DNA of a specific base sequence that's labeled with a radioactive marker. When the solution, or probe, was washed over the nylon membrane, the probe

246

sought out and bonded with complementary single strands – with the killer's complementary single strands."

"So the zipper is zipped back up?" she asked. "But it's radioactive now?"

"The point is that his pattern can now be visualized on X-ray film," I said.

"Yeah, his *bar code*. Too bad we can't run it over a scanner and come up with his name," Wesley dryly added.

"Everything about him is there," I continued. "The problem is the technology isn't sophisticated enough yet to read the specifics, such as genetic defects, eye and hair color, that sort of thing. There are so many bands present covering so many points in the person's genetic makeup it's simply too complex to definitively make anything more out of it than a match or a nonmatch."

"But the killer doesn't know that." Wesley looked speculatively at me.

"That's right."

"Not unless he's a scientist or something," Abby interjected.

"We'll assume he isn't," I told them. "I suspect he never gave DNA profiling a thought until he started reading about it in the papers. I doubt he understands the concept very well."

"I'll explain the procedure in my story," Abby thought out loud. "I'll make him understand it just enough to freak him."

"Just enough to make him think we know about his defect," Wesley agreed. "If he has a defect . . . That's what worries me, Kay." He looked levelly at me. "What if he doesn't?"

I patiently went over it again. "What continues to stand out to me is Matt Petersen's reference to 'pancakes,' to the smell inside the bedroom reminding him of pancakes, of something sweet but sweaty."

"Maple syrup," Wesley recalled.

"Yes. If the killer has a body odor reminiscent of maple

syrup, he may have some sort of anomaly, some type of metabolic disorder. Specifically, 'maple syrup urine disease.'"

"And it's genetic?" Wesley had asked this twice.

"That's the beauty of it, Benton. If he has it, it's in his DNA somewhere."

"I've never heard of it," Abby said. "This disease."

"Well, it's not exactly your common cold."

"Then *exactly* what is it?"

I got up from my desk and went to a bookcase. Sliding out the fat *Textbook of Medicine*, I opened it to the right page and set it before them.

"It's an enzyme defect," I explained as I sat back down. "The defect results in amino acids accumulating in the body like a poison. In the classic or acute form, the person suffers severe mental retardation and/or death at infancy, which is why it's rare to find healthy adults of sound mind who suffer from the disease. But it's possible. In its mild form, which would have to be what the killer suffers from if this is his affliction, postnatal development is normal, symptoms are intermittent, and the disease can be treated through a low-protein diet, and possibly through dietary supplements – specifically, thiamine, or vitamin B_1, at ten times the normal daily intake."

"In other words," Wesley said, leaning forward and frowning as he scanned the book, "he could suffer from the mild form, lead a fairly normal life, be smart as hell – but stink?"

I nodded. "The most common indication of maple syrup urine disease is a characteristic odor, a distinctive maple-syrupy odor of the urine and perspiration. The symptoms are going to be more acute when he's under stress, the odor more pronounced when he's doing what stresses him most, which is committing these murders. The odor's going to get into his clothing. He's going to have a long history of being self-conscious about his problem."

"You wouldn't smell it in his seminal fluid?" Wesley asked.

248

"Not necessarily."

"Well," Abby said, "if he's got this body odor, then he must take a lot of showers. If he works around people. They'd notice it, the smell."

I didn't respond.

She didn't know about the glittery residue, and I wasn't going to tell her. If the killer has this chronic odor, it wouldn't be the least bit unusual for him to be compulsive about washing his armpits, his face and hands, frequently throughout the day while he's exposed to people who might notice his problem. He might be washing himself while at work, where there might be a dispenser of borax soap in the men's room.

"It's a gamble." Wesley leaned back in his chair. "Jeez." Shaking his head. "If the smell Petersen mentioned was something he imagined or something he confused with another odor – maybe a cologne the killer was wearing – we're going to look like fools. The squirrel's going to be all the more certain we don't know what the hell we're doing."

"I don't think Petersen imagined the smell," I said with conviction. "As shocked as he was when he found his wife's body, the smell had to be unusual and potent for Petersen to notice and remember it. I can't think of a single cologne that would smell like sweaty maple syrup. I'm speculating the killer was sweating profusely, that he'd left the bedroom maybe minutes before Petersen walked in."

"The disease causes retardation . . ." Abby was flipping through the book.

"If it's not treated immediately after birth," I repeated.

"Well, this bastard isn't retarded." She looked up at me, her eyes hard.

"Of course he isn't," Wesley agreed. "Psychopaths are anything but stupid. What we want to do is make the guy *think* we think he's stupid. Hit him where it hurts – his goddam pride, which is hooked up with his grandiose notions of his off-the-charts IQ."

"This disease," I told them, "could do that. If he has it, he's going to know it. Possibly it runs in his family. He's

249

going to be hypersensitive, not only about his body odor, but also about the mental deficiencies the defect is known to cause."

Abby was making notes to herself. Wesley was staring off at the wall, his face tense. He didn't look happy.

Blowing in frustration, he said, "I just don't know, Kay. If the guy doesn't have this maple syrup whatever . . ." He shook his head. "He'll be on to us in a flash. It could set the investigation back."

"You can't set back something that is already backed into a corner," I said evenly. "I have no intention of naming the disease in the article." I turned to Abby. "We'll refer to it as a metabolic disorder. This could be a number of things. He's going to worry. Maybe it's something he doesn't know he has. He thinks he's in perfect health? How can he be sure? He's never had a team of genetic engineers studying his body fluids before. Even if the guy's a physician, he can't rule out the possibility he has an abnormality that's been latent most of his life, sitting there like a bomb waiting to go off. We'll plant the anxiety in his head. Let him stew over it. Hell, let him think he's got something fatal. Maybe it will send him to the nearest clinic for a physical. Maybe it will send him to the nearest medical library. The police can make a check, see who seeks out a local doctor or frantically begins riffling through medical reference books at one of the libraries. If he's the one who's been breaking into the computer here, he'll probably do it again. Whatever happens, my gut tells me *something* will happen. It's going to rattle his cage."

The three of us spent the next hour drafting the language in Abby's article.

'We can't have attribution," she insisted. "No way. If these quotes are attributed to the chief medical examiner, it will sound fishy because you've refused to talk in the past. And you've been ordered not to talk now. It's got to look like the information was leaked."

"Well," I commented dryly, "I suppose you can pull your famous 'medical source' out of your hat."

Abby read the draft aloud. It didn't set well with me. It was too vague. "Alleged" this and "possible" that.

If only we had his blood. The enzyme defect, if it existed, could be assayed in his leukocytes, his white blood cells. If only we had *something*.

As if on cue my telephone buzzed. It was Rose. "Dr. Scarpetta, Sergeant Marino's here. He says it's urgent."

I met him in the lobby. He was carrying a bag, the familiar gray plastic bag used to hold clothing connected to criminal cases.

"You ain't gonna believe this." He was grinning, his face flushed. "You know Magpie?"

I was staring at the bulging bag, my confusion apparent.

"You know, *Magpie*. All over the city with all his earthly belongings in a grocery cart he swiped somewhere. Spends his hours rummaging through garbage cans and Dumpsters."

"A street person?" What was Marino talking about?

"Yo. The Grand Dragon of street persons. Well, over the weekend he's fishing around in this Dumpster less than a block from where Henna Yarborough was whacked and guess what? He finds himself a nice navy blue jumpsuit, Doc. Flips him right out because the damn thing's stained with blood. He's a snitch of mine, see. Has the brains to stuff the thing in a trash bag, and's been wheeling the damn thing around for days, looking for me. So he waves me down on the street a little while ago, charges me the usual ten-spot, and Merry Christmas."

He was untwisting the tie around the top of the bag.

"Take a whiff."

It almost knocked me over, not just the stench of the days-old bloody garment but a powerful maple-sweetish, sweaty odor. A chill ran down my spine.

"Hey," Marino went on, "I bopped by Petersen's apartment before I come over here. Had him take a whiff."

"Is it the odor he remembers?"

He shot his finger at me and winked. "Bingo."

For two hours Vander and I worked on the blue jumpsuit. It would take a while for Betty to analyze the bloodstains, but there was little doubt in our minds the jumpsuit was worn by the killer. It sparkled under the laser like mica-flecked blacktop.

We suspected when he assaulted Henna with the knife he got very bloody and wiped his hands on his thighs. The cuffs of the sleeves were also stiff with dried blood. Quite likely it was his habit to wear something like a jumpsuit over his clothes when he struck. Maybe it was routine for him to toss the garment into a Dumpster after the crime. But I doubted it. He tossed this one because he made this victim bleed.

I was willing to bet he was smart enough to know bloodstains are permanent. If he were ever picked up, he had no intention of having anything hanging in his closet that might be stained with old blood. He had no intention of anyone's tracing the jumpsuit either. The label had been removed.

The fabric looked like a cotton and synthetic blend, dark blue, the size a large or perhaps an extra-large. I was reminded of the dark fibers found on Lori Petersen's window sill and on her body. There were a few dark fibers on Henna's body as well.

The three of us had said nothing to Marino about what we were doing. He was out on the street somewhere, maybe at home drinking beer in front of the TV. He didn't have a clue. When the news broke, he was going to think it was legitimate, that the information was leaked and related to the jumpsuit he turned in and to the DNA reports recently sent to me. We wanted *everybody* to think the news was legitimate.

In fact, it probably was. I could think of no other reason for the killer's having such a distinctive body odor, unless Petersen was imagining things and the jumpsuit just happened to be tossed on top of a Mrs. Butterworth's maple syrup bottle inside the Dumpster.

"It's perfect," Wesley was saying. "He never thought we'd find it. The toad had it all figured out, maybe even knew where the Dumpster was before he went out that night. He never thought we'd find it."

I stole a glance at Abby. She was holding up amazingly well.

"It's enough to run with," Wesley added.

I could see the headline:

DNA, NEW EVIDENCE:
SERIAL KILLER MAY HAVE
METABOLIC DISORDER

If he truly did have maple syrup urine disease, the front-page story ought to knock him off his feet.

"If your purpose is to entice him with the OCME computer," Abby said, "we have to make him think the computer figures in. You know, the data are related."

I thought for a minute. "Okay. We can do that if we say the computer got a hit on a recent data entry, information relating to a peculiar smell noted at one of the scenes and associated with a recently discovered piece of evidence. A search hit on an unusual enzyme defect that could cause a similar odor, but sources close to the investigation would not say exactly what this defect or disease might be, or if the defect has been verified by the results of recently completed DNA tests."

Wesley liked it. "Great. Let him sweat."

He didn't catch the pun.

"Let him wonder if we found the jumpsuit," he went on. "We don't want to give details. Maybe you can just say the police refused to disclose the exact nature of the evidence."

Abby continued to write.

I said, "Going back to your 'medical source,' it might be a good idea to have some pointed quotes coming from this person's mouth."

She looked up at me. "Such as?"

I eyed Wesley and replied, "Let this medical source refuse to reveal the specific metabolic disorder, as we've agreed. But have this source say the disorder can result in mental impairment, and in acute stages, retardation. Then add, uh . . ." I composed out loud, "An expert in human genetics stated that certain types of metabolic disorders can cause severe mental retardation. Though police believe the serial killer cannot possibly be severely mentally impaired, there is evidence to suggest he might suffer a degree of deficiency that manifests itself in disorganization and intermittent confusion."

Wesley muttered, "He'll be off the wall. It will absolutely enrage him."

"It's important we don't question his sanity," I continued. "It will come back to haunt us in court."

Abby suggested, "We'll simply have the source say so. We'll have the source distinguish between slowness and mental illness."

By now, she had filled half a dozen pages in her reporter's notepad.

She asked as she wrote, "This maple syrup business. Do we want to be that specific about the smell?"

"Yes," I said without pause. "This guy may work around the public. He's going to have colleagues, if nothing else. Someone may come forward."

Wesley considered. "One thing's damn certain, it will further unhinge him. Should make him paranoid as hell."

"Unless he really doesn't have a weird case of B.O.," Abby said.

"How is he going to know he doesn't?" I asked.

Both of them looked surprised.

"Ever heard the expression, 'A fox never smells its own'?" I added.

"You mean he could stink and not know it?" she asked.

"Let him wonder that," I replied.

She nodded, bending over her notepad again.

Wesley settled back in his chair. "What else do you know about this defect, Kay? Should we be checking out the local pharmacies, see if someone buys a lot of oddball vitamins or prescription drugs?"

"You could check to see if someone regularly comes in to buy large doses of B$_1$," I said. "There's also MSUD powder, a dietary supplement available. I think it's over-the-counter, a protein supplement. He may be controlling the disease through diet, through a limiting of normal high-protein foods. But I think he's too careful to be leaving those kinds of tracks, and in truth, I don't think his disease has been acute enough for him to be on a very restricted diet. I suspect in order for him to function as well as he does he leads a fairly normal life. His only problem is he has a strange-smelling body odor that gets more noticeable when he's under stress."

"Emotional stress?"

"Physical stress," I replied. "MSUD tends to flare up under physical stress, such as when the person is suffering from a respiratory infection, the flu. It's physiological. He's probably not getting enough sleep. It takes a lot of physical energy to stalk victims, break into houses, do what he does. Emotional stress and physical stress are connected – one adds to the other. The more emotionally stressed he becomes, the more physically stressed he becomes, and vice versa."

"Then what?"

I looked impassively at him.

"Then what happens," he repeated, "if the disease flares up?"

"Depends on whether it becomes acute."

"Let's say it does."

"He's got a real problem."

"Meaning?"

"Meaning, the amino acids build up in his system. He's going to get lethargic, irritable, ataxic. Symptoms similar to severe hyperglycemia. It may be necessary for him to be hospitalized."

"English," Wesley said. "What the hell's *ataxic* mean?"

"Unsteady. He's going to walk around like he's drunk. He's not going to have the wherewithal to scale fences and climb through windows. If it gets acute, if his stress level continues to climb, and if he goes untreated, it could get out of control."

"Out of control?" he persisted. "We stress him – that's our purpose, right? His disease gets out of control?"

"Possibly."

"Okay." He hesitated. "What next?"

"Severe hyperglycemia, and his anxiety increases. If it isn't controlled, he's going to get confused, overwrought. His judgment may be impaired. He'll suffer mood changes."

I stopped right there.

But Wesley wasn't going to let me. He was leaning forward in his chair, staring at me.

"You didn't just think of this maple syrup urine disease business, did you?" he pushed.

"It's been in my differential."

"And you didn't say anything."

"I wasn't at all sure," I replied. "I saw no reason to suggest it until now."

"Right. Okay. You say you want to rattle his cage, stress him right out of his mind. Let's do it. What's the last stage? I mean, *what if his disease gets really bad*?"

"He may become unconscious, have convulsions. If this is prolonged, it may lead to a severe organic deficit."

He stared incredulously at me as his eyes filled with comprehension. "Jesus. You're trying to kill the son of a bitch."

Abby's pen stopped. Startled, she looked up at me.

I replied, "This is all theoretical. If he's got the disease, it's mild. He's lived with it all his life. It's highly unlikely MSUD's going to kill him."

Wesley continued to stare. He didn't believe me.

14

I couldn't sleep all night. My mind wouldn't shut down and I tossed miserably between unsettling realities and savage dreams. I shot somebody and Bill was the medical examiner called to the scene. When he arrived with his black bag, he was accompanied by a beautiful woman I did not know . . .

My eyes flew open in the dark, my heart squeezed as if by a cold hand. I got out of bed long before my alarm went off and drove to work in a fog of depression.

I don't know when in my life I'd ever felt so lonely and withdrawn. I scarcely spoke to anyone at the office, and my staff began to cast nervous, strange glances my way.

Several times I came close to calling Bill, my resolve trembling like a tree about to fall. It finally fell shortly before noon. His secretary brightly told me "Mr. Boltz" was on vacation and wouldn't be back until the first of July.

I left no message. The vacation wasn't planned, I knew. I also knew why he didn't say a word about it to me. In the past he would have told me. The past was past. There would be no resolution or lame apologies or outright lies. He'd cut me off forever because he couldn't face his own sins.

After lunch I went upstairs to serology and was surprised to find Betty and Wingo with their backs to the door, their heads together as they looked at something white inside a small plastic bag.

I said, "Hello," and came inside.

Wingo nervously tucked the bag in a pocket of Betty's lab coat, as if slipping her money.

"You finished downstairs?" I pretended I was too preoccupied to have noticed this peculiar transaction.

"Uh, yeah. Sure am, Dr. Scarpetta," he quickly replied, on his way out. "McFee, the guy shot last night – released him a little while ago. And the burn victims coming in from Albemarle won't be in till four or so."

"Fine. We'll hold them until the morning."

"You got it," I heard him say from the hallway.

Spread out on the wide table in the center of the room was the reason for my visit. The blue jumpsuit. It looked flat and mundane, neatly smoothed out and zipped up to the collar. It could have belonged to anybody. There were numerous pockets, and I think I must have checked each one half a dozen times hoping to find anything that might hint at who he was, but they were empty. There were large holes cut in the legs and sleeves where Betty had removed swatches of bloodstained fabric.

"Any luck grouping the blood?" I asked, trying not to stare at the plastic bag peeking out of the top of her pocket.

"I've got some of it worked out." She motioned me to follow her to her office.

On her desk was a legal pad scribbled with notes and numbers that would look like hieroglyphics to the uninitiated.

"Henna Yarborough's blood type is B," she began. "We're lucky on that count because it's not all that common. In Virginia, about twelve percent of the population's type B. Her PGM's one-plus, one-minus. Her PEP is A-one, EAP is CB, ADA-one and AK-one. The subsystems, unfortunately, are very common, up there in the eighty-nine percent and above of Virginia's population."

"How common is the actual configuration?" The plastic peeking out of the top of her pocket was beginning to unsettle me.

She started stabbing out digits on a calculator, multiplying the percentages and dividing by the number of subsystems she had. "About seventeen percent. Seventeen out of a hundred people could have that configuration."

"Not exactly rare," I muttered.

"Not unless sparrows are rare."

"What about the bloodstains on the jumpsuit?"

"We were lucky. The jumpsuit must have already air-dried by the time the street person found it. It's in amazingly good shape. I got all the subsystems except an EAP. It's consistent with Henna Yarborough's blood. DNA should be able to tell us with certainty, but we're talking about a month to six weeks."

I commented abstractedly, "We ought to buy stock in the lab."

Her eyes lingered on me and grew soft. "You look absolutely ragged, Kay."

"That obvious, is it?"

"Obvious to me."

I didn't say anything.

"Don't let all this get to you. After thirty years of this misery, I've learned the hard way . . ."

"What's Wingo up to?" I foolishly blurted out.

Surprised, she faltered. "Wingo? Well . . ."

I was staring at her pocket.

She laughed uneasily, patted it. "Oh, this. Just a little private work he's asked me to do."

That was as much as she intended to say. Maybe Wingo had other real worries in his life. Maybe he was having an HIV test done on the sly. Good God, don't let him have AIDS.

Gathering my fragmented thoughts, I asked, "What about the fibers? Anything?"

Betty had compared fibers from the jumpsuit to fibers left at Lori Petersen's scene and to a few fibers found on Henna Yarborough's body.

"The fibers found on the Petersen windowsill could have come from the jumpsuit," she told me, "or they could have come from any number of dark blue cotton-polyester blend twills."

259

In court, I dismally thought, the comparison's not going to mean a thing because the twill is about as generic as dime-store typing paper – you start looking for it and you're going to find it all over the place. It could have come from someone's work pants. It could, for that matter, have come from a paramedic's or cop's uniform.

There was another disappointment. Betty was sure the fibers I found on Henna Yarborough's body were not from the jumpsuit. "They're cotton," she was saying. "They may have come from something she was wearing at some point earlier in the day, or even a bath towel. Who knows? People carry all sorts of fibers on their person. But I'm not surprised the jumpsuit didn't leave fibers."

"Why?"

"Because twill fabrics, such as the fabric of the jumpsuit, are very smooth. They rarely leave fibers unless the fabric comes in contact with something abrasive."

"Such as a brick window ledge or a rough wooden sill, as in Lori's case."

"Possibly, and the dark fibers we found in her case may have come from a jumpsuit. Maybe even this one. But I don't think we're ever going to know."

I went back downstairs to my office and sat at my desk for a while, thinking. Unlocking the drawer, I pulled out the five murdered women's cases.

I began looking for anything I might have missed. Once again, I was groping for a connection.

What did these five women have in common? Why did the killer pick them? How did he come in contact with them?

There had to be a link. In my soul, I didn't believe it was a random selection, that he just cruised around looking for a likely candidate. I believed he selected them for a reason. He had some sort of contact with them first, and perhaps followed them home.

Geographics, jobs, physical appearances. There was no common denominator. I tried the reverse, the least common

260

denominator, and I continued to go back to Cecile Tyler's record.

She was black. The four other victims were white. I was bothered by this in the beginning, and I was still bothered by it now. Did the killer make a mistake? Perhaps he didn't realize she was black. Was he really after somebody else? Her friend Bobbi, for example?

I flipped pages, scanning the autopsy report I'd dictated. I perused evidence receipts, call sheets and an old hospital chart from St. Luke's, where she'd been treated five years earlier for an ectopic pregnancy. When I got to the police report, I looked at the name of the only relative listed, a sister in Madras, Oregon. From her Marino got information about Cecile's background, about her failed marriage to the dentist now living in Tidewater.

X rays sounded like saw blades bending as I pulled them out of manila envelopes and held them up, one by one, to the light of my desk lamp. Cecile had no skeletal injuries other than a healed impaction fracture of her left elbow. The age of the injury was impossible to tell but I knew it wasn't fresh. It could go back too many years to matter.

Again, I contemplated the VMC connection. Both Lori Petersen and Brenda Steppe had recently been in the hospital's ER. Lori was there because her rotation was trauma surgery. Brenda was treated there after her automobile accident. Perhaps it was too farfetched to think Cecile might have been treated there as well for her fractured elbow. At this point, I was willing to explore anything.

I dialed Cecile's sister's number listed on Marino's report. After five rings the receiver was picked up.

"Hello?"

It was a poor connection and clearly I'd made a mistake.

"I'm sorry, I must have the wrong number," I quickly said.

"Pardon?"

I repeated myself, louder.

"What number were you dialing?" The voice was cultured and Virginian and seemed that of a female in her twenties.

I recited the number.

"That's this number. With whom did you wish to speak?"

"Fran O'Connor," I read from the report.

The young, cultured voice replied, "Speaking."

I told her who I was and heard a faint gasp. "As I understand it, you are Cecile Tyler's sister."

"Yes. Dear Lord. I don't want to talk about it. Please."

"Mrs. O'Connor, I'm terribly sorry about Cecile. I'm the medical examiner working her case, and I'm calling to find out if you know how your sister fractured her left elbow. She has a healed fracture of her left elbow. I'm looking at the X rays now."

Hesitation. I could hear her thinking.

"It was a jogging accident. She was jogging on a sidewalk and tripped, landing on her hands. One of her elbows was fractured from the impact. I remember because she wore a cast for three months during one of the hottest summers on record. She was miserable."

"That summer? Was this in Oregon?"

"No, Cecile never lived in Oregon. This was in Fredericksburg, where we grew up."

"How long ago was the jogging accident?"

Another pause. "Nine, maybe ten years ago."

"Where was she treated?"

"I don't know. A hospital in Fredericksburg. I can't remember the name."

Cecile's impaction fracture wasn't treated at VMC, and the injury had occurred much too long ago to matter. But I no longer cared.

I never met Cecile Tyler in life.

I never talked to her.

I just assumed she would sound "black."

"Mrs. O'Connor, are you black?"

"Of course I'm black." She sounded upset.

"Did your sister talk like you?"

"Talk like me?" she asked, her voice rising.

"I know it seems an odd question . . ."

"You mean did she talk *white* like me?" she went on outraged. "Yes! She did! Isn't that what education's all about? So *black* people can talk *white*?"

"Please," I said with feeling. "I certainly didn't intend to offend you. But it's important . . ."

I was apologizing to a dial tone.

Lucy knew about the fifth strangling. She knew about all of the slain young women. She also knew I kept a .38 in my bedroom and had asked me about it twice since dinner.

"Lucy," I said as I rinsed plates and loaded them in the dishwasher, "I don't want you thinking about guns. I wouldn't own one if I didn't live alone."

I'd been strongly tempted to hide it where she would never think to look. But after the episode with the modem, which I had guiltily reconnected to my home computer days ago, I vowed to be up front with her. The .38 remained high on my closet shelf, inside its shoebox, while Lucy was in town. The gun wasn't loaded. These days, I unloaded it in the morning and reloaded it before bed. As for the Silvertip cartridges – those I hid where she would never think to look.

When I faced her, her eyes were huge. "You know why I have a gun, Lucy. I think you understand how dangerous they are . . .

"They kill people."

"Yes," I replied as we went into the living room. "They most certainly can."

"You have it so you can kill somebody."

"I don't like to think about that," I told her seriously.

"Well, it's true," she persisted. "That's why you keep it. Because of bad people. That's why."

I picked up the remote control and switched on the television.

Lucy pushed up the sleeves of her pink sweatshirt and complained, "It's hot in here, Auntie Kay. Why's it always so hot in here?"

"Would you like me to turn up the air-conditioning?" I abstractedly flipped through the television schedule.

"No. I hate air-conditioning."

I lit a cigarette and she complained about that, too.

"Your office is hot and always stinks like cigarettes. I open the window and still it stinks. Mom says you shouldn't smoke. You're a doctor and you smoke. Mom says you should know better."

Dorothy had called late the night before. She was somewhere in California, I couldn't remember where, with her illustrator husband. It was all I could do to be civil to her. I wanted to remind her, "You have a daughter, flesh of your flesh, bone of your bone. Remember Lucy? Remember her?" Instead, I was reserved, almost gracious, mostly out of consideration for Lucy, who was sitting at the table, her lips pressed together.

Lucy talked to her mother for maybe ten minutes, and had nothing to say afterward. Ever since, she'd been all over me, critical, snappish and bossy. She'd been the same way during the day, according to Bertha, who this evening had referred to her as a "fusspot." Bertha told me Lucy had scarcely set foot outside my office. She sat in front of the computer from the moment I left the house until the moment I returned. Bertha gave up calling her into the kitchen for meals. Lucy ate at my desk.

The sitcom on the set seemed all the more absurd because Lucy and I were having our own sitcom in the living room.

"Andy says it's more dangerous to own a gun and not know how to use it than if you don't own one," she loudly announced.

"Andy?" I said absentmindedly.

"The one before Ralph. He used to go to the junkyard and shoot bottles. He could hit them from a long ways away. I bet you couldn't." She looked accusingly at me.

"You're right. I probably couldn't shoot as well as Andy."

"See!"

I didn't tell her I actually knew quite a lot about firearms.

Before I bought my stainless-steel Ruger .38, I went down to the indoor range in the basement of my building and experimented with an assortment of handguns from the firearms lab, all this under the professional supervision of one of the examiners. I practiced from time to time, and I wasn't a bad shot. I didn't think I would hesitate if the need ever arose. I also didn't intend to discuss the matter further with my niece.

Very quietly I asked, "Lucy, why are you picking on me?"

"Because you're a stupid ass!" Her eyes filled with tears. "You're just an old stupid ass and if you tried to, you'd hurt yourself or he'd get it away from you! And then you'd be gone, too! If you tried to, he'd shoot you with it just like it happens on TV!"

"If I tried to?" I puzzled. "If I tried to *what*, Lucy?"

"If you tried to get somebody first."

She angrily wiped away tears, her narrow chest heaving. I stared blindly at the family circus on TV and didn't know what to say. My impulse was to retreat to my office and shut the door, to lose myself in my work for a while, but hesitantly I moved over and pulled her close. We sat like this for the longest time, saying nothing.

I wondered who she talked to at home. I couldn't imagine her having any conversations of substance with my sister. Dorothy and her children's books had been lauded by various critics as "extraordinarily insightful" and "deep" and "full of feeling." What a dismal irony. Dorothy gave the best she had to juvenile characters who didn't exist. She nurtured them. She spent long hours contemplating their every detail, from the way their hair was combed to the clothes they wore, to their trials and rites of passage. All the while Lucy was starved for attention.

I thought of the times Lucy and I spent together when I lived in Miami, of the holidays with her, my mother and Dorothy. I thought of Lucy's last visit here. I couldn't recall her ever mentioning the names of friends. I don't think she had any. She would talk about her teachers, her mother's

265

ragtag assortment of "boyfriends," Mrs. Spooner across the street, Jake the yardman and the endless parade of maids. Lucy was a tiny, bespectacled know-it-all whom older children resented and children her age didn't understand. She was out of sync. I think I was exactly like her when I was her age.

A peaceful warmth had settled over both of us. I said into her hair, "Someone asked me a question the other day."

"About what?"

"About trust. Someone asked me who I trusted more than anybody else in the world. And you know what?"

She leaned her head back, looking up at me.

"I think that person is you."

"Do you really?" she asked, incredulously. "More than *anybody*?"

I nodded and quietly went on, "That being the case, I'm going to ask you to help me with something."

She sat up and stared at me, her eyes alert and utterly thrilled. "Oh, sure! Just ask me! I'll help you, Auntie Kay!"

"I need to figure out how someone managed to break into the computer downtown . . ."

"I didn't do it," she instantly blurted out, a stricken look on her face. "I already told you I didn't."

"I believe you. But someone did it, Lucy. Maybe you can help me figure it out?"

I didn't think she could but had felt an impulse to give her a chance.

Energized and excited again, she said confidently, "Anybody could do it because it's easy."

"Easy?" I had to smile.

"Because of System/Manager."

I stared at her in open astonishment. "How do you know about System/Manager?"

"It's in the book. He's God."

At times like these I was reminded, if not unnerved. Lucy's IQ. The first time she was given an IQ test she scored so high the counselor insisted on testing her again because

266

there had to be "some mistake." There was. The second time Lucy scored ten points higher.

"That's how you get into SQL to begin with," she was rattling on. "See, you can't create any grants unless you got one to start with. That's why you've got System/Manager. God. You get into SQL with Him, and then you can create anything you want."

Anything you want, it dawned on me. Such as all of the user names and passwords assigned to my offices. This was a terrible revelation, so simplistic it had never occurred to me. I supposed it never occurred to Margaret either.

"All someone's got to do is get in," Lucy matter-of-factly went on. "And if he knows about God, he can create any grant he wants, make it the DBA, and then he can get into your data base."

In my office, the data base administrator, or DBA, was "DEEP/THROAT." Margaret did have a sense of humor now and then.

"So you get into SQL by connecting System/ Manager, then you type in: GRANT CONNECT, RESOURCE, DBA TO AUNTIE IDENTIFIED BY KAY."

"Maybe that's what happened," I thought out loud. "And with the DBA, someone not only could view but actually alter the data."

"Sure! He could do anything because God's told him he can. The DBA is Jesus."

Her theological allusions were so outrageous I laughed in spite of myself.

"That's how I got into SQL to begin with," she confessed. "Since you didn't tell me any passwords or anything. I wanted to get into SQL so I could try out some of the commands in the book. I just gave your DBA user name a password I made up so I could get in."

"Wait a minute," I slowed her down. "Wait a minute! What do you mean you assigned a password you made up to my DBA user name? How did you know what my user name is? I didn't tell you."

267

She explained, "It's in your grants file. I found it in the Home directory where you have all the INP's for the tables you created. You have a file called 'Grants.SQL' where you created all the public synonyms for your tables."

Actually, I hadn't created those tables. Margaret did last year and I loaded my home computer with the boxes of backup diskettes she gave me. Was it possible there was a similar "Grants" file in the OCME computer?

I took hold of Lucy's hand and we got up from the couch. Eagerly, she followed me into my office. I sat her down in front of the computer and pulled up the ottoman.

We got into the communications software package and typed in the number for Margaret's office downtown. We watched the countdown at the bottom of the screen as the computer dialed. Almost immediately it announced we were connected, and several commands later the screen was dark and flashing with a green C prompt. My computer suddenly was a looking glass. On the other side were the secrets of my office ten miles from here.

It made me slightly uneasy to know that even as we worked the call was being traced. I'd have to remember to tell Wesley so he didn't waste his time figuring out that the perpetrator, in this instance, was me.

"Do a find file," I said, "for anything that might be called 'Grants.'"

Lucy did. The C prompt came back with the message "No files found." We tried again. We tried looking for a file called "Synonyms" and still had no luck. Then she got the idea of trying to find any file with the extension "SQL" because ordinarily that was the extension for any file containing SQL commands, commands such as the ones used to create public synonyms on the office data tables. Scores of file names rolled up the screen. One caught our attention. It was called "Public. SQL."

Lucy opened the file and we watched it roll past. My excitement was equaled by my dismay. It contained the commands Margaret wrote and executed long ago when she created public synonyms for all of the tables she created in the office data base – commands like CREATE PUBLIC SYNONYM CASE FOR DEEP.CASE.

I was not a computer programmer. I'd heard of public synonyms but was not entirely sure what they were.

Lucy was flipping through a manual. She got to the section on public synonyms and confidently volunteered, "See, it's neat. When you create a table, you have to create it under a user name and password." She looked up at me, her eyes bright behind her thick glasses.

"Okay," I said. "That makes sense."

"So if your user name is 'Auntie' and your password is 'Kay,' then when you create a table called 'Games' or something, the name the computer gives it is really 'Auntie.Games.' It attaches the table name to the user name it was created under. If you don't want to bother typing in 'Auntie.Games' every time you want to get into the table, you create a public synonym. You type the command CREATE PUBLIC SYNONYM GAMES FOR AUNTIE.GAMES. It sort of renames the table so it's just called 'Games.'"

I stared at the long list of commands on the screen, a list revealing every table in the OCME computer, a list revealing the DBA user name each table was created under.

I puzzled, "But even if someone saw this file, Lucy, he wouldn't know the password. Only the DBA user name is listed, and you can't get into a table, such as our case table, without knowing the password."

"Wanna bet?" Her fingers were poised over the keys. "If you know the DBA user name, you can change the password, make it anything you want and then you can get in. The computer doesn't care. It lets you change passwords anytime you want without messing up your programs or anything. People like to change their passwords for security reasons."

"So you could take the user name 'Deep' and assign it a new password and get into our data?"

She nodded.

"Show me."

She looked at me with uncertainty. "But you told me not to ever go into your office data base."

"I'm making an exception this one time."

"And if I give 'Deep' a new password, Auntie Kay, it will get rid of the old one. The old one won't be there anymore. It won't work."

I was jolted by the memory of what Margaret mentioned when we first discovered someone tried to pull up Lori Petersen's case: something about the DBA password not working, causing her to have to connect the DBA grant again.

"The old password won't work anymore because it's been replaced by the new one I made up. So you can't log on with the old one." Lucy glanced furtively at me. "But I was going to fix it."

"Fix it?" I was barely listening.

"Your computer here. Your old password won't work anymore because I changed it to get into SQL. But I was going to fix it, you know. I promise."

"Later," I quickly said. "You can fix it later. I want you to show me exactly how someone could get in."

I was trying to make sense of it. It seemed likely, I decided, that the person who got into the OCME data base knew enough about it to realize he could create a new password for the user name found in the Public.SQL file. But he didn't realize that in doing so he would invalidate the old password, preventing us from getting in the next time we tried. Of course we would notice that. Of course we would wonder about it, and the idea the echo might be on and echoing his commands on the screen apparently didn't occur to him either. The break-in had to have been a one-time event!

If the person had broken in before, even if the echo was off, we would have known because Margaret would have discovered the password "Throat" no longer worked. Why?

Why did this person break in and try to pull up Lori Petersen's case?

Lucy's fingers were clicking away on the keyboard.

"See," she was saying, "pretend I'm the bad guy trying to break in. Here's how I do it."

She got into SQL by typing in System/Manager, and executed a connect/resource/DBA command on the user name "Deep" and a password she made up – "jumble." The grant was connected. It was the new DBA. With it she could get into any of the office tables. It was powerful enough for her to do anything she wished.

It was powerful enough for her to alter data.

It was powerful enough, for example, for someone to have altered Brenda Steppe's case record so that the item "tan cloth belt" was listed in the "Clothing, Personal Effects" field.

Did *he* do this? He knew the details of the murders he'd committed. He was reading the papers. He was obsessing over every word written about him. He would recognize an inaccuracy in the news accounts before anybody else would. He was arrogant. He wanted to flaunt his intelligence. Did he change my office data to jerk me around, to taunt me?

The break-in had occurred almost two months *after* the detail was printed in Abby's account of Brenda Steppe's death.

Yet the data base was violated only once, and only recently.

The detail in Abby's story could not have come from the OCME computer. Was it possible the detail in the computer came from the newspaper account? Perhaps he carefully went through the strangling cases in the computer, looking for something inconsistent with what Abby was writing. Perhaps when he got to Brenda Steppe's case he found his inaccuracy. He altered the data by typing "tan cloth belt" over "a pair of nude pantyhose." Perhaps the last thing he did before logging off was to try to pull up Lori Petersen's case, out of curiosity, if for no other reason. This would explain why those commands were what Margaret found on the screen.

Was my paranoia running off with my reason?

Could there be a connection between this and the

mislabeled PERK as well? The cardboard file was spangled with a glittery residue. What if it hadn't come from my hands?

"Lucy," I asked, "would there be any way to know if someone has altered data in my office computer?"

She said without pause, "You back up the data, don't you? Someone does an export, doesn't he?"

"Yes."

"Then you could get an export that's old, import it into a computer and see if the old data's different."

"The problem," I considered, "is even if I discovered an alteration, I can't say for sure it wasn't the result of an update to the record one of my clerks made. The cases are in a state of constant flux because reports trickle in for weeks, months, after the case has been initially entered."

"I guess you got to ask them, Auntie Kay. Ask them if they changed it. If they say no, and if you find an old export that's different from the stuff in the computer now, wouldn't that help?"

I admitted, "It might."

She changed the password back to what it was supposed to be. We logged off and cleared the screen so no one would see the commands on the OCME computer in the morning.

It was almost eleven o'clock. I called Margaret at home and she sounded groggy as I questioned her about the export disks and asked if she might have anything dating back prior to the time the computer was broken into.

She offered me the expected disappointment. "No, Dr. Scarpetta. The office wouldn't have anything that old. We do a new export at the end of every day, and the previous export is formatted, then updated."

"Damn. Somehow I've got to get hold of a version of the data base that hasn't been updated for the past several weeks."

Silence.

"Wait a minute," she muttered. "I might have a flat file . . ."

"Of what?"

"I don't know . . ." She hesitated. "I guess the last six months of data or so. Vital Statistics wants our data, and a couple of weeks ago I was experimenting, importing the districts' data into one partition and spooling all the case data off into a file to see how it looks. Eventually, I'm supposed to ship it to them over the phone, straight into their mainframe –"

"How many weeks ago?" I interrupted. "How many weeks ago did you spool it off?"

"The first of the month . . . let's see, I think I did it around the first of June."

My nerves were buzzing. I had to know. At the very least, my office couldn't be blamed for leaks if I could prove data were altered in the computer *after* the stories appeared in the papers.

"I need a printout of that flat file immediately," I told her.

There was a long silence. She seemed uncertain when she replied, "I had some problems with the procedure." Another pause. "But I can give you what I've got, first thing in the morning."

Glancing at my watch, I next dialed Abby's pager number. Five minutes later, I had her on the line.

"Abby, I know your sources are sacred, but there's something I must know."

She didn't respond.

"In your account of Brenda Steppe's murder, you wrote she was strangled with a tan cloth belt. Where did you get this detail?"

"I can't –"

"Please. It's very important. I simply must know the source."

After a long pause, she said, "No names. A squad member. It was a squad member, okay? One of the guys at the scene. I know a lot of squad members . . ."

"The information in no shape or form came from my office?"

273

"Absolutely not," she said emphatically. "You're worrying about the computer break-in Sergeant Marino mentioned . . . I swear, nothing I've printed came from that, came from your office."

It was out before I thought twice. "Whoever got in, Abby, may have typed this tan cloth belt detail into the case table to make it appear you got it from my office, that my office is the leak. The detail is inaccurate. I don't believe it was ever in our computer. I think whoever broke in got the detail from your story."

"Good God" was all she said.

15

Marino dropped the morning newspaper on top of the conference table with a loud slap that sent pages fluttering and inserts sliding out.

"What the hell is this?" His face was an angry red and he needed a shave. "Je-sus Christ!"

Wesley's reply was to calmly kick out a chair, inviting him to sit.

Thursday's story was front-page, above the fold, with the banner headline:

DNA, NEW EVIDENCE RAISE POSSIBILITY STRANGLER HAS GENETIC DEFECT

Abby's byline was nowhere to be found. The account was written by a reporter who usually covered the court beat.

There was a sidebar about DNA profiling, including an artist's sketch of the DNA "fingerprinting" process. I wondered about the killer, imagined him reading and rereading the paper in a rage. My guess was wherever he worked, he called in sick today.

"What I want to know is how come I wasn't told any of this?" Marino glared at me. "I turn in the jumpsuit. Do my job. Next thing, I'm reading this crap! What *defect*? Some DNA reports just come in some asshole's already leaked, or what?"

275

I didn't say anything.

Wesley replied levelly, "It doesn't matter, Pete. The newspaper story isn't our concern. Consider it a blessing. We know the killer's got a strange body odor, or at least it seems likely he does. He thinks Kay's office is on to something, maybe he makes a stupid move." He looked at me. "Anything?"

I shook my head. So far there'd been no attempts at breaking into the OCME computer. Had either man come into the conference room twenty minutes earlier, he would have found me ankle-deep in paper.

It was no wonder Margaret had been hesitant last night when I asked her to print out the flat file. It included about three thousand statewide cases through the month of May, or a run of green-striped paper that stretched practically the length of the building.

What was worse, the data were compressed in a format not meant to be readable. It was like fishing for complete sentences in a bowl of alphabet soup.

It took me well over an hour to find Brenda Steppe's case number. I don't know if I felt thrilled or horrified – maybe it was both – when I discovered the listing under "Clothing, Personal Effects": "Pair of nude pantyhose around neck." There was no mention of a tan cloth belt anywhere. None of my clerks remembered changing the entry or updating the case after it was entered. The data had been altered. It was altered by someone other than my staff.

"What about this mental impairment stuff?" Marino rudely shoved the newspaper my way. "You find out something in this DNA hocus-pocus to make you think he ain't operating on all cylinders?"

"No," I honestly replied. "I think the point of the story is some metabolic disorders can cause problems like that. But I have come up with no evidence to suggest such a thing."

"Well, it sure as hell ain't my opinion the guy's got brain

276

rot. Me, I'm hearing the same garbage again. The squirrel's stupid, nothing more than a lowlife. Probably works in a car wash, cleans out the city sewers or something . . ."

Wesley was beginning to register impatience. "Give it a rest, Pete."

"I'm supposed to be in charge of this investigation and I gotta read the damn newspaper to know what the hell's going on . . ."

"We've got a bigger problem, all right?" Wesley snapped.

"Well, what?" Marino asked.

So we told him.

We told him about my telephone conversation with Cecile Tyler's sister.

He listened, the anger in his eyes retreating. He looked baffled.

We told him all five women definitely had one thing in common. Their voices.

I reminded him of Matt Petersen's interview. "As I recall, he said something about the first time he met Lori. At a party, I believe. He talked about her voice. He said she had the sort of voice that caught people's attention, a very pleasant contralto voice. What we're considering is the link connecting these five murders is voice. Perhaps the killer didn't see them. He *heard* them."

"It never occurred to us," Wesley added. "When we think of stalkers, we think of psychopaths who *see* the victim at some point. In a shopping mall, out jogging, or through a window in the apartment or house. As a rule, the telephone, if it figures in at all, comes after the initial contact. He sees her. Maybe he calls her later, just dials her number to hear her voice so he can fantasize. What we're considering now is far more frightening, Pete. This killer may have some occupation that involves his calling women he doesn't know. He has access to their numbers and addresses. He calls. If her voice sets him off, he selects her."

277

"Like this really narrows it down," Marino complained. "Now we got to find out if all these women was listed in the city directory. Next we got to consider occupation possibilities. I mean, not a week goes by the missus don't get a call. Some drone selling brooms, light bulbs, condos. Then there's the pollsters. The let-me-ask-you-fifty-questions type. They want to know if you're married, single, how much money you earn. Whether you put your pants on one leg at a time and floss after brushing."

"You're getting the picture," Wesley muttered.

Marino went on without pause, "So you got some guy who's into rape and murder. He could get paid eight bucks an hour to sit on his ass at home and run through the phone book or city directory. Some woman tells him she's single, earns twenty g's a year. A week later," this to me, "she's coming through your joint. So I ask you. How the hell we going to find him?"

We didn't know.

The possible voice connection didn't narrow it down. Marino was right. In fact, it made our job more difficult instead of easier. We might be able to determine who a victim saw on any given day. But it was unlikely we could find every person she talked to on the phone. The victim might not even know, were she alive to tell. Telephone solicitors, pollsters and people who dial wrong numbers rarely identify themselves. All of us get multiple calls day and night we neither process nor remember.

I said, "The pattern of when he hits makes me wonder if he has a job outside of the home, if he goes to work somewhere Monday through Friday. Throughout the week his stress builds. Late Friday night or after midnight, he hits. If he's using a borax soap twenty times a day, then it isn't likely this is something he has in his household bathroom. Hand soaps you buy at your local grocery store don't contain borax, to my knowledge. If he's washing up with borax soap, I suspect he's doing so at work."

"We're sure it's borax?" Wesley asked.

278

"The labs determined it through ion chromatography. The glittery residue we've been finding on the bodies contains borax. Definitely."

Wesley considered this for a moment. "If he's using borax soap on the job and gets home at five, it's not likely he'd have such a buildup of this glittery residue at one o'clock in the morning. He may work an evening shift. There's borax soap in the men's room. He gets off sometime before midnight, one A.M., and goes straight to the victim's residence."

The scenario was more than plausible, I explained. If the killer worked at night, this gave him ample opportunity during the day while the rest of the world was at work to cruise through the neighborhood of his next victim and look over the area. He could drive by again late, maybe after midnight, to take another look. The victims were either out or asleep, as were most of their neighbors. He wasn't going to be seen.

What night jobs involve the telephone?

We batted that around for a while.

"Most telephone solicitors call right in the middle of the dinner hour," Wesley said. "It seems to me it's unusual for them to call much later than nine."

We agreed.

"Pizza deliverers," Marino proposed. "They're out all hours. Could be it's the drone who takes the call. You dial up and the first thing the operator asks is your phone number. If you've ever called before, your address pops up on the computer screen. Thirty minutes later some squirrel's at your door with a pepperoni-hold-the-onions. It could be the delivery guy who figures out in a hurry he's got some woman who lives alone. Maybe it's the operator. He likes her voice, knows her address."

"Check it," Wesley said. "Get a couple of guys to go around to the various pizza delivery places pronto."

Tomorrow was Friday!

"See if there's any one pizza place all five women called

279

from time to time. It should be in the computer, easy to track."

Marino left for a moment, returning with the Yellow Pages. He found the pizza section and started scribbling down names and addresses.

We kept coming up with more and more possible occupations. Switchboard operators for hospitals and telephone companies were up all hours answering calls. Fund-raisers didn't hesitate to interrupt your favorite television program as late as ten P.M. Then there was always the possibility of someone playing roulette with the city directory or telephone book – a security guard with nothing better to do while he's sitting inside the lobby of the Federal Reserve, or a gas station attendant bored late at night during the slow hours.

I was getting more confused. I couldn't sort through it all.

Yet there was something bothering me.

You're making it too complicated, my inner voice was telling me. You're getting farther and farther removed from what you actually know.

I looked at Marino's damp, meaty face, at his eyes shifting here and there. He was tired, stressed. He was still nursing a deep-seated anger. Why was he so touchy? What was it he said about the way the killer would think, something about him not liking professional women because they're snooty?

Every time I tried to get hold of him, he was "on the street." He'd been to every strangling scene.

At Lori Petersen's scene he was wide-awake. Had he even been to bed that night? Wasn't it a little odd he was so rabid in trying to pin the murders on Matt Petersen?

Marino's age doesn't profile right, I told myself.

He spends most of his time in his car and doesn't answer the phone for a living, so I can't see the connection between him and the women.

Most important, he doesn't have a peculiar body odor,

and if the jumpsuit found in the Dumpster was his, why would he bring it in to the lab?

Unless, I thought, he's turning the system inside out, playing it against itself because he knows so much. He is, after all, an expert, in charge of the investigation and experienced enough to be a savior or a satan.

I suppose all along I'd been harboring the fear that the killer might be a cop.

Marino didn't fit. But the killer might be someone he'd worked around for months, someone who bought navy blue jumpsuits at the various uniform stores around the city, someone who washed his hands with the Borawash soap dispensed in the department's men's rooms, someone who knew enough about forensics and criminal investigation to be able to outsmart his brothers and me. A cop gone bad. Or someone drawn to law enforcement because this is often a very attractive profession to psychopaths.

We'd tracked down the squads that responded to the homicide scenes. What we'd never thought to do was to track down the uniformed men who responded when the bodies were discovered.

Maybe some cop was thumbing through the telephone or city directory during his shift or after hours. Maybe his first contact with the victims was voice. Their voices set him off. He murdered them and made sure he was on the street or near a scanner when each body was found.

"Our best bet is Matt Petersen," Wesley was saying to Marino. "He still in town?"

"Yeah. Last I heard."

"I think you'd better go see him, find out if his wife ever mentioned anything about telephone soliciting, about someone calling up to say she'd won a contest, someone taking a poll. Anything involving the phone."

Marino pushed back his chair.

I hedged. I didn't come right out and say what I was thinking.

Instead, I asked, "How tough would it be to get printouts

or tape recordings of the calls made to the police when the bodies were found? I want to see the exact times the homicides were called in, what time the police arrived, especially in Lori Petersen's case. Time of death may be very important in helping us determine what time the killer gets off work, assuming he works at night."

"No problem," Marino replied abstractedly. "You can come along with me. After we hit Petersen, we'll swing by the radio room."

We didn't find Matt Petersen at home. Marino left his card under the brass knocker of his apartment.

"I don't expect him to return my call," he mumbled as he crept back out into traffic.

"Why not?"

"When I dropped by the other day he didn't invite me in. Just stood in the doorway like a damn barricade. Was big enough to sniff the jumpsuit before basically telling me to buzz off, practically slammed the door in my face, said in the future to talk to his lawyer. Petersen said the polygraph cleared him, said I was harassing him."

"You probably were," I commented dryly.

He glanced at me and almost smiled.

We left the West End and headed back downtown.

"You said some ion test came up with borax." He changed the subject. "This mean you didn't get squat on the greasepaint?"

"No borax," I replied. "Something called 'Sun Blush' reacted to the laser. But it doesn't contain borax, and it seems quite likely the prints Petersen left on his wife's body were the result of his touching her while he had some of this 'Sun Blush' on his hands."

"What about the glittery stuff on the knife?"

"The trace amounts were too small to test. But I don't think the residue is 'Sun Blush.'"

"Why not?"

"It isn't a granular powder. It's a cream base – you

remember the big white jar of dark pink cream you brought into the lab?"

He nodded.

"That was 'Sun Blush.' Whatever the ingredient is that makes it sparkle in the laser, it's not going to accumulate all over the place the way borax soap does. The creamy base of the cosmetic is more likely to result in high concentrations of sparkles left in discrete smudges, wherever the person's fingertips come in firm contact with some surface."

"Like over Lori's collarbone," he supposed.

"Yes. And over Petersen's ten-print card, the areas of the paper his fingertips actually were pressed against. There were no random sparkles anywhere else on the card, only over the inky ridges. The sparkles on the handle of the survivor knife were not clustered in a pattern like this. They were random, scattered, in very much the same way the sparkles were scattered over the women's bodies."

"You're saying if Petersen had this 'Sun Blush' on his hands and took hold of the knife, there'd be glittery smudges versus individual little sparkles here and there."

"That's what I'm saying."

"Well, what about the glitter you found on the bodies, on the ligatures and so on?"

"There were high-enough concentrations in the areas of Lori's wrists for testing. It came up as borax."

He turned his mirrored eyes toward me. "Two different types of glittery stuff, after all, then."

"That's right."

"Hmm."

Like most city and state buildings in Richmond, Police Headquarters is built of stucco that is almost indistinguishable from the concrete in the sidewalks. Pale and pasty, its ugly blandness is broken only by the vibrant colors of the state and American flags fluttering against the blue sky over the roof. Pulling around in back, Marino swung into a line of unmarked police cars.

We went into the lobby and walked past the glass-enclosed

information desk. Officers in dark blue grinned at Marino and said, "Hi, Doc," to me. I glanced down at my suit jacket, relieved I'd remembered to take off my lab coat. I was so used to wearing it, sometimes I forgot. When I accidentally wore it outside of my building, I felt as if I were in my pajamas.

We passed bulletin boards plastered with composite sketches of child molesters, flimflam artists, basic garden-variety thugs. There were mug shots of Richmond's Ten Most Wanted robbers, rapists and murderers. Some of them were actually smiling into the camera. They'd made the city's hall of fame.

I followed Marino down a dim stairwell, the sound of our feet a hollow echo against metal. We stopped before a door where he peered through a small glass window and gave somebody the high sign.

The door unlocked electronically.

It was the radio room, a subterranean cubicle filled with desks and computer terminals hooked up to telephone consoles. Through a wall of glass was another room of dispatchers for whom the entire city was a video game; 911 operators glanced curiously at us. Some of them were busy with calls, others were idly chatting or smoking, their headphones down around their necks.

Marino took me around to a corner where there were shelves jammed with boxes of large reel-to-reel tapes. Each box was labeled by a date. He walked his fingers down the rows and slipped out one after another, five in all, each one spanning the period of one week.

Loading them in my arms, he drawled, "Merry Christmas."

"What?" I looked at him as if he'd lost his mind.

"Hey." He got out his cigarettes. "Me, I got pizza joints to hit. There's a tape machine over there." He jerked his thumb toward the dispatcher's room beyond the glass. "Either listen up in there, or take 'em back to your office. Now if it was me, I'd take them the hell outa this animal

284

house, but I didn't tell you that, all right? They ain't supposed to leave the premises. Just hand 'em back over when
you're through, to me personally."

I was getting a headache.

Next he took me into a small room where a laser printer
was sweeping out miles of green-striped paper. The stack
of paper on the floor was already two feet high.

"I buzzed the boys down here before we left your
office," he laconically explained. "Had 'em print out everything from the computer for the last two months."

Oh, God.

"So the addresses and everything are there." His flat
brown eyes glanced at me. "You'll have to look at the hard
copies to see what came up on the screen when the calls
was made. Without the addresses, you won't know which
call's what."

"Can't we just pull up exactly what we want to know on
the computer?" I broke out in exasperation.

"You know anything about mainframes?"

Of course I didn't.

He looked around. "Nobody in this joint knows squat
about the mainframe. We got one computer person
upstairs. Just so happens he's at the beach right now. Only
way to get in an expert is if there's a crash. Then they call
DP and the department gets knocked up for seventy bucks
an hour. Even if the department's willing to cooperate with
you, those DP dipsticks are as slow coming around as
payday. The guy's going to get around to it late tomorrow,
Monday, sometime next week, and that's if Lady Luck's
on your side, Doc. Fact is, you was lucky I could find somebody smart enough to hit a Print button."

We stood in the room for thirty minutes. Finally, the
printer stopped and Marino ripped off the paper. The stack
was close to three feet high. He put it inside an empty
printer-paper box he found somewhere and hoisted it up
with a grunt.

As I followed him back out of the radio room, he tossed

over his shoulder to a young, nice-looking black communications officer, "If you see Cork, I gotta message for him."

"Shoot," the officer said with a yawn.

"Tell him he ain't driving no eighteen-wheeler rig no more and this ain't *Smokey and the Bandit*."

The officer laughed. He sounded exactly like Eddie Murphy.

For the next day and a half I didn't even get dressed but was sequestered inside my home wearing a nylon warm-up suit and headphones.

Bertha was an angel and took Lucy on an all-day outing.

I was avoiding my downtown office, where I was sure to be interrupted every five minutes. I was racing against time, praying I came up with something before Friday dissolved into the first few hours of Saturday morning. I was convinced he would be out there again.

I'd already checked in with Rose twice. She said Amburgey's office had tried to get me four times since I drove off with Marino. The commissioner was demanding I come see him immediately, demanding I provide him with an explanation of yesterday morning's front-page story, of "this latest and most outrageous leak," in his words. He wanted the DNA report. He wanted the report on this "latest evidence" turned in. He was so furious he actually got on the phone himself threatening Rose, who had plenty of thorns.

"What did you say to him?" I asked her in amazement.

"I told him I'd leave the message on your desk. When he threatened to have me fired if I didn't hook him up with you immediately, I told him that was fine. I've never sued anybody before . . ."

"You *didn't*."

"I most certainly did. If the little jerk had another brain it would rattle."

My answering machine was on. If Amburgey tried to

call me at home he was only going to get my mechanical ear.

It was the stuff of nightmares. Each tape covered seven twenty-four-hour days. Of course, the tapes weren't that many hours long because often there were only three or four two-minute calls per hour. It simply depended on how busy the 911 room was on any given shift. My problem was finding the exact time period when I thought one of the homicides was called in. If I got impatient, I might whiz right on by and have to back up. Then I lost my place. It was awful.

Also, it was as depressing as hell. Emergency calls ranged from the mentally disenfranchised whose bodies were being invaded by aliens, to people roaring drunk, to poor men and women whose spouses had just keeled over from a heart attack or a stroke. There were a lot of automobile accidents, suicide threats, prowlers, barking dogs, stereos up too loud and firecrackers and car backfires that came in as shootings.

I was skipping around. So far I had managed to find three of the calls I was looking for. Brenda's, Henna's and, just now, Lori's. I backed up the tape until I found the aborted 911 call Lori apparently made to the police right before she was murdered. The call came in at exactly 12:49 A.M., Saturday, June 7, and all that was on the tape was the operator picking up the line and crisply saying, "911."

I folded back sheet after sheet of continuous paper until I found the corresponding printout. Lori's address appeared on the 911 screen, her residence listed in the name of L.A. Petersen. Giving the call a priority four, the operator shipped it out to the dispatcher behind the wall of glass. Thirty-nine minutes later patrol unit 211 finally got the call. Six minutes after this he cruised past her house, then sped off on a domestic call.

The Petersen address came up again exactly sixty-eight minutes after the aborted 911 call, at 1:57 A.M., when Matt

Petersen found his wife's body. If only he hadn't had dress rehearsal that night, I thought. If only he'd gotten home an hour, an hour and a half earlier . . .

The tape clicked.

"911."

Heavy breathing. "My wife!" In panic. "Somebody killed my wife! Please hurry!" Screaming. "Oh, God! *Somebody killed her!* Please hurry!"

I was paralyzed by the hysterical voice. Petersen couldn't speak in coherent sentences or remember his address when the operator asked if the address on his screen was correct.

I stopped the tape and did some quick calculations. Petersen arrived home twenty-nine minutes after the first responding officer shone his light over the front of the house and reported everything looked "secure." The aborted 911 call came in at 12:49 A.M. The officer finally arrived at 1:34 A.M.

Forty-five minutes had elapsed. The killer was with Lori no longer than that.

By 1:34 A.M., the killer was gone. The bedroom light was out. Had he still been inside the bedroom, the light would have been on. I was sure of it. I couldn't believe he could see well enough to find electrical cords and tie elaborate knots in the dark.

He was a sadist. He would want the victim to see his face, especially if it were masked. He would want his victim to see everything he did. He would want her to anticipate in unthinkable terror every horrendous thing he planned to do . . . as he looked around, as he cut the cords, as he began to bind her . . .

When it was over, he calmly flicked off the bedroom light and climbed back out the bathroom window, probably minutes before the patrol car cruised by and less than half an hour before Petersen walked in. The peculiar body odor lingered like the stench of garbage.

So far I'd found no common patrol unit that had

responded to Brenda, Lori and Henna's scenes. My disappointment was robbing me of the energy to go on.

I took a break when I heard the front door open. Bertha and Lucy were back. They gave me a full account and I did my best to smile and listen. Lucy was exhausted.

"My stomach hurts," she complained.

"It's no wonder," Bertha started in. "I told you not to eat all that trash. Cotton candy, corn dogs . . ." Shaking her head.

I fixed Lucy chicken broth and put her to bed.

Returning to my office, I reluctantly slipped the headphones on again.

I lost track of the time as though I were in suspended animation.

"911." "911."

Over and over again it played in my head.

Shortly after ten I was so weary I could barely think. I dully rewound a tape trying to find the call made when Patty Lewis's body was discovered. As I listened, my eyes drifted over pages of the computer printout unfolded in my lap.

What I saw didn't make sense.

Cecile Tyler's address was printed halfway down the page and dated May 12, at 21:23 hours, or 9:23 P.M.

That couldn't be right.

She wasn't murdered until May 31.

Her address shouldn't have been listed on this portion of the printout. It shouldn't be on this tape!

I fast-forwarded, stopping every few seconds. It took me twenty minutes to find it. I played the segment three times trying to figure out what it meant.

At exactly 9:23 a male voice answered, "911."

A soft, cultured female voice said in surprise, after a pause, "Oh, dear. I'm sorry."

"Is there a problem, ma'am?"

An embarrassed laugh. "I meant to dial Information. I'm

sorry." Another laugh. "I guess I hit a nine instead of a four."

"Hey, no problem, that's good, always glad when there's no problem." Adding jauntily, "You have a nice evening."

Silence. A click, and the tape went on.

On the printout the slain black woman's address was listed simply, under her name: Cecile Tyler.

Suddenly I knew. "Jesus. Dear Jesus," I muttered, momentarily sick to my stomach.

Brenda Steppe had called the police when she had her automobile accident. Lori Petersen had called the police, according to her husband, when she thought she heard a prowler that turned out to be a cat getting into the garbage cans. Abby Turnbull had called the police when the man in the black Cougar followed her. Cecile Tyler had called the police by mistake – it was a wrong number.

She dialed 911 instead of 411.

A wrong number!

Four of the five women. All of the calls were made from their homes. Each address immediately flashed on the 911 computer screen. If the residences were in the women's names, the operator knew they probably lived alone.

I ran into the kitchen. I don't know why. There was a telephone in my office.

I frantically stabbed out the number for the detective division.

Marino wasn't in.

"I need his home number."

"I'm sorry, ma'am, we're not allowed to give those out."

"Goddam it! This is Dr. Scarpetta, the chief medical examiner! Give me his goddam home phone number!"

A startled pause. The officer, whoever he was, began apologizing profusely. He gave me the number.

I dialed again.

"Thank God," I gushed when Marino answered.

"No shit?" he said after my breathless explanation. "Sure, I'll look into it, Doc."

"Don't you think you'd better get down to the radio room to see if the bastard's there?" I practically screamed.

"So, what'd the guy say? You recognize the voice?"

"Of course I didn't recognize the voice."

"Like what exactly did he say to this Tyler lady?"

"I'll let you hear it." I ran back into the office and picked up that extension. Rewinding the tape, I unplugged the headphones and turned the volume up high.

"You recognize it?" I was back on the line.

Marino didn't reply.

"Are you there?" I exclaimed.

"Hey. Chill out for a while, Doc. It's been a rough day, right? Just leave it to yours truly here. I promise I'll look into it."

He hung up.

I sat staring at the receiver in my hand. I sat without moving until the loud dial tone went dead and a mechanical voice began to complain, "If you'd like to make a call, please hang up and try again . . ."

I checked the front door, made sure the burglar alarm was set and went upstairs. My bedroom was at the end of the hall and overlooked the woods in back. Fireflies winked in the inky blackness beyond the glass, and I nervously yanked the blinds shut.

Bertha had this irrational idea sunlight ought to stream into rooms whether anyone was inside them or not. "Kills germs, Dr. Kay," she would say.

"Fades the rugs and the upholstery," I would counter.

But she was set in her ways. I hated it when I came upstairs after dark and found the blinds open. I'd shut them before turning on the light to make sure nobody could see me, if there was anybody out there. But I'd forgotten tonight. I didn't bother to take off my warm-up suit. It would do for pajamas.

Stepping up on a footstool I kept inside the closet, I slid out the Rockport shoe box and opened the lid. I tucked the .38 under my pillow.

291

I was sick with the worry the telephone would ring and I'd be summoned out into the black morning and have to say to Marino, "I told you so, you stupid bastard! I told you so!"

What was the big lug doing right now, anyway? I flicked off the lamp and pulled the covers up to my ears. He was probably drinking beer and watching television.

I sat up and flicked the lamp back on. The telephone on the bedside table taunted me. There was no one else I could call. If I called Wesley, he would call Marino. If I called the detective division, whoever listened to what I had to say – provided he took me seriously – would call Marino.

Marino. He was in charge of this damn investigation. All roads led to Rome.

Switching off the lamp again, I stared up into the darkness.

"911."

"911."

I kept hearing the voice as I tossed on my bed.

It was past midnight when I crept back down the stairs and found the bottle of cognac in the bar. Lucy hadn't stirred since I had tucked her in hours ago. She was out cold. I wished I could say the same for me. Downing two shots like cough medicine, I miserably returned to my bedroom and switched off the lamp again. I could hear the minutes go by on the digital clock.

Click.

Click.

Seeping in and out of consciousness, I fitfully tossed.

". . . So what exactly did he say to this Tyler woman?"

Click. The tape went on.

"I'm sorry." An embarrassed laugh. *"I guess I hit a nine instead of a four . . ."*

"Hey, no problem, . . . You have a nice evening."

Click.

". . . I hit a nine instead of a four . . ."

"911."

"Hey . . . He's a good-looking guy. He don't need to slip a lady a mickey to get her to give up the goods . . ."

"He's scum!"

". . . Because he's out of town right now, Lucy. Mr. Boltz went on vacation."

"Oh." Eyes filled with infinite sadness. "When's he coming back?"

"Not until July."

"Oh. Why couldn't we go with him, Auntie Kay? Did he go to the beach?"

". . . You routinely lie by omission about us." His face shimmered behind the veil of rising heat and smoke, his hair gold in the sun.

"911."

I was inside my mother's house and she was saying something to me.

A bird was circling lazily overhead as I rode in a van with someone I neither knew nor could see. Palm trees flowed by. Long-necked white egrets were sticking up like porcelain periscopes in the Everglades. The white heads turned as we passed. Watching us. Watching me.

Turning over, I tried to get more comfortable by resting on my back.

My father sat up in bed and watched me as I told him about my day at school. His face was ashen. His eyes didn't blink and I couldn't hear what I was saying to him. He didn't respond but continued to stare. Fear was constricting my heart. His white face stared. The empty eyes stared.

He was dead.

"Daddddyyyyy!"

My nostrils were filled with a sick, stale sweatiness as I buried my face in his neck . . .

The inside of my brain went black.

I surfaced into consciousness like a bubble floating up from the deep. I was aware. I could feel my heart beating.

The smell.

Was it real or was I dreaming?

293

The putrid smell! *Was I dreaming?*

An alarm was going off inside my head and slamming my heart against my ribs.

As the foul air stirred and something brushed against the bed.

16

The distance between my right hand and the .38 beneath my pillow was twelve inches, no more.

It was the longest distance I'd ever known. It was forever. It was impossible. I wasn't thinking, just feeling that distance, as my heart went crazy, flailing against my ribs like a bird against the bars of its cage. Blood was roaring in my ears. My body was rigid, every muscle and tendon straining, stiff and quivering with fear. It was pitch-black inside my bedroom.

Slowly I nodded my head, the metallic words ringing, the hand crushing my lips against my teeth. I nodded. I nodded to tell him I wouldn't scream.

The knife against my throat was so big it felt like a machete. The bed tilted to the right and with a click I went blind. When my eyes adjusted to the lamplight, I looked at him and stifled a gasp.

I couldn't breathe or move. I felt the razor-thin blade biting coldly against my skin.

His face was white, his features flattened beneath a white nylon stocking. Slits were cut in it for eyes. Cold hatred poured from them without seeing. The stocking sucked in and out as he breathed. The face was hideous and inhuman, just inches from mine.

"One sound, I'll cut your head off."

Thoughts were sparks flying so fast and in so many directions. Lucy. My mouth was getting numb and I tasted

295

the salty blood. Lucy, don't wake up. Tension ran through his arm, through his hand, like power through a high-voltage line. I'm going to die.

Don't. You don't want to do this. You don't have to do this.

I'm a person, like your mother, like your sister. You don't want to do this. I'm a human being like you. There are things I can tell you. About the cases. What the police know. You want to know what I know.

Don't. I'm a person. A person! I can talk to you! You have to let me talk to you!

Fragmented speeches. Unspoken. Useless. I was imprisoned by silence. Please don't touch me. Oh, God, don't touch me.

I had to get him to take away his hand, to talk to me.

I tried to will my body to go limp, to relax. It worked a little. I loosened up a little, and he sensed it.

He eased the grip of his hand over my mouth, and I swallowed very slowly.

He was wearing a dark blue jumpsuit. Sweat stained the collar, and there were wide crescent moons under his arms. The hand holding the knife to my throat was sheathed in the translucent skin of a surgical glove. I could smell the rubber. I could smell him.

I saw the jumpsuit in Betty's lab, smelled the syrupy putrid smell of it as Marino was untying the plastic bag . . .

"Is it the smell he remembers?" played in my mind like the rerun of an old movie. Marino's finger pointing at me as he winked, *"Bingo . . ."*

The jumpsuit flattened on the table inside the lab, a large or an extra large with bloody swatches cut out of it . . .

He was breathing hard.

"Please," I barely said without moving.

"Shut up!"

"I can tell you . . ."

"Shut up!" The hand tightened savagely. My jaw was going to shatter like an eggshell.

His eyes were darting, looking around, looking at everything inside my bedroom. They stopped at the draperies, at the cords hanging down. I could see him looking at them. I knew what he was thinking. I knew what he was going to do with them. Then the eyes darted frantically to the cord leading out of my bedside lamp. Something white flashed out of his pocket and he stuffed it into my mouth and moved the knife away.

My neck was so stiff it was on fire. My face was numb. I tried to work the dry cloth forward in my mouth, pushing it around with my tongue without him noticing. Saliva was trickling down the back of my throat.

The house was absolutely silent. My ears were filled with the pounding of my blood. Lucy. Please, God.

The other women did what he said. I saw their suffused faces, their dead faces . . .

I tried to remember what I knew about him, tried to make sense of what I knew about him. The knife was just inches from me, glinting in the lamplight. Lunge for the lamp and smash it to the floor.

My arms and legs were under the covers. I couldn't kick or grab or move. If the lamp crashed to the floor, the room would go black.

I wouldn't be able to see. He had the knife.

I could talk him out of it. If only I could talk, I could reason with him.

Their suffused faces, the cords cutting into their necks.

Twelve inches, no more. It was the longest distance I'd ever known.

He didn't know about the gun.

He was nervous, jerky, and seemed confused. His neck was flushed and dripping with sweat, his breathing labored and fast.

He wasn't looking at my pillow. He was looking around at everything, but he wasn't looking at my pillow.

"You move . . ." He lightly touched the needle point of the knife to my throat.

My eyes were widely fixed on him.

"You're going to enjoy this, bitch." It was a low, cold voice straight out of hell. "I've been saving the best for last." The stocking sucking in and out. "You want to know how I've been doing it. Going to show you real slow."

The voice. It was familiar.

My right hand. Where was the gun? Was it farther to the right or to the left? Was it directly centered under my pillow? I couldn't remember. I couldn't think! He had to get to the cords. He couldn't cut the cord to the lamp. The lamp was the only light on. The switch to the overhead light was near the door. He was looking at it, at the vacant dark rectangle.

I eased my right hand up an inch.

The eyes darted toward me, then toward the draperies again.

My right hand was on my chest, almost to my right shoulder under the sheet.

I felt the edge of the mattress lift as he got up from the bed. The stains under his arms were bigger. He was soaking wet with sweat.

Looking at the light switch near the blank doorway, looking across the bedroom at the draperies again, he seemed indecisive.

It happened so fast. The hard cold shape knocked against my hand and my fingers seized it and I was rolling off the bed, pulling the covers with me, thudding to the floor. The hammer clicked back and locked and I was sitting straight up, the sheet twisted around my hips, all of it happening at once.

I don't remember doing it. I don't remember doing any of it. It was instinct, someone else. My finger was against the trigger, hands trembling so badly the revolver was jumping up and down.

I don't remember taking the gag out.

I could only hear my voice.

I was screaming at him.

"You son of a bitch! You goddam son of a bitch!"

The gun was bobbing up and down as I screamed, my terror, my rage exploding in profanities that seemed to be coming from someone else. Screaming, I was screaming at him to take off his mask.

He was frozen on the other side of the bed. It was an odd detached awareness. The knife in his gloved hand, I noticed, was just a folding knife.

His eyes were riveted to the revolver.

"TAKE IT OFF!"

His arm moved slowly and the white sheath fluttered to the floor . . .

As he spun around . . .

I was screaming and explosions were going off, spitting fire and splintering glass, so fast I didn't know what was happening.

It was madness. Things were flying and disconnected, the knife flashing out of his hand as he slammed against the bedside table, pulling the lamp to the floor as he fell, and a voice said something. The room went black.

A frantic scraping sound was coming from the wall near the door . . .

"Where're the friggin' lights in this joint . . .?"

I would have done it.

I know I would have done it.

I never wanted to do anything so badly in my life as I wanted to squeeze that trigger.

I wanted to blow a hole in his heart the size of the moon.

We'd been over it at least five times. Marino wanted to argue. He didn't think it happened the way it did.

"Hey, the minute I saw him going through the window, Doc, I was following him. He couldn'ta been in your bedroom no more than thirty seconds before I got there. And you didn't have no damn gun out. You went for it and rolled off the bed when I busted in and blew him out of his size-eleven jogging shoes."

We were sitting in my downtown office Monday morning. I could hardly remember the past two days. I felt as if I'd been under water or on another planet.

No matter what he said, I believed I had my gun on the killer when Marino suddenly appeared in my doorway at the same time his .357 pumped four bullets into the killer's upper body. I didn't check for a pulse. I made no effort to stop the bleeding. I just sat in the twisted sheet on the floor, my revolver in my lap, tears streaming down my cheeks as it dawned on me.

The .38 wasn't loaded.

I was so upset, so distracted when I went upstairs to bed, I'd forgotten to load my gun. The cartridges were still in their box tucked under a stack of sweaters inside one of my dresser drawers where Lucy would never think to look.

He was dead.

He was dead when he hit my rug.

"He didn't have his mask off either," Marino was going on. "Memory plays weird tricks, you know? I pulled the damn stocking off his face soon as Snead and Riggy got there. By then he was already dead as dog food."

He was just a boy.

He was just a pasty-faced boy with kinky dirty-blond hair. His mustache was nothing more than a dirty fuzz.

I would never forget those eyes. They were windows through which I saw no soul. They were empty windows opening onto a darkness, like the ones he climbed through when he murdered women whose voices he'd heard over the phone.

"I thought he said something," I muttered to Marino. "I thought I heard him say something as he was falling. But I can't remember." Hesitantly, I asked, "Did he?"

"Oh, yeah. He said one thing."

"What?" I shakily retrieved my cigarette from the ashtray.

Marino smiled snidely. "Same last words recorded on

300

them little black boxes of crashed planes. Same last words for a lot of poor bastards. He said, 'Oh, shit.'"

One bullet severed his aorta. Another took out his left ventricle. One more went through a lung and lodged in his spine. The fourth one cut through soft tissue, missing every vital organ, and shattered my window.

I didn't do his autopsy. One of my deputy chiefs from northern Virginia left the report on my desk. I don't remember calling him in to do it but I must have.

I hadn't read the papers. I couldn't stomach it. Yesterday's headline in the evening edition was enough. I caught a glimpse of it as I hastily stuffed the paper in the garbage seconds after it landed on my front stoop:

STRANGLER SLAIN
BY DETECTIVE
INSIDE CHIEF MEDICAL EXAMINER'S
BEDROOM

Beautiful. I asked myself, Who does the public think was inside my bedroom at two o'clock in the morning, the killer or Marino?

Beautiful.

The gunned-down psychopath was a communications officer hired by the city about a year ago. Communications officers in Richmond are civilians, they aren't really cops. He worked the six-to-midnight shift. His name was Roy McCorkle. Sometimes he worked 911. Sometimes he worked as a dispatcher, which was why Marino recognized the CB voice on the 911 tape I played for him over the phone. Marino didn't tell me he recognized the voice. But he did.

McCorkle wasn't on duty Friday night. He called in sick. He hadn't been to work since Abby's Thursday morning front-page story. His colleagues didn't have much of an opinion of him one way or another except they found his CB phone manner and jokes amusing. They used to kid him about his frequent trips to the men's room, as many as a dozen during a shift. He was washing his hands, his face, his neck. A dispatcher walked in on him once and found McCorkle practically taking a sponge bath.

In the communications men's room was a dispenser of Borawash soap.

He was an "all-right guy." No one who worked with him really knew him well. They assumed he had a woman he was seeing after hours, "a good-looking blonde" named "Christie." There was no Christie. The only women he saw after hours were the ones he butchered. No one who worked with him could believe he was the one, the strangler.

McCorkle, we were considering, may have murdered the three women in the Boston area years ago. He was driving a rig back then. One of his stops was Boston, where he delivered chickens to a packing plant. But we couldn't be sure. We may never know just how many women he murdered all over the United States. It could be dozens. He probably started out as a peeper, then progressed to a rapist. He had no police record. The most he'd ever gotten was a speeding ticket.

He was only twenty-seven.

According to his résumé on file with the police department, he'd worked a number of jobs: trucker, dispatcher for a cement company in Cleveland, mail deliveryman and as a deliveryman for a florist in Philadelphia.

Marino wasn't able to find him Friday night but he didn't look very hard. From eleven-thirty Marino was on my property, out of sight behind shrubbery, watching. He was wearing a dark blue police jumpsuit so he would blend with the night. When he switched on the overhead light inside my bedroom, and I saw him standing there in the jumpsuit, the gun in hand, for a paralyzing second I didn't know who was the killer and who was the cop.

"See," he was saying, "I'd been thinking about the Abby Turnbull connection, about the possibility the guy was after her and ended up with the sister by mistake.

That worried me. I asked myself, what other lady in the city's he getting hooked into?" He looked at me, his face thoughtful.

When Abby was followed from the newspaper late one night and dialed 911, it was McCorkle who answered the call. That was how he knew where she lived. Maybe he'd already thought of killing her, or maybe it didn't occur to him until he heard her voice and realized who she was. We would never know.

We did know all five women had dialed 911 in the past. Patty Lewis did less than two weeks before she was murdered. She called at 8:23 on a Thursday night, right after a bad rainstorm, to report a traffic light out a mile from her house. She was being a good citizen. She was trying to prevent an accident. She didn't want anybody to get hurt.

Cecile Tyler hit a nine instead of a four. A wrong number.

I never dialed 911.

I didn't need to.

My number and address were in the phone directory because medical examiners had to be able to reach me after business hours. Also I talked with several dispatchers on several occasions over the past few weeks when I was trying to find Marino. One of them might have been McCorkle. I'd never know. I don't think I wanted to know.

"Your picture's been in the paper and on TV," Marino went on. "You've been working all his cases, he's been wondering what you know. He's been thinking about you. Me, I was worried. Then all that shit about his metabolic disorder and your office having something on him." He paced as he talked. "Now he's going to be hot. Now it's gotten personal. The snooty lady doctor here's maybe insulting his intelligence, his masculinity."

The phone calls I was getting at late hours . . .

"This pushes his button. He don't like no broad treating him like he's a stupid ass. He's thinking, 'The bitch thinks she's smart, better'n me. I'll show her. I'll fix her.'"

I was wearing a sweater under my lab coat. Both were buttoned up to the collar. I couldn't get warm. For the last two nights I'd slept in Lucy's room. I was going to redecorate my bedroom. I was thinking of selling my house.

"So I guess that big newspaper spread on him the other day rattled his cage all right. Benton said it was a blessing. That maybe he'd get reckless or something. I was pissed. You remember that?"

I barely nodded.

"You want to know the big reason I was so damned pissed?"

I just looked at him. He was like a kid. He was proud of himself. I was supposed to praise him, be thrilled, because he shot a man at ten paces, mowed him down inside my bedroom. The guy had a buck knife. That was it. What was he going to do, throw it?

"Well, I'll tell you. For one thing, I got a little tip sometime back."

"A tip?" My eyes focused. "What tip?"

"Golden Boy Boltz," he replied matter-of-factly as he flicked an ash. "Just so happens he was big enough to pass along something right before he blew out of town. Told me he was worried about you . . ."

"About me?" I blurted.

"Said he dropped by your house late one night and there was this strange car. It cruised up, cut its lights and sped off. He was antsy you was being watched, maybe it was the killer . . ."

"That was Abby!" I crazily broke out. "She came to see me to ask me questions, saw Bill's car and panicked . . ."

Marino looked surprised, just for an instant. Then shrugged. "Whatever. Just as well it caught our attention, huh?"

I didn't say anything. I was on the verge of tears.

"It was enough to give me the jitters. Fact is, I've been watching your house for a while. Been watching it a lot of late nights. Then comes the damn story about the DNA link. I'm thinking this squirrel's maybe already casing the doc. Now he's really going to be off the wall. The story ain't going to lure him to the computer. It's going to lure him straight to her."

"You were right," I said, clearing my throat.

"You're damn right I was right."

Marino didn't have to kill him. No one would ever know except the two of us. I'd never tell. I wasn't sorry. I would have done it myself. Maybe I was sick inside because if I tried I would have failed. The .38 wasn't loaded. Click. That's as far as I would have gotten. I think I was sick inside because I couldn't save myself and I didn't want to thank Marino for my life.

He was going on and on. My anger started to simmer. It began creeping up my throat like bile.

When suddenly Wingo walked in.

"Uh." Hands in his pockets, he looked uncertain as Marino eyed him in annoyance.

"Uh, Dr. Scarpetta. I know this isn't a good time and all. I mean, I know you're still upset . . ."

"I'm not upset!"

His eyes widened. He blanched.

Lowering my voice, I said, "I'm sorry, Wingo. Yes. I'm upset. I'm ragged. I'm not myself. What's on your mind?"

He reached in a pocket of his powder-blue silk trousers and pulled out a plastic bag. Inside was a cigarette butt, Benson & Hedges 100's.

He placed it lightly on my blotter.

I looked blankly at him, waiting.

"Uh, well, you remember me asking about the commissioner, about whether he's an antismoker and all that?"

I nodded.

Marino was getting restless. He was looking around as if he were bored.

"You see, my friend Patrick. He works in accounting across the street, in the same building where Amburgey works. Well." He was blushing. "Patrick and I, we meet sometimes at his car and go off for lunch. His assigned parking place is about two rows down from where Amburgey's is. We've seen him before."

"Seen him before?" I asked, baffled. "Seen Amburgey before? Doing what?"

Wingo leaned over and confided, "Seen him smoking, Dr. Scarpetta." He straightened up. "I swear. Late morning and right after lunchtime, Patrick and me, we're sitting in the car, in Patrick's car, just talking, listening to tunes. We've seen Amburgey get into his black New Yorker and light up. He doesn't even use the ashtray because he doesn't want anybody to know. He's looking around the whole time. Then he flicks the butt out the window, looks around some more and strolls back toward the building squirting freshener in his mouth . . ."

He stared at me, bewildered.

I was laughing so hard I was crying. It must have been hysteria. I couldn't stop. I was pounding the top of my desk and wiping my eyes. I'm sure people could hear me up and down the hall.

Wingo started laughing, uneasily, then he couldn't stop either.

Marino scowled at both of us as if we were imbeciles. Then he was fighting a smile. In a minute he was choking on his cigarette and guffawing.

Wingo finally went on, "The thing is . . ." He took a deep breath. "The thing is, Dr. Scarpetta, I waited until he did it and right after he left his car I ran over and collected the butt. I took it straight up to serology, to Betty, had her test it."

I gasped. "You did what? You took the butt to Betty? That's what you took up to her the other day? To what? Have his saliva tested? What for?"

"His blood type. It's AB, Dr. Scarpetta."

"My God."

The connection was that fast. The blood type that came up on the mislabeled PERK Wingo found inside the evidence refrigerator was AB.

AB is extremely rare. Only four percent of the population has type AB.

"I was wondering about him," Wingo explained. "I know how much he, uh, hates you. It's always hurt me he treats you so bad. So I asked Fred . . ."

"The security guard?"

"Yeah. I asked Fred about seeing anybody. You know, if he'd seen anybody going inside our morgue who wasn't supposed to be there. He said he saw this one dude on an early Monday evening. Fred was starting his rounds and stopped off to use the john down there. He's coming out just as this white dude's coming in, into the john, I'm saying. Fred told me the white dude had something in his hands, some paper packets of some sort. Fred just went on out, went about his business."

"Amburgey? It was Amburgey?"

"Fred didn't know. He said most white folks look alike to him. But he remembered this dude because he had on a real nice silver ring with a real big blue stone in it. An older guy, scrawny, and about bald."

It was Marino who proposed, "So maybe Amburgey went into the john and swabbed himself –"

"They're oral," I recalled. "The cells that showed up on the slides. And no Barr bodies. Y chromosome, in other words – male."

"I love it when you talk dirty." Marino grinned at me, and went on, "So he swabs the inside of his cheeks – the ones above his friggin' neck, I hope. Smears some slides from a PERK, slaps a label on it –"

"A label he got from Lori Petersen's file," I interrupted him again, this time incredulously.

"Then he tucks it inside the fridge to make you think you screwed up. Hell, maybe he's the one breaking into the computer, too. Unbelievable." Marino was laughing again. "Don't you love it? We'll nail his ass!"

The computer had been broken into over the weekend, sometime after hours on Friday, we believed. Wesley noticed the commands on the screen Saturday morning when he came in for McCorkle's autopsy. Someone had tried to pull up Henna Yarborough's case. The call, of course, could be traced. We were waiting for Wesley to get the goods from the telephone company.

I'd been assuming it was McCorkle who might have gotten in at some point Friday evening before he came after me.

"If the commissioner's the one breaking into the computer," I reminded them, "he's not in trouble. He has the right, ex officio, to my office data and anything else he cares to peruse. We'll never be able to prove he altered a record."

All eyes fell to the cigarette butt inside the plastic bag.

Evidence tampering, fraud, not even the governor could take such liberties. A felony is a felony. I doubted it could be proved.

I got up and hung my lab coat on the back of the door. Slipping on my suit jacket, I collected a fat folder off a chair. I was due in court in twenty minutes to testify in yet one more homicide case.

Wingo and Marino walked me out to the elevator. I left them and stepped inside.

Through the closing doors I blew them each a kiss.

Three days later, Lucy and I sat in the back of a Ford Tempo heading to the airport. She was returning to Miami, and I was going with her for two very good reasons.

I intended to see about the situation with her mother and the illustrator she had married, and I desperately needed a vacation.

I planned to take Lucy to the beach, to the Keys, to the Everglades, to the Monkey Jungle and the Seaquarium. We'd watch the Seminoles wrestle alligators. We'd watch the sun set over Biscayne Bay and go see the pink flamingos in Hialeah. We'd rent the movie *Mutiny on the Bounty*, and then tour the famous ship at Bayside and imagine

Marlon Brando on deck. We'd go shopping along Coconut Grove, and eat grouper and red snapper and Key lime pie until we were sick. We'd do everything I wished I could have done when I was her age.

We'd also talk about the shock of what she'd been through. Miraculously, she had slept through everything until Marino opened fire. But Lucy knew her aunt was almost murdered.

She knew the killer got in through my office window, which was closed but unlocked, because Lucy forgot to lock it after opening it several days earlier.

McCorkle cut the wires to the burglar alarm system outside the house. He came in through the first-floor window, walked within feet of Lucy's room and quietly went up the stairs. How did he know my bedroom was on the second floor?

I don't think he could have unless he'd watched my house in the past.

Lucy and I had a lot of talking to do. I needed to talk to her as much as she needed for me to talk to her. I planned to hook her up with a good child psychologist. Maybe both of us should go.

Our chauffeur was Abby. She was kind enough to insist on driving us to the airport.

She pulled in front of the airline gate, turned around and smiled wistfully.

"I wish I were going with you."

"You're welcome to," I responded with feeling. "Really. We'd love it, Abby. I'll be down there for three weeks. You have my mother's phone number. If you can get away, hop on a plane and we'll all go to the beach together."

An alert tone sounded on her scanner. She absently reached around to turn up the volume and adjust the squelch.

I knew I wouldn't hear from her. Not tomorrow or the next day or the day after that.

By the time our plane took off, she would be chasing

ambulances and police cars again. It was her life. She needed reporting like other people need air.

I owed her a lot.

Because of what she set up behind the scenes we discovered it was Amburgey breaking into the OCME computer. The call was traced back to his home telephone. He was a computer hack and had a PC at home with a modem.

I think he broke in the first time simply because he was monitoring my work, as usual. I think he was rolling through the strangling cases when he noticed a detail in Brenda Steppe's record different from what Abby reported in the paper. He realized the leak couldn't be my office. But he so desperately wanted it to be, he altered the record to make it appear that way.

Then he deliberately keyed on the echo and tried to pull up Lori Petersen's case. He wanted us to find those commands on the screen the following Monday, just hours before he called me to his office in front of Tanner and Bill.

One sin led to another. His hatred blinded his reason, and when he saw the computer labels in Lori's case file he wasn't able to restrain himself. I'd thought a long time about the meeting in my conference room, when the men were going through the files. I'd assumed the PERK label was stolen when several cases slipped off Bill's lap and scattered over the floor. But as I went over it I recalled Bill and Tanner sorting out the paperwork by the proper case numbers. Lori's case was not among them because Amburgey was perusing it at the time. He took advantage of the confusion and quickly tore off the PERK label. Later, he left the computer room with Tanner but stayed behind alone in the morgue to use the men's room. He planted the slides.

That was his first mistake. His second mistake was underestimating Abby. She was livid when she realized someone was using her reporting to jeopardize my career.

It didn't matter whose career, I suspected. Abby simply didn't cotton to being used. She was a crusader: truth, justice and the American way. She was all dressed up with rage with no place to go.

After her story hit the racks, she went to see Amburgey. She was already suspicious of him, she'd confessed to me, because he was the one who slyly gave her access to the information about the mislabeled PERK. He had the serology report on his desk, and notes to himself about the "fouled-up chain of evidence," and the "inconsistency of these results with those from earlier tests." While Abby was seated on one side of his famous Chinese desk, he stepped out, leaving her alone for a minute – long enough for her to see what was on his blotter.

It was obvious, what he was doing. His feelings for me were no secret. Abby wasn't stupid. She became the aggressor. Last Friday morning she had gone back to see him and confronted him about the computer violation.

He was cagey, feigning horror that she might print such a thing, but he was salivating. He could taste my disgrace.

She set him up by admitting she didn't have enough to go on. "The computer violation's only happened once," she told him. "If it happens again, Dr. Amburgey, I'll have no choice but to print it and other allegations I've heard, because the public will have to know there's a problem at the OCME."

It had happened again.

The second computer violation had nothing to do with the planted news story, because it wasn't the killer who needed to be lured back to the OCME computer. It was the commissioner.

"By the way," Abby told me as we got the bags out of the trunk, "I don't think Amburgey's going to be a problem anymore."

"A leopard can't change its spots," I remarked, glancing at my watch.

She smiled at some secret she wasn't going to divulge.

"Just don't be surprised when you come back to find he's no longer in Richmond."

I didn't ask.

She had plenty on Amburgey. Someone had to pay. She couldn't touch Bill.

He had called me yesterday to say he was glad I was all right, that he had heard about what had happened. He had made no references to his own crimes, and I had not so much as alluded to them when he calmly said he didn't think it was a good idea for us to see each other anymore.

"I've given it a lot of thought, and I just don't think it's going to work, Kay."

"You're right," I agreed, surprised by my own sense of relief. "It just isn't going to work, Bill."

I gave Abby a big hug.

Lucy frowned as she struggled with a very large pink suitcase.

"Shoot," she complained. "Mom's computer's got nothing but word processing on it. Shoot. No data base or nothing."

"We're going to the beach." I shouldered two bags and followed her through the opening glass doors. "We're going to have a good time, Lucy. You can just lay off the computer for a while. It's not good for your eyes."

"There's a software store about a mile from my house . . ."

"The beach, Lucy. You need a vacation. Both of us need a vacation. Fresh air, sunshine, it will be good for you. You've been cooped up inside my office for two weeks."

We continued bickering at the ticket counter.

I shoved the bags on the scale, straightened Lucy's collar in back and asked her why she hadn't carried her jacket. "The air-conditioning in planes is always too high."

"Auntie Kay . . ."

"You're going to be cold."

"Auntie Kay!"

"We've got time for a sandwich."

"I'm not hungry!"

"You need to eat. From here we're stuck in Dulles for an hour and there's no lunch on the plane from there. You need something in your stomach."

"You sound just like Grans!"